The Girl in the Painting

Kirsty Ferry

Where heroes are like chocolate – irresistible!

Published 2017 by Choc Lit Limited
Penrose House, Crawley Drive, Camberley, Surrey GU15 2AB, UK
www.choc-lit.com

A CIP catalogue record for this book is available
from the British Library

ISBN 978-1-78189-360-9

Printed and bound by Clays Ltd

'Even so, where Heaven holds breath and hears
The beating heart of Love's own breast, –
Where round the secret of all spheres
All angels lay their wings to rest. –
How shall my soul stand rapt and aw'd,
When, by the new birth borne abroad
Throughout the music of the suns,
It enters in her soul at once
And knows the silence there for God!'

Extract from *The Portrait*, Dante Gabriel Rossetti.

For my family and friends who have always supported me and my writing. Thank you for everything, you mean the world to me.

Acknowledgements

Thank you so much to the whole team at my lovely publishers, Choc Lit – from the reading panel who actually liked the book enough to go "yes!" (Jo C., Robyn, Izzy, Olivia, Betty and Sharon), to my editor, to my cover designer and to the wider Choc Lit Family who are always there for a rant or a moan or to deliver a confidence boost. Thank you also to my friends who read *The Girl in the Painting* before I submitted it and who all gave me very valuable feedback. Nobody said it was utter rubbish, which is always a good sign! Thank you also to the readers of my first Choc Lit novel, *Some Veil Did Fall*, who asked me 'what happens next – and when is the sequel coming out?' Here it is – and I hope you like it! The biggest thanks of all, though, must go to my family – to Shaun and James, and to my Mum and Dad – who have, in varying degrees, put up with my endless demands for chocolate and coffee and my ramblings on the Pre-Raphaelites – without whom this novel wouldn't have worked at all well. Yet I must stress that it's all made up. It's fiction. These people existed: Lizzie and Dante and John and all the rest. They were legends and they have their own stories. They might not have done what I have made them do – they might have been quite different personalities to how I have portrayed them. But they are and were wonderful, exciting, fascinating people and I hope they wouldn't be too upset to see how I've written about them. In fact, I hope they would be flattered to have found themselves in a novel. It's nice to think so, anyway!

Prologue

He will find me here, in my bed. The room is dark and the patterns on the wallpaper do not show in this February dusk. And I am so, so sorry that he has to find me. He shouts and I hear him thundering up the staircase.

He calls for me: 'Daisy! Daisy!' but I cannot move. My body is weak and frail beneath the weight of the blankets. My breathing is shallow.

'Please, let me sleep,' I want to tell him. No more pain. Let me sleep, my love, let me sleep … The door into the room slams open. I know it is him, but I cannot bear to open my eyes. I am so tired. So very tired. He calls my name again.

Then he screams 'No!' over and over again. Hands seize me; he shakes me, he pulls me out of the bed, hoisting me upwards, calling to me all the time. I flop around like a rag doll, my head lolls to one side. I don't want to open my eyes. I can't open my eyes. He slips away from me and all is silent.

It will be so beautiful.

Part One

Chapter One

Cori Keeling had lived in London for five weeks and had yet to visit the Tate Britain. Which was crazy, because visiting the Tate was one of the main things she had intended to do when she moved down to London from Northumberland.

But her house was still a muddle of packing boxes and bits of furniture and she hadn't yet managed to find the time to leave it all to indulge her inner artist. She was sleeping on a mattress in the lounge because the bedroom had just been re-plastered and the wallpaper was half off the walls in the other rooms, and there were still bare boards in what was going to be her office space on the second floor.

The kitchen needed a good scrub as well – the cupboards wafted that awful smell of old packets of soup and spilt instant coffee whenever you opened them – and there were sticky patches of some unknown substance in the grouting between the tiles.

Cori picked at another strip of paper and a chunk of plaster came off with it. She dropped it on the floor with the rest of the old wall covering and sighed. She didn't know what she'd been thinking when she decided to take this place on. '*This property has been owned by the same family for fifty years and is in need of some TLC.*' The brochure hadn't mentioned the fact that nobody had lived in the place for the last year and, she was willing to bet, the rooftop garden hadn't been maintained since long before that year.

The front door of the mews house was dodgy and sometimes wouldn't shut properly without her full weight behind it, and the garage had a distinct odour of damp –

but that was fine. It was all fine, because it was her house and her project and it was all just perfect.

Shutting the door on the mess that would eventually be her bedroom, she climbed over a pile of paint, brushes and neatly folded paint-stained dust sheets. The decorators had left it all there yesterday, when they had abandoned the job for the weekend.

But it was depressing. It really was.

'Stuff Project Mews House,' she said out loud. 'I need a coffee.'

One of the many positive things about being in London was that there were plenty of coffee shops near Cori's new home, so she didn't even have to fight her way into the obnoxious kitchen to boil the kettle.

Just at the edge of her square she could turn left or right onto Kensington High Street and have a choice of little patisseries and bakeries that dotted the street. She nipped into the first one she came to and ordered a takeaway latte.

It was as she was leaving and sipping the foam through the little hole in the plastic lid of the cup that a taxi pulled up, just beside her.

A young girl with skyscraper heels, a tiny skirt and a very large bag climbed out of the taxi, smiled briefly at Cori and *click-clacked* her way down the pavement. Cori, momentarily envious of the girl's purposeful aura and arrow-straight aim towards, she assumed, the designer shop of choice, found herself grabbing the door of the taxi, standing poised on the edge of getting in and going – well, *somewhere*.

'Tate Britain, please,' she heard herself say as she climbed inside. The driver nodded, and indicated, pulling out into the traffic. And Cori couldn't help but feel a little thrill of excitement.

* * *

5

The taxi stopped just outside the Tate and Cori stared up at the Millbank entrance, looking at the cream-coloured pillars and the architecture of the building.

'Thanks,' she said to the taxi driver. He muttered something back to her, but she was already halfway out of the cab and across the forecourt before it registered that he had spoken. She heard the cab pull off and stood for a moment longer, savouring the fact that she was here; she was actually here. After all that talking about it with her granny and all the plans she had made, she was finally here. It was a moment she thought she would probably never forget.

She'd been before; a few years ago when she'd visited the Tate as a student, but she'd had to plan that, had to arrange transport and accommodation. But now she was a grown woman of twenty-nine, living in London and she could visit whenever she wanted to.

Inside that building, she knew, were some of the greatest Pre-Raphaelite paintings in the world. The ones she was most interested in were Millais' *Ophelia*, and basically all of Dante Gabriel Rossetti's work, including the ethereal *Beata Beatrix* and the loose, rough pencil sketches depicting Lizzie Siddal – Rossetti's wife, lover, muse and, Cori thought, his kryptonite.

Someone, years ago, had commented that Cori was Lizzie's double and that – as well as the fact that one of her wayward, redheaded relations had apparently had an affair with Rossetti – had sparked her interest in, or some might say her slight obsession with, the Pre-Raphaelite Brotherhood; or the PRB, as most people called them.

Cori shuddered despite the warmth of the early spring day and drained her coffee cup hoping that the paintings she would soon rediscover would take her mind off Evan and the mess that had gone before. She thought his cold eyes and his final few comments to her would never leave her memory and tossed her coffee cup into a nearby rubbish bin as if she could throw away the wasted years with him just as easily. Part of the reason she had moved to London was so that she could forget him.

Today though, she thought, pushing the unpleasant memories to the back of her mind, was the first day of the rest of her life and Evan didn't factor in her future at all.

Not like *Ophelia* and Lizzie. They could now be a huge part of it, with nobody judging her. With these thoughts, she took her first step as a local towards the gallery entrance.

7

Chapter Two

The Tate Britain was cool inside the huge, airy foyer. A staircase led up to the treasures above and Cori headed towards it, the soles of her Converse trainers squeaking on the tiled floor.

She knew that the Millais Gallery and the Pre-Raphaelite collection were on the first floor and she determined to go straight there. So resolute was she that she didn't see a man in the corridor coming straight towards her until they almost collided.

The man was tall, about six foot, and Cori found herself looking up at him. He had fair hair that was a little too long, and haunted, navy blue eyes that widened slightly as he saw her. He was clutching a clipboard.

The man smiled and the darkness lifted out of his eyes briefly. 'Sorry, my fault,' he said and stepped to one side to let her pass, throwing his arms out and gesturing her past with his clipboard. His voice was warm and polite and his accent definitely sounded as if he belonged in the south of the country as opposed to the north. She assumed he might work at the gallery.

'No, it's mine. I'm not looking where I'm going,' said Cori, with a smile. And then, because she wanted to hear his voice again, she asked: 'The Pre-Raphaelites are along here, aren't they?'

'They are,' said the man. 'Straight along.'

'Thanks,' said Cori. The man nodded and she put her head down and hurried away, feeling a little blush creep up on her cheeks.

Seeing him had been quite a nice way of eradicating

Evan's face from her mind; full marks to the Tate so far, she thought.

Simon Daniels stood in the corridor and didn't move for a few minutes.

Instead, he watched the girl hurry along the corridor, her long, red corkscrew curls flying out behind her almost to her waist. An image of Rossetti's sketch of Lizzie Siddal plaiting her hair came into his mind. If the girl who had just spoken to him brushed her hair out of the curls into loose waves, it would almost be as if Lizzie had stepped out of a painting and come to life. Transport Lizzie Siddal into the twenty-first century and dress her in a pair of skinny jeans and a sloppy jumper that hung off one shoulder and exposed the strap of a back vest top, and she'd be there.

There had been a smear of white emulsion paint on her leg as well, he had noticed, and a blob of it on her trainers too. Simon was an artist – he noticed little details like that. He wondered whether she was an artist as well. But that brought an image of Sylvie into his mind and he felt his face close up again. He didn't want to think of Sylvie.

Simon turned and headed in the opposite direction. He was heading to the coffee shop to informally meet one of the curators, along with a Rossetti expert they'd brought in. There was a new Rossetti painting due to arrive at the Tate and the idea was that it would be the centrepiece of a new exhibition. As the resident Pre-Raphaelite expert – unofficially so, anyway – Simon had been asked to share some of his ideas.

On the clipboard in front of him was a photograph of the new painting but as he glanced down at it, all he could focus on was the girl with the flame-red hair who had just disappeared into the crowds along the corridor.

'There you are,' said Cori under her breath as she walked

into the Millais Gallery and saw the painting of *Ophelia* straight in front of her.

It was as beautiful as she had remembered. She felt that flutter of excitement again as she saw Lizzie Siddal drifting down the river to certain doom, clutching a pathetic little posy of flowers.

There's rosemary, that's for remembrance. Pray you, love, remember.

The words came to Cori from the depths of English lessons at school. *Hamlet* had been sickeningly fascinating due to the fact that the stage had been littered with bodies at the end – but for all of Hamlet's madness, feigned or otherwise, it was Ophelia Cori remembered best. *Get thee to a nunnery* indeed. Cori smiled.

Theories abounded over why Ophelia was such a popular subject for the Pre-Raphaelites. Cori liked to think that she was a tragic, romantic heroine who had captured their imaginations – nobody could do tragedy and beauty and madness quite like Ophelia. And did Ophelia really understand she was committing suicide while she sang so innocently to herself? Who would ever know?

Cori was desperate to reach out and touch the painting, but shoved her hands into her pockets instead. She tilted her head to the side, looking at it, trying to spot all the symbolism Millais had added, looking for the faint outline of where she knew a water vole had been painted but later erased, paddling alongside Lizzie.

She knew there was a pencil sketch of the vole under the mounting on the top left and sighed. Oh, how wonderful to be able to take the frame apart and see it, along with the bold strips of colour Millais had painted there as well. The vole, however, had been erased as nobody apparently knew what it was. Guesses from his peers, she understood, had ranged from hares to rabbits to dogs and cats. So the vole had been painted over.

Millais seemed quite a character – she liked what she had read about him. He certainly didn't appear to have the magnetism that Rossetti had, which, she reasoned was perhaps why Rossetti's paintings were so much bolder and wilder. Millais was, she suspected, very much a safe, commercial artist; but it had served him well.

Cori had a special liking for Dante Gabriel Rossetti, due in part to that old family legend that the relative she'd been named after, redheaded great-great-great-aunt Corisande – Cori wasn't quite sure how many Greats there were, to be fair it was a few Greats ago, anyway – had enjoyed a heady, albeit brief love affair with the artist. There had been rumours Rossetti had painted her portrait, but nobody had ever proved that it was the original Corisande and Cori reserved judgement on that one.

The modern-day Cori tore herself away from *Ophelia* and moved towards *Mariana*, that vision in blue who looked like she, Cori, felt today – fed up with the mess in her house and desperate to escape.

That thought made Cori smile. She'd never likened herself to *Mariana* before – because *Mariana* wasn't posed by Lizzie Siddal.

Simon headed into the coffee shop and spotted Hugo, the curator, sitting next to a girl with long dark, glossy hair, held back by a black and white spotted scarf. The girl was sitting with her back to Simon, deep in conversation with Hugo – mid-thirties, light brown hair, rapt expression – who was nodding occasionally and looking very interested in what the dark-haired girl was saying.

For a minute, Simon's heart somersaulted. Sylvie had hair like that – she'd spend hours with the ceramic hair straighteners and wasn't happy until her hair fell perfectly down from her centre parting, the layers cutting in by her chin and framing her face. Her sloe black eyes would always be smoky-dark; mascara and eyeliner carefully applied to contrast with the pouting pale pink lipstick. She was as sultry and curvaceous as Angelina Jolie – and knew it.

'Please, no,' he muttered. One foot in front of the other, he made his way over to the table, his heart pounding. That would just be typical. She'd reappeared to taunt him some more.

'Ah, Simon!' said Hugo, catching sight of him. 'This is Isobel McCullogh. She's come to give us some advice on the new exhibition – and she comes highly recommended by Lissy de Luca, so I'm sure she will be most helpful to us.'

The woman turned and smiled at Simon. 'Nice to meet you,' she said in a lilting, Scottish accent. And it was only then that Simon exhaled. He hadn't realised he had been holding his breath: taking on an assumed identity wasn't something he was aware that Sylvie had actually done, but until he'd seen Isobel McCullogh's face, he hadn't been able to relax.

It was definitely a different woman though. Isobel McCullogh had a heart-shaped face with a ready dimple in her cheek when she smiled and wide brown eyes the colour of horse chestnuts.

And even while Simon was smiling and shaking her hand and reciprocating her greeting, all he could think about was the girl with red hair who was somewhere in the crowds upstairs; and the fact that when he got his hands on Lissy he would willingly wring her neck.

Chapter Three

Lissy thought that her plan might be successful this time. She knew Isobel from her work in other galleries, and was absolutely sure that she was exactly what Simon needed in his life.

All Lissy had to do was throw Isobel and Simon together in a project which combined their joint passion and step back. Light the blue touch paper and watch the sparks fly, so to speak. Isobel was pretty, intelligent and loved art. She was friendly and, most importantly, single. A match made in Heaven, as far as Lissy was concerned.

Lissy had made Simon into a pet project of sorts. She had known him for a while now, working as she did as a volunteer at the Tate. She had been there to pick up the pieces when he and Sylvie had broken up. She had helped him move his stuff out of the home he shared with Sylvie, donated a small tabby kitten to him named Bryony and seen him installed in a rented flat.

'It's just to live in for now,' he'd told her, his face drawn and his eyes shadowed. It had hit him hard, no matter what he had secretly suspected, to actually find his girlfriend with another man – in his own bed.

'You're well rid of Slutty,' Lissy had told him, helping him lug an easel into the small second bedroom of his new flat. 'It'll soon feel like a bad dream and you'll move on.'

'Maybe,' he'd said.

'Shall we put this here?' Lissy had asked, all five feet nothing of her trying to tug against the strength of a fairly muscular, six-foot tall man, in order to put the easel in the perfect spot for the daylight to shine on it.

'No,' Simon had said, easily pulling it back. 'I'll just leave it here for the minute.' He'd propped it in the corner and piled boxes up around it while Lissy watched him, pursing her mouth disapprovingly, and the kitten pawed at a pile of rags inquisitively before climbing onto them and curling up for a nap.

'You need to start painting again,' she'd scolded.

'I will,' he said. 'Soon.'

The easel had stayed there, abandoned, for a few weeks. But painting and creating was like a drug to Simon; he couldn't stay away for long, so gradually he had started painting again.

Lissy had been delighted; until she had seen some of his work on a stall in Portobello market.

'Simon. Your work is very touristy. It's very nice but very soulless,' she told him.

'At least I'm painting,' he had answered, defensively.

'Yes, but that's not proper painting,' she'd replied. 'That's not what you *do*. You're playing it safe.'

'I'll get there,' he said.

Lissy knew what he was capable of – she'd seen the work he'd produced when he'd been with Sylvie, and this souvenir-style art was just not Simon.

Somewhere, deep down, was a man with a passion who had lost it along the way. Lissy wanted the old Simon back, and to her the answer was simple. He needed a channel to unleash that passion; so she had spent a good few months trying to fix him up with an appropriate channel.

Isobel was the latest attempt and she hoped it would work. It would have been, she thought, so much simpler if she, Lissy, actually felt a spark for Simon herself. But she didn't and she never would and she knew that feeling was mutual.

'Isobel?' Lissy appeared around the corner, just as Isobel was packing up her laptop and pulling the papers together after the meeting in the cafe.

Isobel looked up and smiled. 'Hey, Lissy,' she said. 'Good to see you. I hoped I would.'

'I'm on a flying visit,' said Lissy, clutching a takeaway cup of coffee. She took the lid off and blew on it, sending waves of rich espresso aromas towards Isobel. 'I'm heading off to Staithes tomorrow, in North Yorkshire, to help them archive some bits and pieces and I've got a million things to do first. So I just nipped in, hoping I'd catch you or Simon. How did it go, then? Did you get plenty of feedback from Simon?'

'Oh yes!' said Isobel. 'I'm not surprised you wanted him involved. He's quite the expert on the Pre-Raphaelites, isn't he?'

'He is indeed,' said Lissy. 'And did you arrange to meet again?'

'Of course,' replied Isobel, enthusiastically. 'We'll get together when we have a better idea of when the portrait will be delivered and plan a strategy. It should be a really exciting exhibition. I can't wait to see the new painting. I've seen the photograph, but it'll be so different in real life!'

Lissy smiled, a little tightly. 'Good. But I meant did you arrange to *meet* again?'

Isobel looked at her a little blankly. 'Yes. I just explained that.'

'No! Are you going to see him again? Romantically!' said Lissy, exasperated.

Isobel's eyes widened and she stared at Lissy; then began to laugh. 'No. No, I'm not going to see him romantically, Lissy! Don't be silly. Honestly! Is that what you intended? Were you trying to set us up?'

Lissy blushed and looked down at her coffee. 'It would have been an added bonus,' she said. 'That's all. I thought you'd get on well and one thing might lead to another.' She looked up at Isobel. 'Tell me that I wasn't wrong!'

Isobel laughed and shook her head. 'You're wrong,

Lissy,' she said. She tucked the papers into her briefcase and packed her laptop away behind them. 'Simon seems a nice guy, but really, we were very professional with one another. I didn't think of him like that for one moment. And I didn't get the feeling he felt like that about me, so sorry about that, sweetheart.' Then she grinned, the little dimple in her cheek deepening. 'But I am going for dinner with Hugo tonight, so *that* part of it went very well indeed!'

After the meeting, Simon had hurried back upstairs to the Pre-Raphaelite collection, hoping to catch sight of the red-haired girl again.

He was to be disappointed, though. He scanned the crowds in the corridors and looked for the girl amongst them. He thought he saw her, walking into a room where a wall was dedicated to Rossetti's sketches of Lizzie Siddal; but when he hurried over and looked inside, there was no sign of her.

'Damn,' he muttered. He'd already popped his head through most of the doors to the rooms on that floor, all to no avail. He'd have one more look in the Millais Gallery, he told himself – and if she wasn't there, he'd—

'Simon.' The sound was imperative and he knew the voice well.

'Lissy,' he responded, turning to face her.

'Isobel,' she said.

'And?' he responded.

Lissy stared at him for a moment. 'I can't answer that in one word,' she said, 'so instead I shall ask you outright – what the *hell* were you doing not asking her out? Now *Hugo* is having dinner with her. And that's not how it should have been.'

'Ah, yes. *That* Isobel,' he said. He shook his head. 'No, Lissy. Stop it. I knew exactly what you had been planning when I saw her sitting there, and it wasn't going to happen.

She seems like a nice girl, but that's as far as it goes. No reason for either of us to want to see the other out of school.'

'But she's perfect for you!' said Lissy. There was a definite hint of a whine in her voice.

'No, she's not,' said Simon. He nodded towards Lissy's cup. 'And be careful with your coffee, please. I'm not having you spill it on *Ophelia*.'

Lissy sniffed and glared up at him. 'I'm in the corridor,' she said, acidly. '*Not* in the Millais Gallery. And I'm trying to help,' she said, forcing the plastic lid back on the cup. 'You can't go on painting those awful London scenes any more. Before we know it, you'll have painted a Pearly King enjoying a knees-up and then I shall have to stop speaking to you. I'm sorry, Simon. I would.'

'Nothing wrong with Pearly Royalty,' said Simon. He began whistling 'The Lambeth Walk' very quietly and Lissy's eyes narrowed.

'Just stop it,' she said. 'Please.'

Simon shrugged and looked around him. The red-haired girl was definitely not in the corridor – he had a feeling about the Millais Gallery though.

'Look, Lissy. I'm busy. I've got things to do, so much as I'd love to stand here and have a conversation about my love life – or lack of it – I need to do some work.'

Lissy sighed. 'All right, I get the hint,' she said. 'I'm off to Staithes in the morning, so we'll catch up when I'm back, okay?'

'Okay,' said Simon.

Lissy stood on tiptoe and kissed him swiftly on both cheeks. 'Ciao for now,' she said and raised her cup to him. 'I'll bin it when I go downstairs, don't worry.'

'I won't,' he said.

Lissy nodded and turned on her heel. Simon watched her striding along the corridor, her stilettos tapping out a rhythm on the wooden floorboards.

Her heart was in the right place, he thought. But until he actually found someone he could connect with, the scenic London pictures would be all that appeared on his canvasses. And for all of Lissy's good intentions, even he didn't know what he wanted, so how could Lissy even attempt to find him someone?

But that girl with the red hair might be a good place to start.

His eyes drifted down the corridor, all the way along towards the Millais Gallery and his heart quickened.

Cori had explored the other rooms, glorying in the Pre-Raphaelites and their muses and finally decided to move back to *Ophelia* before she returned home.

It was as if the portrait was a magnet, drawing her towards it. If she stared at it long enough, she could almost see the tendrils of Lizzie's hair rippling in the water; almost smell the freshness of the earth and the grass and recognise the perfume of the flowers she clutched to her; the pungent scent of rosemary; the sweet fragrance of violets.

How would Lizzie have felt when she saw this painting for the first time? How would she have dealt with being catapulted to fame as one of the PRB's 'stunners' – as they were known at the time – as Rossetti's muse, as the face of a generation? As a celebrity, Cori supposed. She allowed her imagination to run riot a little, just to see if she could sense some of it.

Yes; she was lost in it. But there were, she reasoned, worse places to be lost.

She was in there. In front of *Ophelia*. Simon blinked. It was almost as if he was looking at Lizzie Siddall, looking at herself in a mirror.

There was never a shortage of red-haired ladies inspecting these pictures. He had seen Pre-Raphaelite sisters of all shapes and sizes, and ladies with hair a thousand different shades of red.

But nobody had ever come close to what he saw now.

'Can I just ask you your opinion about *Mariana*?' asked an earnest looking man who suddenly appeared at Simon's elbow. 'It's just, I was wondering whether you felt Millais had ...'

The words washed over Simon, even as he nodded and agreed and mechanically answered the man's questions.

And the next time he looked, the red-haired girl had gone.

Chapter Four

Cori dreamed she was Ophelia that night. She slept on the mattress in the lounge with her sleeping bag pulled up to her chin. It would be so nice, she had thought drowsily, when she could sleep in a bed again.

It must have been the thought of a warm bed and the excitement of going to the Tate that did it. She dreamed she was in the tin bath Lizzie had lain in while she was posing for Millais, and then the bath opened out and she floated away down a river, singing songs to herself.

She reached out and grasped a reed from the riverbank, then it turned into a rose which scratched her palm and she had to let it go. As she did so, the current swept her away, swirling and whirling downstream and she wondered if she really wanted to die after all?

Then strong arms pulled her out of the water and she lay in those arms and felt safe – and then she opened her eyes and she was in a bedroom with a flickering fire and candles everywhere and there was a sprig of rosemary on the pillow next to her.

There's rosemary, that's for remembrance. Don't forget me ...

It was at that point Cori woke up, her heart pounding and wondered, for a moment, where she actually was. And then the second thought that came to her was the fact that Ophelia's lines had been misquoted somewhat in that dream.

'Ridiculous,' muttered Cori. 'It should be "*Pray you, love, remember.*"' She lay in the sleeping bag blinking in the pre-dawn milkiness that was coming through her thinly curtained windows. That was something else she needed to sort out – some decent curtains.

It was at moments like this, when she woke up in those eerie hours, that she missed the familiarity of her family home the most. During the day, everything was different. It was bright and busy and all sorts of things were going on to distract her; usually in the shape of workmen, ladders and paint pots.

She sat up in the sleeping bag and drew her knees up to her chin. Hugging her legs, she stared into the pigsty of a lounge, her hair tangling around her shoulders and down her back.

The place would look like home soon enough, she thought. And if the workmen were quite happy to supervise themselves, there was no need for her to sit in here with them, was there? She didn't have that much worth stealing and it would be pretty easy to find the culprits if anything did end up going missing. And she was insured, anyway.

She needed some cushions and a rug and some new curtains – most definitely. Along with some new bedding, she thought, and some more cushions to scatter around the bedroom. Because why not? You could never have too many cushions.

And because she knew sleep would evade her and it was a long time until she could get up and do much more than find a 24-7 coffee bar or grocery shop in the vicinity, she decided to make some notes. Notes were good. She could plan what she needed to buy.

And the Tate opened at ten. So she really only had to fill in time until then.

Maybe that tall, fair-haired guide would be there again? She smiled into the lounge. It was nice to dream.

Chapter Five

It was inevitable, really, that the Tate would become part of Cori's regular routine.

The house was coming together gradually, and she found it less distressing going out and coming back to improvements, rather than sitting in the place watching men slapping paint around and constantly asking for tea.

A couple more weeks down the line and she had polished floorboards in the room she had designated as her office, which meant she could organise her workspace and get back to some semblance of normality. She had used some of her time wandering around London to make contacts and had a few things she wanted to follow up – which was much easier to do linked up to a computer than using a smartphone all the time. And considering she was a web designer, a working computer was kind of essential.

The painting of *Ophelia* at the Tate never changed; yet Cori found herself drawn back to her. It was so easy just to pop in to the gallery, use the cafe, mooch around the gift shop and look at beautiful paintings. She could get quite used to it, actually. No matter how many times she went into the PRB galleries, she always found something new to study. And if she happened to catch sight of that rather nice guide she had bumped into in the corridor – as she had done on several occasions – so much the better.

On one particular sunny, cheerful day, when much of the work in her house was completed, Cori decided to buy her granny a postcard of *Ophelia*. Her granny knew, of course, what the painting looked like; but Cori thought it might be quite nice to send her the postcard, just so she knew Cori was thinking about her.

She turned the card over in her hand and read the details on the back. The postcard could never do *Ophelia* justice, of course, but her granny would understand. The card, however, had the edge bent over –and it was silly as it could easily get damaged in the post but Cori didn't want to send damaged goods to her granny. She looked around, wondering if anyone would spot her swapping it for one at the back of the display; but all she saw was the tall, fair-haired guide she had bumped into walking past the door. He was on a mobile phone and was frowning, but for a brief moment their eyes met and she felt her heart jump.

Ophelia was forgotten as the man faltered and looked as if he was coming into the gift shop. Cori felt her jaw slacken a little – but then he stopped, ran his fingers through his hair and turned away, hurrying back in the direction he had come from, his body language implying he was having a rather heated discussion with whoever it was on the phone.

Cori swore under her breath and cursed the person he was talking to. She had felt almost sure he was going to come into the shop and speak to her.

Ah, well. Once again, she could dream.

'Sylvie you can't call me at work,' Simon said, trying to control his temper. 'Yes, you know I'm on my break. I'm always on my break at this time. It's not news.' He was prowling along the corridors, full of fury. 'I don't care. We've had this conversation before and the answer is still the same. I've got nothing of yours at all. No. No, you can't have the new address and come over to check. Sorry. Whatever was yours, I just left at Chelsea. Yes, that includes your oil paint set. No, I'm not bloody using it! I've got my own!'

He shook his head. The woman was unbelievable. Hell

would freeze over before he would let her into his flat. Because then one thing would lead to another and it was easier just to have a clean break.

She, however, had taken to calling every so often with random excuses. She had never once apologised or even referred to the fact she had been sleeping with another man, quite brazenly, in their bed. She was remorseless; in fact, Simon wondered whether she had enjoyed the thrill of it all and being discovered was the ultimate prize. She'd left the front door unlocked and the bedroom door open, for goodness sake. What message did that send out?

He'd avoided blocking her number thus far for some reason best known to his subconscious, but now he was certain that was the first thing he was going to do when he hung up. In fact—

He looked up and saw he was outside the gift shop. He also saw the girl with the red hair turning a postcard over in her hands. Today she was wearing a pair of frayed denim shorts and a white broderie anglaise top. Her hair was plaited, the tail of the plait curling back on itself, just above her waist.

The girl looked up just as he spotted her. He hesitated and began to walk towards her, not quite knowing what he was doing. How on earth could he even speak to her, when he was dealing with a psychopathic ex on the phone?

He forced himself to turn away from the gift shop, heedless of the relentless quacking sound in his ear as Sylvie further tried to justify why she should visit Simon.

He ran his fingers through his hair and shook his head. This was it; this really was it.

He closed his eyes and took a deep breath, cutting Sylvie off, mid-justification. 'Goodbye, Sylvie. I've got nothing left to say to you. Now, or in the future. Goodbye.'

Simon pressed the end call button and immediately went into the contact settings. *Block caller*. There. It was done.

Simon exhaled and stared at the phone. He then looked towards the gift shop. Maybe he still had time? He hurried to the shop, but all he saw was the back of her, walking out of the exit and into the street, her plait swinging jauntily from side to side.

'Damn!' He leaned against the wall, closing his eyes and raising his face to the ceiling. 'Damn and blast it!'

He had to get back to work. His break was over and there was no way he could rush out into the street to try and find her.

But as his emotions began to settle, he felt an odd sort of stillness coming over him. He opened his eyes and stared straight ahead. Then, really concentrating, he focussed on the paintings that lined the corridors. He knew there was more of the same in the building – he was surrounded by so many beautiful works of art and yet they had been wasted on him these past six months.

It had all been about Sylvie and about what he'd lost. He'd had no thought about the future or the present and all that had to change.

He looked down at his hands, not really seeing them but picturing images in his mind of a red-headed girl with hair like molten lava. He saw her smiling; he saw her standing in front of the pictures that echoed her image; and he saw her captured on canvas – painted in oils, by him. His fingers itched to paint her, to paint every individual strand of that hair and capture all the highlights and tones within it.

And he swore that the next time he saw her, he was going to speak to her.

Cori wrote the card out for her granny while she was sitting on a bench by the Thames.

The river was slate grey, despite the blue sky and she could see bridges and hear traffic all around her. Red buses crawled over the bridges and people scurried about like ants. The smell coming off the river wasn't that pleasant though, but she was willing to ignore it.

Her heart lifted and she stretched her legs out in front of her, just looking at the view. It wouldn't be long now before the mews house was finished. In fact, her pleasant task for that evening was to make the bed up in her actual bedroom.

She had asked the workmen – Paulo and Solomon, if you please – to move the frame in there and put the mattress on for her if they didn't mind. They had smiled and agreed and she had paid them in chocolate biscuits. A win-win situation. She had new sheets and duvet all ready to put on the mattress and new cushions piled up ready to scatter around.

First, though, she would post the card to Northumberland. And in order to do that, she would need to buy some stamps. There was a newsagent on the corner and she stood up and sauntered towards the shop. She might buy herself a family bar of chocolate as well to celebrate with and maybe a bottle of wine. She wasn't a big drinker, but she would raise a glass tonight, she thought, in her nice new bed. Yes, life was looking brighter.

It would be pretty much perfect if she'd managed to get the attention of that guide at the Tate though, she thought with a frown. Never mind. She had lots of time yet.

Cori pushed open the door into the shop and smiled at the man behind the counter. She collected her chocolate and wine and went over to get her stamps and pay. There was a rack of magazines and newspapers set up next to the till and she scanned the front covers as she waited for a lady who was buying each of her twin boys a pocket money toy car.

Cori's attention was caught by a strapline on one of the newspapers.

The Millais Mystery. Was Ophelia *really Lizzie?*

For a moment the excited chatter of the little boys faded

away and Cori was unaware of anyone else in the shop. Even the face of the tall, fair-haired guide at the Tate took a back seat for a moment.

'Can I help? Miss? Miss?'

She blinked as the man behind the counter smiled at her, his teeth white in his dark face.

'Oh. Sorry. Yes. A book of first class stamps, please,' she said. 'And these.' She placed the bottle and the chocolate down with a clumsy clatter. 'And this. Thank you. Yes. I'll take this as well.' She placed a copy of the newspaper down next to her shopping and smiled back at the man. 'Yes. Great. Thank you.'

'You're very welcome,' said the man. He nodded at the wine and chocolate. 'A good night, yes?'

Cori, though, was looking at the newspaper. 'Yes,' she agreed, re-reading the strapline and feeling a delicious sense of anticipation. 'I think it will be a very good night indeed.'

Chapter Six

After the best night's sleep she'd had for ages in her newly decorated bedroom, Cori was enjoying her first cup of tea of the morning, staring at yesterday's newspaper on her coffee table with that thought provoking strapline: *The Millais Mystery. Was Ophelia really Lizzie?*

Cori turned to the inside page again and read the article but even when she had finished she still didn't know the truth of it. Was the girl in the famous *Ophelia* portrait that she loved so much really Lizzie Siddal or not?

This article seemed to suggest that the painting hadn't been completed using the original model. According to the journalist, a diary had been discovered, and it implied that someone called Daisy Ashford had been substituted to finish the job.

It is important to realise, the journalist had written, *that we cannot prove anything from this diary alone. Stranger things have happened and we must keep an open mind. Whatever the truth,* Ophelia *remains one of the most iconic pictures of the Victorian era and is a triumph for the Pre-Raphaelite movement.*

Cori smiled and rolled the newspaper up. She stuffed it in her bag and, turning her back on the bombsite that was her lounge, decided the rest of the unpacking could wait for yet another day.

Heading down the stairs, stepping over several books on art and the Pre-Raphaelite Brotherhood in general, she set out to pay yet another visit to *Ophelia*. She sometimes wondered how she'd ended up as a web designer instead of working in a gallery; her degree was in art history, after all, and, despite all the time she had spent studying the Pre-Raphaelite Brotherhood, she was fairly certain she had never come across a Daisy Ashford in any of the documents.

Chapter Seven

TATE BRITAIN

In the Millais Gallery there was a huge crowd clustered in front of the *Ophelia* painting and, from what Cori could hear, most of them were rather annoyed that the canvas was much smaller than they had anticipated.

Since reading the article, even Cori had started to wonder whether the model was Lizzie Siddal or Daisy Ashford. But now she found herself bobbing around the outskirts of the crowd, feeling a particular sense of annoyance that she couldn't get close enough to have a proper look and try to work out who the girl was.

Finally, a man moved out of the way and her heart jumped as she caught a tiny glimpse of the girl's face. Lizzie, or Daisy, or whoever it was in the painting, had a perfectly smooth complexion, so pale it was ethereal and the most beautiful red hair flowing like weeds through the water. A tree behind her echoed her pose as her hands curled gently, slightly out of the water – the girl was caught in the moment of madness that foreshadowed her suicide and Cori was, as always, entranced. She pushed further into the crowd and found herself standing more or less eye to eye with Ophelia.

'It's pretty stunning close up, isn't it? Can you see the texture on the foliage?' A man's voice spoke quietly next to her. Cori's stomach flipped. She recognised the voice from that moment in the corridor; the encounter where she had almost mown him down. 'Millais wrote a famous letter to his patron's wife when he was working on it,' the man continued, 'saying he had been threatened with a notice about trespassing in that field and destroying the hay. We should be grateful he never got arrested over it.'

'It's her face that always catches my attention, to be honest,' replied Cori. 'She's so lifelike.' She turned her head, her heart bouncing around like a jumping bean. And yes. She was gratified to see the owner of the voice was indeed the fair-haired man and her heart bounced around a bit more. The gallery identity badge attached to his shirt pocket read Simon Daniels.

'She's generated a lot of interest,' Simon continued. 'I think it's due to that article – the Becky Nelson one. It's gone viral on the Internet.'

Cori patted her bag. 'Yes. I've read it. I've got the newspaper in here. It does make you think, though.' But to be fair, all she was actually thinking about at that moment was Simon's eyes.

'It does,' replied Simon. 'It makes a good story. So who would you say was the model? Lizzie or Daisy?'

'I don't know.' Cori shook her head. 'Lizzie was so famous after sitting for this. If it's not her, it calls into question a lot about the Pre-Raphaelites, doesn't it? Lizzie's whole legend, in fact. And if it was this Daisy Ashford – she wouldn't have been very happy if Lizzie got all the praise.' She smiled at the fair-haired man, hoping she hadn't bored him too much with her theory. Evan had often told her to stop when she was in full PRB flow. 'But as you say,' she said, trying to round off her chatter, 'there's a story in there somewhere.'

She hefted her bag onto her shoulder and gave one last, reluctant glance at *Ophelia*. 'Oh well, I'll just have to have a proper look when all the excitement's died down.'

'Well, it's always nice to see you,' said Simon. 'Sorry, that sounds odd. What I mean is, when you work here, you get to recognise people.' He indicated his name badge. 'I've noticed you in the PRB section a few times.'

'Oh!' Cori was secretly thrilled about that comment. 'But is it not just my hair you've recognised?' she asked, hardly daring to think otherwise. 'It's rather difficult to miss.' She raised her hand and lifted a bunch of curls away from her shoulder. She pulled them around to the side and looked at them askance.

Simon shook his head. 'No. It's not just your hair,' he said. 'To be honest, you remind me of Lizzie Siddal. I've studied the PRB quite a lot and she was the first person I thought of when I saw you. Especially when you were in front of *Ophelia*.'

Cori looked down at her maxi-dress; it was a flimsy white fabric, shot through with silver threads – perfect for the warm London weather. And quite a good match to the fabric of *Ophelia*'s dress as well.

'I suppose I've borrowed a bit of her style,' she agreed. 'Don't worry; you're not the first to say I look like her. I usually take it as a compliment.'

'It was meant as one,' said Simon. He smiled, rather shyly. 'Listen, would you like to get a coffee sometime? I've just finished my break or I would try to persuade you to come down to the cafe now.'

Cori stared up at him. 'Really?' She noticed how the look in his navy blue eyes hinted at more than sharing just an academic interest in the PRB and marvelling at her likeness to Lizzie Siddal. There was a spark of genuine passion there; the man was keeping something hidden deep down. Cori had the feeling that 'something', whatever it was, had been squashed out of him and needed to breathe again. Plus, now she was close enough to appreciate him, she had noticed that his fair hair was definitely a little too long and also curled slightly around the back of his neck, as if it too was trying to falsely restrain itself. She'd always liked that half-messed up look in a man.

'You know what,' she said, 'I think I'd actually quite like

that. I just moved down here recently and it would be good to get to know a few people.'

Since she had split up with Evan, she had been more than cautious about who she let into her life, but she had promised herself that she wasn't going to pass up any opportunities in London, if she could help it. And this was rather too good an opportunity to miss. Hadn't it been this man, as much as the Tate itself, which had drawn her back so many times?

'I'm Cori,' she said. 'Cori Keeling. It's short for Corisande.'

'Cori? That's a pretty name,' replied Simon. 'And so is Corisande. I've never heard it before – although maybe once.' He looked at her curiously, his eyes flicking over her hair again.

'Hmm. Sometimes I hate it, sometimes I love it. More often than not, I think I sound like an herb. I was named after a fifteenth-century French king's mistress and a pretty wayward great-great-great-aunt somewhere along the line. It was rumoured she'd had an affair with Rossetti. Again – it's all about the hair.' Cori laughed and shook her head. 'If you've studied Rossetti in any great depth you might have dug up my aunt, hidden away as a footnote somewhere in history.'

'That's probably it,' said Simon.

Cori nodded. Her name had been her granny's choice; Cori's mother had abandoned her at a few days old and she hadn't really seen her daughter since.

'I sometimes think they may as well have called me Parsley,' Cori said.

'No, I think Cori suits you,' said Simon. 'Look, I'd best go as I think that woman is about to have an argument with that chap with the camera, but you know where I am. Hopefully,' he said, a smile lighting up his face and making his eyes crinkle a little at the edges, 'I'll see you soon.

You'll have to come to see the new Rossetti we're expecting anyway. I'll make a point of watching out for you. And we'll get that coffee, I promise.'

'That sounds great,' replied Cori. 'Oh. And if all else fails …' She took her bag from her shoulder and began to rummage around. 'Here. That's my business card. Just in case we miss each other.'

Simon took the card and tucked it into his shirt pocket. 'Thanks. But I'll not miss you,' he said. The little spark in his eyes flared and died back.

And with that, he turned away and disappeared into the crowds around the painting.

Chapter Eight

ALMOST NOTTING HILL, LONDON

Simon hadn't stopped thinking about Cori since their first proper meeting.

That night, he went into his makeshift studio and looked at all the paintings he had completed recently. They were tourist favourites: Tower Bridge; the Victoria Embankment on a winter's evening, strung with lights between the lampposts; Covent Garden; the Serpentine, snaking, as its name suggested, through Hyde Park. They sold and they sold well on the Portobello market stall his friend ran. But they weren't enough. They lacked the passion and the drive he had once had and, to his eyes, they were dull, lifeless images that a photograph could have captured equally effectively.

Sylvie had a lot to answer for. His heart just hadn't been in his painting since the break-up. He missed his old workspace as well – the light had streamed into the Chelsea garden flat they had bought together, and the small second bedroom of his current home was nowhere near as good to work in. Sylvie had been the inspiration, the driving force behind his work. They had met at the Slade School of Fine Art; he had been swept away by the talented, dark-haired Parisian and they had made plans – big plans.

This had all been very well, until he came home from the Tate six months and three days ago, and walked into the middle of Sylvie's latest love affair.

The trouble with being an artist and seeing things no one else generally saw, was that something like that stuck in your mind, perfectly executed in every detail. He saw the sinews in her neck as she arched backwards, her full mouth slightly parted. He saw the sweat glistening on both their bodies – and the amused look in Sylvie's sloe-black eyes as she pulled a shirt on to cover herself. It had been her lover's shirt, Simon had realised; and he didn't know if that was more insulting than her wearing Simon's shirt.

The image had been a mental block to his creativity ever since. Simon hadn't managed to put anything down onto canvas apart from the trite, souvenir pictures he produced for Portobello in all that time.

He took a deep breath and moved a half-finished sketch of Nelson's Column off the easel onto the floor, and put a large, blank sheet of stiff paper in its place; then he grabbed the softest, darkest piece of charcoal he could find. He decided if he couldn't ignore the picture, he would paint it out. He would get it out of his head and onto the canvas. He would erase Sylvie and all her sultry Angelina Jolie sensuality from his memory and his life.

Then, once the image had taken shape and he had drawn every curve and every bead of sweat on those two bodies, he would load a brush with thick, black paint and cover the whole of it. Then he would rip it up and start something new.

Chapter Nine

TATE BRITAIN

'Someone looks tired,' said an amused voice behind him. 'Didn't you sleep well?'

It was the next day, and Simon hadn't dared leave the Millais Gallery all morning, just in case Cori showed up. He turned and saw Lissy.

Lissy's family had connections somewhere, and as such she tended to come and go as she pleased at the Tate and nobody questioned her. She did, however, love the place and it clearly showed in her boundless knowledge and enthusiasm. Simon didn't think she had a paid career at all, anywhere – but she dabbled in many things, she told him, and one day she might find something she wanted to settle to.

'Good morning, Lissy,' Simon replied. 'No, I didn't sleep well. But I was working – so it's nothing interesting for you to speculate over, I'm afraid.'

'Oh, Simon.' Lissy sighed. 'What are we going to do with you? Honestly, if I could get my hands on Slutty I'd wring her neck. She's put you off girls, hasn't she?'

Simon shook his head. 'I wouldn't say that. I'm just ... proceeding with caution.'

'Six months is a *lot* of caution,' said Lissy.

'How long has it taken you to get over Stefano?' replied Simon. 'We're talking three years now? Maybe four? I don't see you rushing into anything serious.'

'I don't want to talk about him,' replied Lissy, sniffing. 'He's an idiot. But at least I'm having fun and that's what you should be doing.'

'Well, maybe I should be,' he said.

Lissy blinked. 'That's the first time you've ever agreed with me about it!' she said, suddenly delighted. 'What's her name?'

'Her name?' asked Simon. 'What makes you think there's someone I should be naming?'

'Because I'm not stupid,' replied Lissy. 'There's paint in your cuticles and it's green and white. That means you've moved on from the tourist trap paintings and done something different. Probably involving grass or trees or something pleasant. You're not covered in brick colours or building colours.'

'Hyde Park is green,' said Simon.

'And white? And – oh look – yellow?' asked Lissy, peering at his hands more closely. 'Bright colours. Nature colours. Happy colours. So – what's she called?'

Simon shook his head. Lissy astonished him. It wasn't even worth trying to fight it.

'Okay!' He raised his hands up and spotted a little red smear as well, just on his third finger. 'You win. She's called Cori. It's short for—'

'Corisande,' fired back Lissy. 'I believe she was the mistress of a French king in the fourteenth century.'

'Fifteenth,' replied Simon. Lissy glowered at him. She hated being corrected. And, to give her her due, she was often very much correct. But not in this case. Simon cheered himself inwardly.

'She told you that, did she?' asked Lissy.

'Yes, she did,' replied Simon. 'Yesterday. She was interested in *Ophelia*. We had a chat about the PRB.'

Lissy looked thoughtful for a moment. 'The PRB? And you say she was called Cori? What does she look like?'

Simon didn't hesitate to answer; Cori's face was on his mind all the time. He felt he knew it better than his own – and she had definitely haunted his dreams last night.

'She looks just like Ophelia. Long red hair, big eyes, pale complexion.' He smiled at the thought. 'I've seen her a few times in here. Yesterday was the first time I managed to speak to her.'

'So what you're saying is that she doesn't look like Ophelia.' Lissy prodded him in the chest with her forefinger. 'She looks like Lizzie Siddal. Or ...' she moved her finger away from his chest and wagged it at him '... we might now say she looks like Daisy Ashford. That's very interesting. Very interesting indeed.'

And then, to Simon's puzzlement, she nodded, turned on her heel and walked off towards the exit.

Chapter Ten

KENSINGTON

Cori was trying to locate some of her resources for work. She currently had three boxes open and discarded in her lounge and still hadn't found what she needed.

The beauty with being a self-employed web designer was that you could work from home, and this was what Cori did. However, the downside was that if you couldn't work, you couldn't make money.

It wasn't an enormously insurmountable problem at the minute, thankfully. She had the mews house now and the sale had left her a bit of extra money – well, quite a lot of extra money, if she was honest – to use until she got back to it again. The little room – well, large room – at the top of the house was screaming out to be made properly into her office; and it was her office, to all intents and purposes, it just wasn't fully functional yet.

At the minute, the computer was the only thing in there that she had set up, but at least the house was starting to look like her own. It was pretty quirky inside, now she had her mismatched furniture in place and had bought some extra bits and bobs. She had somewhere to sleep, sit and eat now – and not all at the same time, in the same place, which was how it had been up until about three weeks ago.

Cori's mobile rang and she cursed, looking around the room, wondering where on earth the phone had hidden itself.

She finally located it underneath a cushion, which she threw angrily across the room; then she checked the number on the display and saw it was her granny. 'Hi, Granny!' She knew she sounded breathless and distracted.

'Cori? Have I called at a bad time?' Her granny sounded contrite. 'Sorry, love. Just wanted to see how you were getting on.'

'No, it's fine,' replied Cori. She lowered herself into her favourite armchair and moved another cushion out of the way. 'You just caught me, though. I'm heading out soon.'

'Ooh, anywhere nice?' she asked.

'Well, actually,' said Cori, 'I'm going to the Tate.'

'Again?' replied her granny. Then the old lady laughed; it was a particularly dirty sort of chuckle, Cori thought, for a woman of her age. 'There must be something there that you really like, eh?' she said.

'Yes. The paintings,' said Cori, defensively. She felt her skin prickle as she blushed. It wasn't all about the paintings now though, was it? She hadn't had too long a conversation with Simon Daniels, but she knew exactly what that cultured, dark chocolate voice sounded like and had, she admitted to herself, wished it had been his voice on the other end of the phone this morning. Hell, his voice and his face – especially his eyes – had been invading her thoughts since she met him.

'Nothing else?' her granny asked. 'No new friends I need to know about?'

This time Cori's cheeks didn't just prickle, they burned. 'Nothing else,' Cori said, tightly. Then she closed her eyes and lifted her scarlet face to the ceiling, exasperated with herself. It was useless to try to hide anything from the woman who often knew her better than she did herself. 'Well, okay. Yes there is something else.' She opened her eyes and fixed them on the door to the staircase. 'Or someone else, I suppose. He's called Simon and he works at the Tate and he's asked me for coffee. He's interested in the PRB.'

'Oh, very nice!' said Granny. Cori could just imagine her relaxing into the sofa for some more gossip, possibly even punching the air as her suspicions were confirmed. Nothing was beyond the realms of possibility with her granny.

The woman had driven down to visit her last month, for goodness sake. She'd tackled the M25 and everything.

'It's good that you're moving on from Evan,' continued her granny, throwing Cori slightly. 'That man was no good for you. What do they say nowadays? It was a toxic relationship?'

Cori smiled into the phone, feeling a great rush of affection for the woman at the end of the line. 'Definitely toxic,' she said. Her granny didn't know half of it – she'd welcomed her granddaughter back with open arms when it all fell to pieces and Cori left the house she and Evan had lived in.

The house had been an old vicarage in a chocolate box village with a river running along the bottom of the garden and it should all have worked out perfectly. But Granny had never probed too deeply – she didn't know about the pregnancy scare or the fact Evan had coldly told her to 'deal with it' because he 'didn't want to have a baby with her'.

Granny just knew Cori had ended up back on her doorstep and said it was over.

And then Cori had decided to move to London and make a fresh start. And why not?

True to her word, after a lengthy conversation with her granny, Cori headed off to the Tate. As she closed the door to the mews house extra-firmly – the old wood had a terrible habit of warping and not shutting properly – she had to take a deep breath to steady her nerves. Simon, she reminded herself, was highly unlikely to be another Evan.

She walked to the tube station and barely registered anybody else on the street as she left the quiet little square in Kensington and joined the flow of foot traffic. Instead, she was thinking about Simon. There was no harm, she justified to herself, going back to the gallery and seeing if he was around. It was free entry, after all. And if he wasn't there, then she didn't mind spending some quality time with the Pre-Raphaelites.

If he was there, he might meet her for a coffee as he'd said, sooner rather than later.

Which would be very nice indeed. And, if he wasn't able to meet her, she'd simply head off to the V&A. She had some leads she wanted to follow up about a commission for an upcoming exhibition and she would make the most of the day.

So, with an alternative end to her expedition in mind if it didn't all go according to plan, she walked into the Tate, secretly hoping, however, she wouldn't end up at the V&A – at least not today.

He had been discussing the symbolism in *Ophelia* with a greasy-haired bohemian-type art student. The student had, like so many others, rediscovered *Ophelia* on the back of the diary article and had brought his girlfriend with him to see it. They'd been a nice young couple, but a sixth sense told Simon to abandon the discussion and turn around.

He looked along the gallery and there she was. Her hair was loose today and she was wearing a long, green, flowing skirt and a white vest top. It gave the impression that she was floating through the room towards him and he thought that he had never seen anything so beautiful in all his life.

He wished he could stop time; just freeze-frame that moment and capture it, dreamlike, in watercolours.

He walked through the gallery to meet her halfway, the people in the room blurring into the edges of his vision. He knew he was smiling and he couldn't stop himself.

And the best thing? She was smiling as well.

'Cori,' he said. 'You came.' Later, he'd think how ridiculous it was that he couldn't come up with anything more imaginative to say. But she didn't seem to mind.

'Of course I did,' she said, stopping just in front of him. 'I'd never pass up an opportunity to talk about the PRB.'

'Me, neither,' he said. 'Can I interest you in that coffee at all?'

'I think you could,' she said.

'Well, that's perfect timing. I do believe I'm due my lunch break.'

'Definitely perfect timing,' she replied.

And she was still smiling.

Chapter Eleven

The thing with Costa coffee shops was that they were the same the world over. Cori could order what she wanted, no messing, and not be distracted by anything new or different; apart from, of course, if that new or different thing was Simon.

They had left the Tate and Simon had taken them to a little Costa, quite nearby, that he often spent his lunch hours in. Cori was already halfway through a large latte, and realised she was buzzing; and it wasn't just the caffeine that was doing it.

Sitting there, in a window seat, with Simon opposite her was the most comfortable she'd been in a man's company for quite a while.

He didn't look as if he was bored either. The conversation had been easy, their interests very similar. By now, he knew she was a slightly frustrated web designer with an adventurous granny and she knew he was originally from Sussex but had gone to Slade and began working at the Tate after that. He also had a doctorate in the PRB, but tended not to use the title very much.

'One day,' he said, 'my intention is to have my own exhibition somewhere. A proper exhibition.' He'd spread his hands out on the table and looked down at them.

Her eyes followed his and she noticed he had smears of paint on his fingers. They were long, artistic fingers.

'What I'd really like to do,' said Simon, 'is to reinterpret some of the Pre-Raphaelite paintings. I'll do it someday.' He looked up and smiled. Again, those fathomless eyes. Cori felt her jaw slacken a little as she fell into the navy blue depths. She wondered what it would be like to wake up and see those eyes first thing in the morning, half-heavy with sleep, looking into hers. 'I've just got to get my inspiration first,' he said. And those eyes *were* actually looking into hers. That little spark deep inside them flickered again and Cori couldn't look away any more.

My goodness.

She pressed her hands against the latte mug and hoped Simon wouldn't see them shaking.

'The thing is,' he said, 'I haven't done any proper painting for about six months. However, I—'

Rat tat tat.

They both looked up, startled, as somebody knocked on the window, right next to them. A small, dark-haired person was waving madly and grinning through the glass like a very attractive pixie.

Cori took in the bobbed hair with the pink streak down the side and the effortless designer look the girl had. She also noticed the girl's amazingly curious eyes – one blue and one green – and, although Cori knew very little about designer labels, this girl clearly did. Whatever brand she was wearing looked stunning. Cori knew that she personally would never, ever try to get away with skin-tight jeans and towering stilettoes; but this girl managed it and managed it well.

She always had done.

'Lissy!'

Cori and Simon both said it at the same time.

Lissy, as if she'd read their lips, smiled and waved maniacally this time.

'Wait there!' she shouted through the glass. She must have been shouting quite loudly as they heard her through the glazing. 'I'm coming in!'

Cori and Simon simply stared at each other.

'That's Lissy de Luca,' said Cori, rather unnecessarily.

'It most certainly is,' replied Simon. 'Bloody hellfire.'

* * *

'Fancy meeting you here!' said Lissy. Then she laughed; it was a little, tinkling laugh, as if she'd made a huge joke. 'Well, not so much of a surprise to see *you* here, Simon.' She turned to Cori. 'He's always here on a lunchtime. It's very easy to track him down. But *you*, Cori Keeling. I would never have thought to see *you* here!' She elegantly slid into the seat next to Cori, and smiled at them both somewhat triumphantly. 'Cori and I went to university together. We were on the same art history course,' she told Simon. 'She's always looked like Lizzie Siddal – clearly, you were right about that, most definitely. And she knew so much about the PRB it was unreal. I had my suspicions it was the same Cori when we were talking this morning as I really didn't think there could be two Coris like that. Especially when you said about the French king's mistress. That's *exactly* what she told me when we met as well. So, Cori. What *are* you doing in London? And if I may say so, it's wonderful to see you again.'

Cori stared at Lissy and heard Simon give a little groan of embarrassment. She chanced a look at him. His head was in his hands and he was shaking it slowly.

It had been how many years since she had seen Lissy? She thought the last time she had spoken to her was possibly their graduation ceremony, which was maybe eight years ago? It had to be that long. She was twenty-nine now, almost thirty; Lissy would be the same age. Good grief. And yet Lissy had just picked up again where she'd left off. It wasn't surprising, really, that Cori had bumped into her in the London art world. If anyone belonged there, it was Lissy de Luca. She had always seemed destined to be there – right in the middle of it all.

'I live here now,' said Cori. 'I just moved down a couple of months ago.'

'And are you enjoying everything the galleries and museums have to offer you?' asked Lissy. Although she said it innocently enough, there was a hint of amusement in her eyes and Cori had a feeling she didn't just mean was she enjoying the actual artworks. Lissy was as bad as Granny.

'So far I am,' Cori answered, carefully. 'And hopefully it'll continue.'

Lissy reached across and squeezed her arm. 'It will if I have anything to do with it,' she said. 'Speaking of which, what did you think of that article about *Ophelia*?'

'Excuse me,' said Simon. 'Sorry to interrupt the reunion, but—' He looked up and pushed his hand through his hair so it stuck up on end. He looked slightly shell-shocked, as he well might do, thought Cori. Although, if she was honest, she would like to know exactly what he'd said to Lissy about her. 'Would you like a coffee, Lissy?' He spread his hands out again, helplessly this time, as if he was resigned to the fact Lissy would be sharing what was left of his lunch hour.

'Ooh, an espresso would be simply perfect, darling!' said Lissy. 'Thank you.'

'Okay,' he said. He looked at Cori. 'Can I maybe get you another latte?' He had a slight crease between his eyebrows as if he was uncertain she would accept anything else from him, considering he had apparently discussed her with Lissy.

Cori smiled at him; she was sure, somehow, that whatever he had said was, at the very least, complimentary. 'I'd love one,' she said. 'But only if you've got time to have one with me.'

'He's got time,' interjected Lissy. 'It's absolutely fine. We'll go back together, they'll be very cool about it. I promise.'

Simon looked at her. 'The ironic thing is, she's right,' he said.

'I am,' replied Lissy. 'Oh, actually, I'll have a double espresso instead, if you don't mind. Thanks, darling.'

Simon nodded and stood up. Cori watched him push his seat away from the table and head off to the counter. Lissy, it was apparent, hadn't really changed in all those years. She was still confident and outspoken and, despite all that, still very likeable.

'Simon's one of the good guys,' said Lissy, interrupting her thoughts. 'I've known him for a while now. He deserves a nice girl in his life. Slutty was vile.'

'Slutty?' Cori stared at Lissy. 'Who on earth was Slutty?'

'His ex. She's called Sylvie really. But I call her Slutty.' Lissy shrugged, dismissing the woman. 'He's better off without her. But you! When he started describing this amazing girl he'd seen in the galleries, I just knew it had to be you. And I was sure I'd find him here – he's always here at lunchtimes – and I just wondered if he'd actually managed to see this amazing girl he spoke about, because that was clearly what he was desperate to do. Then I saw you here and bonus!' She clapped her hands. 'Yay!'

Cori laughed. 'You know, I'm not surprised you're involved with the Tate, Lissy. But I am actually surprised that I haven't bumped into you before now. We must have kept missing each other.'

'I don't have a set pattern, I just turn up,' said Lissy. 'And I've been around some other galleries as well. I can't stay in one place for too long. I start to miss the pictures at my other galleries.' She leaned her elbows on the table and rested her chin in her hands. She let her gaze rove over Cori and nodded. 'Yes. Still like Lizzie. Gosh, I'm *so* pleased we met again!'

'Lizzie Siddal was stunning,' said Cori, 'but the whole Lizzie legend makes that Daisy Ashford story all the more interesting, doesn't it?'

'I know! And what an exciting time for you to be here!' said Lissy. 'Right here on the doorstep as the whole thing unfolds.'

'Ah,' said Simon, appearing with the drinks. 'I wondered how long it would be before Daisy Ashford was mentioned.

Looks like I got back just in time. At least my lunch break wasn't gate-crashed needlessly.' He put the tray on the table and lifted Cori's latte off it first. Carefully, he placed the mug in front of her, then took the tiny espresso cup off and placed that in front of Lissy.

'Oh, thank you, darling,' said Lissy, picking the cup up. The artificial light in the coffee shop winked off her perfectly manicured, sugar-pink nails and she pursed her Cupid's bow lips as she blew on the coffee. 'Lizzie was the original supermodel,' she continued, after an elegant sip of the strong, dark liquid. She didn't even leave a lipstick mark on the white cup. 'I've heard her called that before. Even down to the drug habit and eating disorder.'

'Lissy!' Simon laughed. 'Stop generalising!'

'Well, okay. Maybe they haven't *all* got a habit,' said Lissy, pulling a face. 'But she did. It's well documented. Maybe she was a fraction taller than you, Cori? And I don't think your features are *quite* as sharp,' she pondered, 'but Lizzie had a very strange beauty. She was compelling, I think.'

'Exactly. She was so unique. And I just think that if Daisy looked enough like Lizzie to fool the world, well – anything is possible, isn't it?' said Cori.

'Indeed it is,' said Simon. '"It seems a thing to wonder on", as Rossetti himself put it.'

'Oh, I *love* that poem!' said Cori, sitting up straighter. 'It's so powerful. He must have really adored her to write about her like that.'

'*The Portrait*,' sniffed Lissy as if she wanted to prove her knowledge alongside Cori and Simon. 'Everybody knows that poem. "This is her picture as she was: it seems a thing to wonder on, as though mine image in the glass should tarry when myself am gone."' Lissy recited the poem as if she had learned it by rote, speaking the lines tonelessly at the approximate pace of a galloping horse.

Cori hid a smile behind her coffee cup. No, Lissy hadn't changed.

'Anyway,' said Lissy, putting her cup down, 'let's get back to Daisy Ashford. The diary clearly implies that she was a model for Millais when he painted *Ophelia*. Though there is, of course, no way of proving it.'

'I suppose not,' agreed Cori. 'But how amazing would it be to see that diary and dig a bit further? You never know, my great-great-great-aunt may be mentioned in it somewhere. Having said that, we're not sure at what point she supposedly had the affair with Rossetti. And I'm not entirely sure how many "greats" away she is either.'

'But one of your actual ancient relatives had an affair with Rossetti?' repeated Lissy. 'How marvellous! I don't remember you saying anything about that.'

'I'm fairly sure I would have mentioned it, Lissy,' said Cori, amused. 'It's my family's greatest claim to fame.' Lissy had never really been one for listening to other people though. She'd always been racing around the campus, flitting from one thing to another like a butterfly.

'That's *so* interesting!' said Lissy, looking at Cori with renewed respect. 'Gosh you could be related to him – the descendant of an illegitimate Rossetti child. Imagine that!'

'I think I'd have a little more artistic talent if I was,' said Cori. 'If I am related, then all I inherited from them was my name and my hair colour.'

'I never saw any mention of a Corisande in the diary,' said Lissy, thoughtfully, 'but then she may have just been mentioned as a nameless lover.'

For a moment, the world stopped turning. Had Cori really heard Lissy correctly? She opened her mouth to ask the question, but Lissy railroaded on.

'My sister-in-law has the diary, you know. She's the one who wrote the article.'

'But that was Becky Nelson,' said Cori.

'Yes. Becky's married to my brother, Jon,' said Lissy.

'Then surely she would be Becky de Luca?' said Cori, quickly working the logical stuff out. 'Or did she keep her maiden name?' Whatever she'd done, there was no way she would ever have linked Becky Nelson to Lissy de Luca.

'No.' Lissy shook her head and the pink streaks danced amongst the glossy darkness. 'Jon's my half-brother. We've got different fathers. So he's Jon Nelson. He's a photographer. I grew up with Becky – she's still my best friend after all these years. And sort of a sister now as well. Oh! And I'm going to be an aunty soon. I can't wait! Can I Simon?' She clapped her hands again. '*So* exciting. Can't you remember Becky, Cori?'

It was Cori's turn to shake her head, still thrown by the revelation. 'No,' she said. 'Did she ever visit you? Ever come up at any point where I would have met her?'

'Probably not,' said Lissy. 'In fact, no. No. I'm not the best at keeping in touch.' She had the grace to look ashamed – or as about as ashamed as she could ever look – and shook her head again. 'We talked through e-mails and texts mainly while I was at university. It's much better now I see her more regularly. But we still rely a *lot* on e-mails and texts.'

Cori was trying to process the information, as was Simon it seemed.

'So, Lissy, backtrack a little, would you?' he said. 'Let's return to the diary. Becky's got it – how? How did she get it? And no—' he looked at Cori, his eyes confused now but oh so hypnotic. His hair was still sticking up a little, though, and Cori fought back the urge to smooth it down for him by sitting firmly on her hands. 'Cori, I didn't make the connection either. I promise. And Lissy – you never said anything!'

'Hmm. I was desperate to really,' Lissy said, frowning. 'But if I did people would have probed and made things awkward and you know what it's like. I wouldn't have had a *moment's* peace at the gallery.' She rolled her eyes. '*So* difficult.'

Cori wondered wryly if it had been difficult for Lissy to keep her mouth shut, or just difficult to decide what to do about it all. She suspected it was the first thing.

'And I'm afraid,' Lissy continued, far too innocently, 'that I have to take credit for finding the diary in the first place – but Becky brought it all together. I think she should write a book about it, as well as the one she did about the Carrick family. But she says she won't. She is *so* stubborn.' Lissy shook her head. 'You just can't tell her. She insists upon hiding behind her words. And it's not like she's horrendously ugly or anything, she'd look fabulous in the publicity shots if she would only let me give her a proper makeover.'

Cori almost felt sorry for Becky. She thought that having Lissy as a sister-in-law might mean a high maintenance relationship somewhere along the line; and she imagined an ongoing battle of wills wouldn't be too far off the mark either.

'Anyway. Becky loves bits of junk and old things. She always has done. That's probably why she married Jon,' said Lissy as if the thought had just occurred to her. 'She'd shown no interest in him all the time we were growing up. Who knows how these things work. One weekend together, years later, and that was it.' She shook her head as if she was still trying to understand how her friend could have fallen for her brother.

Cori and Simon exchanged a smile.

'Anyway, I found the diary in a gallery. One of those little hidden places that are truly gems. It was in Yorkshire – near Staithes, which isn't far from Whitby. They had an artists' colony up there and I was helping out with the archiving in the museum for an exhibition. I found that book in a trunk full of bits and pieces someone had donated eons ago. Way before the current owners took over. It was buried under some old playbills, shoved in the corner, right at the back of the room.' She grinned an evil little goblinesque grin. 'Let's just say I borrowed it.'

She took another sip of espresso and put the cup down again. 'So it came home with me, and then I took it to Becky and told her she could borrow it because she might find it interesting. She thinks it was a lucky find in a junk shop. I shan't enlighten her. She said last week she was finished with it, so I could pick it up next time I was in Yorkshire. And I'm planning to go up this weekend. Do you want to come too? I can tell her I bumped into my old friend Cori, who's from Northumbria and now living in London, but she's a bit homesick, so I'm bringing her with me at the weekend for some company and some good old northern sea air. And then when I get the diary back, you can borrow it straight away.'

Cori just stared at her. 'Lissy! I don't know …' she began.

'Lissy!' Simon said, angrily. 'Maybe Cori can't just drop everything and swan up to Yorkshire—'

'It's not just Yorkshire, darling. It's Whitby!' said Lissy. 'Everybody loves a trip to Whitby!'

'Lissy!' Simon said again.

'Hold on. Whitby?' said Cori. 'I love Whitby. I haven't been in ages!'

'There you go, then. Perfect,' said Lissy, triumphantly.

Cori reminded herself that she had sworn she would grab every possible opportunity afforded to her in London so she could fully break free from Evan. She had accepted a coffee with Simon. She had begun networking to get her commissions built up. And she had, literally, just reconnected with Lissy, after a fashion. This was just another opportunity, wasn't it? She loved Whitby; always had done. And yes, some nice, fresh sea air might blow the cobwebs away a little bit. Literally. Her house seriously was a tip.

And it wasn't like she didn't know Lissy. They had shared three years of their lives together, probing the PRB and the Impressionists and many other art movements as well. They'd been good friends at university; shared almost every secret they'd had between them.

Then Lissy had dropped off the radar. Cori was, however, a great believer in Fate. She had, she chose to think, reconnected with Lissy for a good reason. So—

'You know what; count me in, Lissy,' she said. 'I'm not going to overthink it.'

'And what about you, Simon?' Lissy turned to him, blinking wide, innocent eyes. 'Do you want to come as well? It should be a good day out – all friends together, sort of thing. And I don't think you're scheduled to work this weekend, are you?'

'No, you are right, I'm not scheduled to work,' said Simon. 'But you're unbelievable, Lissy. You can't just expect everyone to fall in line with your plans. We might have been busy this weekend.' He looked helplessly at Cori, and her stomach somersaulted. Had he been contemplating asking her out at the weekend? That would have been very nice indeed. 'And anyway,' he continued, 'who's to say your Becky's even happy for us all to call in?'

'No, look, it's fine,' said Cori, quickly. 'I have to say, I'm very happy to go to Whitby. It doesn't even matter if we don't see Becky. I just all of a sudden want to go to Whitby. And Simon. It would be great if you came as well.'

She hoped he'd understand that, Whitby or not, she wanted to spend a bit more time with him this weekend. A lot more time with him, if she was honest.

It had been really lovely seeing Lissy and the story she had just told them was amazing. But it was Simon she had wanted to meet today and Simon she wanted to get to know better.

A four-hour trip on a train each way to Whitby and back might be a jolly good way of actually doing that.

Simon watched her for a moment, as if he was contemplating the very same thing. 'All right,' he said, eventually. His eyes never left her and she felt herself grow scarlet again. 'I'll come as well. If you guys are happy to have me.'

Cori just nodded. Their gaze never broke. 'I'm happy with that,' she said. 'Very happy.'

'Great,' said Simon. A little smile twitched at the corner of his mouth. 'I'm glad we're all happy.'

Lissy smiled. 'Fantastic. Becky won't have a problem with it at all, I'm sure. She's quite sociable. She'll probably give you biscuits. Can't stop her eating the things at the minute. I'll text her right now and tell her to expect all three of us.' She started to rummage in her bag to find her mobile phone but Simon tried to intervene, the look between him and Cori finally breaking as he transferred his attention to Lissy.

'Please. Don't put pressure on Becky like that!' he said. 'And don't think you can text her right now and expect an answer within ten minutes or so. Cori and I can always do something else if it's a problem.'

'Oh, I don't expect her to answer straight away,' said Lissy, locating her mobile and pressing some keys as she spoke. 'She'll probably have her phone lying around somewhere out of sight. She'll answer me when she gets around to it. But at least my part of the deal is done, if I actually send a message. There.' She smiled at them. 'It's done. Now let's just sit back and wait for her to agree.'

56

Chapter Twelve

Two hundred and fifty miles away, in a comfortable, messy lounge above a photographic studio in Whitby, Becky Nelson's fingers were flying over a laptop keyboard. She was two-thirds of the way through writing an article about the wonderful Countess of Warwick, who scandalised Edwardian society by complaining that her lover's wife was pregnant.

Becky couldn't help being in awe of the Countess and deeming her, despite her faults, a truly amazing woman. Becky had just reached the part where the Countess was trying to blackmail King George V to help clear her debts – she had, after all, been lover to his father, King Edward VII and felt it was the least she deserved – when she became aware, out of the corner of her eye, that her mobile phone was jumping around the desk, vibrating madly.

Becky groaned inwardly. She lifted her hand off the keyboard and none too gently flicked the offending phone away, so it skittered along the desk out of sight. She was in Daisy Greville's world, not this world, and she wanted to finish the article. She mused briefly on the fact that she had stumbled across Daisy, Countess of Warwick, when she was looking for information on another Daisy – the Daisy Ashford who had shot her to supernova stardom in certain circles. But as far as she was concerned, the Lizzie/Daisy/*Ophelia* task was one job done, and more jobs waited in the wings.

It seemed that not everybody thought that way, though. The Internet hits were frightening, not to mention the fact that people had been hounding her for interviews and completely random strangers had been e-mailing her and asking for sight of the diary. Only two days ago, someone from the local cafe had approached her and asked her if she would sign their copy of the article. Becky thought that things couldn't get much more bizarre, until a man on television claimed to be a conspiracy theorist and said that yes, it was indeed true that Daisy Ashford had been the model for *Ophelia*, because the real Lizzie had been abducted by aliens and it was all a huge cover-up by the Government at the time.

So when she saw the phone blinking and announcing yet another message, Becky decided to ignore it for a little while and concentrate on Countess Daisy instead.

Half an hour later, she was done. Becky stretched like a cat and scraped her seat back from the desk. She stood up and reached for the coat she had abandoned first thing this morning and slipped it on. She picked up her purse and headed down the rickety stairs to the studio where her husband, Jon, was apparently spared – for the moment, anyway – from the steady trade of tourist traffic. The studio was empty and he had piles of photographs all neatly packaged on the counter next to him, ready for people to collect.

He was on the telephone accepting a booking, it seemed, for a wedding some months hence and looked up as she approached. He waved and smiled, and Becky crooked her thumb and forefinger together and mimed drinking coffee. Jon's eyes lit up and he gave her a thumbs-up sign. She smiled at him and pushed the door open, taking a deep breath of sea air and heading towards the local cafe. It was the same one where Lucy the barista had asked for her autograph – but they sold the best coffee in Whitby and Becky couldn't hold the fact that Lucy was now slightly star-struck against the cafe.

So it wasn't until Becky had returned, and spent some time helping out in the studio, that she finally went back upstairs to her workstation and remembered the skittering phone. She swore and picked it up, swiping the screen lock off. One new text message. From Lissy. Saying that she was travelling up to Whitby with a couple of friends this weekend and she hoped it was all right if they all popped in.

I know Cori from uni, the text message elaborated. She's the absolute double of Lizzie S and knows heaps about PRB. And Simon really really likes her as well. Lol! Got to try and matchmake – his ex was a cowbag. Good opportunity to get them together, don't you think? xxxxx

No problem, Becky replied. And remember, you can take the diary back with you as well. Xxx

The message came straight back.

Hurrah! Hoped you'd say that. See you Saturday love you muchly. Mwah! Xxx

Love you too Lissy! Xxx typed Becky, shaking her head. Lissy was very exuberant, even in her texts.

She would never change. Becky ran her hand thoughtfully over her bump and imagined Lissy babysitting as she had frequently insisted she was going to do.

One smear of chocolate on Lissy's designer clothes would probably put her off the idea for good – but it would be fun to watch her try, at any rate.

'Hopefully this should work out well,' Lissy had said on the phone to Cori, Friday evening. 'I'm going to make a weekend of it and do lots of baby shopping in York, and you guys can do what you like afterwards. Becky says she's definitely going to give me the diary back, so it can be your turn to borrow it. Anyway, do you think you'll stay over? I can recommend a really nice hotel if you want it – Carrick Park. Becky and Jon love it there. You can phone up now and book a room. If it's meant to be, they'll have a vacancy.'

Cori had laughed. 'What are you trying to do, Lissy? Do you not think that's a bit fast? Throwing us together for a whole weekend like that? I don't even know if Simon is that interested in me!' Secretly, she hoped he was – but she wasn't going to admit that to Lissy. However, her comment paid off.

'I'm not trying to throw you together,' Lissy had said, affronted. 'I never said you had to share *one* room, did I? But you know – you could do if you wanted. I happen to know Simon is really keen. I can't drag him away from the Millais Gallery just in case a certain someone appears. And he stares at *Ophelia* the whole time, just imagining that certain someone's face.'

'Lissy!' Cori had said. 'Stop it. Right now.'

But again, secretly, she had been thrilled.

So that was how it came to be that Lissy was currently leading the way up a small side street in rain-soaked Whitby, and walking into a tiny, narrow building that seemed to be a photographer's studio.

'Here we are!' Lissy said as she held the door open for Cori and Simon. Somewhere, a bell rang announcing their entry and a man popped his head out of a little room.

'Lissy!' The man dashed towards them, flinging the door open. His face split into a huge smile and he held his arms out to welcome Lissy. Cori assumed the room had to be the darkroom, judging by the smell of chemicals that assailed her nostrils. She wrinkled her nose and looked around the studio. It was an intriguing little place, and actually seemed larger on the inside than she had first thought.

'Hello, Jon!' cried Lissy. 'Jon, these are my friends, Cori and Simon – I've told them all about you, so they're popping in to say hello. Becky said it was fine. Then I'm not sure if they're heading off into the town afterwards.'

'We might do,' said Simon, holding out his hand to Jon. 'I've never been to Whitby before, but Cori said she knows it pretty well, so I'll trust her judgement.'

'Nice to meet you,' said Jon, shaking Simon's hand. He turned to Cori. 'And you, Cori. Becky said Lissy was bringing some friends.' He smiled at Cori. 'She said you went to university together. I think I remember you from the graduation, but Lissy wasn't the best at introducing people to us. Not after two bottles of champagne, anyway.'

'No, it wasn't my best moment,' said Lissy, frowning. She turned to Simon. 'Let's just say I had a very nice black eye the day after and I couldn't remember a thing about how I got it.'

'You fell off your stilettos and hit the bar face-on,' said Jon. 'It was quite comical, really.'

'For you, maybe,' said Lissy, sniffing. 'Cori, Simon, I suggest you have a look at the pictures around the walls or gaze in awe at the beautiful costumes. They are far more interesting than idle gossip.'

'Oh, it's not idle gossip,' said Cori. 'It was me you spilt your drink on as you fell. So, yes, Jon, you probably do remember me. Usually it's my hair that people remember.'

'There you go, then,' said Jon, grinning. His eyes were exactly the same as Lissy's – one blue, one green.

'Right, that's enough!' said Lissy. 'Go away and look at pictures. No more talking about me, please.'

Cori laughed and began to look around as Lissy had suggested. Her attention was soon caught by a photograph on the wall of a pretty, dark-haired girl sitting at a desk. There was an old-fashioned writing slope in front of her, and her face displayed a strange sort of concentration.

'Do you like it?' Jon came over. 'That's Becky. It was taken a couple of years ago now. It's my favourite photograph.'

'It's lovely,' said Cori. 'I love her dress.'

The man looked at the picture and his face softened. 'Yes, it's a beautiful dress,' he said. 'It's a special one.'

'And you do those dressing-up shots as well, I guess,' said Simon. He was peering at some more pictures on the wall.

'I sense a theme here. The costumes are stunning. I'd love access to this sort of thing – it would make painting these styles so much easier if you could see them for real.'

'I agree. Black lace, velvet and jet,' said Cori. Her eyes had already settled on the racks of clothes that stood by the wall. 'All very nice indeed. True Gothic splendour.'

Simon looked at her. 'You'd suit that look, I think.'

'Perhaps she would,' interrupted Lissy, 'but what I want to know is whether Becky is around or not.' She looked over at a wardrobe and leaned a little, trying to peer around it. Cori spotted a door propped open and behind it a well hidden and, it had to be said, fairly unsteady looking staircase leading up on to another floor.

'Where else would she be?' answered Jon. 'She's not out on any of her journalistic jaunts today. We knew you were coming, so she said she would stay upstairs and catch up on some bits and pieces. And I hope, Lissy, that you're happy I've lost my assistant for the day.' He turned to Cori. 'We work together. Well, when I say work together, I work down here and her domain is the laptop in the flat upstairs, unless she gets bored. In which case she wanders off or comes down to see what's going on. I'll just go and let her know you're here. I think it's nearly coffee time, anyway.' He turned and half-lolloped, half-bounded across the room and up the stairs.

'Any excuse to stop for coffee,' Lissy said with a sigh, shaking her head. She hoisted herself up onto the counter and sat by the till, swinging her legs so her heels bashed off the old, chipped wooden front of the counter.

'You know, all the times I ever came to Whitby and I passed this street, I never thought I'd visit like this,' said Cori, slightly in awe of the place; it had such a nice feeling to it.

'Life has a funny way of directing us,' replied Simon. 'Oh!' He rustled around in his jacket pocket and brought out a neatly typed piece of A4 paper. 'Remember the letter I was telling you about at the gallery. The one Millais wrote when he was painting *Ophelia* saying that he had been threatened with trespassing in the field. It might give you some context if you haven't had a chance to look it up yet. I particularly like the bit where he says he is "in danger of being blown by the wind into the water, and becoming intimate with the feelings of Ophelia when that Lady sank to muddy death."' Simon grinned. 'It's yours. I copied it for you. It was originally written to Martha Combe, his patron, Thomas Combe's wife.' He held the letter out to her and Cori took it, delighted.

She opened her mouth to respond but her attention was caught by two figures coming down the stairs. Jon was in front, and a woman was behind him. As she stashed the letter in her bag, Cori realised that this was the same girl from the photograph she had just been admiring. She was pretty – not as stunning as the photo made her out to be – but it was definitely her, even though she had apparently cut her chestnut hair a bit shorter since the photograph had been taken.

Cori's eyes were automatically drawn to the girl's neatly rounded tummy. Lissy had said she was going to be an aunty soon – and Becky was, Cori judged, about six or seven months pregnant. The same as she, Cori, would have been, had the scare been real. She felt a little pang. She would be lying if she said she'd actually hoped it wasn't a scare; it was the truth that she had been genuinely upset when she found out she wasn't pregnant.

The only good thing, she supposed, was that she had made the break with Evan over it and moved away. And she'd found out what Evan was like before it had actually reached the stage of parenthood, nappies and sleepless nights. Somehow, she couldn't see him settling to that sort of life any time soon.

'Becky!' cried Lissy, jumping off the counter and running to the girl. She pulled her towards her in a bear hug, which seemed way out of proportion to Lissy's actual size. Then she held her away and looked at her tummy approvingly. 'Gosh, look at you now! Anyway, this is Cori, my friend from uni, and this is Simon, from the Tate. And this,' she indicated the dark-haired girl, 'is the famous journalist, Becky Nelson; my lovely sister-in-law. She wrote the *Ophelia* article.'

'I'm not famous,' said Becky. 'I just wrote an interesting article, that's all. I wish I was getting paid per hit on the Internet. I'd be wealthy by now.'

'You wrote an interesting book as well,' said Lissy. 'That one about Ella. Oh, it's lovely – you know, Cori, that one I mentioned about the Carrick family? You and Simon will have to read it some time. She won't promote herself, you know.'

Becky smiled and tucked a strand of hair behind her ear, then pushed her hands in the pockets of her jeans. 'Not my style, Lissy. I keep telling you. Anyway – Lissy told me a bit about you guys. She said you're both interested in the PRB. I don't blame you. Lissy knows more than I do, obviously, but I enjoyed writing the article.'

'I bumped into Cori when she was looking at *Ophelia*,' said Simon. He was standing very close to Cori, Cori realised. She could feel the warmth coming off him and was quite happy to stay like that for a little longer.

'Yes, Lissy said as much,' replied Becky. 'It's ages since I saw *Ophelia* myself, but I've certainly got people talking about it. I suppose that's a good thing!'

Jon laughed, and laid his hand on Becky's arm. 'Of course it is,' he said. 'It's always good to encourage people to study artworks. Look, I've just got to finish developing these plates for someone, then I'll be up for coffee, okay?' He turned and disappeared back into the darkroom.

Becky watched him go then turned to Cori and Simon. 'Do you want a coffee?' she asked. 'The kettle's on, so it's no bother.'

Cori looked at Simon. 'Well, if you're sure you don't mind,' she said. 'I'm quite happy to have one. Unless Simon wants to go and find one in the town?'

'I'm happy to have one here. Then we can have another one later,' said Simon.

Becky laughed. 'Did Lissy tell you that's how I bumped into Jon again? He spilled my coffee in the middle of Goth Weekend and he insisted on buying me another. He's lucky he didn't ruin my camera. Come on, we'll head up to the flat. Just mind the stairs, they're lethal if you're not used to them.'

She turned and led the way up such an uneven, narrow mish-mash of steps that Cori stumbled halfway up. Simon tried to catch her before she fell flat on her face, but was too late. She knocked a framed picture off the wall and it bounced towards the bottom of the stairs.

'Oh, crikey! I'm sorry. It's fine, I haven't damaged anything, don't worry,' she said as she tried and failed to push past Simon and rescue the picture. Luckily, Simon had already caught it and handed it back to her.

'Oh, don't worry, I doubt she even heard it,' said Lissy, popping her head out of a tiny hallway at the top of the stairs. 'She's just about deaf as a post. You wouldn't know it, would you?'

'Wow,' said Cori, feeling herself grow hot with embarrassment. 'I'm sorry, I—'

'God, she's had plenty of time to get used to the idea,' said Lissy. 'I wouldn't worry about it. We don't. It's sometimes quite a good excuse to be naughty,' she continued. 'Jon smashed a super-posh mug of hers last week in the kitchen. She never flinched. She was in the lounge at the time. I don't even think she's noticed it's missing, to be honest.'

'I notice enough, Lissy,' came Becky's voice from along the corridor. 'Don't underestimate me.'

'Whoops,' said Lissy.

Cori blushed again, this time on Lissy's behalf. But at least she had made it safely up the rest of the stairs without wrecking anything else. She followed Lissy into what she assumed was the lounge she had just mentioned. It wasn't the biggest of rooms, but had marvellous picture windows overlooking the streets of Whitby and a comfortable-looking three-piece suite, arranged so the occupants could look at the view.

'Sit down. Coffee all round? Just milk, no sugar, yes?' Lissy didn't wait for an answer but waved at the sofa, taking charge and inviting them to sit down before she headed into the small, galley kitchen, which led off from the lounge.

Cori noticed that a desk stood by the wall, with an open laptop on it. Reams of paper were scattered around the floor with more paper piled up on a little bookcase next to the chair. Cori noticed that the chair was facing the door. Becky clearly disliked being surprised by unwanted visitors.

'This is unbelievable, isn't it?' said Simon. He looked around, apparently in awe of the place. 'How wonderful. I'd love somewhere like this. Kind of sparse on the ground in London though, I would imagine. How old would you say it is?'

'Two hundred years? Three hundred, maybe? I don't know – but yes, it's fabulous.' Cori twisted around and watched as Lissy basically got in the way in the tiny kitchen, bustling around with a mug in each hand and not much purpose. Then Lissy drifted off out of the room, muttering something about telling Jon to hurry up. Cori assumed she was going to get him, perhaps wave a mug under his nose or something and tempt him upstairs. Personally, she wouldn't fancy trying that staircase with two hot mugs of coffee.

There was a clatter as Becky came out of the kitchen

balancing a tray full of coffee and biscuits – just as Lissy had predicted. She kicked the door shut behind her and Simon stood up to help but she shook her head and came through the lounge to them, apparently concentrating on not spilling anything.

'I'm fine thanks,' she said. 'And it's a seventeenth-century building. So what's that? Nearer to four hundred years?' She placed the tray on the small coffee table and stood up, regarding it triumphantly. Then she nodded towards a mirror hanging by the door of the kitchen, reflecting Cori and Simon on the sofa – and clearly, Cori realised, reflecting their conversation. 'Nothing's sacred in here. They think it is, but it isn't.' Becky grinned and sat down on an armchair. 'There has to be some benefits. Don't tell them about it – it's too much fun.' She leaned forward and took a mug, then sat back again, curling her feet underneath her. 'Lissy also told me you looked a lot like Lizzie Siddal. I love your hair. I tried to dye mine that colour once and it was hideous. Never again.'

'Lizzie and all the PRB "stunners" made it fashionable,' said Cori. 'I was teased all the time at school, though. Bunch of heathens.'

Becky laughed. 'We live and learn. They're probably all jealous now.'

'Perhaps,' said Cori.

'Well, I hope they read my article and felt guilty,' said Becky. 'Obviously people like Lizzie were celebrities in their day. That's probably why Daisy Ashford wanted to be like her. I think I've inadvertently started some cult or other about this Daisy thing.'

'I suppose it's the natural reaction to the Lizzie Siddal connection,' said Cori. 'She's fascinating. Now that I'm living in London I am a regular visitor to the Tate and the Millais Gallery, and especially *Ophelia*. Way back, or so family legend has it, one of my relatives had an affair with

Rossetti. A great-great-great-aunt. I don't know whether it was before, after or during his relationship with Lizzie, but ever since someone told me I looked like her I've been ever so slightly obsessed. Not in a weird way, but the PRB were my passion at uni and I still read everything I can get my hands on about them. Your article was one of the most interesting things I've read for a long time. It was something I didn't already know.'

Becky nodded. 'Sometimes things can grab your imagination like that. Or we get connections to objects and we just don't know why. You see that writing slope over there?' She nodded to a small, battered box on a shelf by the fireplace. 'Well, that's how I felt about that. The more I got to know about the slope and the people who had used it, the more things in my own life started to make more sense to me. Then I wrote a book about the Carrick family who owned it and it felt good to get their story out there after so many years. I think they would have been happy too.' She glanced up towards the door. 'Oh, here's Jon. I knew it wouldn't take him long. He can sense a coffee cup a mile off.'

'Lissy told me it was ready,' said Jon, 'only I've now lost her downstairs. She's spotted the new costumes and she's poking through them.' He took the spare chair and sank back into it. 'Anyway, it does me good to have a break. Tourist season means it's manic here. You should see the place at Goth Weekend.' He shook his head and smiled. 'You can't move for black taffeta. I love it.'

'Goth Weekend is amazing,' said Becky. 'I love it too. It's even better when people don't spill coffee on your camera. You should come, Cori. And you, Simon. We could get you dressed up downstairs – take a picture of you both. You'd look fantastic, Cori, especially with your hair loose. You'd look really Pre-Raphaelite then. Like Miranda out of Waterhouse's 1916 *Tempest*. Wouldn't you agree, Jon?

We'd have to go medieval rather than Victorian though, but we could stand you on the beach for it.'

'I don't know about that!' said Cori. 'I'm not model material.'

'I think the PRB would have loved you,' said Simon. He was watching her with something like amusement in his eyes. 'You'd look perfect for Miranda,' he said. 'Obviously, the model wasn't Lizzie, but she was a gorgeous lady. Her identity has always been a bit of a mystery.'

'It sounds like the sort of thing Julia Margaret Cameron photographed,' said Cori. 'But, Simon; if I have to be Miranda and I have to stand on the beach in a storm, what would you do? Would you just stay in the studio and paint pictures where it's warm?'

'I'd do whatever it took to look authentic,' he said. 'It's all art, at the end of the day. I'm not sure I'd be happy in a suit of armour though. I'd maybe stick to Victorian Goth if I had to.'

And actually, as far as Victorian Goth went, Cori could actually see Simon in a top hat and a frock coat; and what about herself, if she ever ventured into Victoriana after her Miranda costume?

She thought she might go for one of those wonderful corseted creations. It would push what little bust she had upwards and pull her in at the waist so she wasn't quite so straight up and down.

She thought about the corset and the amount of flesh it could potentially expose. Her granny's voice came into her mind, saying something old-fashioned about dumplings and boiling over, and she quickly looked down, pretending to study her coffee cup so people couldn't read her face and guess at her thoughts. Oh my. She heard her name again and looked up.

'Anyway, I'm going to shut up about taking photos before I terrify Cori any more,' said Becky, smiling at Cori.

'You have some very interesting ideas, Becky,' said Jon. 'I like them.' He quirked a smile. 'Anyway, before we do terrify you,' he said, looking at Cori and Simon, 'I have to say that I can't even begin to imagine what working with my sister is like, Simon. It must be horrific.'

'Actually, Lissy's amazing to work with,' said Simon. 'It's like having an over-enthusiastic puppy around the place. The customers love her.'

'She's awful,' said Becky, shifting position and laying her hand across her tummy. 'She'll never change. Yet she keeps on getting results!'

Jon nodded in agreement. 'You can't dispute that,' he said.

Cori watched them, so comfortable in each other's company and was willing to bet Lissy had been involved in their story somehow.

A little voice inside her suggested Lissy was trying to matchmake her and Simon – and she kind of hoped it was true – and also that it would work.

Chapter Thirteen

Simon decided that he loved this little flat above the photographer's studio. If he was ever lucky enough to own a building where he could sell his art downstairs and paint upstairs, he would be a happy man.

And if, for instance, he had Cori to pop up and see every so often, his life would be perfect. He imagined Becky and Jon Nelson must have a pretty strong relationship. It couldn't be easy, working with your partner and spending 24-7 with them, even if sometimes Becky did apparently go off on 'journalistic jaunts' as Jon called them. Simon was willing to bet Becky wouldn't go away any longer than she had to.

Simon slid a glance over to Cori. He saw how she was perched on the edge of her chair, totally absorbed by the conversation and he loved her energy. Today, she had her hair tied up in a messy sort of bun. Again, he itched to capture it on paper. Charcoal, he thought, a simple line drawing with the corkscrew tendrils flowing away from her perfect face. She laughed at something, then, as if she knew he was watching, she turned slightly and caught his eye. He was too slow to look away – but he found she didn't look away either. They looked at each other, eyes locked, until Becky's voice interrupted his thoughts.

'Look, I was going to give this to Lissy to take back today, but you might as well have a read of it, Cori.' She reached over the arm of the sofa and lifted a battered, leather bound journal onto her knee. She lowered her eyes briefly as she ran her hand over the embossed cover and then looked up again at Cori. 'Knowing Lissy, she'd probably pass it straight on to you anyway. You might find your aunt in there – or at least something nobody else has discovered. Then you can have the next round of glory.'

'Really?' Cori looked taken aback. 'Is that Daisy's diary? Are you sure?'

'Quite sure,' said Becky. 'Enjoy it. Write about it. Do a Masters in the PRB. Or something.' She shrugged her shoulders. 'Just have fun with it. It really is very interesting, but I've got too many other projects on the go to do any more with it right now.'

Cori laughed, a little nervously. 'But what happens if I discover something that does actually blow the *Ophelia* story out of the water? So many people will just hate me.'

'You don't have to tell the world, do you?' said Becky. 'Maybe don't write a dissertation on it after all. Perhaps it'll be enough for just one person to know the truth; maybe two.' Simon saw her cast a quick glance up at Jon. 'You have to decide. And if more people need to know, I'm sure you'll pick the right time to talk about it.'

'Three people might need to know,' said Lissy, 'at *least*.' Simon was aware of a perfumed blast as Lissy swept past him and sat on the floor by Jon. 'Don't forget me. I'm the one who makes all the fabulous discoveries. I found that diary.'

'Yes, Lissy. It's all about you,' said Jon. He looked at Simon. 'Is she like this at work? Always poking around antique shops and boring you with the details?'

'Worse,' replied Simon. 'We call her the Junk Shop Junkie.'

'I couldn't possibly bore anyone!' cried Lissy. She looked at Becky, her eyes wide and innocent. 'Tell them. Tell them, Becky. Tell them how interesting I am.'

'Actually, can I pass on that one?' said Becky. Lissy opened her mouth, probably to complain, but Becky raised her hand and waved her comments away. 'I'm joking. Yes. You're very interesting. Okay. There you go, Cori.' She leaned over the coffee table and passed the diary to Cori. 'You probably know more about the PRB than me, but if you want to get in touch to discuss anything, you know where I am.'

Cori touched the book reverently. But then, more than that, Simon saw a slanting ray of sunlight break through the clouds over the rooftops and pour in through the windows of the flat. It didn't seem to be an accident that it alighted on Cori and shot gold through her hair and pink in her cheeks. Simon blinked. He knew then that he was truly lost.

As if he'd even doubted it for a single second since the moment he first saw her.

Cori held Daisy's diary in her hand and it felt as if she had held it a hundred times before. Her fingers fitted exactly in the slight indentations on the cover and she seemed to instinctively know the feel of the tooling pattern around the edge.

She opened it, and caught sight of an entry from April 1861.

Today we visited Hastings and Fairlight Downs. It is so nice here away from the smog and bustle of London. Sometimes I just want to breathe fresh air and forget everything. I feel alive here, and I like that feeling. I promised I would show Henry the sights in Hastings, but he made me draw and paint the sea before we had any fun at all. He takes his duties too seriously at times, but I can forgive him for that. He had also packed a picnic, which was a very pleasant surprise. My painting, of course, was admired by him – as indeed it should have been.

Cori couldn't help but smile. A day trip to the coast, away from London, with someone who enjoyed painting. That sounded familiar.

'Who's Henry?' she asked, looking up at Becky.

'He's Daisy's art tutor,' said Becky. 'At least, that's the impression I get. She doesn't seem to have been the best student though. She's usually complaining that her work is awful and it's all Henry's fault, of course, poor man.'

'Sounds like me,' said Cori, with a grin. 'I'm hopeless. I'm very jealous of people who can draw and paint. Which makes me quite sure that I am not a descendant of some illicit Rossetti affair. But still,' she closed the book and clutched it to her chest, 'I shall enjoy seeing if I can spot Corisande anywhere and, even better, getting my hands on a primary resource. Thanks again.'

'You're very welcome,' said Becky.

Becky watched Cori handle the diary and she also saw the sun alight on Cori through the window.

For a split second, Cori wavered out of focus. And it may have been Becky's imagination, but she thought she saw another Cori, slightly to one side of her; another red-haired girl, leaning over and looking at the book in the same way that Cori was. Becky moved forward and the image was gone.

Her heart pounding, she looked at the little group of people in the room wondering if anyone else had seen it. Lissy was chewing the corner of her thumbnail whilst saying something nonsensical to her brother and Jon in turn was draining his coffee cup and nodding. Simon was looking at Cori, a smile hovering around his lips and Cori, unaware of his reverence, glanced up again and saw Becky looking at her. She smiled and it lit up the room.

No, thought Becky, smiling back. *Don't be stupid, Becky. There's nothing there.*

Chapter Fourteen

LONDON

They'd spent the rest of the day in Whitby being 'proper tourists', as Cori called it.

They'd gone out of the harbour on one of the little yellow boats for a pleasure cruise, and visited the Dracula Experience. They'd tried the sideshows at the beach and walked through the whalebone arch. They'd even had fish and chips, out of a polystyrene carton, on the sand.

'You haven't lived until you've done this,' she'd told Simon.

He had laughed and said he wanted to come back for a longer trip and paint the Abbey next time.

'Hastings is more my neck of the woods,' he'd said. 'I've painted the Downs a couple of times. I can never get the light right though.'

Cori had felt a little jolt as she remembered the diary entry she'd read and the similarities amused her, so she told him about it and he laughed as well. She and Simon had even had a picnic at the coast too today – of sorts. And the seagulls had some of it as well.

Cori was looking forward to reading more of the diary when she got home. But today, at Whitby, was all about spending time with Simon. Not too bad a place for a proper first date, if that was what this was.

'You might want to save the diary until you're back in London,' Becky had advised her as they had left. 'Unless you feel like fending off any Lizzie fans on the train. You never know who might be in the carriage with you.'

But it turned out the train wasn't too full of people, Lizzie fans or otherwise. It was, in fact, a very pleasant journey.

'So what are you thinking you might discover in that book that Becky hasn't already found?' asked Simon. He was sitting opposite her, a bottle of water each on the table between them, and the crumby remains of more biscuits in the middle of the table.

Cori shrugged. 'I don't know. The logical thing is to see if my aunt appears, but I sincerely doubt she will – and my secret wish would obviously be that I discovered enough to decide whether Daisy Ashford was the model for *Ophelia* or not.' She grinned. 'Not that I'd tell anyone if she was. I'm not that brave.'

Simon shook his head. 'I don't think you have anything to worry about,' he said. 'I think it's all Lizzie, really.'

'I'll find out,' said Cori. 'I just can't wait to start looking through it. It'll make them all come alive, I think.'

'One day, I'll take you on a Pre-Raphaelite tour of the city,' said Simon. 'You're not just limited to the big museums. They lived around Bloomsbury so I'll show you their homes if you like. And their studios and the smaller galleries. Anywhere you want to go, I'll take you.'

'Even to Tolworth?' asked Cori. 'So we can see where Millais nearly drowned?'

'Even to Tolworth,' said Simon. 'Sylvie was never really interested. She—' He stopped talking and looked out of the window, a strange look flitting across his face. 'She preferred the more modern works – Jackson Pollock, Salvador Dali. Andy Warhol.'

So this, then, was the Slutty that Lissy had mentioned.

'Wow,' said Cori, after a moment. 'Really in-your-face stuff then?'

'You could say that,' said Simon. 'It matched her personality. She was loud, she was confident, she was beautiful and very colourful.' He looked away from the window and back at Cori. 'We broke up about six months ago. I think she managed to kill my creativity. Hence why

I've recently just been painting tourist pictures that sell in Portobello market.' He laid his hands out on the table and looked at them. Cori noticed there were more splashes of colour on them, engrained into his nails.

'Do you miss her?' she asked, hardly daring to listen to the answer.

'Miss her?' Simon looked up and stared at Cori. 'Not at all. No way. She was having affairs left, right and centre. It ended when I found her with one of the guys in our bed. Before that, I'd kind of ignored the fact. Poured it all out onto the canvas because I couldn't face asking her outright. So no, I don't miss her. I miss my flat and my workspace and the light there – but I don't miss her.'

'That's good,' said Cori. And it seemed woefully inadequate, but it seemed to be the best comment she could come up with, under the circumstances.

She felt, though, as if she needed to offer something back to him. 'I broke up with my partner about the same length of time ago,' she said. 'He was called Evan. My granny said he was toxic.' She smiled, remembering her granny's voice on the phone. 'She was right.'

'And there's nobody else at the minute then?' asked Simon.

'No,' she said. She was very tempted to add 'at least not yet', but she didn't quite dare.

'That's good,' said Simon. Cori looked at him quickly. There was a smile playing around his lips as he echoed her comment. 'Now, in the absence of any raging Lizzie fans you need protection from in this carriage, I'm going to take this opportunity to go to the buffet car.' He pushed the biscuit wrapper away. 'I think I need chocolate. How about you?'

'Perfect,' said Cori. She leant forward and lowered her voice. 'But how do you know there are no Lizzie fans here?'

Simon just nodded across at a middle-aged lady who

was alternately knitting and dozing, and a family of four, including two small children playing a card game across the plastic table they sat around.

'Okay, I may be wrong about that, but I'm sure you could take them out if need be,' he said and winked.

Cori tried to smother a laugh and turned it into a cough. Simon stood up and walked off down the aisle, heading towards the buffet car. Cori waited until the door of the carriage had slid shut behind him and pulled her bag across the seat towards her. She rummaged around and found what she was looking for. Then she pulled it out.

The binding was old but fairly sturdy, considering its age. She stared at it for a moment, her heart beating fast and opened the diary randomly.

Henry and I went for a ride in the carriage today. The horses were terribly flighty and I complained to the driver, but he said they were just excited to be out. We travelled to Hyde Park but it was rather dull and there was nobody very interesting there. Henry suggested we bring the easel tomorrow and try to paint the Serpentine but it is really very dreadfully dull and I don't want to. I wish Henry would teach me to paint something rather more interesting than scenery. He says he paints all sorts of things when he is on his own. But he says I have to master the basics first. But that is dull, dull, DULL!

Cori was rather disappointed by this entry. Whether she expected to see Daisy's relationship with Millais spring out of the page, or even a hint of the original Corisande's relationship with Rossetti, she wasn't sure. But an innocent day trip in a carriage, followed by a brief discussion on what this Henry chap apparently painted? It was no more than she was doing now.

Oh well. She was sure there would be some more interesting entries in the diary. Cori looked up and saw Simon coming back through the door from the buffet carriage. She thrust the diary back into her bag and sat back in the seat, trying her best to look as if she hadn't just broken her word to Becky and sneaked a look at the diary. She didn't know how successful she had been or whether Simon would realise; but she was definitely looking forward to the chocolate.

It was just past ten o'clock when they finally pulled into King's Cross station. Over twelve hours since they had left.

'Was it worth it, then?' asked Simon, waiting for her on the platform as she stepped down from the train. 'I wish we could have spent a bit longer up there, don't you?'

'It was very much worth it,' replied Cori. 'But I know what you mean.' She sighed. 'And I really liked Becky. I can't believe Lissy kept that connection to herself!'

'Hmm,' replied Simon. 'Knowing Lissy, she was probably just waiting for the right moment to drop that information into casual conversation.'

'Well, she certainly did that,' said Cori.

'Definitely,' replied Simon. 'And I have a feeling Lissy planned this whole thing. I think her intention was to get you the diary and to throw us together somehow.' He smiled. 'I've enjoyed myself.'

'Me, too,' said Cori, feeling herself colour and glad that the cool, night air was blowing some of the treacherous red out of her cheeks. That was the worst thing about being a fair-skinned redhead; you couldn't hide your blushes very easily.

'Lissy's great,' said Simon, 'but she's pretty determined to get what she wants. Was she like that at uni?'

'Very much so,' said Cori. 'And she was always going out with really unsuitable guys as well. Is she with anyone at the moment?' Cori was curious – Lissy wasn't acting like she was in a relationship, but you never knew.

'Lissy's still in love with her ex, but she won't admit

it,' said Simon. 'He's Italian – but the thing is, whenever you put her and another Italian temper together, there are always explosions. That's why none of her relationships last. She's always drawn to the same type, but she's never happy for long because none of them are Stef.' He grinned. 'Those sort of relationships must be fun while they do last, though. If you're into high-octane, high-maintenance stuff, that is. Lissy's like a hurricane. I don't know how anyone could cope with her for long. Now me – I had that with Sylvie. And I don't want to go back to it.'

'No. I wouldn't want another Evan,' Cori said. 'But he was different. He lacked any emotion whatsoever. I started to really dislike him towards the end. I don't know – is sociopath too strong a word?' She pulled a face. 'Anyway, where do you live? I'm in Kensington. We could share a taxi back?' she suggested. 'If you live close enough?'

'I'm in Notting Hill. Well, as near to Notting Hill as dammit,' said Simon. 'So it's doable.'

'If you like, we can head towards Kensington first; then you can pop in and I'll make you a coffee,' said Cori. Too late, she realised how forward that might have sounded; but it hadn't stopped her at uni so why should it stop her now? 'Or you might just want to go home, I suppose. It's late. Sorry.' Embarrassed, she opened her bag and feigned rummaging for her phone, her keys, her purse; basically anything that meant she didn't have to look at Simon in the harsh glare of King's Cross station's lights. It was fine. She'd go back and read the diary. It might be better if he didn't come anyway. Probably best all round, in fact.

'Actually, yes, that sounds perfect.' Simon's answer was as fast as it was unexpected.

Cori looked up, pausing in her rummaging. The diary, for a split second, was forgotten, her attention taken by Simon's navy blue eyes and fair hair. There was definitely something inexplicable fizzing between them.

'You sure?' she asked, wondering how she had actually managed to find her voice.

'I'm sure,' he said. 'Fasten your bag and let's get out of here.'

Cori didn't need telling twice. The firm grip of his hand on her elbow as he steered her out of the station and towards the taxi rank was warm and comfortable.

Yes. The diary could definitely wait a couple of hours more.

Chapter Fifteen

KENSINGTON

'So this is where you live?' They were standing outside a three storey, white mews house in a quiet corner of Kensington.

Simon assumed Cori owned one of the floors. He guessed it might be the second storey; the one with the wide, leaded window overlooking the courtyard they were standing in.

'Yes, this is home,' she said. 'I moved in a couple of months ago, but I'm still unpacking and getting everything sorted, so you'll have to excuse the mess.'

She smiled up at him apologetically as she pushed open the front door. She stood to one side and ushered him into a small entrance hall. The door stuck a little as she tried to close it behind them and she used her foot to give the door some extra leverage, eventually managing to shut it securely.

'I need to sort that out,' she said, 'but never mind. I'll get there.' She turned to the right and snapped on a light in the kitchen. He assumed, therefore, she must have the bottom floor. 'Let me just put the kettle on and we can head upstairs to the lounge,' she said.

'Up to the lounge?' Simon noticed a flight of stairs heading up and Cori gestured to them.

'Yes, just up there. It's quite comfortable, but I still need to put my own stamp on the place. I'm hoping to turn the second floor room with the big window into a proper office eventually. It's part of the way there. I'll give you the guided tour shortly.' She filled the kettle and set it to boil, then took two mismatched mugs out of the cupboard. She pulled a jar of instant coffee towards her and got a spoon out of a drawer. 'Just milk, isn't it?'

'Just milk, thanks,' said Simon, still marvelling at the fact she seemed to have access to the whole building. It made his one and half bedroom flat look rather sad in comparison. Stuck in the middle of a rather featureless, purpose built modern block near the colourful Portobello Road, the flat had been marketed as two bedrooms, but a person would be hard pushed to get even a single bed in the box room – which was the room he had converted into his studio.

'I'd have been just as happy to take you to a coffee bar, you know, if you aren't ready for visitors. The truth is, I'm just happy to be able to spend a little more time with you anywhere – here or somewhere else.'

Cori laughed, and flushed that lovely dusky pink across her cheeks. 'It's nice to have you here. I haven't invited anyone else here yet, apart from my granny, of course, but she just kind of turned up – so it can get a bit lonely. I'm still trying to come to terms with being here myself. I can't quite believe I actually did it. I came into some money quite unexpectedly and I've always wanted to relocate to London. It was a good chance and it was a long way from Evan. And it's so much closer to everything I'm passionate about. I'll see how it goes, but,' she stood, hands on her slim hips, surveying her bright, modern kitchen, 'I think I've got good vibes about it all.'

She turned to him. 'Come on, I'll take you up to the lounge and then I'll pop back down here when the kettle's boiled.'

Simon was just about to protest that it was fine and he was more than happy to wait, when Cori lifted her hand and pointed at the door. He turned and walked out of the kitchen, realising Cori was right behind him. She followed him to the bottom of the staircase and he stood to one side as she squeezed past him to show him upstairs.

As she passed close by he caught a hint of her perfume – something light and fresh that reminded him of the ocean. He had no choice but to follow her up the stairs. He headed upwards then came out of a dog-leg onto a tiny landing and finally walked through a door into a huge, airy lounge. There was already a lamp on in the corner, courtesy of, Simon assumed, some sort of timer device. Lamplight spilled out over the comfortable sofa and the soft, duck egg blue rug in the middle of the floor.

Cori was plumping some cushions up on the sofa and turned to him as he entered. 'Here you go. I know we've been sitting for a while, but I promise this is more comfortable than the train and my coffee is definitely better than theirs was. I won't be long.' She hurried over to the stairs and he heard her thudding down them, back to the kitchen. He didn't sit down, though. He walked over to the window and looked out at the little square and the houses opposite.

A few lights were on in the windows, and neat plant pots and bay trees decorated the pavements outside the front doors. He could see people moving about inside the houses, shadows of other peoples' lives, just happening around him. And all these people had their own stories – maybe their own nemesis, their own Sylvie to fight. But life went on, didn't it? And rediscovering his creativity was a start for him.

He closed his eyes, allowing himself to imagine a life where he lived somewhere like this, with someone like Cori. Today was the first time he'd really allowed himself to let go of the repression Sylvie had generated and to actually consider a future with someone else. He opened his eyes again. It felt wonderfully liberating. And he felt strangely at home in this mismatched, messy house.

A moment later, Cori crashed back through the lounge door, balancing two cups. 'Sorry. The milk was off so I had to start again.' She hovered in the lounge, seemingly wondering what to do with the cups and where to put them. Simon gestured to a small coffee table with coasters already neatly arranged on it and Cori placed the cups down.

'Here – yours is the red one.' She pushed it closer to him and sat down on a squashy, chintz-covered chair. Simon saw by the state of the cushions that it was probably her favourite seat. 'I'll give you the guided tour afterwards.'

He took a seat on the sofa and sank into it; it really was remarkably comfortable. 'So have you started your web design work again, or are you taking some time off to enjoy the "proper touristy" things first?' he asked.

Cori laughed. 'Work's ticking over nicely, actually. And because I don't answer to anybody, I can do touristy things as well as work. It suits me down to the ground. Obviously, I answer to my clients, but you know what I mean.' She smiled. 'I've got some commissions coming up for the V&A and an exhibition they're running with some West End theatres. It sounds like a really exciting project, and I've managed to set up a meeting with someone called Elodie Bingham-Scott to talk through it all.'

'That's an impressive name!' said Simon.

'Isn't it? She sounds really nice though. She's one of the best costume designers in the business so they want her on board. And you know how I feel about the PRB artworks, so I'm hoping to see some costumes included similar to the ones they would have used on their models.'

'Sounds perfect for you,' Simon said.

Cori nodded. 'Yes, I hope it's going to be a flagship commission for me, which is a really pretentious way of saying it's important for me to get it right as there's a lot riding on it. So my intention is to have all my work stuff upstairs on the second floor in my office, which means I won't be tempted to wander off and have coffee breaks every five minutes. There's a big set of double doors onto my roof terrace as well, so the idea is that in the summer I can go outside for lunch. I'll put a few tubs and baskets out there, and a table and some chairs and then it will be good for entertaining as well. I'm hoping at some point I'll make enough friends to do that.'

'I'm sure you can count Lissy and me in that category,' said Simon. 'I've never known Lissy to give up on the idea of a party.'

'Me neither,' replied Cori, with a laugh. 'You can both come and be entertained,' she said.

'Sounds good,' said Simon and was gratified to see Cori grin at him over the top of her mug.

'Now, because you are a friend and I've been kind enough to invite you to a party, can I show you the flat and expect approving comments and not veiled complaints over the fact it's a bombsite?'

'I'll do anything to make you happy,' he said.

And he actually meant it.

After they'd finished their coffees, Cori led the way upstairs on to the second floor. It was a huge space, with patio doors leading out onto the roof terrace, and the roof angled in over the corners, making you feel you were in an attic of sorts. There was a convenient amount of eaves storage and a good space to fill with bookshelves. She already had her desk set up there, and the computer was surrounded by notebooks and scribbled ideas.

Outside, the roof terrace was practically invisible in the darkness; and what she hadn't told Simon was that she also had access to an exclusive garden square, about two hundred yards away. The idea that she, Cori Keeling, had achieved all of this from such a strange set of circumstances still made her reel. But she did realise how lucky she was, that was for sure.

'This is it,' she said, waving her arm expansively around the room. 'My little den of iniquity.'

Simon looked around and his gaze settled on a pile of books on the floor near the computer. Balanced on the top was a graphics tablet, a long lead attaching it to the computer.

'Oh, you're a digital artist as well!' he said. He moved over and looked at the spines of the books. '*Recreating the Masters in Photoshop. Digital Painting: A How To Guide. An Easy Guide to Computer Art.* They look interesting.'

'They look simplistic!' said Cori. She blushed and moved in front of them. 'You weren't supposed to see those. I kind of stopped seeing them a couple of weeks ago, because they've just sat there for ages, you know? I'm absolutely rubbish at it!'

'It takes practice,' said Simon. 'Look, it's something I've been experimenting in. Well, I had been experimenting before the Sylvie thing happened. If you ever want to have a play around with it, I'm happy to help if you get stuck.'

'Thanks,' said Cori. 'I'm really bad at it. This is what makes me think I am in no way related to Rossetti. And to save any further mortification on my behalf, do you want to come and have a look at the garden instead? It does need some work on it, though.'

Cori moved over to the door and turned a key in the lock. The door creaked open and a gust of pleasantly mild air blew in, bringing with it that lovely fresh smell you get after a shower of spring rain.

She looked behind her and was pleased to see Simon crossing the room to join her. 'And once you see out here, you've seen most of the place. Well, most of it except the bedrooms, which I really couldn't show you due to sheer embarrassment. They're even messier than the lounge.' She sighed wryly. 'All four of them. Never mind,' she said. She stood back and let Simon walk past her. He leaned on the railings and looked at London.

Cori knew how gorgeous it was, all spread out before

the viewer in a patchwork of light and rooftops. This, more than anything, had clinched the deal for her with the house. It was a mild night, the sun was just setting and she was alone on the rooftop with Simon in this amazing city. Life, she thought, was looking pretty damn perfect.

'I'd love to paint this,' he said. 'It's a view of London that people don't see.'

There was a faint hum – the noise of cars and buses travelling through the capital, and she could see traffic lights running through their sequences in the streets below.

'It is rather special,' she replied quietly, scared she might break the spell.

They watched the evening for a few moments longer, then Simon turned towards her. His face was shadowed by the setting sun, every angle on his face looking as if it was chiselled out of a beautiful piece of marble.

Cori's heart started to beat a little faster and she had a fleeting vision of him leaning into her and kissing her, because, seriously, what would have been a more romantic end to the day if not a warm kiss and maybe a warm body pressed against hers; or even just warm arms wrapped around her on the breezy rooftop as they admired the patchwork below them?

'Cori,' he said, and there was that unfathomable look in his eyes again.

'Yes?' she replied, hardly daring to breathe.

'Cori, I—'

Then there was an almighty crash from behind them.

They spun around to see the door into the house banging open and closed, open and closed, as if it was caught in its own little whirlwind, whipped up on the rooftop.

'Bloody hell!' said Cori. 'I don't think the door's strong enough to sustain that somehow.' The glass panes were rattling in the frame and a terracotta pot had shattered, just in front of it. The pot must have hit the door, as the bottom pane of glass had spidery cracks leading out of the centre and Cori swore again as she hurried over to it. 'Oh, no!' she said, leaning down to inspect it. 'I'll have to get someone out to deal with that now.' She kicked the remains of the pot out of the way, annoyed beyond belief. What absolutely terrible timing. She turned to Simon, knowing, however, the moment was truly lost. 'I'm sorry,' she said. 'Really, really sorry.'

'No, it's fine,' said Simon. He thrust his hands in his pockets and shrugged. 'These things happen. And anyway, it's getting late. I should probably go.' Cori knew the unspoken part of that sentence was something like *'before things get out of hand.'* Because she knew, and she guessed he knew as well, that whatever magic spell had been woven around them on that rooftop was just getting ready to overtake them completely. A few moments more, and she would have been lost. They both would have been.

'Enjoy reading the diary,' he said as she fought back the urge to stamp her feet and throw a full on tantrum. 'I'd almost forgotten about it.' He smiled, his eyes clear and slightly apologetic. 'That's what today was about after all, wasn't it? We can catch up another time.'

'Yeah, I suppose so,' she replied.

But I wanted you today! She wanted to scream at him. *You can't leave me!*

And then she blinked. Of course he could leave. She had no reason to keep him there and he had no reason to stay. They could meet up again. It wasn't the end of things at all. Just the beginning – she hoped.

Simon stood outside Cori's house, wondering which was the best way to go and get a taxi.

Or maybe he would just walk; but it was about three miles and he guessed it would take him an hour or so to cover the distance – and he really didn't want to be alone with his thoughts for that length of time.

He decided he would just head north and see where he came out. He could flag a taxi down as he went.

She'd been looking at him with those teal coloured eyes and one of her curls had escaped from its fastenings, and it hung temptingly just down the side of her face. How easy it would have been for him to take it and smooth it back for her and say something or do something. And he had been just on the verge of that.

Then that door had slammed.

And that had been the end of it.

He puffed his cheeks out and exhaled. On that rooftop he had glimpsed the future. A future where Sylvie was just a bad dream and Cori was everything else. He wondered whether they would ever connect like that again or whether it was the culmination of a long day and the magic of a May evening, looking out over the lights of London. In his heart, though, he knew that they would, that she was the woman he had been searching for all his life – but he had to take it slowly. Cori was vulnerable and he didn't want to do anything that might scare her away.

He looked back over his shoulder as he pulled his coat collar up and prepared to walk out of the courtyard. He could feel cobbles under the soles of his shoes, slippery after the rain as he headed out of the courtyard towards the main street. Her whole house was lit up from his tour and he knew the light would still be spilling out onto the roof terrace.

And immediately before he turned right at the end of the cobbles, he couldn't help but look back at her house again, tucked in the corner of the courtyard; just as the lights snapped off on the second floor, plunging the whole storey into darkness.

Simon paused for a moment, then headed out towards the hustle and bustle of London.

Chapter Sixteen

That was the light off, anyway. Now she didn't have to see the stupid door out onto the stupid roof terrace where she had been so thwarted. Ugh! Cori slammed all the doors behind her, not caring if the neighbours would hear or not. She doubted they would, and if they did, they would be far too polite to mention it next time they saw her anyway.

She stomped off downstairs, past the lounge where she could still see Simon's empty cup on the coffee table and she felt shamefully hot tears of rage spring to her eyes. She blinked them away and stomped some more, just to make herself feel better. It was the first time she'd ever felt a proper connection to anyone since she'd split up with Evan. And it was definitely the first time she had felt comfortable enough to consider taking the relationship to the next level. But then the stupid door had slammed, just as if something was trying to stop them.

Cori stomped all the way into the kitchen and pulled a bottle of wine out of the chiller. She unscrewed the cap, poured a generous glassful, swigged back the first three centimetres or so of it and refilled the glass even higher. The alcohol hit her between the eyes and she blinked.

She wasn't very good with alcohol and usually got very drunk, very quickly, when she did bother with it. But tonight was an exception. She'd had a lovely day with lovely people and come all the way back here with the loveliest one of all … and now he'd gone. Well, what the hell had she expected? That something magical would happen out there? Well, actually, yes. And it very nearly had.

Cori picked up the bottle and read the label, not really taking it in. It was a white and good to drink on its own, apparently. She knew the first bit, obviously, and was willing to prove the second bit.

In fact, she was going to take the bottle and the glass and collect Daisy's diary and go to bed. Then she might be able to forget about the horrible end to the day. It was just after eleven. She might get a good go at the diary if she set her mind to it, or at least something of an overview.

Setting the bottle and the glass down, Cori bent over her bag and pulled the journal out. Despite the clear conspiracy to stop her going further with Simon, she felt a flutter of excitement in her stomach. At least Daisy Ashford would give her something else to think about, rather than spending the evening fixating on Simon Daniels and his inexcusably beautiful eyes. And you never knew – Corisande might appear somewhere.

The effects of the wine were already starting to make themselves felt, however, and she fumbled as she tried to open the book.

The diary fell to the floor, opening at an entry dated May 1847.

Henry told me my artwork left something to be desired. He tried to tell me nicely but I am sure he did not mean it that way. I am beyond furious. I have tried and tried to improve myself with ALL of these different techniques, yet NOTHING WORKS. He has assured me that he will help me as oil painting is something he has dabbled in himself. But I am BEYOND HORRENDOUS at this technique. I really am annoyed and do not want to study any more under Henry as I feel entirely inadequate. I think I shall give all the art classes up and then that will show them. I want to study under a proper artist and model for that artist as well. I do not need to hear how bad I am. I do not need to be reminded of my so-called inadequacies. I despise painting and I give up!

'Not too far away from the way I feel about my digital art techniques, then,' said Cori to the empty room.

Then she scooped up the diary, tucked it under her arm and carried the bottle and the glass up the stairs, through the lounge, into the hallway and into her bedroom.

Once she was in bed and had managed to feel a bit more settled, Cori opened the diary with the intention of reading it properly from the beginning, rather than dipping in at random.

The first few pages were nothing out of the ordinary. Accounts of shopping trips and rides out in the carriage with Henry; information regarding new furnishings for a house and the excitement of moving to London, away from her home in the country; and a description of the work needed to bring the place up to her standards.

Everything is brighter today. I am to be mistress of the family home in Kensington! read one entry. *Imagine that. My father does not want to move to the city and I do not want to stay with him in the country. The countryside is dull but London is vibrant and alive and I feel a connection here.*

The house has been sadly neglected for some months, so my first task is to ensure the servants realise I am to live here permanently now and they must therefore keep the house as I wish it to be kept. The garden needs quite a lot of work, and it is rather overgrown in places, but as I have full responsibility for the house and its environs, it is something I look forward to dealing with.

Dear Henry will be looking after me as well, so I am grateful that he is to be part of my new life. I do actually feel an extraordinary sense of freedom. Only good things can happen to me now I am here. Who knows, I may meet some wonderful new friends and cause a sensation in London Society! Henry might even take the art world by storm. I might even take the art world by storm. The art world, in fact, will be at my feet. An artist may fall for me and I shall love and be loved by him and it will ALL be perfect. I suspect what I am saying is that anything is possible and I truly look forward to it!

Cori smiled, slightly drunkenly. Daisy seemed like every other young woman who had moved to London to make a new start. It was a world full of excitement and promise; and good grief, if the *Ophelia* story was true, Daisy had definitely set the London art world alight. Cori couldn't wait to study Daisy's diary properly.

And by properly, she reasoned that it would probably make more sense without the aid of alcohol.

She skimmed through the diary a little more, hoping to find at least a mention of the PRB and the start of the really exciting part of the story. Eventually, the first words relating to the PRB jumped out at her and her eyes widened.

Today I met Mr Rossetti in a millinery shop in Cranbourne Alley, London. Mr Deverell, Mr Rossetti's friend and fellow artist, told me that I was to be his next model ...

'Well, now,' Cori murmured to nobody in particular. 'I can see how Becky's exposé happened, Daisy!'

In that instant, Simon was not exactly forgotten, but consciously pushed firmly to the back of her mind. Cori scanned down the page and realised her heart was beating way too fast. It was incredible, absolutely incredible, she realised, to be holding this leather bound journal in her hands and to be reading something a girl just like herself had recorded so long ago. She flipped the pages back to the flyleaf. Written in ink so old it had faded to brownish-grey in places was the inscription: *The Journal of Daisy Annabel Ashford, aged 17, committed to paper in the year of our Lord, 1847.* This, then, was the year Daisy had been shipped out to London on her own. Seventeen was a reasonable age in those days, considered Cori. Girls were marriageable then, so it made sense.

Cori looked at the entry about the millinery shop again. That was dated 1849, two years after the diary started. So Daisy would have been nineteen. The same age Lizzie Siddal was when she was discovered in a millinery shop. And, in actual fact, she realised, from her previous studies, it had all been in the same year.

'So you're saying you really were discovered, Daisy?' Cori asked out loud. 'It seems very similar to the Lizzie story, I have to say.'

There was a loud clatter from the corner of her bedroom and Cori jumped. She held her breath, and looked over at the area. She exhaled slowly as she saw a pile of PRB reference books had slid from their carefully stacked tower onto the floor. They were not so carefully stacked, then, as she had thought. She shook her head and went back to the diary.

Cori thumbed through a few pages. It was nothing like she had anticipated. Some of the entries puzzled her; she could see that Daisy had been very friendly with the PRB artists – in fact, it seemed as if she had been part of their group. Yet why then had she never appeared in any of the documentation about them? Unless Cori had been looking in the wrong places, of course. But one would think with all the research she had already done, Daisy's name might have cropped up somewhere. Whatever the story was, though, it looked as if things were going to get exciting in Daisy-world.

In an entry for 1851, for example, Cori read: *I visited John at his studio today. He has a wonderful studio in his family home ...*

And in January 1852: *I hear Lizzie is indisposed. I offered to help poor John out. He is at a most difficult part of the portrait, in which he represents Ophelia ...* This, then, Cori thought, was the time Daisy had apparently posed for the portrait. To have this in her hands was the most incredible feeling. She read the rest of the entry avidly, certain phrases jumping out at her.

I see he has added some daisies to the foreground! … John suggested I take the place of Lizzie for the time being, just until she regains her health. Of course, I agreed. I would do anything to help my friends. Poor Dante, he is trapped by her, yet I am reluctant to raise the matter with him just yet. She is not the most stable of characters and I fear for both their sanity at times … The background was painted in Tolworth! But Lizzie and I were painted in his new studio in Cheam. Now, fancy that!

Cori flicked through some more pages, seeing entries here and there that demanded her attention. The girl's writing was difficult to decipher. Sometimes it was small and tightly formed; at other times, it snaked around the pages creating all sorts of strange patterns. There were badly executed sketches in some of the margins and splodges of ink which she had dragged the nib of the pen through and made into intricate shapes and the presentation only got worse as the diary progressed.

One of the entries concerned Lizzie's trip to France; a period, Cori knew, that had been when Lizzie and Rossetti were struggling in their relationship. Daisy had apparently moved in to fill the breach left by her.

Whilst I was staying with him, he painted me; it is not much more than a sketch at the moment but he humoured me. I asked him to make the portrait special, to make it just for me, and he laughed and did so. I was reluctant to return home, but I could not impose upon him any longer.

'Go Daisy!' muttered Cori, taking a sip from her glass. She was in Daisy's world and could almost feel the warm, sensual body of Dante next to her. The man, she knew, had oozed sexuality. She wasn't surprised the original Corisande had apparently fallen for him. A delicious shiver ran down her spine as she thought of Simon and she smiled.

I have always aspired to be like Lizzie, to be as wonderful and to be as talented and to be as loved as she is, wrote Daisy at one point. *Why can she not see that she is destroying everything I have built for us?*

'Oh, poor Daisy,' said Cori. 'Bad Lizzie …'

Something like a giggle filtered out of the darkness and Cori looked up.

'*Bad Lizzie indeed.*' It was like a whisper filling her ear, followed by a breath on her cheek. Then, just as soon as it had happened it was over. Cori looked at her wine glass and pulled a face. It was empty, as was the bottle next to it.

She wasn't surprised she was hearing things. She felt very drunk and a lot sleepy. But tonight, it felt nice. She snuggled into the bed and flicked to the last entry. A few words floated before her eyes and she squinted, trying to read them. *Oh, Lizzie, what have you done?*

'What indeed,' slurred Cori. Her eyes closed and her grasp on the diary slackened. Her arm slipped from the bed and the diary dropped onto the ground with a soft thud; she was asleep before it even reached the floor.

Chapter Seventeen

Cori woke up with a raging hangover. She groaned as she turned over in bed and found herself staring at an empty wine bottle and a glass with a faint patina of gunk around the bottom. She was a rubbish drinker; always had been, always would be it seemed.

And what on earth had possessed her to drink all that stuff in the first place? Oh, yes. She blushed and, flipping the pillow over, buried her burning cheeks into the cool underside; it had been Simon, hadn't it? The fact that she had let him just walk away last night and really, he should have been right here beside her; he should have been waking up with her, loving her. But he wasn't.

She lifted her head off the pillow and squinted at the big window. She hadn't closed the curtains last night and the watery morning sun was filtering through the glass. It hurt her eyes and she burrowed further beneath the duvet, feeling horribly sorry for herself.

She rolled over, curling into a ball and opening her eyes inside the warm cave of her duvet. Maybe she could just stay here forever and simply die of alcohol poisoning. She wondered if she did indeed die of alcohol poisoning, whether anybody would miss her. And at what point might someone remember there was once a girl called Cori who'd had a passing acquaintance with them and had disappeared from the face of the earth?

Carried away by her own ridiculous fantasies, she began to panic a little, imagining herself suffocating horribly in the cocoon of bedcovers. She fumbled around until she caught the edge of the duvet and lifted it up so a little bit of light came through. She wriggled to the light and lay there, her nose and mouth welcoming the air and gulping it in as if her body was actually starved of oxygen.

Simon might remember her, she supposed. But what if he was the one who ended up finding her wizened up, decomposing, mummified body? Because he and Lissy were the only people she really knew down here and he was the only person who actually knew where she lived. She hadn't passed that information on to Lissy yet. Lissy just knew it was Kensington – she didn't know the finer details.

Cross with herself, she pulled the rest of her wretched body out of the duvet-gap and ended up sitting on the side of the bed, her head pounding. She fumbled for a glass of water she kept on the bedside table and, lifting it to her lips, she drained it. She pulled a face as the liquid rushed into her body and semi-hydrated her poor aching head. Ugh.

And how on earth would anyone actually get into her house to find her? They would have to break down the door. She really didn't like where this train of thought was headed.

Still wallowing in these depressing thoughts, she spotted Daisy's diary, lying open at the side of the bed where it had fallen last night.

This new medicine is extraordinary, the entry said. *I feel wonderful when I drink it and can see how beneficial it might be to one. However, the nausea and tiredness after the effects have worn off are most unpleasant. I find I sometimes forget things and cannot particularly concentrate very well until I have a little more – and then I feel wonderful again. It is truly magical!*

As the nausea began to rise in Cori's body, she shuddered. She hated hangovers. And she was willing to bet that whatever the medicine was that Daisy was referring to, it had a good percentage of alcohol in it.

She leaned over very carefully to close the diary and saw her mobile phone lying on the floor next to it. She hadn't switched the phone off last night and the light at the top was blinking. She reached over to pick it up and groaned as she felt a weight like a ton of rock shift around in her head. *Never again.*

Through half-squinted eyes she looked at the screen and saw a text message. Her tummy did a little flip when she realised it was from Simon. Thanks for a great day. Hope to see you soon? She couldn't help smiling a little. But why on earth was he questioning her at the end of it? Did he think she might say no? Absolutely not. She really wanted to see him again.

Although, if they were ever able to recreate that moment on the rooftop, it would be a bloody miracle.

It hurt her eyes to concentrate on the tiny buttons, but she eventually managed to type a response. Had a great day too. Her fingers hesitated before she typed the next bit, but then she took a deep breath. Would love to see you soon. She re-read it. Then, squeezing her eyes shut and telling herself it wasn't really coming on too strong with him, she pressed *send*.

It was only when she saw the 'sent' screen staring back at her that she realised she was still holding her breath. She blew a soft breath out through pursed lips and laid her phone down. It was done. She hoped it was enough for the minute.

Simon had found a taxi, just as he had hoped and had sat in the back of it, fingering his phone, wondering what to do.

Once or twice, he took the screen lock off and clicked on the 'call' icon. He got as far as calling Cori's number up on the screen, but that was it. He was grateful that she'd given him the business card the first time they met and had put her number into his phone as soon as he got the chance. But he never actually pressed 'call' that night in the taxi.

Once he had been delivered to the featureless block

of flats he really didn't like that much, he sat in his bijou lounge for ages, thinking long and hard about what to put in a text message. He finally settled on something fairly nondescript and neutral, which didn't cover at all how he felt – but he wasn't quite sure how to proceed. All sorts of powerful feelings had hit him out on that roof garden and although Sylvie's mocking smile floated in front of his mind's eye, he blinked it away.

His eyes drifted to the small corridor that ran down the middle of his flat, and beyond that he looked at the door to his second bedroom, knowing what was in there.

He had to do it; so before he could second-guess himself or talk himself out of it, he quickly typed the words and pressed send.

Thanks for a great day. Hope to see you soon?

'That should cover it,' Simon said to Bryony. His little tabby stared at him with glittering black eyes as if she knew exactly what he was thinking about; as if she knew he had phrased the second part of the text as a question, thus giving Cori the chance to opt out if she wanted to. And would he see her soon? He bloody well hoped so. This time, it was her face that drifted into his mind. Those teal eyes smiling up at him and that glorious copper-coloured hair framing her perfect face.

God willing, he would have another chance like he'd had last night. And this time, he hoped he would at least be able to kiss her.

When the message came back the next morning, Simon couldn't help but smile.

Had a great day too. Would love to see you soon.

And as luck would have it, he had the perfect reason to send her another message at lunchtime.

New Rossetti delivered today – needed to hold back the screaming hordes, even though it's still under wraps. Won't be revealed to anyone before exhibition though – sorry about that. Would have loved for you to see it. Shame you couldn't have been here though and screamed along with the hordes.

She answered, almost immediately.

New Rossetti? Can't wait to see that one. Have heard it's amazing. Can't wait for exhibition. Keep the hordes away so I have a clear path to it please! #friendsinhighplaces.

Simon couldn't stop the grin from spreading across his face. Cori and he were on the brink of something wonderful and, on another level, the painting he was working on was flowing as if someone, a much better artist than him, perhaps, had taken the brush and moved Simon carefully out of the way so they could create their own masterpiece. He felt as if he had no control over the process whatsoever and he was, he realised, enjoying it.

His sleep pattern, on the other hand, was well and truly disrupted. He was probably functioning on adrenalin alone, but he didn't care. He felt more alive than he had done in the last six months.

And every time his conscious mind came back to focus on the painting, he was amazed and stunned in equal measures to see what he was creating.

Chapter Eighteen

TATE BRITAIN

Cori had told Simon she was working on some smaller commissions she needed to get finished before the work for the V&A started.

'I'm hoping to clear some stuff so I'll be ready for Elodie Bingham-Scott,' she'd said on the telephone a few days later. 'Then my mind won't be so full of engineering companies and football clubs that I can't do the costume exhibition justice. I'll probably be too busy to pop in to the gallery for a few days, just in case you're looking for me.'

'That's fine. We'll just meet after work one afternoon if you want?' he'd suggested. 'Our Costa is open quite late.'

'Our Costa,' she'd repeated. Then, with a smile in her voice: 'Sounds good to me. Our Costa it is then.'

And today was the day they were finally meeting. Simon was taking the opportunity of a quiet moment to study the *Ophelia* painting, noticing again the flowers and the drooping willows framing the perfect countenance of Lizzie Siddal. Or Daisy Ashford, perhaps. But try as he might, he couldn't see anyone but Lizzie Siddal in the portrait.

It was as he was pondering this, that he heard Lissy's voice echoing through the gallery. 'There you are, Simon, I've been searching for you.' He turned and saw her walking purposefully towards him. She nodded at the painting behind him. 'Do you know, my sister-in-law admits she hasn't seen *Ophelia* for ages? I told her to come down and take a look. I'm always inviting her and Jon down to spend a few days with me, and all I keep getting is excuse after excuse after excuse.' She frowned. 'I really can't see the problem. I go up to Whitby whenever I get the opportunity.'

'Well, maybe they can't just pick up and go whenever they feel like it?' suggested Simon. 'Jon has a business to run, hasn't he? And I'm sure Becky's pretty busy as well.'

'She goes off on her journalistic jaunts, as Jon calls them,' grumbled Lissy. 'She could jaunt down here.' She looked up and switched on a smile, moving gracefully to one side as an elderly man nodded at her and tottered up to the portrait. He leaned in so close to it, that Simon thought the old boy's nose might connect messily with Ophelia's belly button.

'It's an opportunity too good to miss, now that they've finally met you,' continued Lissy, watching the old man with a faint moue of disbelief as he produced a tissue and proceeded to blow his nose loudly, centimetres from the priceless painting. 'You could tell them all about the symbolism. Don't you think the likeness between Cori and Lizzie is pretty astonishing close up?'

Simon smiled, looking at Ophelia but thinking about Cori. 'Yes. That's exactly why I think Cori is so entranced by it all,' he said, 'as well as having that flagrant aunt of hers involved with Rossetti, of course. But having said that, I do only see Lizzie here and I don't see any indication of Daisy Ashford at all. This Ophelia looks pretty much like the photographs and the other portraits of Lizzie.' He turned back to Lissy. 'So maybe it's all just a story anyway? I've never come across any suggestion of Daisy Ashford in my studies.'

'Or perhaps Millais just painted in Daisy's body or her hair or something into this picture. You know, like a Victorian body double,' replied Lissy. 'Rossetti did it – he sort of airbrushed stuff. He painted over the face of one of his mistresses, didn't he?'

'Very good,' said Simon. 'Now name the portrait.'

'*Lady Lilith*,' shot back Lissy. 'Model number one,

Fanny Cornforth. Model number two, Alexa Wilding.' Her eyes followed the old man. He shuffled on to another painting and she visibly relaxed. 'And he also painted over a couple of actual photographs of Lizzie too, in order to make paintings. Baboom! Are you impressed?'

'Very impressed,' said Simon. 'Though Rossetti felt very guilty about that and decided he needed to apologise for it. Never mind. If Millais did a similar thing with Lizzie and Daisy, he did a good job. You know, talking about body doubles, I've been seriously thinking about recreating some of the PRB work as new paintings – updating them a little bit. It's been a plan of mine for ages, but I shelved it after breaking up with Sylvie.'

Lissy looked at Simon in astonishment. 'What? Updating something like *Ophelia*? She shouldn't be updated. It's like doing Shakespeare in 1970s disco gear. It's just *wrong*.'

'I wouldn't update them too much,' said Simon. He walked over to *Ophelia*. 'Especially with something as unique as *Ophelia* or even *The Lady of Shalott*. I'd stay as true as I could to the originals, but I'd try to capture the essence of them as well as moving with modern times.'

'Would you ask Cori to pose for you?' Lissy's voice suddenly dripped honey.

Simon smiled and turned squarely to face her. 'Of course,' he said. 'Why not? Her Aunt Corisande probably did it for Rossetti. Cori might do the same for me. I've already mentioned to her that I was thinking about doing it.'

'I knew it.' Lissy grinned. 'If you do decide to do that, though, *please* don't leave her in a tin bath with the water getting cold and forget about her. Do you know, in her diary Daisy implies that was the moment she stepped in to help out – in the period when Lizzie was recovering?'

'Yes, that was in Becky's article,' replied Simon. 'I'll have to ask Cori more about it when I see her. She's made a start on the diary, but she says she hasn't discovered her aunt yet.'

'Ohhhh – so you're seeing her soon, are you?' asked Lissy. That little goblinesque grin was back and she folded her arms. 'How wonderful. Oh – and speak of the devil.' She raised her hand and waved.

Simon looked along the gallery and indeed there was Cori. Her hair was loose and she was wearing that white and silver maxi-dress again. For a moment, he could have sworn it was Ophelia herself coming towards him.

As Cori approached she waved back at Lissy and smiled. Simon found himself smiling back.

'Hello,' Cori said when she was close enough. 'I didn't realise you were both going to be here. I finished a bit early, so I thought I'd just pop in and see *Ophelia* again, and tell Simon I'll meet him in the foyer later.'

'That works for me,' said Simon. 'It's lovely to see you.' And he meant it. So would it be too much to drop a kiss on her, right here, right now?

He looked up. Lissy was talking to a visitor, smoothly and discreetly giving him and Cori space and simultaneously transitioning from member of the public to volunteer guide. Everyone else in the gallery was predisposed, lost in the beauty of the masterpieces all around them. Cori was looking up at him, waiting for him to continue with the conversation.

But he didn't.

He leaned down and kissed her instead.

Chapter Nineteen

Cori left Simon at the gallery and although it was a terrible cliché, she definitely felt as if she left with a spring in her step. That kiss was worth waiting for.

She had decided to go for a walk and then head back to the Tate in time for the end of Simon's shift. She had tried to concentrate on the other paintings but they had all blurred into one beautiful, colourful mess. It seemed that everything was brighter today.

Daisy had thought that as well, when she moved to London, hadn't she? She was right –everything *was* brighter and Cori's new life in London was suddenly full of promise.

She smiled to herself.

An artist has fallen for me, and I have fallen for an artist.

She thought she might be paraphrasing what Daisy had written in her diary somewhat, but the sentiment was the same. Daisy and she, it seemed, not only looked alike but were also in quite similar situations. Little phrases kept coming back to Cori and she frowned. She needed to start reading the diary properly instead of just dipping into it when she had a spare moment. She couldn't forget about Daisy Ashford, not when their lives seemed to be following the same star.

Which all seemed a little dramatic, but also very true.

She paused, standing stock still in the middle of the pavement. Simon might actually paint her one day – now *that* would be quite an achievement. She had a vague image of herself lounging in a bath, dressed as Ophelia, wearing the maxi-dress she had on at the moment.

Simon had said he wanted to update some of the PRB paintings and *Ophelia* might be as good a place as any to start.

Henry might take the art world by storm.

And so might Simon, thought Cori, with a little excited flutter in her tummy. She began walking again, weaving through the streets and not really taking in much of the scenery, too busy imagining herself modelling for Simon and seeing herself captured in oils or watercolours or whatever he did.

She blushed, thinking she was maybe taking the fantasy too far when she visualised herself posing for a life drawing with very little clothing on. 'Oh my goodness,' she said, loudly, to nobody in particular. A woman stared at her and gave her a wide berth as she passed her in the street.

And then the spectre of the faceless yet probably extremely attractive Sylvie floated into her mind. Cori pulled a face. After Sylvie's influence on his creativity, would Simon really want her, Cori, to start encouraging him in his art? What if she told him to do something and it was entirely wrong? He wouldn't be happy with her.

He might think she was a little mad, a little bit Ophelia-like – trying to move in and pick up where the gorgeous Sylvie had left off and she was clearly very unqualified to do so. She knew a lot about the PRB, but very little about producing good artwork herself.

Well, she was a lot of things, but she wasn't mad.

'I wasn't mad either.'

Cori's step faltered and she looked around. A girl's voice had clearly spoken, but she couldn't see anyone in the street close enough to her for it to have been them. She hoped she hadn't spoken out loud again.

'Concentrate, Cori. Or you *will* look like you're mad,' she told herself. She started walking again, and then she stopped short as the same voice echoed in her mind.

'*She said I had monomania.*'

This time Cori actually stopped and stared around her. There was definitely nobody there and 'monomania' wasn't a word she would generally use in polite conversation.

She'd looked it up once out of interest when she'd read about a Victorian murderess who had been incarcerated in Broadmoor. It was an old way of saying you were, basically, mad. The murderess had poisoned some chocolates and it turned out she was completely obsessed by her married lover. She had—

'*Married lover?*' The voice snapped at her, somewhere near her ears. '*No, I would never have upset their marriage. You mustn't insinuate that! They were separated when I loved him. Then I gave him back to her.*'

Jeez! Whoever was here was engaging with her thoughts now!

'Get out of my head!' hissed Cori, spinning around. 'Whoever the hell you are, get *out* of my head!'

'*But Corisande!*' The voice was desperate now; very young and very pleading. And it also sounded scared. '*Corisande, you know who I am. It's Daisy. You know how Dante and I loved each other. You read it. I told you through my diary. Please don't say you didn't believe me. Look. I've proved it. You know I'm real. Look – see where we are. I can even show you how I felt when I took my medicine. It was the same medicine Lizzie took. She gave me some of hers, you know. She was so kind to me!*'

Cori's heart began to beat faster and a wave of nausea swept over her. She reached out to steady herself on something before she ended up crumpling into an ungainly heap on the ground in the middle of London. She really did think she was fainting. Everything was going black and she had the most terrible stomach cramps. She felt dizzy and she couldn't breathe properly.

Her hands grasped cold metal railings and she

concentrated hard, trying to regulate her breathing, feeling her heart judder and spasm inside her. Finally, she managed to take a proper deep breath. The black mist was fading a little and she stood still, staring at the railings in front of her. The house was on the corner of an alleyway and a road. Briefly, she found herself hoping that if she did disgrace herself and throw up or pass out, she could at least stagger into that alleyway and do it there.

When she felt she could lift her head, she raised it and found herself staring at a blue front door with a big, shiny, brass number seven on it. Her gaze travelled to a blue plaque that sat squarely in the centre of four dazzlingly white bricks between two beautiful big sash windows. Were they Georgian? They might have been.

But it was the plaque which arrested her attention.

In this house the Pre-Raphaelite Brotherhood was founded in 1848.

And it was just about at that point, when Cori did indeed manage to stagger into the alleyway, bend over and throw up.

Chapter Twenty

'Simon?' Her voice didn't sound like her at all. 'Can you come and get me? Please? I'm lost.'

Simon was in the foyer of the Tate, waiting for her. Instead, she was on the phone, telling him she was stuck somewhere random in the middle of the city. 'Of course I can. Where are you?' he asked, already walking out of the door.

'If I knew that I wouldn't be lost,' she said, with a touch of her usual asperity. 'It's Gower Street. I don't know where Gower Street is. I mean I've heard of it, with the PRB, and all that.' She stifled a sob. 'I'm outside number seven. But I don't know where it is in London and I don't know how I got here and I don't feel very well. I'm sorry. I'd get a cab but I'm worried I might throw up in it. Sorry – not that I want to throw up in your car.'

'It's okay. I know,' he said. 'You're in Bloomsbury. I guess you couldn't wait for my tour. Just sit tight and I'll come for you. My car's just around the corner from me.'

'I can't even find a tube station.' She started sniffing and her voice wavered. Definitely not like her. 'And I still want you to show me the PRB places.'

'I'll still take you, it's okay. But yeah, tube stations aren't easy to find around there. However, I can tell you that Gower Street is right in the middle of two of them. Goodge Street or Tottenham Court Road. Or then there's Russell Square station, but that's a bit of a walk away. Only recommended if you fancied keeping fit.' Simon knew he was simply talking at her to stop her from panicking, and he kept the phone pressed to his ear as he unlocked the car. 'Don't worry, it's easy enough for me to get to you. I'll be there before you know it. I think you've just found a road and kept walking,' he told her. 'I'll be there in about ten minutes. Don't move, okay? Now, can you tell me whereabouts you are on the street? Are you still by number seven or did you wander off?'

'I'm so sorry. I just don't know my way around and I got all confused. I did wander away but I'm back now. I'm at number seven and I'm next to somewhere called Gower Mews,' she said. Her voice was still shaky, but at least she seemed to have stopped crying. He could hear her breathing heavily as she walked around to try and position herself. 'And if I stand with my left side next to this house, I can see a big white building on a corner of a crossroads. You know how far along I am, don't you? It's a long road and there are buses everywhere. Sorry.'

'Sounds like the London School of Hygiene and Tropical Medicine,' said Simon.

'Ha. Bloody hell, and it's got *Ross* carved up on the wall, right up high on it.' She tried to laugh. 'Should have been Rossetti.'

'That would have been good, wouldn't it?' said Simon. 'But you're completely in the wrong direction for your place. And even for my place.' Simon put the phone on speakerphone and started the engine. 'I'm sure, when I get there, we can find a coffee shop or something. I'm pretty certain there's a few just down from that crossroads, where the Tropical Medicine place is. And failing that, there's bound to be a pizza place. There are always pizza places.' He was driving now, mentally judging how far he was away from her.

The car was crawling along Oxford Street. Just a sharp right onto Tottenham Court Road, Simon knew, right onto Store Street and right again. He kept her chatting, until he eventually turned onto Gower Street, and suddenly there she was. Standing outside number seven, turning around, looking up and down the street as if she was searching for something. His car, of course, Simon reasoned.

He pulled messily into the kerb a few houses away and stepped out onto the street, picking up his phone and still talking into it. 'So, yes, it's not far and I should be there around about … now.' At 'now', he tapped her on the shoulder and she spun around. She was a horrible sickly colour, yet behind the pallor, her face was all red and blotchy. 'Surely it wasn't that bad getting lost here?' he asked her.

'Oh, Simon, you have no idea how horrible it was!' she cried, throwing herself at him. Luckily, he opened his arms in time to catch her. 'It was horrible. Just horrible.'

'But this is a nice area,' said Simon, wrapping her in his arms. 'Remember the Bloomsbury Group? What could possibly be bad about Bloomsbury? And if it wasn't for Millais' home on Gower Street, we wouldn't have the PRB as we know and love it.'

It had been the wrong thing to say.

'Damn the PRB!' Cori said.

'Okay, I can see that maybe wasn't what you wanted to hear,' said Simon, frowning. 'Look, there'll be a Costa or a Starbucks on Tottenham Court Road if you want to get away from here. Let's go there. I'll treat you to a big latte or something, it'll make you feel better.'

Cori nodded. 'Yes, please. A coffee would be lovely, I—'

'*Coffee? No, tincture of opium would make things better. It makes everything better.*'

'What was that?' Simon stood back and looked at Cori. 'Did you say something? Something about tinctures?'

'Oh God!' Cori began to drag Simon away from number seven. 'No, I didn't say *anything* about tinctures!'

'Because I could have sworn someone said tincture of opium,' Simon said, looking around him.

'Tincture of *opium*?' Cori asked. 'What on earth is that?' She was still dragging him along, head down, trying not to look at anything around her.

Simon laughed. 'Tincture of opium is better known as laudanum. You'll know all about laudanum from Lizzie Siddal. Remember how everyone knew she'd overdosed herself with the stuff? I doubt they ever proved it was suicide though. Laudanum is the cure-all Victorian medicine – but it's highly dangerous, and liable to kill you.'

One of Daisy's diary entries came back into Cori's mind as her thoughts raced ahead of her.

I feel wonderful when I drink it and can see how beneficial it might be to one. However, the nausea and tiredness after the effects have worn off are most unpleasant.

And then those words came back to her.

I can even show you how I felt when I took my medicine. It was the same medicine Lizzie took. She gave me some of hers, you know. She was so kind to me!

'Laudanum?' Cori's steps faltered. 'Another name for laudanum? So she would have used that as a medicine? Oh God.'

'I told you I could show you how I felt.' The voice was breathy; triumphant; and just in her ear.

She had dropped Simon's hand, sworn very loudly, and started to run as fast as she could.

Chapter Twenty-One

They hadn't gone for coffee anywhere after all. Cori had been in no fit state.

She remembered, embarrassed, the fact that the stomach cramps had continued and she had been forced to stop, bending double in the middle of the street, whilst she retched uselessly. Wave after wave of misery and depression consumed her and again she wanted to curl up into a ball and just die, quietly, so that nobody would bother her ever again.

'I think I just need to go home,' she had said to Simon, sitting as far away as possible from him in the passenger seat when he had eventually bundled her into his Mazda. 'I'm so sorry. I was really looking forward to seeing you. I just don't know what's come over me.' Big fat tears had started to roll down her cheeks and she hadn't even bothered wiping them away.

'Don't worry about it,' Simon had said. 'It's probably a bug. You know, that norovirus thing. It just hits you out of nowhere. One minute you're fine, the next – *bam!* You're not.' He'd looked over at her, his navy blue eyes kind and that had made her feel worse. 'We don't want to risk infecting a whole coffee shop. Best wait until you feel better.'

He'd taken her right to her front door, asked her if she wanted anything before he went and she hadn't even invited him in. Ironically, Simon was the only thing she wanted, but there was something else she *needed* to do and she needed to be on her own to do it. If only her brain would stop mushing up and she could think straight. And, dear Lord,

115

she had *never* been so tired in her whole life.

'I'll see you later. Tomorrow, maybe? Whenever,' Cori said. 'Thanks again.'

Then she forced open her front door, and went straight upstairs. She was pulling Daisy's diary out of the bookcase, just as she heard the car engine start again and drive off. Norovirus bug be damned – Bloomsbury? Gower Street? Daisy's voice and her tinctures and the sense she was being followed – no, *directed* – to somewhere she had only read about.

I'll show you how I felt.

She dragged herself to the bedroom and threw the diary on the floor to read later. Before that, she needed to sleep. She crawled between the covers fully clothed and was asleep before her head hit the pillow.

Cori awoke hours later and, opening her eyes against the darkness of the room, she realised she felt human again; she felt like herself. And she also felt ready to tackle the diary. This time, she was going to read it properly – without the wine.

She studied the book until her eyes itched and the words blurred in front of her. The entries were fractured. They were in chronological order, but the book seemed to span several years. It was most certainly not a daily journal from a young lady. It was, in fact, mainly an obsessional account of Daisy Ashford's friendship with the PRB.

Once she'd settled into her life in London and written about a few day trips and a handful of little domestic issues, the PRB was all she talked about. As if every time she had a meeting with one of them, she wrote it down. Whatever had happened in between didn't seem to exist or was glossed over meaninglessly.

The domestic entries finally ceased all together and it was just pages and pages, all about the PRB. It was as if Daisy was dipping in and out of their lives and sharing every drama they ever encountered. She seemed so close to the group, that Cori couldn't believe her name had never come up anywhere before in relation to them.

'This cannot be normal,' whispered Cori, turning another page and reading Daisy's account of a meeting between her and Lizzie Siddal in 1861. 'I mean, what about the rest of her life? Surely, she must have done something with it?' She wondered whether Daisy had married, whether she had children – whether there were any other records pertaining to her life. Everything was about the PRB; and especially Lizzie. *I have always aspired to be like Lizzie*, said one line.

Cori turned again to the back page, and then flicked some pages back until she came to the last date; February 11th, 1862. The date had been circled again and again in heavy black ink, and there were watery smudges on the paper, as if someone had wept over the book.

Cori's heart lurched as she re-read the first three words: *Lizzie is dead.* She slammed the book shut and stared out across the room, suddenly feeling a nasty chill creeping across her shoulders.

She shivered and looked around her. But how, she tried to tell herself, had she expected the diary to end? The whole thing was clearly based on Daisy likening herself to Lizzie. *I have always aspired to be like Lizzie.* Once Daisy's heroine had gone – what point was there in continuing the diary? None. None at all. Then Cori had the most sickening thought, which she hoped was desperately, desperately wrong. *What was the point in Daisy continuing?*

Cori looked at the clock. Was it too late to ring someone? she wondered. Simon, perhaps? She took a deep breath and picked up her phone. Her fingers hovered over the buttons, but then she laid the phone down beside her and looked at it instead. No. She couldn't ring Simon. She didn't want to impose on him any more today.

So she picked up the phone and dialled Lissy's number instead. She stared idly off into the middle distance thinking over the diary entries as she waited for Lissy to pick up. She couldn't remember hanging one of her dresses up on the curtain rail before she fell asleep, but she must have done, because the shape of it stood out black against the curtained windows. Oh, well. She'd hang it up properly in the morning. And there must be a bit of a draught, actually, because it was moving in the breeze.

She blinked and looked down at the diary. Another job to do, she thought. Note to self – draught excluder for windowpanes.

Lissy was lounging in her apartment, flicking through a gossip magazine. Her legs were curled up elegantly beneath her and a large glass of Dom Pérignon was beside her. She didn't usually go for champagne on her own, not after the 'Graduation Incident', as Jon had taken to calling it – but she felt today had been rather successful.

She loved going to the gallery, but to see Cori and Simon together was so exciting; she giggled to herself, turning one corner of a page over to mark it for later. She wondered if it was too early to buy a wedding hat. Or maybe a fascinator, because they were a bit more in fashion, weren't they?

Her thoughts were interrupted by the ringing of her phone and she tutted. She glanced at the clock – it was just after eleven. Who on earth would be calling her at that time of night? She uncurled herself and walked over to the windowsill where she had left the phone earlier. She'd been peering out at the street, wondering why the traffic was so backed up and Jon had called her. They'd chatted a while, and then she'd got distracted and therefore the phone had been abandoned. She picked up the phone now and saw the name on the display. She raised her eyebrows. Cori.

'Hello, Cori,' she said, heading back to her comfy sofa

and preparing for a long, girly gossip with her old friend. 'What a nice surprise! Is everything all right?' She sat down and curled up again, eyeing her champagne hungrily. Perhaps Cori could come over one night and they could have some more of the same?

'Lissy? I'm so sorry. I know I should wait until tomorrow, but I need to ask you something about Daisy.'

'Ask *me* something?' replied Lissy. 'What about Simon? Isn't he there? Can't he help?'

'No. No, Simon's not here.' The girl's voice was guarded. Lissy closed her eyes and raised her face heavenwards. Unbelievable. They hadn't even spent the night together. It should have been so perfect – they were meeting for coffee, one thing should have led to another. Honestly! What else did she have to *do* for God's sake?

It would *definitely* have happened in Lissy-world, she knew that without a doubt. And those two were so well matched. She blamed Simon, she decided. In fact, no, she blamed Slutty. Seriously, the woman had practically destroyed Simon's faith in himself. She'd have to have words with him when she saw him. She was certain Cori hadn't been that reticent at uni.

'Well, where *is* he?' Lissy asked, rather too sharply. 'Why is he not there?'

'He's gone home. Lissy, look, I'm sorry. I shouldn't have called. I'll find out myself somehow. It's all right.'

'No!' Lissy interrupted. She sighed. 'No. Wait. Tell me. What is it? It's fine.'

'It's just – well – Daisy's diary ends on the eleventh of February, 1862.'

'Now why is that date significant to me?' pondered Lissy out loud.

'It's the date Lizzie died,' said Cori, her voice dropping to a whisper. 'Daisy seems really upset by it.'

'Ah! Of course.'

'Did Becky find anything else out about Daisy after the diary ended?' asked Cori. There was a peculiar, tight little note to her voice that Lissy couldn't quite place.

'Well, now, that's a good question,' said Lissy, surprised. 'I don't know. I haven't asked her. Becky just saw it as an interesting article, I suppose. I suspect she won't have progressed it. She's so busy at the moment that it would have been put on a back burner if she'd thought that way.'

'Can you? Can you ask her? I mean, would you mind?'

'No. No, of course not. But it will have to wait until tomorrow. I can send her an e-mail or text her, but she won't answer, you know what she's like. If I e-mail, I get more of a response ...' Lissy's voice tailed off. The other end of the phone suddenly went very quiet; but she could still hear ragged, irregular breathing, so she knew Cori was still there. 'Cori?'

'Yes? Yes? Lissy?' Her voice sounded odd; rather distant and distracted, in fact. 'Sorry – I forgot. I forgot what I was doing for a moment ... there's something. Someone ... What the ...? No. It's fine. It's just the wind. I thought ...'

Lissy sat up, unfolding her legs. She sat forward clutching the phone to her ear. 'Cori. Is there anything in particular you want to know about Daisy?' she asked. She was getting a funny uneasy feeling in the pit of her stomach and she didn't like it very much.

'I don't know. It's Daisy. Yes. I need to know.'

There was a rustle of paper as if she was turning the pages of a book. Lissy knew Cori's mind was elsewhere. It certainly didn't seem to be on the conversation.

'Sorry. I'm really tired. I'm so tired. I think I should probably go now.' There was a breathless little laugh. 'I'm starting to think I'm seeing things. I thought there was something in my bedroom. Anyway. Yeah. Lissy – how did Daisy die?'

'I ... I'm afraid I don't know,' she replied. She looked

out at the lights of London through her huge bay window, twinkling here and there amongst the massive trees of the garden square she overlooked; but she didn't really see them. 'I'll try to find out. Cori?' Lissy's voice softened.

'Yes?' Cori's voice seemed strained.

'Take care, won't you?'

'Take care? Yes. You too. Goodbye.'

The call disconnected, and Lissy looked down at the phone.

'Oh, bloody hell,' she said. 'Bloody, bloody *hell*.'

Chapter Twenty-Two

WHITBY

The icon flashed on the screen; one new e-mail. Becky pulled a face. She had barely sat down and switched the PC on and there was something there demanding her attention already.

Sometimes, it was tempting to switch the Internet off and just get on with her work. But, she realised, the e-mail was from Lissy and Lissy's e-mails always had that aura of urgency around them – Lissy had discovered that it was much quicker to e-mail than text if it was important. And, of course, it was hopeless to telephone her. So Becky couldn't really ignore it. Well, she could, but would her life be worth living if she did? And, yes, it had one of those annoying red exclamation marks next to it. Definitely *Urgent*. She sighed and clicked to open it.

You have to come down to visit me! Immediately. No arguments this time, no excuses. Okay? I have an emergency with Cori. You can stay with me. Oh – and if my brother complains about losing custom, tell him I'll pay whatever he thinks he would have made over the couple of days you'll be here. And I know you can bring your work with you, so ... Becky groaned and stopped reading. Typical Lissy, demanding this, that and the other. And another visit to London, of all places.

It wasn't so bad now she was used to it, but in the beginning, when she realised her hearing was definitely getting worse, she had hated visiting London. She had hated the crowds and she had hated all the conversations going on around her, and most of all she had hated being privy to them all, even if it was accidental.

The ability to lip-read wasn't just something she could switch on and off; it was just something she had grown used to over the years. And it could be bloody annoying at times. But – she had given Cori that diary, hadn't she? So – and she did feel a little churn in her stomach at that point – she *was* kind of responsible in a way, wasn't she?

Lissy hadn't been specific, but Becky had a sudden creeping, uncomfortable feeling about it all. She remembered the ghostly image of the girl leaning over the diary when Cori had been in the flat. Becky had tried to put it all out of her mind and think it was just a trick of the light, but there was something about it that she couldn't just dismiss. And Jon and Lissy were probably the only two people in the world who she could express those feelings to. Similarly, if Lissy had any inkling of any issues in that vein, who was she going to turn to?

Becky's mind drifted back to that October weekend two years ago, when her intention had been only to visit Whitby for Goth Weekend and write a couple of articles. She'd just split up with Seb and sworn off men for one reason and another, and then she'd bumped into Jon again. He'd been dragged into everything that had happened, but not once had he left her to deal with any of it alone. She knew she had been lucky. She honestly didn't know how she could have coped with Ella Carrick's ghost otherwise. What if Cori had attracted the attention of someone otherworldly as well?

Becky closed her eyes and tried, consciously, to bring the image of the ghostly girl back to her mind. She had been tall. She had a waterfall of loose, wavy red-gold hair and she'd been very, very slim. She'd been wearing something pale, almost silvery. It was a dress – high necked, long sleeved, fitted to the waist and then the skirt had flowed to the ground, fading into the shadows ...

Becky opened her eyes. She felt sick, which was, for once,

nothing to do with too many biscuits or being pregnant. She felt sick because she remembered another dress – Ella's wedding dress – the one Jon had a replica of in the studio, and the one she had worn to have her photograph taken as she sat by the antique writing slope. The one she wore in the photograph downstairs, on the wall.

If Jon and Lissy hadn't been there for her, where would she be now?

'I have no choice,' said Becky to the laptop screen. She pressed print and watched the paper slide out of the printer. She got up and retrieved it, then headed downstairs.

Jon was smiling at a pair of young women who had clearly just finished their transaction. He handed over a package to one of the girls who was blushing and giggling, twirling her long, fair hair around her fingers.

Becky leaned against the banister at the bottom of the stairs watching them. She pushed her own hair behind her left ear and almost immediately cursed herself. She was trying to break that damn habit. It didn't really make much of a difference to hearing what was going on and it probably never had done anyway, if she was honest. She heard nothing through that ear at all – she hadn't done so for years.

The blonde girl had finished flirting now, and Jon was quirking that amazing smile at the blonde, the same smile that had won her, Becky, over in the beginning.

Maybe we'll see you around Whitby? The blonde was saying.

Maybe, Jon replied.

Damn, she *was* bloody good at lip-reading, though; and pah! They'd be lucky. Becky tried not to laugh and waited a moment longer until the girls left the shop. Jon turned to put something away and caught sight of her standing there. He quirked an even more brilliant smile at her and came over.

124

'Hey, Gorgeous,' he said, taking her in his arms. 'To what do I owe this pleasure? Coffee time, perhaps?'

Becky punched him lightly on the arm, then responded by wrapping her arms around his body. He felt good. 'No, not yet. We've had an urgent summons to London,' she said. 'I thought you might want to see it. Oh, and she has all the excuses resolved before we even have a chance to excuse ourselves, funnily enough.' She unwrapped an arm and presented him with the printout. 'We don't have much choice. Not given the circumstances.'

Jon released her and took the paper. His eyes scanned the document quickly, then he rolled his eyes heavenwards. 'We have no choice. None at all,' he said. 'Oh, well. Fancy a trip to the capital, my love? We'll get to stay in Lissy's new four million pound penthouse. That's quite a nice feeling.'

'I prefer our little penthouse here,' said Becky, 'but,' she pulled a face, 'I guess we should start packing.'

Chapter Twenty-Three

KENSINGTON

Cori woke up with that horrible, hungover feeling again. In her half-asleep state, she probed the corners of her mind to see whether she had actually foolishly overindulged again last night, or whether there was another explanation.

She eventually realised, as she came fully awake, that she hadn't drunk a bottle of wine again but she had taken a God almighty flip out in Gower Street instead. She cringed as she recalled it and as for poor Simon ...

I'll show you how I felt.

Ugh. She tried to blank out the memory of that voice. Now, in daylight, it just seemed a silly sort of incident that could easily be explained away. She could put it down to overworking or overexcitement or simple over-imagination. She was thinking too much about that *Ophelia* painting mystery and just needed to step away from it all.

Cori picked up her phone and saw that Simon had sent her a message early this morning, wishing her a speedy recovery and telling her once again that norovirus was rife and he was saving that latte for another time when they could both enjoy it properly.

Feeling better today, thanks, she typed. Just woken up. Gonna take it easy, just in case. Got to see the theatre lady later as well.

So you won't be in Tate today then? he'd responded.

Doubt it, she texted. Sorry. Would have liked to see you.

Don't be sorry. Just beat that virus! I'll see you soon, ok?

Ok, she said. Thanks again. Her fingertips hovered over the 'x' key, then she added three of them at the end.

126

Xxx came back to her.

She smiled, then lay back in bed and remembered the phone call to Lissy, which made her cringe again.

Hey ho. They'd all be fed up with her before long. She was just about fed up with herself, actually. There were too many things going around her mind for her to focus on one thing at a time.

Granny would have told her to stop burning the candle at both ends, or something equally wise. But she had lots to think about – like Daisy Ashford, and Simon, and meeting Lissy again, and the whole excitement of working with the V&A, and being so close to the heart of the PRB. Not to mention, she thought, with a little pang of regret, the fact she'd met Becky Nelson and couldn't help obsessing ever so slightly about the baby she might have been carrying as well, had things turned out differently.

Cori swung her legs out of bed and looked up at the window, knowing there was something bugging her from last night. But there was nothing there this morning.

Yawning and rubbing her eyes, she shuffled into the hallway, intent on heading downstairs and switching the kettle on. Once she'd had some coffee, she could function better. And today she had to be on top form, because she was meeting Elodie Bingham-Scott.

As she passed the lounge door, there was a *flumph* sort of noise – the sort of noise that you get when a book falls on the floor. She swore under her breath and blamed either an underground train – if any actually went under her house, which she was a little unsure about – or a dodgy floorboard in the old building unbalancing something.

She peeked in and saw a heavy book lying on the rug. It was, she realised, the exhibition catalogue from the Pre-Raphaelite Exhibition the Tate had run in the early eighties. She had bought it second-hand, and to this day remained stunned by the beautiful reproductions of the paintings and drawings and all of the interesting pieces of information the book had shared.

It must have slipped off her bookshelf. Everything was stuffed into the shelves any old how at the moment. She shut the door on it and continued down the stairs to the kitchen.

One coffee later, she had poured herself another mug and was traipsing back up the stairs wondering if a Teasmade machine was too indulgent to have in a person's bedroom nowadays or if it was simply just a rather dated contraption for the twenty-first century, when she decided to retrieve the book and have a leisurely look at it over her coffee. She wanted to revisit some of those paintings so badly, she realised, it was almost a physical need.

Cori pushed open the door to the lounge, looked inside – and literally screamed. Neat squares of paper had been laid out on the lounge floor; dozens of pictures from the book had been removed and placed in identical lines, running from one edge of the rug to another. A sea of redheads and medieval fantasies stretched out across her lounge floor and she began to shake.

As the mug crashed to the floor and shattered, Cori only had one thought in her head.

Daisy Ashford was here.

Elodie Bingham-Scott was exactly as her name suggested; small, bubbly, curvaceous and blonde. Her hair hung almost down to her waist in a long, wavy, golden mane that, Cori thought, looked so artlessly styled it had probably taken her or her hairdresser hours to achieve.

Elodie led Cori through a maze of corridors into the back of the National Theatre and into her comfortable office. Cori had originally thought that her office would have been lined with wardrobes or had costumes everywhere, but she was disappointed to see that it only had a few fabric swatches lying on a desk and some fashion designer sketches next to them.

Elodie must have seen Cori glance at the pictures, because she walked over and picked one up.

'That's for our production of *Camelot*,' said Elodie. She handed it over to Cori who gazed at the picture of a ridiculously skinny sketched-out figure wearing a flowing medieval style dress. 'That's Guinevere. I'm going for green, red and gold for her.'

'And that's what the fabric is for?' asked Cori. She still felt a little shaken by the incident this morning, and the last thing she wanted to see, really, was a medieval picture. At least Elodie hadn't produced a Pre-Raphaelite painting for her to study, even though that was possibly where she had taken her inspiration from.

'It is indeed,' said Elodie. 'When we've finished here, we can go and see the storeroom if you like. It's full of clothes like that. We did *Hamlet* not so long ago. It was a short run, so we just recycled some of the older costumes. I wish that *Ophelia* article had come out before we closed – it would have been a great marketing tool.' Elodie didn't have a London accent. Cori tried to place it, and guessed it was Norfolk or Suffolk or somewhere around that region and vaguely wondered how she had ended up in a London theatre. 'We've still got the *Hamlet* costumes on site,' Elodie continued, 'so you'll get a chance to see them before we take them up to the warehouse, if you want.'

Cori put the sketch back on the desk, her hand trembling, ever so slightly.

She opened her mouth to say no, it really didn't matter about seeing those particular costumes, thanks, but instead heard herself ask, 'Do you have Ophelia's costume?'

Elodie smiled. 'We do. But the *Hamlet* we did was contemporary, and Ophelia was a heroin addict, so she wasn't at all glamorous. Bit of a wasted life, really.'

129

Elodie's face started to flicker, just as if Cori was starting to get a migraine. Cori broke out into a sweat, and tried to focus on something else; something more relevant to the task in hand, but all she could imagine was herself wearing Ophelia's dress in the painting and sinking into a bath of water.

A whirlwind rushed past her, and seemed to race towards the door behind. She pressed her hands into her knees, trying to listen to what Elodie was telling her. Then she became conscious of the fact that Elodie Bingham-Scott had stopped talking and was, instead, looking at her oddly.

'Are you all right?' she asked. 'You've gone white.'

'I'm fine,' said Cori, forcing a smile.

Cori jumped as a pile of papers slid off a desk at the end of the room and fluttered to the floor. The door swung open and she thought she saw the sweep of a silvery-white dress disappear around the corner before it slammed shut.

Elodie's lovely office was beginning to feel claustrophobic and it was definitely on the chilly side.

'Is this theatre haunted?' Cori burst out, unable to stop herself asking.

'It is,' said Elodie. 'I see them all the time. They don't bother me and I don't bother them.' She smiled. 'I'm used to it – I've seen them all my life. My house has a ghost. He's harmless. But her—' she pointed to the door '—she's new. I haven't seen her before.'

'What did she look like?' asked Cori, not really wanting to know the answer.

'I didn't get a good look,' said Elodie, 'I just saw her dress, really – and she was dressed to impress. It's not a dress I recognise.' Then she smiled dismissing the apparition. 'I usually just ignore them. If they want me for anything, they can come and find me.'

Cori was worried that Daisy already had.

Chapter Twenty-Four

TATE BRITAIN

Cori was beginning to feel a little bit like a stalker. She was back at the Tate, heading straight up to the Millais Gallery, focussed only on finding Simon.

Monomania. That word came back to her again and she shivered.

She walked into the gallery and stared around. Another guide she didn't recognise was in there, talking to a middle-aged lady who was wearing hiking boots and carrying a backpack.

'Damn!' she said under her breath. She stood in the middle of the parquet flooring looking around for Simon.

'He's not here.' Lissy melted out of a crowd and walked over to her, clutching a clipboard. 'I take it you've come to hunt out the divine Dr Daniels?'

'Where is he?' she asked. As her voice echoed through the gallery, she sounded, she thought, a little desperate.

'I have no idea,' said Lissy. 'Possibly painting. Possibly having a coffee. Possibly just enjoying not being at work today. He said he had something he needed to sort out urgently, so he's taken the day off. That's why I'm here. He asked if I would cover for him, so I had words with the powers that be and here I am.' Lissy shrugged. 'He didn't say why.'

'He asked if I was coming in today,' said Cori, 'and I said no.'

'Then that's probably why he took the day off,' said Lissy, smiling knowingly. 'What was the point in being here when he knew you weren't coming in?'

Cori had no response to that. Instead she shook her head and wandered over to *Ophelia*, leaving Lissy standing in the middle of the room.

'Are you Daisy?' she asked, under her breath as she stared at the perfect features and the flawless complexion. '*Are* you?' She wasn't sure if she was talking to the girl in the portrait, or that shadowy figure that was hanging around, just on the edge of her consciousness.

The horrible nauseous feeling started to come over her again, but she was unable to move away from the picture. She heard a voice coming to her as if it was a very long way away, then felt herself just falling, falling, falling into that picture. Into the river; floating off downstream, where she would be lost forever and nobody would find her.

'There's rosemary, that's for remembrance. Pray you, love, remember.'

'Cori!' She jumped, startled as she heard her own name. She blinked as Lissy appeared; right in front her face, staring at her with those odd eyes of hers.

'Lissy,' she said. 'Hello.'

'Cori, let's get out of here,' said Lissy. She frowned. 'You don't look very well. Simon said you'd been ill yesterday. I can't have you throwing up in my gallery, so I'll tell you what we're going to do. We're going to leave here and I'm going to take you shopping. Shopping *always* makes me feel better.'

Cori just looked at her. 'If you think that's best,' she said.

'I think that's best,' said Lissy. 'And regardless, you're not staying here. You look fit to drop. No. We're going to get some fresh air. And the best place for fresh air in London, in my opinion, is Brompton Road. Two seconds, my love, then I'll be finished and we can go.'

Cori didn't even bother arguing. She just turned her back on *Ophelia*, intending to follow Lissy.

132

'No!' said that voice again, angry this time. '*I haven't finished yet! I haven't told you about the daisies. That's my favourite line! Come back, Corisande. Please; come back.*'

Cori put her head down and stuck her fingers in her ears, all the way out of the gallery.

But it didn't really make any difference.

Chapter Twenty-Five

SOUTH KENSINGTON

Lissy's penthouse was amazing. There was no other word for it.

It was the top two floors of a Victorian mansion and it overlooked a neat garden square. It had been completely modernised and renovated inside, with the result that the ceilings were high and the rooms spacious – and the second bedroom was probably the same size as the entire Whitby flat, Becky thought ruefully.

And that was all without the extra little mezzanine floor, jutting out halfway between the two floors.

'Jon, do you never get jealous that Lissy got the rich daddy?' she asked, her words echoing around the huge, airy room. And the bed; dear Lord, the bed! It was massive. She could probably lie lengthways across it and still have space. She ran her fingers across the cool Egyptian cotton sheets and was horrified to see a wrinkle appear. She tried to smooth it out, failed, then laid a cushion over it to hide it.

'Nope,' said Jon. 'Never. I know – weird, isn't it? I can't blame Lissy or my dad, wherever he is, for that, can I? Lissy doesn't flaunt it.'

Becky raised her eyebrows and gestured around the room.

'Well, okay, she doesn't flaunt it *generally*,' Jon said, with a laugh. 'So she's got a nice house; good luck to her. At least we get to borrow it for a couple of days.'

Becky went over to the window and looked out at the pretty, leafy trees. Beyond those, though, she spotted the traffic crawling down Old Brompton Road and a seething mass of people wandering around the streets.

'I like our sea view better,' she said. She shuddered and turned to Jon. 'But I guess it's Cori we're here for.'

'Do we know what it's all about yet?' asked Jon.

Becky shook her head and sat down on the remarkably comfortable window seat. 'All I know is that Lissy said it was an "emergency".' She made little bunny ears with her fingers as she spoke. 'A Cori-type emergency. You saw the e-mail. It's anybody's guess.'

Jon wandered over to the window and stood next to her, peering out himself.

His brow furrowed. 'I'm sure Lissy will take great pleasure in telling us all about it,' he said. 'She had better have a good reason for dragging us down here, that's all I can say.'

He held his hands out and Becky put hers into them. He pulled her to her feet and smiled. Then he looked across at the door and the frown came back. 'Hold on, there's somebody coming. Lissy must be back.'

She hadn't been in to let them into the house. Trustingly, she had left the door open and evidently given instructions as to their names and what they looked like to the concierge downstairs, who had in return presented them with a visitor's parking permit.

Becky had swept up the marble staircase towards Lissy's apartment utterly speechless. She had the irresistible urge to step off the plush, cream coloured carpet that lined the middle of the staircase and walk on the bare marble, wanting, bizarrely, to feel the slipperiness of it beneath the soles of her shoes.

She had waited for Jon on the second landing. 'I'm a little underdressed for these stairs,' she said, only half-joking. 'To think this was originally one house!'

'I think some of them are still only one house,' said Jon.

135

Becky had blanched at that thought and continued up to the next landing to Lissy's front door, shaking her head in disbelief.

And now, the lady of the house had apparently returned. A moment or so later, Jon spoke again. 'Come in!' he said. 'We made it.' The bedroom door opened and Lissy peered in, her fist still clenched from the knock on the door.

'You *did* make it! And all in one piece too! Thank you so much for coming so quickly,' she cried, flying across the room and hugging them. 'Was the traffic all right?'

'It was fine,' said Jon. 'It's good to see you. Even better to see you've got your own parking space. You should use it.'

'Why would I want to bring my car into town?' asked Lissy, pulling a face. 'There are taxis galore, a fabulous tube system and aeroplanes if I need to go further afield. Anyway, Daddy said I could leave my car at home.'

'Home' was a huge mansion in the country. Daddy had a massive garage that could easily accommodate Lissy's little MG in one tiny corner.

Lissy began to wander about the room, chattering on about something to Jon, and Becky took the opportunity to quietly sidle away, intending to move towards the style-heavy kitchen she had spotted at the other side of the lounge. She would make coffee and make herself useful. At the best of times, it was impossible to keep up with the jumps in Lissy's conversation and if it was important, they would find her and tell her. Knowing Lissy, she would get to the point eventually.

Becky padded across the blonde wood parquet flooring towards the staircase and wondered how someone as chaotic as Lissy could maintain such a perfect house. As she came down onto the mezzanine floor she looked over the small balcony and saw the mountain of shopping bags Lissy had dumped in the middle of the floor along with a pair of rather fabulous Louis Vuitton shoes, lying in a heap next to them. She smiled wryly. Yep, that was Lissy. It was clearly the housekeeper that kept the place shipshape.

She skirted the graveyard of designer gear and went into the kitchen. There had to be the means of making a drink in here somewhere. It was as she was pondering, looking into a glass-fronted unit for inspiration, that she saw her.

There was a shadowy figure reflected behind her in the kitchen doorway; a figure with long, curly hair. She spun around, convinced for a moment it was the spirit woman she had seen back in her own flat in Whitby; until she realised it was Cori.

'Cori!' She almost laughed with relief. She hadn't realised quite how jittery that spirit woman she had seen in Whitby had made her. 'You gave me a shock.'

'Hello, Becky,' said Cori. 'What are you doing here?'

It wasn't exactly an enthusiastic greeting. There wasn't any hostility there, precisely, but more of a distancing. Cori's eyes didn't seem to be focussed fully on Becky. In fact, the best way Becky could describe it was to say she seemed spaced out.

'Oh, we're just here visiting Lissy,' she said, vaguely. Heaven forbid the girl knew she was the purpose of the journey. 'How are you? Have you been shopping together?' It was a pathetic response, and Becky felt herself flush with embarrassment at it.

'Shopping,' repeated Cori. 'Yes. We've been shopping.' There was an awkward pause and Becky felt the urge to either run away or fill it with some inane comment, but because Cori was blocking the doorway, Becky had to opt for the inane comment.

'Did you buy anything nice?' she asked.

Cori stared at Becky, wondering what on earth she was doing in the apartment. Last time she had seen her, she had been in Whitby. She seemed at home in Whitby; she seemed uncomfortable here, like she didn't belong. For a moment, Cori was back in Whitby, in the little apartment collecting the diary and … what had happened after that?

Sometimes, I forgot things.

Cori stared at Becky a moment longer then blinked. A spark of sense and energy suddenly returned. 'My word,' she said. 'Oh, I'm so sorry, Becky. It's nice to see you again. Lissy's had me around the shops for two hours and I think I'm just tired and stupid today.'

'Two hours is nothing for Lissy. She can shop for England,' replied Becky.

Cori nodded. 'I know. I'd originally popped into the gallery to see Simon but he was on a day off, so I couldn't see him. But then I spotted Lissy and she said she was just finishing and if I just waited for two seconds, she'd be off and we could go out. So I texted Simon while I was waiting and said I was sorry I'd missed him and I was heading off with Lissy so I would call him later.' She blinked as Becky's features began to blur a little and she felt a wave of nausea wash over her. It was as if there were three people in that room. Becky. And her. And a shadow – a shadow very close by, just in the corner of her eye; much like the one that had stormed out of Elodie Bingham-Scott's office.

Cori swallowed the feelings down, and continued in a rush, trying to keep the shadow in her field of vision as it glimmered in the corner. 'But then Lissy came out and we left, and I said I needed some stuff for my house, and she said she knew some great places, so that's where we went and I managed to get some great bargains, but I …' Cori trailed off, seeing the confusion flit across Becky's face. She shut her mouth. 'Sorry.'

'No, it's fine,' said Becky. She smiled, but Cori could tell it was a little strained. 'I caught most of it. I'm assuming, then, that you've been shopping, and Lissy forced you into it and now you're exhausted. I was just about to make some coffee, if you think that might help you revive a bit. But I can't find anything.' She turned back to the cupboards and did that nervous little gesture with her hair again. 'There has to be some somewhere. She can't drink nothing. And she knew we were coming, so ...'

Cori walked over to Becky and began helping her to pull drawers and cupboards open. Between them, they found some mugs, located a fridge and some tins of ground coffee. They stared at the little row of tins, all marked Fortnum & Mason, and then stared at each other. The tins looked too pretty to break open.

'I just wanted Nescafé,' said Becky.

'A cup of tea would have done me,' replied Cori. 'I'm going right off coffee.'

Becky widened her eyes. 'You're not ...?' she asked.

'What? Oh! Oh – no. Good Lord, no. No way.' Cori sucked her tummy in and stood up straight, mortified at the fact Becky might think her pregnant, even if that was what she secretly wished herself. 'No. Daisy wrote that she liked tisanes. I think they're some sort of posh tea. She keeps talking about them, and how good they are for you. It just made me think that I needed to cut back on the caffeine and try that approach instead.'

'Oh!' Becky laughed. 'You had me worried. Having said that, I haven't gone off the stuff, so it doesn't happen to everyone.'

She smiled at Cori, perfectly innocent of Cori's innermost desires and Cori forced a smile back, but couldn't quite bring herself to answer her.

I wish I'd been with child as well, just like Lizzie was. But it never happened.

Cori jumped and turned her head in the direction the voice had come from.

'Oh, look – just sod it,' said Becky. 'I'm going to open this coffee.' She began to poke a knife under the seal, then

139

stopped poking and gestured to another cupboard with the knife. 'I think I saw tea bags in there. Or a tea caddy or something, if that's what you want instead.' The sun was streaming in the window by now and glinting off the shiny, silver blade.

The light caught Cori's attention and she couldn't stop staring at it. 'I'm finding the diary very interesting, you know,' she replied. 'It's not just the fact that Daisy's teaching me all about tisanes.' It was as if her voice was coming from far away. 'I'm getting to learn so much more about everybody in the PRB and I'm really getting a feel for Daisy's life. Yes. I think I'd like tea.'

'Okay – well the tea bags or tea leaves or whatever are in there, as I say. Just choose whatever you want. I doubt Lissy will mind.' Becky moved the knife back towards the coffee tin and leaned over it. 'Bloody tight fit this,' she muttered, finally popping the lid off. It rolled onto the grey and white marble surface and made a horrendous clatter. Becky smacked her hand down on it and swore.

Cori blinked, the noise bringing her focus back to the present. 'Nothing's broken,' she said, surveying the scene. 'Not to worry.'

'Thank goodness. This place has me on edge,' said Becky, frowning. 'It's too tidy. But I'm surprised Jon hasn't come in. The noise of a coffee jar opening and the smell of the stuff – he's like a moth to a flame. But I guess there's a bit more distance between us down here and him upstairs, than we'd have at home.'

'Do you live at the studio, then?' asked Cori, passing Becky a chrome and glass cafetière.

'Live there? No. No, we don't live there. It's convenient and we're very lucky to have it, especially if the weather's bad or we have a late night and don't feel like driving; but generally we just work from it. It has a lovely atmosphere to work in.' She heaped some spoonfuls of coffee into the cafetière and flicked the switch on the nearby kettle. 'It's maddening if I have to go away anywhere for work and leave it all behind though. I'm always happy to get back.'

Cori had located an interesting looking tea which was fortunately contained within a tea bag and, in the absence of seeing a teapot anywhere, popped it straight into a cup. 'Did you write that article about Daisy in your studio?' she asked.

Becky smiled. 'I write most of my articles in the studio,' she said, 'unless I need to do something in the field, sort of thing. But, yes, Daisy's article was written there and it all came really easily to me.'

'Did you feel like she was talking to you?' asked Cori, carefully. She looked down, and made a big production of filling the cup and cafetière up from the kettle.

'No,' said Becky. Cori was pretty sure Becky had answered just as carefully. 'Why do you ask?'

'No reason,' she said. 'Look.' She changed the subject and smiled brightly at Becky. 'That's the tea done and the coffee ready to stew in the pot.'

'I'll go and find Jon and Lissy,' replied Becky, 'and then we have to decide where to serve the drinks. I think the dining table in the bay window looks nice.' She grinned suddenly. 'You did bring your maid's outfit, didn't you? Because I left mine in Whitby.'

'Dammit,' said Cori. 'I knew there was something I'd forgotten.'

But, despite the jokes, somewhere, hovering just on the edge of Cori's subconscious was the spectre of Daisy. And it seemed very wrong to be bringing her here, to Lissy's home, without Lissy's knowledge. Because she did feel as if she was with her again; and it wasn't pleasant.

Does one refer to this as a tisane or a tincture? I do not know. The names and the meanings escape me now. I

141

believe tisanes are made with natural, herbal ingredients, but then so is this. Does it truly matter?'

Becky found Jon and Lissy in the bedroom, still talking.

'I didn't realise you'd brought Cori along, Lissy,' she said, walking over to them. Her feet sank into the deep carpet and she realised the carpet was what made the room smell so very new and very expensive. 'She said you'd been shopping together.'

Lissy lit up the room with her smile. 'Oh! Yes. She popped into the gallery to see Simon and—'

'Stop!' Becky commanded. She held her hand up. 'I've already had the story from Cori. It's clearly very complicated, but it's nice you two have picked up where you left off.'

Lissy looked guiltily at the floor and shifted her weight from one foot to the other. 'Ah. Yes. She still hasn't got much taste in soft furnishings,' she said. 'She needs some professional guidance.'

Becky smiled. 'You're a terrible liar. Don't pretend you haven't got a heart. It's not just a jolly shop with an old pal. You feel bad about the whole diary thing, don't you?'

'Well. Okay. Maybe a teeny, tiny bit,' said Lissy, pulling a face. 'I felt sorry for her today. And I just thought if she was with me she might open up a bit. She's just not herself. I would think, as her oldest friend in London, she would trust me if something was going on.' Lissy looked self-righteous, as only Lissy could.

Becky let that comment pass. 'So what exactly is happening?' she asked. 'You dragged us down here, telling us you had an emergency. I think we need to know what that is.'

Lissy shrugged. 'Yes, I suppose you do need to know. Simon says Cori freaked out when she got lost yesterday. And she rang me late last night asking about some things to do with Daisy. I don't know if there was anything else. Oh, she said she thought she saw someone in her bedroom, and that sounded pretty odd, but she's said nothing since. She did look a bit strange in the gallery today though. I spoke to her for ages, but she wouldn't answer me – just stared at that *Ophelia* picture like she expected Lizzie to open her eyes and climb out of the frame.' Lissy shuddered. 'It would be like a scene from a horror movie, wouldn't it? Lizzie, all weedy and wet and dripping everywhere. And probably decomposing by now.' She mimicked the ghastly Ophelia creeping around and looked a little like a zombie. Then she shuddered again. 'One thing I do know, though, is that whatever's happening has been really sudden. She was fine last week. I'm a bit worried it *is* something to do with Daisy. '

'When spirits want your attention, they can be pretty intense,' said Becky. 'If that's what it is, of course. But whatever's going on, she needs to talk about it.'

'Is she not just highly strung?' chipped in Jon. 'Sorry!' He held up both hands as the women glared at him in unison.

'Was I highly strung when we met up again?' asked Becky, coldly. 'When I told you that the ghost of Ella was talking to me?' She took great satisfaction in watching him squirm and shake his head. 'Good. Thank you. We have to give Cori the benefit of the doubt here. You should know that. Anyway; we've made some drinks, and Cori is probably setting them out on the dining table as we speak. I think we need to go and see her, don't you?' Lissy and Jon nodded. It was a bit strange seeing two identical and yet unique sets of eyes moving up and down in such different faces, but it was nice as well.

Becky smiled. 'Excellent. Come on, let's go.'

Cori had laid the cups and saucers out carefully around the table and she was standing staring at them when Becky came back in with Jon and Lissy. Cori must have found some biscuits as well, because there was a selection laid out in the middle of the table, looking particularly delicious on the creamy coloured china.

The biscuits were Becky's favourites and she knew that it would be easy to polish off most of them in one sitting. She idly wondered how polite it was to a) have broken into your hostess's expensive coffee and b) be contemplating eating all your hostess's treats as well. She looked at Cori, ready to congratulate her on her findings and Cori caught her look.

A smile flashed up before it disappeared again. 'They all match,' she said. 'The stuff in my house doesn't match.'

'I don't suppose anyone cares really,' said Becky. 'It'll be you they come to visit, not your matching crockery.'

'I quite like things not matching. At home,' her face flickered a little, 'I mean at Granny's house, everyone had their own mug when they visited.'

Becky wondered if Cori was feeling a little homesick. It wouldn't help if she was feeling that way and also dealing with other things that might or might not be related to the diary.

'Nothing matches in our place above the studio either,' said Becky. 'I don't think it's a problem. Makes it more homely, I think. I'm happy amongst it all, anyway.' She glanced at Jon.

Jon caught Becky's glance and smiled at her, gesturing to the seat next to him. Lissy had already installed herself at the head of the table – yes, even on a round dining table, Lissy still managed to assume the head of it. Becky slipped in beside Jon and he squeezed her hand under the table.

'So the new Rossetti painting has been loaned to us from America,' Lissy said as she pulled her cup towards her and reached out for the cafetière. 'It's a new discovery and we are all really excited about it. It's going to be the centrepiece of an exhibition, which is due to run in the summer. Nobody can see it until then, which is a crying shame in my opinion.'

Becky thought the way that Lissy had basically claimed the Tate as her own was quite comical; but, instead of finding out any more interesting information, Becky found herself watching Cori.

Cori was stirring her drink over and over again. She never raised the cup to her lips. She was more or less sitting there watching the stuff go cold. Jon, on the other hand, had already spilt some of his vastly expensive coffee and the shiny, wet mark showed up terribly on the highly polished surface of the table. It didn't take him long to lean in it as well and smear it around with his shirtsleeve, but Lissy didn't seem to notice it; and if she had, she was clearly unconcerned.

Becky, however, noticed the way that Cori kept staring out of the huge bay window as if her mind was drifting elsewhere; then she would shake her head slightly and try to pull her attention back to the little group around the table. Lissy could talk for England and she was usually quite interesting, but Becky's main concern at that particular moment was Cori. Her tea had gone cold and she hadn't touched the chocolate biscuit Becky had put in front of her to try and tempt her. Eventually, Becky reached out and laid her hand gently on Cori's forearm.

'Are you all right?' Becky asked. 'Your arms are freezing.' She rubbed Cori's arm to try and get some heat into it. Cori nodded vaguely, then looked out of the window again.

Feeling a little frustrated, Becky tried again. 'Cori. Are you sure you're all right? You haven't touched your tea and, well, you just don't look *right*.' Almost as soon as she said it, Becky bit her lip. What an awful thing to tell someone; even though Lissy had clearly thought the same. 'I'm sorry.' This time Becky shook her head. 'Ignore me.' She turned back to Jon and Lissy, intending to find out more about the new exhibition, until she felt cold fingers pressing on her own forearm. Becky looked back at Cori, surprised she had even bothered to try and respond.

'I don't like feeling like this,' Cori said. 'This isn't me. I feel like I don't even know what day it is at the moment.' The way she leaned forward towards Becky and the way her eyes flicked across to Jon and Lissy then back to her, made Becky think she didn't want anyone else to hear her story. 'I can't stop thinking about the diary. Daisy's getting into my head. She sounds so convincing in places, but so mad in others. I'm having difficulty separating truth from fiction and it's like she's with me, all the time. I never feel alone, if you know what I mean. Didn't you feel it when you read it? Or is it just me?'

Becky raised her finger to her own lips and shook her head imperceptibly. It was obviously something Cori wanted to share with her; but where was the best place to do it privately?

Cori understood. She stared at Becky, her greenish-blue eyes angry and scared, silent questions bubbling up in them. *Where can we talk? What can I do? Is it just me?* Becky couldn't help but notice the faint smudges of black beneath her eyes; the girl looked exhausted.

'Cori, come and help me clear up,' she said too loudly, yet still hoping it sounded convincing. 'Grab those cups and we'll go into the kitchen.'

'Oh, just leave them!' Lissy said. 'Agnes won't mind cleaning them up tomorrow.'

'Agnes?' replied Becky. 'Oh no, poor Agnes will have plenty to do. And we might want the cups again later.' Her excuses were feeble and she knew it. But no matter; Lissy had asked her down here urgently, and so Lissy had to try and understand why she needed to take Cori into the kitchen. She cursed inwardly, wishing she could simply spell it out to her, but Lissy wouldn't have a clue. Lissy had stubbornly refused to try and learn any sort of sign language whatsoever. But again, no matter. Cori was reaching over and collecting the cups, her face not giving anything away; eager, Becky knew, to carry the charade along.

'But—' Lissy said.

'Jon! Ask Lissy about that … thing. That picture you were interested in,' Becky said, suddenly. Jon looked at her confused. He opened his mouth to speak, but she ducked her head away and hurried after Cori, clutching her own cup in her hands.

Once they had escaped from the dining area, Becky felt she could breathe again. She watched Cori locate and stock a well-hidden dishwasher and saw how her hands were shaking.

One of the precious cups almost slipped out of her grasp and fell onto the floor. The quarry tiles would have shattered the thing, had Becky not managed to reach out and rescue it before that happened. Becky placed the cup carefully in the dishwasher, along with her own, and looked up at Cori, concerned. Cori's eyes suddenly filled with tears and she wrapped her arms around her stomach, the colour draining out of her face and her whole body tensing as if a pain had cramped up the whole of her insides.

'What is it?' Becky asked, standing up. She had absolutely no experience of any of this behaviour at all. Dear Lord, what if Cori *was* pregnant and just didn't know it? She had heard of it happening to some people. She desperately hoped that Cori wouldn't take it into her head to give birth, right in the middle of Lissy's immaculate kitchen. Her emotions definitely seemed to be all over the place.

Cori closed her eyes and seemed to take a couple of deep breaths until her shoulders relaxed and she opened her eyes again. 'They smashed a cup at your house,' she said, 'and she said you hadn't realised. Yet here you are saving her cups at this house. I smashed a mug at my house too, just this morning. One of my art catalogues was ripped up and I got a shock and I ended up smashing my mug.'

'Yes, I think I told you I had noticed there was a mug missing at the studio and Lissy dropped herself in it when you came to visit, remember? But where does all that fit in with you?' she asked.

'What?' said Cori. 'Oh, it doesn't. It's just a coincidence. In the same way as I've been hearing and seeing Daisy ever since I brought the diary back to London. Then, yesterday, I ended up wandering around London and Simon had to come and find me.'

'It's easy to get lost in London,' said Becky. 'I do it all the time – it's the scariest thing in the world for me. It makes me panic, so I know how you must have felt.'

Cori nodded, apparently in agreement. 'You know, Simon and I had a perfect time in Whitby,' she continued, 'and then after that, I invited him in for coffee and I took him onto the roof and showed him the garden, but we didn't get to take that any further because the door slammed and a pot smashed. And now I'm wondering whether that was even real or if it was Daisy just starting to make herself known. I don't know, maybe she was jealous? And it's Daisy – it's Daisy all the time, and she's talking to me and telling me things and she's in my head and I seriously think I'm losing my mind!'

'Cori!' Becky put her hand on the girl's arm. 'I hate asking. I hate it. But can you just … slow down. Please.' Becky did hate asking. It annoyed her intensely. But she wanted to know what on earth Cori was trying to say and all the words were running together. Combine that with Cori's hiccupping sobs and the streaming nose and Becky was lost. It was no good to either of them if she only got half a story and tried to make up the bits she missed.

Cori covered her face with her hands. Becky had to fight the urge to scream at her to take them away. How the hell could she hope to talk to her like that? Instead, she reached out and pulled the girl's hands away.

Cori was visibly upset and shaking even more. 'I feel sick. I feel really sick,' she said. 'It's her, isn't it? She's doing it to me. I looked it up. I don't think she's happy just hanging around me any more. She's making me feel things as well. She told me she'd show me how she felt. What if that's what she's doing?'

'Cori. Do you want to go for a walk?' Becky asked, frantically. 'Get out of here completely and get some fresh air?'

'But last time I went for a walk, that's when I got lost. I ended up in Gower Street,' said Cori. Her eyes filled with more tears. 'Bloody Gower Street, where Millais had his studio.' She gave what was more than likely a bitter little laugh. 'And there I was, right in front of number seven. And you know what the plaque said?' Becky shook her head, and Cori continued. 'It said, "In this house the Pre-Raphaelite Brotherhood was founded in 1848."'

'I'm sure it's a really interesting place to visit,' said Becky. 'I can imagine it's good to see where it all started.'

Cori shook her head vehemently. 'No, you see, that's how I know there's a big problem here.' She looked Becky straight in the eyes. 'I'd never been to that part of London before and I still don't have a clue how the hell I got there.'

Chapter Twenty-Six

Becky managed to get Cori and herself out of Lissy's penthouse, on the pretext of finding a local shop to buy some more milk.

Lissy looked at Becky vaguely as she pulled on a coat and announced her intentions. 'Haven't I got any milk?' she asked. 'Oh well, yes, by all means, go and get some.'

Becky leaned over to kiss Jon goodbye and discreetly made a little sign. *You stay*. He looked hurt for a second, then, as Becky nodded to the kitchen where Cori was standing, chewing her thumb with one arm still clutched around her stomach, he understood.

Becky then turned to Lissy and, with her back to Cori, whispered, 'I'll try to get her to tell me what's going on? Try to discover why she's acting so oddly and whether or not it's to do with Daisy's diary or something else.' Lissy nodded. It was the reason she and Jon were here after all.

They left the building and Becky smiled and nodded at the concierge sitting at his neat little desk. The place was like a high-end hotel – she still couldn't believe people lived like this.

'Where shall we go?' Becky asked more to make conversation than anything. Cori, hunched up and bundled up in her coat shrugged her shoulders. She looked as if she barely had the energy to move and her nose was all red from the crying. 'Okay. I'll make an executive decision then,' said Becky. 'This way.' She turned left and headed out towards where she thought Old Brompton Road was. If they headed towards civilisation they might find somewhere they could talk. It seemed fairly surreal to Becky – the fact they had left Whitby that morning, driven all the way down here and now she was walking the streets of London. She felt pretty exhausted herself, never mind Cori.

She reached out and rubbed Cori's arm again. 'It's okay,' she said.

Cori nodded, but kept her eyes to the ground as if she couldn't be bothered to raise her head. She stumbled a little and Becky steadied her, her eyes scanning the shopfronts and the little offshoots of streets lined with tall, elegant buildings looking for somewhere to go. She swallowed down some panic and risked another look at Cori. She was seriously floppy now and Becky tried to pick up the pace, half-dragging her along, praying that she would find somewhere to take her.

'Oh thank God!' she muttered as she caught sight of a mobile coffee cart. Another coffee was the last thing Becky wanted but Cori was shivering and definitely looked in need of something and something quickly; the coffee cart was better than nothing.

'Are you eating properly?' Becky asked Cori as she paid for a single-shot Americano and a nasty herbal concoction that Cori had pointed listlessly at when given a choice in the matter. 'If I don't eat I don't feel very well.'

'I think so,' Cori said. 'I can't remember. But I feel sick all the time and sometimes I don't want to eat.'

Becky bit her lip. It was on the tip of her tongue to ask once again if the girl was pregnant. She was pleased she hadn't asked that, though, when Cori came out with her next words.

'I think it's the laudanum,' she said. 'I think she used to take it and she's showing me what it was like. But I wish she'd stop.'

'*What?*' Becky squawked. 'Say that again. I thought you said "laudanum".'

'I did,' said Cori. 'You have to understand me. I've never taken it. I don't even drink that much wine. I can't handle it.' Cori's eyes flickered and they began to glaze over, just like they had in Lissy's kitchen earlier. Her pupils began to

151

shrink until they were nothing more than little pinpricks and Becky watched in amazement as she lost Cori, right in front of her.

'I feel sick,' Cori murmured. It was hard to make out what she said with all the traffic noise around them; her voice was quiet and her lips were dry and barely moving. Cori began to sway and Becky grabbed hold of her arm. She looked around helplessly, trying to quash the sense of panic that was rushing into her. She saw a little garden square opposite. The gate wasn't quite shut, but it was obvious that random trespassers weren't generally going to be welcome.

'Come on,' Becky said, not caring about the consequences. She would lie and say she thought it was Lissy's square or something if she was challenged. But the main thing was to get Cori in there, away from everybody and sitting down.

She manoeuvred Cori over to the square, taking quick little worried looks at her and hoping she wasn't going to fall down in the middle of the road. Cori's eyes were half-closed and she was stumbling along beside her; but at least she wasn't resisting. She dropped her paper cup halfway there, though, and the vile smelling herbal stuff dribbled away down a drain.

Becky, still balancing her Americano in her hand, got Cori safely to a bench and forced her to sit down. 'I'm sorry, Cori, but I think I read that this is the best way to deal with feeling faint,' she said, realising she probably sounded more matter-of-fact than she felt. Becky placed her cup on the ground, then put her hand at the back of Cori's head and pushed her head down between her knees.

Becky looked around and, feeling rather stupid, leaned forward to join her; but at least if Cori wanted to turn her head to say something, she would be there. And if not, she was close to her coffee. Jon would have laughed at that. God! She wished now she had brought him with her. She had no clue what she would do if Cori suddenly became really ill.

Eventually, though, Cori did say something; she turned her head and focussed briefly on Becky. 'I told you, it's the laudanum. It's Daisy. It's how she felt when she took it. She ...' She dropped her head again and put it in her hands. She started to shake her head, and Becky guessed she was moaning about feeling sick again.

Becky sat up and looked down at the girl. It was making her back ache too much to stay all hunched up like that and, besides that, the baby was kicking an almighty protest at being squashed up.

So instead, Becky pulled out her mobile phone. She might not use it for calls any more, but she still had to check her e-mails; they were usually discussing the commissions that were the source of her income. Becky looked at the icons and selected the Google search one. She typed in the words 'laudanum antidote' and waited for the screen to load.

Her eyes widened as she saw page after page load about laudanum and the effects it could have on a person: nausea, tiredness, confusion, depression, lack of appetite, stomach cramps ... She pulled a face at bloating, constipation and a more frequent urge to urinate and wondered why people had done that to themselves. It did seem more and more like the worst parts of pregnancy though, and Becky found that inappropriately humorous – although she, thank goodness seemed to be getting away without most of the horrible stuff.

The lists went on: dizziness, hives, hallucinations, cold and clammy skin ... Becky shuddered. It was Cori, today, all laid out in front of her on a phone screen. She whizzed the pages up until she found the one she needed. A gentleman in a Victorian scientific journal had advocated the use of coffee. It was a stimulant, and negated the soporific effects of laudanum. More and more people continued to advocate this, as Becky continued checking, the journalist in her wanting to ensure there was a broad range of people who said exactly the same thing before she used the information.

Some people suggested a stomach pump and others suggested imbibing warm water or emetics, but in the absence of either a stomach pump or a handy emetic, she opted for forcing strong, black coffee into the victim, the application of cold to the spine – here, she pulled Cori's arms out of her cardigan, and untucked her shirt from her jeans, rolling it up to expose her back, which was the best she could manage – and walking the sufferer around the square, talking rubbish to her to keep her attention.

Becky neither knew nor cared if Cori was responding. She just kept hoping Daisy would have her fun, move on and leave Cori alone. This was all thanks to that bloody diary.

When the dizziness and the sickness started to fade, Cori realised she was shivering. She was on her feet and something was pumping through her veins bringing her back to life. Caffeine; it had to be. She could still taste the bitter flavour of strong, black coffee in her mouth.

'Oh, welcome back,' said a voice to her left.

'Becky?'

'Who else did you expect to see?' asked Becky. 'I'm just about fed up of walking around in circles now – so I'm pleased you're a bit more human.'

Cori looked around and saw she was in a kind of park and then found that there was an uncomfortable lumpy feeling around her ribcage. She realised her shirt was rolled up like a giant sausage and, feeling her face colour as she wondered how much of her body she had exposed to the general public, she tugged it down.

'Ah, yes. Sorry. I did that,' said Becky. She pushed her hands in her jeans' pockets and shrugged. 'I had to cool you down. Apparently, it's an antidote to laudanum.' Her eyes slid away from Cori's, as if unwilling to acknowledge she had been party to the little exhibition Cori had provided for her.

Cori swore under her breath and put both hands to her cheeks. They were burning hot.

'I'm so sorry, Becky,' she said, her voice wavering. 'I wish I hadn't had to drag you into all of this.'

'It's okay,' said Becky. 'Stranger things have happened; but I need to get you back. And we need to see how you are for the rest of the evening. I'm a bit worried that it'll happen again. And,' a bitter little laugh, 'it's not like I can call an ambulance or anything if you flake out here. Well, I could, but it would be pretty much a one way conversation for them.'

'Jeez, Becky, I don't know what to say.'

'Say nothing.' Becky frowned. 'Let's just go.' She looked around uncomfortably. 'We didn't get that far. It's not going to take us long to get back to Lissy's, but we need to head back.' She shifted her gaze to Cori and a little note of panic flitted across her eyes. 'Oh, hell. Look, Cori. We have to get back. I think it's best we go now ...'

Cori blinked as Becky's face seemed to go in and out of focus, and she felt the cramps in her stomach again. Her mind recalled a few minutes ago.

Hadn't she been in another garden? But there had been water there. She knew she was wearing a long dress, which she could feel getting heavy around the hem and her shoes were filling with water. Then all she could see was the sky above her. It was inky black and the stars pricked out their constellations and glittered a thousandfold more than they had ever glittered before ... she'd been reciting some beautiful words about the stars and the water. She could remember some of them and she adored them.

... Her eyes were deeper than the depth
Of waters stilled at even;
She had three lilies in her hand,
And the stars in her hair were seven.

Then she'd felt hands pulling at her, dragging her away

from the water and the stars all blurred and dimmed and then …

'Cori. Come on.'

Hands tugged at her again, leading her towards a gate. Someone was worried, Cori could tell by their voice. But all she wanted to do was stay there and …

'Walk, Cori. Just keep walking. It's not far, I promise. Keep it together, sweetheart. Come on.'

Like an automaton, Cori gave herself up to the motion of one foot in front of the other, seeing nothing, aware of nothing, being guided along like a blind person. God, she felt sick; so sick. Her head was buzzing and it must be the caffeine; because if that wasn't in her system she would be lying there, on the grass, sinking into blessed oblivion …

Sleep sank them lower than the tide of dreams,
And their dreams watched them sink, and slid away.
Slowly their souls swam up again, through gleams
Of watered light and dull drowned waifs of day …

Her body was crippling her movements and her mind was just a muddle of words and rhymes and desperate tiredness …

And the next thing she knew, she was sitting on the floor in Lissy's downstairs cloakroom and there was an argument raging outside the door.

'Should we take her to hospital?' asked someone. A male voice; Jon's, she realised.

'I don't think it's anything a hospital can help her with,' said a female voice. That was Lissy.

'Well, we can't just let her go home like that.' Becky, this time. 'You didn't see her. What if it happens when she's alone?'

'I've got plenty of room here,' replied Lissy. 'We'll make a bed up and she can stay with us. Do you think it's Daisy, though? Am I right?'

'I have no idea.' Becky again. 'It seems like it. She was out of it. I mean, *completely* out of it. She was telling me about Daisy taking laudanum and it really seemed like she was on the stuff too. Then I found out that coffee's an antidote, so I made her drink my Americano and she was okay for a little while.'

'Do you think Simon knows?' Jon this time, concerned. 'Because maybe we need to tell him.'

'Nooooooo,' groaned Cori quietly, hidden in the bathroom 'You can't tell *Simon*!'

'Maybe we shouldn't tell him yet,' said Becky.

'Thank you,' muttered Cori.

'We need to be sure,' continued Becky, 'but you say she wasn't like this before?'

'No. She was really sensible at uni.' Cori imagined Lissy's mismatched eyes widening in horror at the thought of what her old friend was like now. 'Well, I say sensible. She wasn't backwards in coming forwards, if you know what I mean.'

'Lissy!' Becky again, snappy.

'Well she wasn't. And she definitely wasn't into drugs. I would have *known*.'

'It sounds a bit weird,' said Jon, 'but then anything's possible. Has she got an overactive imagination or—'

'Jon!' Becky, even more angry. 'We've had this conversation before!'

'Sorry, just wanting to check,' replied Jon, affronted.

'Well, it possibly *is* Daisy,' said Becky. 'If she wasn't like this before and it's all happened since she got that diary, it's just *logical*.' Cori heard very definite, very loud footsteps, as Becky apparently paced around the corridor thinking out loud.

'I suspect you're right,' replied Lissy. 'It's definitely all happened since then. That's why I wanted you down here to see for yourself. So I know it's not just me …'

The voices drifted away and Cori reached up and pulled a soft, fluffy towel from the heated towel rack. She buried her face in it, inhaling deeply the scent of fabric conditioner and washing powder. She needed to think; she needed to get her head around whatever was happening to her. But she knew she couldn't think properly if she was either incarcerated in a hospital or staying here. She knew they meant well but would probably mount shifts outside the bedroom all night to keep an eye on her. There was only one thing for it.

She clambered shakily to her feet and pressed her ear against the door. She could hear the voices coming from the lounge area now and she chanced opening the door a crack. Peering along the corridor, she saw there was nobody there to stop her and she took a deep breath. She opened the door wider, just enough to squeeze out and stood in the hallway, her knees practically knocking together.

She inched down the hallway, quietly picking up her handbag from where she must have dropped it earlier. All the parcels of goodies she had bought for the mews house were also dumped on the floor but she couldn't risk trying to get them all out tonight. She saw one which she knew contained her beautifully squashy, mismatched Orla Kiely cushions and cursed under her breath as her hand shook, trying several times to grab the handle of the bag before succeeding. The rest of the packages would have to wait – if Lissy ever allowed her to come back to this place again, of course.

She steadied her breathing again as she seized the door handle and turned it quietly. As the door opened, she threw a silent prayer of thanks heavenwards and slipped out of the apartment. She pulled the door quietly closed and hurried away. She was thankful she was wearing her Converse – she didn't like the idea of clattering down these halls with heels on – and she ran down the stairs, straight past the concierge and out into the street. She turned in the direction she had gone with Becky, half-remembering it was heading towards a main road and ran until she lost herself amongst a throng of people.

The world started pulsing in and out again and her legs suddenly felt like lead – but she fought the all-too-familiar feelings long enough to identify a black cab at the roadside, hail it and fall into it, muttering her address.

She slumped in the back of the cab trying to fight the nausea and regulate her breathing. The cabbie clearly thought she was drunk. He didn't try to make conversation and he didn't go the scenic route. So it wasn't long before she found herself outside her own home.

Pushing a bundle of notes into the man's hand she murmured a thank you and weaved over to her doorway. The cabbie fortunately pulled away just as she doubled up in agony. Then she spent a good few minutes trying to force her front door open, crying with frustration. Eventually, she managed it, wobbled inside and banged the door shut behind her. And good God, she was pleased to shut the door on that day.

Then and only then, did she allow herself to sink down onto the floor and huddle there, crying until she was fit to burst.

Chapter Twenty-Seven

KENSINGTON

'*Don't cry,*' the voice said.

'Go away!' Cori shouted, still sitting on the floor. She jerked her head up and stared around her. There was a faint glow from upstairs and her heart began thumping, thinking that Daisy was actually going to manifest herself there and then in her lounge. It took her a good few minutes to realise it was the timer light on the standard lamp.

Cori closed her eyes and let her head fall backwards. After a moment, she forced herself to stand up and managed to drag herself up the small staircase into the lounge. Her head spinning, she staggered over to the sofa and lay full-length on it. Too late, she realised she had left her gorgeous new squashy cushions downstairs but she couldn't bring herself to raise her body from the sofa and retrieve them. She wanted to ring someone. She wanted to call Simon or her granny or anybody – but they'd all think that she was mad. And she had the worst room-spin ever.

'*You're not mad,*' the voice said again.

'Just leave me alone!' Cori shouted into the empty room. She heard a faint sigh and pushed her face into the not-so-squashy cushions. There was a yielding noise and a creak as if someone was sitting down on one of her well-upholstered chairs and Cori caught her breath. Against her better judgement she lifted her head, terrified at what she might see. But there was nothing there; except the diary. And she couldn't remember even putting it there, right in the centre of the seat. So she buried her head further into the cushions and screamed and screamed in the hope that she could simply drown it all out.

When Simon had approached Cori in the gallery that first day, he somehow knew that whatever type of fool he made of himself over her, he wouldn't care about it. He just had to try to make her happy.

And tonight, he was probably going to make the biggest fool of himself ever, but he was willing to risk it for her.

He pulled up outside her house in his two-seater and reached across to pull the giant bouquet of flowers out across the gear stick. The wrapper caught a little and ripped, and a few leaves shed onto the upholstery along with one or two flower heads. Simon fluffed the remaining foliage up and carried it more carefully out of the car and up to Cori's door.

He had been busy today. He'd had the day off and he'd not stopped. But he'd had time to go home and shower before he turned up on her doorstep, so that at least was a bonus; God, he hoped she'd like what he'd done.

He knocked on the door, his heart pounding and the flowers weighing heavily in his clutches. He pulled at the foliage again, trying to pretty it all up and managed to pull a whole piece of fern out of place. Swearing quietly, he shifted the weight of the bouquet again and knocked once more, harder this time.

As he knocked a third time, the door eventually gave under the rusty old hinges and Simon found himself staring at the tiny crack at the side, wondering if he should just push it that little bit more. He looked around, saw no neighbours peering out of their windows at him and gave the thing a good shove.

The door opened more fully and he stumbled into the tiny hallway. Cori really needed to get that door fixed, as well as the rooftop one. That was the thing with old houses;

they needed maintenance. He promised himself that he would come back and mend those doors for her. 'Cori!' he called. 'Hey! It's me. It's Simon. Are you in? Your door was open.' It wasn't a complete lie. It was just a little more open now.

He shut the door behind him and stood in the hall, listening carefully. It was a big house, and if she was on the top floor, she'd never hear him; but similarly, he didn't want to head upstairs and startle her.

'Cori?' He tried again. Nothing. He took a step onto the staircase and, one hand on the rail, one clutching the flowers, leaning forward to try and hear any sounds of movement upstairs. He thought he *could* hear something, actually, if he held his breath and concentrated. It was like a snuffling, then a muffled, strangulated animal sound.

'Cori? Okay. I'm coming upstairs, just so you know,' he shouted. He saw a little utility room off to the side and put the flowers carefully on the bench just inside. His toe nudged something soft on the floor and he looked down, seeing a bag with brightly coloured cushions spilling out if it. Cori loved her cushions; he knew that much. So he picked the bag up and loped up the staircase, two at a time.

Simon walked into the lounge and saw Cori, prostrate on the sofa, her head buried in even more cushions. Her shoulders were shaking and that weird noise was, in fact, coming from her. Now he was closer, it sounded like crying.

'Cori? It's me. Simon. Are you okay?'

There was a beat and her knuckles whitened on the fabric she clutched. 'Simon?'

'Yes. It's me.'

'I'm fine.' The voice came from under the cushion.

'No, you're not.'

'Yes, I am.'

'Cori?'

'Who sent you?'

'Nobody.'

Cori paused. She took a deep, shuddering breath and threw the cushion away onto the floor. She uncurled herself, sat up shakily and looked at him; her eyes were wet and her face blotchy. 'Did they say anything about me?' she asked. She seemed more concerned by that than the fact he was actually standing in her lounge.

'Did who say anything about you?' replied Simon. 'I haven't spoken to anyone.'

'If the subject comes up, okay, there was a good reason for it.'

Simon could see himself reflected in her irises by the lamplight. 'I haven't spoken to anyone,' he repeated, 'but I brought you some flowers. And you left your cushions downstairs. You really need to get your front door fixed.'

'I know.' Cori shifted position and twisted her fingers together on her lap. 'I'm sorry. I've had a horrible day. It's good to see you. *Really* good to see you. I don't care at this point how you got in, I'm just glad you did.' She attempted a smile and looked at the bag of cushions. 'You know me so well. I needed these so much tonight, but I just couldn't summon up the energy to go downstairs and get them.' She stopped abruptly, compressing her lips together and looking away from him.

'Do you want to talk about anything?' asked Simon, taking a seat opposite her. 'I have no plans.' Well, he did, but if she needed to talk, they could wait.

'No, thanks.' Cori shook her head. 'Not right now. But like I said, I'm pleased you're here.'

There was a dangerous wobble to her voice and Simon reached out, touching her hand. 'It's okay,' he said. 'Whenever you need to talk, I'll be ready to listen.'

Cori looked at him. 'Will you come out onto the roof with me?' she asked.

Simon hadn't expected that at all. 'The roof?' he asked.

'Yes. I need to get out of this room.' Cori's gaze shifted behind him, then moved around the room. 'It's like I can't breathe in here. I feel like there's somebody watching me, just out of sight.'

'Somebody watching you? Who?' asked Simon, cautiously. He knew, of course, what she was going to say. His eyes settled on the leather diary and he knew also that Cori's eyes had followed his. It sat there on the chair, looking all innocent and he couldn't quite let himself comprehend what was going through Cori's mind about it.

'Daisy,' said Cori. She looked at him, as if she thought he was going to get up and leave. When he stayed put, she pressed on, a little warily. 'Believe me, I don't usually condone all this haunted object rubbish. I'm usually the world's most practical person; but I feel like Daisy's doing stuff. Stuff I don't like. It's either that or I'm going completely and utterly mad. It's since I started reading that bloody diary. I kind of wish I hadn't brought it here.'

'I'm sure it's …' he started. But then he realised he wasn't really sure at all. 'Are you … don't get me wrong, Cori, but I know how much you love the PRB, especially with your aunt's connection to Rossetti. Are you not making connections when there's really just a logical explanation?'

'I wish that was the case. But sometimes it's as if I've slipped out of my world and into hers. It's difficult to explain. You know, like finding myself in Gower Street and knowing about things I haven't experienced. Like laudanum addiction.'

Simon shivered. He remembered that conversation they'd had about tinctures and the voice he had imagined speaking to him.

'But haven't you been immersing yourself in the PRB for a good few weeks now?' he suggested. 'Maybe it's just on your mind too much?' But before she could answer, something caught his eye from the direction of the chair and he snapped his head around. It had been a flash of silver, like a column of light, but there was nothing there. He dismissed it, thinking it had been a car headlamp from the courtyard and turned his attention back to Cori.

She was still looking at the diary. 'Yes, I might be imagining it. Or it's real and I'm certifiable. But whatever, I'm going outside,' said Cori. 'Are you coming?' Without waiting for an answer, she practically threw herself off the sofa and ran up the stairs to the second floor.

Cori just needed to be out of that room. She needed to gulp in some fresh air, even if it was dirty, polluted, London fresh air. Brompton Road hadn't quite cut it, she thought ironically.

She needed to be away from Daisy, to try and separate herself from her if she could. But she was running out of places to escape to. She barged through the door into the office room and ran straight over to the garden door. She threw it open and stumbled outside.

It was still warm out there, even though the sun was dropping behind the horizon. Cori leaned on the railings and closed her eyes, concentrating on the warmth of the metal curled between her fingers. It was quiet. Her mind at last was quiet. There was nobody in her head except herself, thank God.

'Cori?' It was Simon. He had followed her upstairs and out onto the garden terrace.

Cori squeezed her eyelids shut. 'I'm sorry, Simon,' she said. She opened her eyes again and stared out at the skyline. 'I'm sorry you got mixed up in this.' She attempted a laugh, but it came out in that horrible strangled fashion again. 'Sylvie would have been a breeze compared to me at the moment. When I left Northumberland, I was normal, you know. I was pretty well balanced and sane. My gran would have killed me otherwise. I just don't know what's happened to me.'

'You're perfect the way you are,' said Simon. 'That's why I like you. And Sylvie was anything but a breeze. I'd rather have you than her, any day.' He laughed a little, and he sounded embarrassed. 'I brought you some flowers tonight.' He came and stood by her, matching his stance to hers and she was grateful for his presence. He was so close, she could have wiggled her little finger and touched him. 'I put them in the little room downstairs, opposite the kitchen.'

'The estate agent called it the boot room,' said Cori. 'At home, we call it a utility room. I only have one pair of boots and that's rather a big room for one pair of boots.' She turned so she was facing him. 'And if you go through there, you end up in my garage. Can you believe it? A garage here in London, in a mews house?' She laughed, shaking her head. 'Unbelievable. The place is too big for me really, but I loved it when I first saw it. It needs some TLC though.'

'Yes, your front door leaves a lot to be desired,' said Simon. 'Anybody could get in. I mean – look at me. You could probably have me arrested for breaking and entering.'

'No, I'm pleased you did it,' said Cori. 'And I *am* looking at you.' There was the tiniest shake in her voice. 'I like looking at you.'

'I like looking at you too,' he said. He moved even closer to her and took her chin in his hand. Then he dropped his head, still holding her chin, so he was only centimetres away from her.

She could feel his breath on her skin and smell a minty, toothpaste kind of smell that mingled with his aftershave. The combination made her feel funny inside. 'Actually,' he continued, 'it's more than just liking to look at you. That day I spoke to you at the Tate – I'd seen you so many times before and promised myself that day was the day. I told you I get to know the regulars. But the reason I knew you, was because you walked in the room and the sun came out. Six months I'd spent feeling bitter about Sylvie, but when you appeared the bitterness went away and I was grateful to her. She'd set me free, although it felt like she hadn't at the time.' Cori felt him shudder as he took a deep breath. 'And, if you're willing, I want you to come somewhere with me right now,' he said.

Cori was more than willing – desperate to go with him, in fact. It didn't matter where; she would be there in a heartbeat.

'Where do you want to go?' she asked.

'Over there.' Simon nodded to a garden square, just below them and across the road.

'That square?' Cori pointed to it. 'There?'

'Yes. That square there.'

'That's the garden square for this block of houses,' said Cori. 'It's private. So I need to get my key. Otherwise we're stuck.'

Simon smiled into the dusk. 'Yes. A key. A key would work.'

'Fine. It's in the kitchen. Would you …?' She didn't want to go through the house on her own. With him there, it felt better and she felt safer.

'Of course,' he said. He looked down at her and smiled. Then he held his hand out. She took hold of it and as their fingers caught she felt a little shock current jump between them. Her lips parted slightly as the sensation caught her and she risked a glance up at him. He looked as if he'd felt it too, and it gave her a warm tingly feeling that had nothing to do with electricity.

Chapter Twenty-Eight

THE GARDEN SQUARE

Cori had unhooked the heavy iron key from a rack in the kitchen and followed Simon out into the courtyard. She smiled, looking at his car. There was a trail of foliage leading from the driver's door to the front door of her house and she remembered what he said about the flowers in the boot room.

He drew her to him and put his arm around her waist as they walked towards the garden square. She realised that he was the one who seemed to be leading her there. His pace quickened a little and there was an energy coming off him. Excitement? Apprehension? She couldn't really tell, but he was buzzing with something.

'This is it,' she said as they walked up to the wrought iron gate. 'It's quite nice inside. They'll be preparing for the Open Garden Squares Weekend soon, so there will be people coming and going all the time during that period. We should do the tour that weekend – I'd like to see what the other squares look like. How about we do a deal and I'll take you around the squares if you take me around the PRB sights.' She stopped short, briefly remembering the square she had embarrassed herself in earlier with Becky and then checking herself for assuming Simon would want to spend the weekend with her, trawling around garden squares. 'Unless you're busy that weekend, you might be working,' Cori said. 'I'm not really sure when it is or anything.' She started to put the key in the lock of the gate and then realised that it was unlocked.

'I don't know when it is either,' he said, stepping back

168

to let her open the gate fully, 'but I'll make damn sure I'm not working or doing anything else that weekend .We could make a day of it. Take a picnic or something. I mean – it's quite a common thing to do in these gardens. See – it looks as if someone's left a hamper here exactly for that purpose.'

He stopped and pointed to a wicker hamper placed at the base of a tree.

'Oh, what a shame! Someone's forgotten it,' said Cori.

Simon bent over and opened it. 'It's still full of food,' he said. 'Look.'

Cori went over and peered into it. She could see strawberries and a bottle of champagne, a box of chocolates, some tiny sandwiches all cut into triangles, something that looked like a quiche and a large fruit cake, already cut into slices.

'I'll have to ask around the houses to see who it belongs to,' Cori said. 'What shall we do with it?'

'Pick it up and take it with us?' replied Simon. Before she could protest, he closed it up, fastened the buckles and picked it up. 'Let's have a wander over this way,' he said. With his free hand, he took hers, guiding her towards a winding pathway that she knew led to a willow arch near a fountain and a summerhouse.

As they turned a corner she caught her breath. The willow arch was strung with tiny solar lights, all in the shape of stars. A little stream, a kind of mini-serpentine, flowed from the fountain through the square and the lights twinkled and glittered, reflecting in the dark pool of the fountain and the gentle sweep of the stream; and more than that, she saw a picnic rug already spread out beneath the arch. There were plates there, champagne flutes and napkins folded into tiny swans. And a huge pile of cushions to sit on.

'Simon …' she started. 'We have to go. We can't stay here. Someone's coming. I bet it's their picnic we've pinched. We have to take it back.'

Simon laughed and caught her arm. He drew her in closer so she fitted in between his arms and against his chest. Once again, she felt his wonderful warmth through her clothing. She could live and die in those arms.

Memories of another picnic. The smell of fresh cut grass and fresh air. A tang of salt, blowing across the Downs, carried on a sea breeze. A wicker hamper and some laughter. Fleeting images of a man whose arms were strong and capable, whose fingers were long and artistic. She could live and die in those very arms and it would be safe. She would be safe. He wanted her. He wanted her so very, very badly and she thought that she would give herself to him, just as soon as she knew what to do about Dante ...

Cori opened her eyes wide and stared into the dusk over Simon's shoulder. Was that a figure there? A red-haired girl drifting through the makeshift starlight, trailing her hands through the roses and the honeysuckle? Her dress was silvery-white, reflecting in the water of the fountain as she leaned over to look into the depths.

Cori's heart began to pound, and she wrapped her arms around Simon, linking her fingers and digging her nails into her own skin to try and stop Daisy's memories taking over her mind. She blinked and the woman was gone, but the image remained. She tried to focus on Simon, to hear what he was saying, God knew, she wanted to hear it.

'We don't have to go anywhere,' he murmured into her hair. 'It's ours. It's our little picnic. Just don't ask me how I managed to do it all without being arrested for trespassing.'

Her heart bounced around frantically in her chest as she tried to concentrate on the moment and deny Daisy any access to her thoughts. 'But how did you know about the garden? How did you get in? When did you do it? All of this? It's beautiful.' She ran out of words and questions and just stared.

'I did a little research. I discovered which square it was –

I had a feeling you'd have one somewhere. And when I tried the gate it was unlocked, so I came back and did all this today when I was off work.' He whistled through his teeth and surveyed it. 'I'm just really pleased nobody came and spoiled it all when I went home. I was desperate to get you here. I channelled our old friend Rossetti and *The Blessed Damozel*. She has starlight in her hair as well, just like you. It's a Rossetti pastiche, I think.'

'Thank you. Thank you so much. No one has ever done anything like this for me before.'

Simon nodded, still staring at the scene. 'You're worth so much more, but this is all I could do for now. And to quote some academia at you, if you're interested, Rossetti's poem was famous before his painting. Some say he wrote the poem before Lizzie died and some say he wrote it afterwards. I don't know how much of Lizzie went into it as inspiration, but the painting wasn't commissioned until 1871, nine years after Lizzie's death.'

Cori was entranced; the spectre of Daisy Ashford within her mind faded as she managed to dredge the image of the painting up from the depths of her memory. 'I knew the poem but I didn't know the story behind the painting,' she whispered.

Simon smiled. He put the hamper down on the floor and took Cori's hand, drawing her to the rug and kneeling down, so she had no choice but to kneel with him, face to face. 'Can you recall in the poem that he says, *"Her eyes were deeper than the depth of waters stilled at even; She had three lilies in her hand, and the ..."*'

'*"... stars in her hair were seven,"*' murmured Cori. 'Yes. I've always loved that poem. Almost as much as I love *The Portrait*.' She looked up at Simon. 'We've made another connection, haven't we? One just for us. The poem and the painting and this wonderful surprise. Thank you again. I needed this. I needed to escape.' She scoured the edges of the darkness for the girl in the silvery-white dress, but there was nothing there. Maybe she had been a trick of the light. It would be easy to see things amongst the shadows and dipping tree branches. Maybe there had never been a girl there tonight? But, just in case ...

Cori took a deep breath. 'Simon. Please, I hate to ask, but after this, after our picnic, can I come to your place? Just for tonight? Then I can think about Daisy tomorrow. It might all seem different after some time away.'

There was a beat and Simon looked at her. His eyes darkened and he reached out, putting one hand on each side of her face. His thumb stroked her cheeks and she felt her heart rate quicken.

'Of course you can come to my place. You can stay longer than a night, you know. You can stay as long as you like. I'll move my paintings out of the spare room, and make up the futon for you.'

Cori reached out and placed her forefinger over his lips. When he closed his mouth and took the hint to stop talking, she removed her finger, then placed one hand on each of his shoulders. She pulled him closer to her, so he had no choice but to lean into her and again just be centimetres away from her. His hands were still on her face and they knelt there, locked together.

'I don't want the spare bedroom,' she said, looking straight into his eyes. 'I want to stay in your room. With you.' She saw Simon's eyes widen, saw the faint rim of his contacts covering his irises and felt her pulse race and her stomach flip. 'Is that okay?' she asked. She half-dreaded the reply, yet she knew that she had no need to.

'That's more than okay,' he said, his voice hoarse. 'In fact, that's damn near perfect.'

Cori didn't know how she did it, but she managed to eat some of the picnic food.

She had been on edge the whole time, wondering if Daisy would make herself known again, and make her feel sick and dizzy and stop it all from happening; but she hadn't felt her presence at all, not since she imagined the figure by the fountain and all because she had convinced herself that everything had just been in her imagination.

She tried not to think too deeply about the memories of that other picnic; the one Daisy had apparently attended.

At last, here in the square with Simon, she felt she could relax. She lay back on a pile of cushions and folded her hands behind her head. She thought the London sky had never looked so beautiful with the branches of the trees just bursting into blossom and silhouetted against the darkness. She traced the elegant shapes with her eyes and heard a soft sigh. For a moment, a little grip of panic seized her, but then she realised the sigh had come from herself, not Daisy.

'I could stay here all night,' she said, trying and failing to count the stars. 'It's safe and it's kind of warm and I have cushions.'

Simon, lying next to her on his back laughed gently. 'It's up to you,' he said, 'but you know the offer is still there to come to my place. If you prefer to stay here, though, I'll stay with you. If you'll let me.'

'I want nothing better,' said Cori. She turned on her side and faced him. 'This was the best evening I've had ever. I never thought this kind of thing happened in real life.'

'It does when the right people are involved. I've never done anything like this before,' admitted Simon. 'I've done many things, but I've never broken the law for a girl. Breaking and entering a private square – well, there you go.'

'You rebel,' said Cori, sleepily. She yawned, covering her mouth and shaking her head. 'I'm so sorry. This is the most relaxed I've been for ages. And after this afternoon; well, I never thought it would be possible to relax ever again.

Oh, no!' She sat up suddenly. 'Becky. And Lissy. They won't know where I am. They'll be worried about me.'

'What?' Simon sat up, looking confused. 'Why would they worry?'

'I kind of ran out on them,' replied Cori. 'Something happened this afternoon. And I ran away.' She patted her pockets and looked around the rug. 'I don't have my phone. I need to let them know I'm okay.' She half-stood up and Simon pulled her back down.

'Don't worry. Look. I've got my phone. I'll call Lissy and tell her you're with me. She'll be fine.' He took his phone out and pressed a button. His face was bathed in a whitish glow as the screen came on. 'Oh. A voice-mail.' He looked at Cori and raised his eyebrows. 'Now, I wonder who that will be from.'

As he held the phone up to his ear, Cori rolled onto her stomach and groaned. She so did not want him hearing about her idiocy this afternoon, not after they'd had such a lovely evening. She wouldn't blame him for running a mile. More than a mile. And never stopping.

Even from where she lay, thanks to the perfect silence around her, Cori could hear Lissy's voice squawking out of the speaker. She seemed to be yelling at a group of people in the background who were all yelling back, at the same time that she was trying to speak into the phone. Usually Lissy's messages, as Cori knew, calmly resonated with her purring, sexy little voice; but this time she was anything but purring.

'Simon, Cori's escaped. She was in the loo and she's gone and she ... what? What did she say ...? Where? Dear Lord, did she? Simon, as I was saying, Simon, darling, she's escaped from the loo and we're a tad worried. She's been acting ... what? She's what, Becky? Bloody hell! Well, anyway, Simon, she's—' At that point the call cut off.

'Oh God.' Cori squeezed her eyes shut and reached

blindly for a cushion, flapping her hand around until she caught one by the edge and dragging it over her head.

Simon must have clearly realised by that point she had, for some reason, been trapped in the loo and had escaped. If it didn't sound so serious, it would have been comical.

'I wasn't trapped in the loo, I escaped from the loo. There's a difference,' she muttered from beneath the cushion. 'And I still need to apologise to them.' Good grief, it was going to be so much harder telling him about the true extent of the insidious Daisy and her bloody laudanum now. He probably thought she was mad enough as it was, running away from people's toilets.

'I'll text her,' said Simon. 'I'll just tell her you're with me and you're fine. Then we'll go and get your things from your house and we can head off.' He ran a finger up and down her spine and she shivered with that electricity again. 'Maybe I can leave the decorations up in the garden for another time, eh?'

'That sounds good,' said Cori from beneath the cushion. 'All of it.'

Chapter Twenty-Nine

ALMOST NOTTING HILL

It hadn't taken long for Cori to pack an overnight bag and leave the mews house with barely a backward glance.

'I have to warn you, my place is a bit smaller than yours,' said Simon, driving through the London streets, 'so we might be a little cramped. And seriously, I can easily clear the spare room if you want.'

'No,' said Cori, shaking her head, 'don't bother.'

'Well, if you're sure,' he replied.

'I'm sure.' And besides, it would be nice just to be with someone that night; someone real and solid and *breathing* for God's sake. She shivered, thinking about Daisy and what her diary seemed to imply.

And here she was, Cori, in the twenty-first century, going home with an artist. How strange was that?

'Here we are,' said Simon, driving through a pair of high gates. 'The Stalag Seventeen of Notting Hill. I moved here after I split up with Sylvie. It was only supposed to be short term, but I was desperate and I wasn't thinking straight so I rented this place.'

'It's not that bad!' said Cori. She looked up at the high rise – it wasn't horrible, certainly not as grim as Simon was making it out to be; it was just characterless compared to her home. But as this was practically a new-build, it all looked very clean and neat, and she wondered if that was what the creative side of Simon was privately rebelling against.

'It doesn't compare well with my last place,' he said, 'not for working in, at least. I'm doing it a disservice, I suppose. It's all right. It could be worse.'

'Where did you live before?' asked Cori.

'Chelsea. We had a garden flat and the back room was my studio. But when I moved out I never thought I'd need that sort of studio space again. What I've got here seemed enough. But it's not. Not any more.'

Simon parked the car in a carefully marked out bay and turned the engine off.

He turned to Cori and smiled. 'People keep telling me I don't need a car because of where I live and work, but I like to get out of the city when I can. And if I wasn't supposed to have a car, I wouldn't have access to my very own parking bay, would I?'

'It's good to have transport,' said Cori. 'I'm going to get a car sorted just as soon as I can. I want to be independent and go further afield. Plus, I know I'm lucky to have a garage and it's a shame not to use it.'

'Do you know,' said Simon, 'people actually sell and rent out private garages and off-road parking areas to people in this town? Crazy, isn't it?'

'Really crazy,' she replied. 'And is it more crazy that people buy them?'

'Perhaps,' said Simon, laughing, 'but maybe I can't blame them. Parking is horrendous in London. Anyway, let's get inside and I'll show you around. Not that it will take a great deal of showing. What you see with my place is pretty much what you get.'

'I don't mind,' said Cori. As long as I'm with you, she wanted to add.

And as long as I left Daisy at home with that bloody diary.

There was an elevator that moved silently up through the floors. As Cori had suspected, it was a nice, new building and everything worked perfectly. She was willing to bet that her old creaky door wouldn't be replicated here anywhere.

As if he was reading her mind, Simon suddenly raised his forefinger and looked at her. 'Your front door – I'm going to come over and sort it out for you. I don't like the idea of you being in there all alone and that door opening to let random strangers in.'

'Oh! Oh, thanks.' Cori smiled at him and adjusted her overnight bag on her shoulder. 'It's another one of those "I know I have to do it" jobs. But I've just never had the time. I guess I should add the rooftop door to the list as well. Do you fancy having a go at that one too?'

'Always up for a challenge,' said Simon.

'Great,' said Cori. 'I'll have to tell my gran it's all in hand. The front door was hard to lock when she was here and I've never heard the end of it.'

'You're close to your gran?'

Cori nodded. 'Yes. She brought me up. I can't remember the last time I saw my mum; and my dad – well, I don't even think my mum knew who he was.' She frowned. 'Drugs have a lot to answer for.'

'Oh.' Simon nodded. 'It must have been difficult.'

'Not really,' said Cori. 'My gran was more of a mum than my real mum could ever have been. I owe my gran everything and I'm lucky to have her in my life.'

'That's good to hear,' said Simon. 'And you know that you've got me in your life now as well, right?' He looked down at her, his eyes warm and not as guarded as they'd been when she'd first met him.

'I'm pleased I decided to go to the Tate,' she said.

'Me, too,' said Simon. They stared at each other for what seemed like ages, but must only have been seconds, because the soft *ding* of the elevator made Cori jump. She realised she had been centimetres away from Simon's face again. One moment more and she would have been kissing him.

They stood facing each other as the door slid open and Simon took hold of her hand. She knew he didn't even have to ask outright. In the time they'd spent in the garden under those twinkling stars, she pretty much guessed that they both knew exactly what the other one wanted. 'Are you sure?' he asked. 'Really sure you want to do this?'

Cori nodded. 'Completely sure,' she said.

'Okay,' he said, 'this way.' His hand felt warm in hers as he led her along the cream painted corridor towards a door at the far end.

His key slid into the lock noiselessly and the door opened on smooth hinges.

Cori didn't know what to expect when she stepped inside, but the flat was neat and tidy and well looked after. The kitchen was more or less integrated into the lounge and she could see there was one cup in the sink. There was a litter tray in the corner of the room and unaccountably – or maybe nervously – she laughed.

'You have a cat!' she said. 'I never put you down for a cat person.'

'I think the cat actually owns me,' said Simon, frowning. 'She's called Bryony.' He slid the chain shut on the door and turned to face her. 'She's a house cat so she doesn't go out. She's probably in the spare bedroom. That's where she likes to go during the day if she's not sitting on the windowsill or peering out onto the balcony. If you really do want that room, I can—'

'Just stop asking me that,' said Cori. 'I've made up my mind. Stop trying to change it for me.' She took a deep breath and walked over to him. She reached up and touched his cheek. 'Really. It's what I want. *You* are what I want. Don't spoil it.'

'Okay. Do you want—'

His words were cut off as she closed her eyes and kissed him.

'Do I want what?' she asked, pulling away from him, a little smile tugging at the corner of her lips.

'I was going to ask if you wanted a drink or anything, but ...' Simon dipped his head down and met her lips again. 'I think that conversation might just have to wait.'

'I think you're right,' she murmured against his mouth. She closed her eyes and relaxed into him. She didn't care. She didn't care about Daisy or her diary or her own rickety door or her mess of a house ... she just cared about the moment. And that moment was all about Simon.

Chapter Thirty

SOUTH KENSINGTON

After Cori had disappeared, Becky was torn between being furious with Cori and being furious with herself. She stalked around the lounge, cursing everything she could and shaking her head at Jon's well-meaning words.

'I swear, she wasn't herself in that park. Why the hell didn't we watch her so she couldn't leave? God!' Becky threw herself onto the sofa and scowled. 'Ugh!' She leaned forward and covered her head with her hands. 'I wish I knew what sort of hold that Daisy woman *has* on her!'

She sat up and looked at Jon and Lissy, holding her hands up. 'What can we do?' she asked. 'What on earth can we do? I should have *known*.'

'We could find out what hold Daisy *does* have on her?' suggested Jon. 'I can't think of anything else.'

'Oh!' Lissy interrupted, reaching her hand out and waving it as if to get some attention. 'There was something I meant to ask you!' She sat upright and opened her eyes wide. 'Did you do any research on Daisy after I gave you the diary? Did you get any more information about her?'

'No! Why would I? I wasn't going to pursue it,' said Becky. 'It was an interesting article. That's as far as it went with me. It's everybody else who's built it up.'

Then Lissy's eyes literally lit up. Becky could not believe it; it was as if a light went on inside them.

'Then I shall pursue it,' said Lissy. She stood up and Becky watched her disappear up the small staircase to the mezzanine floor. She switched on a laptop and fussed around it for a few minutes.

Jon smiled sympathetically and stood up, heading off into the kitchen.

Becky threw herself back in the sofa, closed her eyes and wished she'd had a bit more forethought. Damn Cori! How could she have let her go like that? She felt responsible for her and seriously felt like kicking herself. She opened her eyes again and saw Jon bringing a half-empty bottle of wine into the lounge along with three glasses. And it was red wine! What if they spilled it on Lissy's floor? She felt like crying, she really did.

'I can't have that. You know I can't,' she growled at him.

'Half a glass isn't going to hurt the baby,' he said. 'Look, I'll put water in it if you want.'

'No. It's fine,' she said. 'I don't need water in it.'

'Thought so,' said Jon. He divided the wine between the three glasses and passed one to Becky. 'You look like you need it,' he said. 'And I'm sure the baby will forgive you, just this once.'

He sat down beside her and gratefully she laid her head on his shoulder. The fingers of her free hand crept up to his chest and she laid her palm over his heart, closing her eyes again briefly. The rhythmic beating soothed her, but she couldn't settle.

'It's my fault.' She spoke into his chest. 'I should never have given her that diary.' His hand found her hair and stroked it. She enjoyed feeling the sensation of his fingers tangling in it and once again thanked her lucky stars they had found each other again.

'I think I saw her, Jon.' There was an imperceptible pause in the stroking. 'I think I saw Daisy. That first day, when Cori first took hold of the diary. I should never have given it to her. I should have let Lissy take it away. She's so careless she would have lost it and Cori would never have had it.' She pushed herself up from his shoulder and looked at him. 'So that's why I blame myself.'

He took her face in his hands and shook his head. 'No, you can't blame yourself for that. Lissy would have given it to Cori anyway. It would have happened regardless.'

She searched his face, trying to work out if he was being genuine or not; she eventually decided he was. 'Maybe,' she said, 'but what can we do now?'

'See what Lissy comes up with?' he said. He nodded over her shoulder. 'And there she is.' Becky turned and saw Lissy running gracefully down the stairs.

She had a sheet of paper in her hand and her face was glowing. 'I found her! I found her on the records!' she said. 'Here. Daisy Ashford. Never married. Lived in London. Born 1830, died first quarter, 1862. That, my friends, is when Lizzie died as well. What a coincidence.'

'What a coincidence indeed,' echoed Becky. 'I don't suppose it says what she died of, does it?'

'Not this top page,' said Lissy, shaking her head and accepting the glass of wine Jon held out to her, 'but there's a newspaper report on the second sheet. Hold on.' She scanned it and a look of horror clouded her beautiful face for a moment. Lissy looked directly at Becky and held the sheet out. Becky noticed Lissy's hand was shaking slightly and hoped she wouldn't ironically spill red wine on her own carpet. 'It says it was a laudanum overdose, Becky,' Lissy said, 'and a suspected suicide. Look. It goes on to transcribe the whole inquest.' Lissy retracted her hand, read a little more and finally shook her head. 'What a terrible waste of a life. Looks like she was addicted to the stuff, and she was found by her art tutor, that Henry Dawson chap she always talks about. Apparently he was "inconsolable" in the dock and had to be helped in to testify. How tragic. He says she had been really happy for months beforehand and it was a huge shock. I bet it was.' She gave a filthy, hollow sort of laugh. 'And I bet he wasn't just her art tutor. It implies that he had his own set of keys.'

'Look, we're getting into gossip now!' said Becky. She reached out and snatched the paper away from Lissy. 'Let me read it.'

Becky took herself off to the bedroom. She had a feeling she would prefer some privacy when she looked through the report and curled up on the window seat after locking the door behind her.

She unfolded the papers and smoothed them out. With a little shudder, she put the death notification on the floor face down, and looked at the inquest report instead. The first thing she noticed was that only a handful of witnesses had come forward – servants, pharmacists, a doctor, a Mr Alfred Ashford and Henry Dawson. Not many people to talk about Daisy – and subsequently, it seemed, not many people to mourn her.

'Dear Lord,' murmured Becky. She skimmed the wordy introduction: 'By virtue of my Office of Coroner ... to enquire on behalf of our Sovereign Lady the Queen, touching the death of Daisy Ashford now lying dead within my jurisdiction ... this Warrant, Given under my Hand and ...'

Becky shuddered. Daisy Ashford now lying dead. It was so impersonal. Poor woman. And she was only a couple of years older than Becky.

Beneath that was the list of names called to witness for the Coroner. She saw Alfred was the girl's father, and Henry Dawson, touchingly, was listed as 'Art Tutor and Dear Friend of Miss Ashford.'

The servants all said the same thing – she had been in the habit of locking herself away in her room and they often found empty phials of laudanum lying around the house. Or tucked underneath her pillow, or hidden amongst her linen or in the drawers of her bureau. She was subject to massive mood swings and strange behaviour, displayed temper tantrums, obsessional delusions and wilfulness. The word 'addict' sprang into Becky's mind; correspondingly, she felt tears spring to her eyes. This was getting worse.

One pharmacist said she was in the habit of coming to him at least once a week and buying laudanum from him, and two more pharmacists from different parts of London echoed his sentiments. Apparently she became irate and unreasonable if there was no laudanum in stock; but as they were being paid for the laudanum, they chose not to take it further. Bloody legalised drug dealers, Becky thought angrily.

The housekeeper said Daisy had been cheerful the previous night. It was only after Mr Dawson had brought the morning paper to her that she became upset and left the house. She had returned later on that afternoon and gone immediately to her room. Her lady's maid said she still seemed upset and refused any food, but that in itself was not unusual.

Several people corroborated that they 'knew of no hurt to her'. Basically, Becky thought, they mustn't have expected anybody else to harm her.

Mr Ashford was next. His testimony was short and unhelpful.

'The deceased was my daughter, although we did not have and never have had a close relationship. I knew not what she did in London. She ceased to be my responsibility many years ago. May I say on record that I am not surprised this has happened and I believe it to be one hundred per cent self-inflicted. It is most certainly the deceased's fault and I also believe her mental state was continually imbalanced. This is the natural end to such an abhorrent lifestyle and I am pleased I have been justified in my thoughts.'

'You utter swine,' growled Becky, laying her hand protectively over her bump. The doctor was next.

'I did not know the deceased well, it having been several

years since I attended her in some intense capacity, but I was sent for on Tuesday evening about half past four. At first sight I believed she was in a comatose state – but upon further examination, it was apparent she was deceased. The smell of laudanum emanating from the body and around the room was very distinct. I believe that she died from the effects of a very large dose of laudanum. An empty two ounce phial labelled "Laudanum Poison" was lying beside the body. There was no sign of anyone having been involved in the death except Miss Ashford and I believe, given the testimonies relating to the mental state of the deceased that day, the action was deliberate.'

And the final words went to Henry Dawson. The Coroner had indeed noted the fact, as Lissy had said, that he had been distraught and needed to be helped to the stand.

'The deceased was my lifelong friend and pupil and her name was Daisy Ashford. I spent the evening with her on Monday and I left her perfectly well and happy at about ten o'clock. I last saw her alive on the Tuesday morning and she asked me to return at three in the afternoon, but I was finishing a commission and lost track of the time. I took a cab from my home to hers and arrived around four fifteen. I let myself into the house, as was my habit, and called for her. The housekeeper can confirm I was not on the premises before that time. Hearing no response, I checked the downstairs living area and looked out into the garden, still calling for her. I then went upstairs to her bedroom and knocked on the door. Again, there was no response and I knocked again. There was still no response, so I opened the door. She was lying on the floor, partially clothed and at first I thought she had fainted. I went to her and realised she was not breathing. I checked her heart and pulse and there was no sign of life. There was a strong smell of alcohol and something else I did not recognise in the room. I covered Daisy with a blanket and ran out into the hallway, shouting for assistance. There was an empty phial on the floor next to her and it was marked "Laudanum Poison". I truly did not know she was in the habit of taking laudanum. I did not know, until I heard the witnesses today. How did I not know? We had been so close for the last few months and very happy and I did not know.' (At this point the Coroner had noted Mr Dawson had broken down and needed to be given some time to recover. Mr Dawson continued his testimony after a few minutes had elapsed and he had composed himself a little.)

'I am sorry. This has all been an immense shock to me. I cannot quite grasp that she is dead. I shall now attempt to continue. The doctor was sent for and he came shortly afterwards. I do not believe she wished to die. I do not believe it was intentional. Daisy admired Mrs Rossetti, and I can only think she was distraught at the news of her passing that morning and wished to still her thoughts. I do not believe my Daisy meant to kill herself.'

'What a bloody mess,' said Becky, the tears running down her cheeks. The verdict was, in the end, suspected suicide. It should maybe have been ruled as accidental death, Becky thought; but as most of the witnesses, apart from Henry, had expressed in some way that the poor woman was mentally unstable, it was ruled as suspected suicide.

Henry, Becky thought, could clearly see no wrong in her. The poor, poor man. And Daisy herself – well, this gave a whole new angle to her possibly not being at rest.

Chapter Thirty-One

ALMOST NOTTING HILL

It was ridiculously early in the morning when Cori woke up. It took her a moment to realise where she was. There was a glow coming through the window which she realised was a streetlamp and a warm body next to her that she remembered was Simon.

The lamplight cast shadows on his face and she looked at his sleeping profile for a few moments. His fair hair looked darker in the shadows and his lashes were long and thick, almost resting on his cheekbones. He shifted in his sleep and turned towards her. He threw one arm around her and she closed her eyes, taking a deep breath. If only this thing with Daisy wasn't happening – she could actually feel very happy here.

The spectre of Evan at least was finally erased. She'd never spent the night with anyone since and she'd almost forgotten what it felt like to feel warm and cared for and loved.

Cori opened her eyes and looked at Simon again. She imagined him lying in her bed in the mews house; imagined him amongst all the clutter and the cushions and the bright colours that graced her house.

Not one thing matched and she liked it that way.

Thinking of Evan, however, had unsettled her, because that led onto babies and Becky and, naturally, Daisy's diary. And that way, as Shakespeare had once said, madness lay.

Angrily, Cori wriggled out from under Simon's arm and threw the sheet off her body. She grabbed a shirt from the chair in the corner and pulled it over her head. It was

Simon's shirt and she closed her eyes, inhaling deeply as the scent of him wrapped itself around her.

She walked over to the window, covering the distance in three steps and leaned on the windowsill, twitching back the blinds and staring out over London laid out far below her. They said that New York was the city that never slept, but she would happily beg to differ. She could see taillights and headlamps weaving through the streets, the windows of far off buildings illuminating the skyline and she knew that on the paths below her people would be walking to wherever they needed to go at that time in the morning; to go to work or to go home or to find a coffee shop that was open 24-7 to try and chase their hangovers away before they had kicked in properly.

Cori found herself imagining what the city would have been like when Daisy and the PRB lived here.

'I'll show you, I'll show you everything.'

Cori froze. The nausea began creeping over her again and the lights outside disappeared into pinpricks.

'It didn't all happen in London, though. We visited Hastings as well. I can show you the church where Dante and Lizzie married, and I can take you to Fairlight Downs. Dante's friend, William Holman Hunt, painted it beautifully. Of course, I knew him better as William. I met him at Gower Street.'

The voice was conversational, rational. It was as if it was talking to her as a friend; a confidante.

'You look a lot like Lizzie as well,' it continued. *'We have so much in common, Corisande. I am sure people used to mistake Lizzie and me for one another. I was in Dante's company so frequently, it isn't surprising.'*

Cori clapped her hands to her ears. There was no escape. No escape from Daisy.

'But poor Lizzie. She was so ill when they got married she had to be carried to the church.'

'Shut up!' Cori hissed. And then there was a crash from the room next door. Cori swore, sweat breaking out all over her body. 'What are you *doing* here?' she said, almost crying. 'Go away!'

'*Come on, come and see what he's doing,*' said the voice.

'No!' said Cori. 'I won't.'

'*You have to,*' it said. '*Come with me.*'

It was as if she was taken there.

Her feet moved one in front of the other and she found herself at the bedroom door. 'Please stop it,' she sobbed. 'I don't know what you want. Why can't you leave me alone?'

'*I'm not going to hurt you!*' said the voice. '*Just come with me and you can see it. I told you that we have so much in common.*' Then the voice hardened. '*Of course, he's doing it all wrong. I'll have to do something about that. But I want you to see it first.*'

Cori realised she was in the small corridor outside the bedroom, heading towards another white, featureless door. As she stood in front of it, the door opened and she jumped, ramming her fist in her mouth to stop herself from screaming.

Something small and furry shot out of the door and brushed past her bare ankles, mewing loudly. The cat. Of course, it was the cat knocking something over in there. With shaking hands, she felt around for a light switch on the wall. Her fingers settled on the cold plastic fixture and pressed down on it. The room was flooded with light and that was when Cori got another shock.

The room was a mess. An utter tip. Much like her house was. There were canvases stacked up against the wall and palettes full of dried paint lying around on various surfaces. Brushes of all sizes stood upright in glasses and half-squeezed tubes of paint were piled up beside them.

An easel stood by the window and Cori walked over to it. She could barely move in the tiny room and wondered briefly how Simon had actually thought he could clear this room and locate a futon. She didn't know where he would have put all the contents if she had decided she wanted to sleep there. She stepped over artists' materials and sketchbooks and broken pieces of charcoal and finally stood in front of the easel; and what she saw on the canvas made her gasp.

Simon had recreated the famous *Ophelia* picture by Millais, but it was so very different. The strokes were looser and the background not so detailed. He had, instead, concentrated on the girl who lay in the water. The girl looked very, very familiar. She had long, red, curly hair and greenish-blue eyes. Her skin was white, with a faint blush on her cheeks and she had a nose that was very, *very* like …

'It's me!' whispered Cori, touching the painting carefully. It was painted in oils and she could feel the smooth peaks and rougher textures beneath her fingertips. It must have taken him a while – and he'd done it all from memory. Knowing how much he loved the original, it was no surprise that he had managed to convey the river as perfectly; but to recognise herself in that painting and to see how much care had been taken with her likeness was indescribable. But it actually made Cori's skin crawl to imagine Daisy prying around the flat and discovering it first. Maybe Daisy had even been there when … when they were … *ugh!* The thought was unbearable.

Daisy's response was a low chuckle. '*Never mind about that,*' came her voice again. '*What are we going to do about this picture?*'

'Nothing,' Cori said, turning back to the door. 'We're not doing anything. Why am I even talking to myself like this?'

'*You're talking to me,*' said Daisy. The door clicked shut, centimetres away from Cori and, too terrified even to scream, a strangled gurgle came from somewhere deep in her throat. She spun around, suddenly conscious of a strange light in the tiny room.

A vague outline of a tall, slim girl in a silvery-white dress stood in front of the easel. She turned her head towards Cori and smiled. She reached out a hand and extended her forefinger in the direction of a paintbrush. Cori saw it lift, then it was as if the girl was guiding it somehow. It dipped gracefully into a pot of white paint and somehow threw itself at the canvas.

'No!' cried Cori, finding her voice. 'You can't!'

'*I can and I will,*' said Daisy. She reached out her other arm and pointed it at Cori. Cori felt herself stumbling backwards until she was pinned against the door. '*He's done a lot of things correctly, but he hasn't got this right.*'

It was like a black, depressive fog had descended on Cori; it was even more intense than the horrible feeling Daisy's otherworldly laudanum had brought on in the park. Her stomach cramped like someone had taken a corkscrew to her intestines and twisted her insides around it. Cori involuntarily bent double, fighting against the urge to throw up, yet simultaneously fighting for air as her lungs constricted within her chest.

Waves and waves of dizziness came at her, and her body suddenly felt like lead. Her legs crumpled beneath her and it was a hundred times worse than the worst drunken state she had ever been in. With no Becky to hold her up this time, she slid onto the floor semi-conscious, the image of the girl standing at the easel fading and the sound of the paintbrush slapping relentlessly against the canvas.

Chapter Thirty-Two

Simon stretched in bed. It was the first time in a long time that he could ever remember falling asleep with a smile on his face and waking up with one too.

He lay still in the May morning, just listening to the birds outside the window, followed by the roar of a jet engine streaking across one of Heathrow's flight paths. Ah, well. You couldn't have everything.

He rolled over, fully expecting his arm to land on and subsequently curl around Cori's soft, warm body.

Instead, his arm landed on cold sheets and empty space. 'Cori?' He sat up, looking around the room. Ridiculous – it's not like she could have got lost in the room. Or even, for that matter, in the flat. Maybe she was in the bathroom. Yes – that might be it. He swung his legs out of the bed and listened carefully. He couldn't hear the hum of the shower or the boiling of the kettle. So where on earth was she?

He padded out into the tiny hallway and peered into the kitchen and lounge. Nothing. The bathroom door was wide open and the second bedroom door was firmly shut. Well, there was no way she could be sleeping in there. In fact – he looked around the place – there was no way she could be anywhere. There was still one cup in the sink, the cat was staring at its food bowl meowing pitifully and there was no sign of ... of anything. No overnight bag. No coat. No clothes. Nothing.

Simon swore and hurried over to the door. The chain was hanging loose from the doorframe, and he always slid it shut. In fact, he knew he had done that last night, when they had walked in. He placed his hands on the doorframe and his forehead on the door feeling the chill of it against his skin.

She'd gone. Just like that. After everything they'd shared last night. Simon swore again, more loudly this time and stepped away from the door. There had to be a reasonable explanation for it. She wouldn't have just walked out on him. Would she?

He headed into the bathroom and switched the shower on, going through the motions of his daily routine without even thinking about it. Then he had a horrible feeling in the pit of his stomach. The second bedroom. He usually left the door ajar so Bryony could come and go as she pleased. The cat loved lying on a pile of soft cloths he kept in there. Hadn't the door been shut tightly when he looked earlier?

What if Cori had seen the painting? The other *Ophelia*? He knew he had been taking a risk painting it without asking her permission and he hadn't even mentioned it to her last night. He had meant to; he had meant to take her in there and approach it properly – but what if she'd seen it by mistake and thought he was some nutjob obsessional person? That he had invited her back to kidnap her or keep her prisoner until he finished the most detailed parts of the girl's face?

'Oh, please, no,' he said. He crossed the corridor in a few steps and threw open the door, his heart pounding and his mouth dry.

Nothing. There was nothing out of place. There was no sign of anyone having been in there at all. He walked over to the painting and ran his fingers across the girl's dress, then traced her hair with his forefinger. Now he knew what that hair felt like for real, covering the pillow next to him, tangled in his fists.

He stared at the painting a moment longer, frowning. He leaned forward. He thought that collection of white daisies at the bottom of it was a bit too in your face now. He'd painted far too many, hadn't he?

That's what happened when the mood just took you over

and you painted without really seeing what it was on the canvas. It was all in your mind and in your heart, and when you looked at it afterwards, you sometimes saw things like this. Sometimes, they were happy accidents, like the way the sun dappled Cori's hair, or the way her hands unfurled a little in the water, her fingers trailing amongst the flowers.

But today, seeing those daisies in daylight, he realised they weren't exactly his best work. He couldn't worry about it now. He would worry about Cori instead. Where the hell was she?

He walked into the lounge and picked up his phone from the dining table. He hoped she had texted him or called him, but the screen was blank; just his usual dull, boring screen saver which he hadn't even personalised – not even with a picture of Bryony.

As if she knew Simon was thinking about her, the cat meandered over and meowed even louder, wrapping herself around his legs. Automatically, he bent over and ran his fingers from the top of her head, along her spine, to the tip of her tail. She arched her back and began purring, then nudged his leg after a moment or two, apparently reminding him she was the most starving cat in the history of the world.

'Yeah, yeah,' he said, walking over to the kitchen, the cat keeping pace. 'Where did she go then Bryony? Do you know?' The cat meowed and took up her vantage point at the bowl, looking up at him expectantly. 'You think I should call her, Bry?' he asked, putting his phone down and scooping food into the cat's bowl. 'What's that? You do? Yeah?' He straightened up and stared out of the tiny window that looked out onto the balcony. Somewhere out there in London was the girl he loved. And, surprising even himself, he realised that he couldn't just stop the feeling. He knew he should be angry and upset and all the other emotions the situation demanded, but he just felt lost; and he knew there had to be something else going on. He turned back to the bench and eyed his phone.

Damn it, he was going to call her. And if he couldn't speak to her, he was going to drive around to her house and see her that way. Come hell or high water, he was going to find out just what was going on.

Chapter Thirty-Three

SOUTH KENSINGTON

Becky just couldn't work. Despite the fact she had her laptop and had access to Lissy's Wi-Fi, as well as any space in the house she wanted to work in, the words just wouldn't come.

She had chosen the dining table with its big, beautiful window where the sun streamed in and its view out over the neat, little square, with Old Brompton Road seething in the distance; but she hated it. She longed to go back to Whitby, to sit amongst her muddle of papers and piles of notes and, yes, to even find herself amongst Jon's well-meaning stream of constant hot coffee, which inevitably grew cold as she lost herself in her work. But it was hopeless to try and settle to anything here.

She thought much of it was to do with reading that inquest last night. She'd hardly slept in the end, what with all the unpleasant thoughts continually whirling inside her head and the baby bouncing around like it was on a trampoline – which was probably the result of drinking the red wine. Even now, it seemed to have a fist or an ankle somewhere up near her ribcage and be relentlessly kicking or punching her insides as if it had just discovered an exciting new game.

After one particularly well-placed thrust, Becky pushed her chair away from the table and stood up, walking over to the window. She stared out at the road and the traffic and carefully placed the tips of her fingers against the windowpane. Maybe a bus would go by and judder the window and cause a bit of a diversion for her. Yes, she was willing to do anything for a bit of procrastination. Well, a bus did go past, but the window never budged and Becky moved her hand away sighing.

She looked around her and realised suddenly what part of the problem was. It was just too damn sterile in there. It was unsettling and she hated it. There was nothing, absolutely nothing out of place and she felt like she was intruding by trying to use the space effectively. At least at home, she could wander down to see Jon or help out in the studio or go for a walk over the cliff paths to blow the cobwebs away. What could she do here? And, more to the point, what could Jon do here?

At present, he was apparently off taking pictures, but she had no idea where he actually was. Lissy was at the gallery and Becky was supposed to be working. But, worst of all, she had no idea what else she could do for Cori – she had seen that the girl was having a horrible experience and that too was part of the problem.

Simon, however, had reported late last night that Cori was much better and had decided to spend the night at his place. Lissy had practically jumped for joy and Becky had at least been able to relax a little, knowing that was the case. But that newspaper report they had found still troubled her. Daisy Ashford didn't seem to be at rest at all; which was an odd thing to think, but somehow Becky knew that was the issue.

And she still felt completely trapped in this beautiful apartment. She knew she should be out there doing something, but what? She looked out of the window again and then her heart skipped a beat. Walking along the path out of the square was Jon, laden down with his camera equipment, his hands in his pockets and looking as if he hadn't a care in the world. In fact – she squinted her eyes – was he *whistling*?

Becky laughed. She ran over to the table and grabbed

her phone. *Look up* she texted. *Now! At the window!* She pressed 'send' and hurried back to the massive bay window. She saw him hesitate and look down at his pocket, then pull his phone out. He read it and looked up.

She began to wave at him, and he started to laugh. He waved back and made a little heart shape by crooking his forefingers and thumbs together.

Wait for me, I need to escape, Becky told him. *I'm coming down.*

Jon smiled and gave her the thumbs-up sign, and Becky hurried back to the table. She shut the lid on the laptop and grabbed her bag. She shoved her phone in as an afterthought and headed out of the house, pulling the door shut and locking it behind her. She raced down the stairs and out into the fresh air.

Jon was waiting for her by the park gate and she dashed over the road to meet him. He opened his arms and she flew into them laughing.

'I couldn't bear it any longer,' she told him. 'It's horrendous up there. It's so stuffy and I can't work. At all. I mean it. I just can't work.' She shook her head. 'I'm stagnating here. It's supposed to be this fabulous city with all this energy and I'm just not taking advantage of it. I just want to go home.' She pushed her hair behind her ear without thinking and stared around her. 'Which way?' She looked back at Jon, waiting for an answer.

'The river?' he suggested. 'The Embankment? We could have a look at the bridges, do some touristy things. Have a coffee.' His eyes sparkled.

'Perfect,' she said. 'I'll let you lead.' She slipped her hand into his and looked up at him. 'I don't mind telling you that this situation with Cori is actually scaring me. I think Daisy's dangerous. When Ella started trying to talk to me, it was different. She found a way to connect through that writing slope and she needed to talk to me so I could help her. She wanted me to tell the truth about what happened to her, so she and Adam could move on. And much as I feel sorry for her, Daisy just seems like a drug-addled fantasist and she's impressing that personality on Cori. I don't know what she's trying to achieve.'

Jon pulled her closer, wrapping his arm around her and it felt so right. 'Are you absolutely sure Cori's not just over-imaginative or something?' he asked.

'You didn't see her yesterday. I swear I thought she was going to die on me,' Becky replied. 'If I had needed help, I just don't know what I ...' she tailed off, shaking her head. 'I'd have been useless!'

'You're not useless,' said Jon. 'You're just what Cori needs right now.'

'I'm not convinced,' replied Becky. 'I think she needs Simon. I don't think Daisy's going to give up easily, and I think Cori's going to crack if she doesn't get help. I don't think I'm enough. She needs Simon like I needed you. But it's a lot for him to take on. I wouldn't have liked to deal with all that by myself. My own problems were enough, without having Ella's as well! I think what I'm trying to say is that I was lucky you were there for me.'

'Well, that's very kind of you to say so,' said Jon, smiling. 'I'm glad you accepted that first coffee I offered you. Where would we be now if you hadn't have done that?'

'I'd still have ended up with you,' said Becky. She reached up and pushed the ever-present bit of hair away from his eyes. 'We just would have met up again somewhere else. It was never not going to happen. It just might have not happened *yet*.' She shuddered, recalling her thoughts from when she had received Lissy's desperate e-mail – and once again she felt grateful.

'It would never not have happened,' Jon replied. He leaned down and brushed her lips with his. 'Come on. Let's just get in the car and go somewhere else instead. We'll drive away from the centre and find some greenery or some water or something. How does that sound?'

'I can't wait,' she replied.

They were just finishing lunch in a coaching inn they had stumbled across somewhere within the commuter belt, when Becky sat back in the chair and contemplated loosening her waistband even more. Her bag was on the chair next to her and Jon suddenly leaned over.

He cocked his head to one side and pointed to the bag. 'There's a funny noise coming from your bag. Is it your mobile?' he asked.

'Ugh,' she replied, flicking a disgusted look at the bag. 'Useless thing.'

'Good grief, it's like you're scared of it!' Jon laughed. 'Open the bag. Get it out. Read the message.'

'Look! My bag's still shaking,' she said, touching the fabric. 'It's not stopping!' She pulled her mobile out and stared at it for a second. 'Here.' She thrust it at Jon. 'You deal with it. It's Cori.'

Jon took it from her. 'Five texts and two missed phone calls?' he said. 'Well, we're lucky to catch this one.' He pressed the answer button and spoke into it. 'Hey, Cori. It's Jon. Yes. Yes, she's here.' He looked at Becky, frowning. 'Yeah. Just tell me, it's fine. No, no worries. Yeah, I'm sure she doesn't think you're really into that sort of stuff. Yeah, I know. She doesn't check texts very often. No that's fine. I know you wanted her to know.

'What? No, I'm sure she doesn't think you're obsessed. Mono-what? Mono*mania*? No, I'm sure you haven't got that either. Look, Cori, hey, it's fine. Don't cry. No, really. Cori?' He held the phone to his ear a moment longer, scratching his head with his free hand and looking confused. Finally, he hung up and passed the phone back to Becky. 'She's gone. She just started crying and it cut off.'

'That doesn't sound good,' replied Becky. She looked at the phone and began to flick through the texts. They all said the same, every single message: I'm sorry. I feel awful. Please forgive me. I never meant it to happen. Silently, she handed it back to Jon and leaned forward, resting her chin on her hands, looking at him for his reaction.

'Well, now,' he said, eventually. 'I think she's sorry. What exactly did she do that was so bad?'

'Just had that episode in the park,' said Becky, frowning.

Jon nodded towards the phone. 'It's off again,' he said. He passed it to Becky and the horrible buzzing reverberated all through her fingertips and up her arms. *Ugh!*

'Oh God,' she said. 'She's saying the same thing again. I'm sorry, I'm sorry ...' She gave one of her expressive hand gestures, trying to wave the comments away. 'I don't like it, Jon. That's not normal behaviour, is it?' She looked up at him. 'Do you think ...?'

'Come on.' Jon pushed his chair back and stood up, understanding. 'Let's go and see her. Oh. We don't know her address.' He frowned. 'Fatal flaw in the plan.'

'I'm already on it,' said Becky. She was pressing buttons on the phone. 'Lissy will know it by now. She knows everything. She'll have made it her business to get Cori's address so she can see what her house is like.'

Two minutes later, the address came through.

Becky smiled and held the phone aloft. 'I knew it,' she said. 'Result.'

'Not so useless now, is it?' Jon teased, pointing at the phone.

He managed to turn around and hurry away, just in time to prevent Becky retaliating verbally in a not-so-pleasant manner.

Chapter Thirty-Four

KENSINGTON

Becky was practically out of the car before Jon had pulled the handbrake on. She had become more and more twitchy as the journey progressed. Seven more messages had come through before Becky had finally switched the power off on the phone and thrown it onto the back seat.

'This is it,' she said as they pulled into the little street. 'Come on.'

'It's a nice house …' Jon began, but it was too late. She was away, hurrying across the cobbled courtyard and up to the front door of the house.

'Becky, slow down!' he shouted. 'Are we sure this is the right place anyway?' But he knew he was talking to himself. Shaking his head in exasperation, Jon locked up and went after his wife. Still when Cori had said 'mews house', he had expected some tiny little place like the apartment over the studio in Whitby – maybe next door to a kebab house or 24-7 off-licence. He hadn't expected this place.

He eyed up the three-storey white house tucked into the corner of the courtyard off Kensington High Street and raised his eyebrows. Very nice, indeed. It even had an integrated garage to the side. And that top room – he could tell the light would stream in there for most of the day. If it all worked out for them, well – who was to say Simon couldn't use that as a studio?

'Jon, it's open!' Becky was standing, holding the door handle. The door was ajar and she looked at Jon. 'Where is she? Can we go in?'

Jon shrugged. 'I don't know, and I don't know,' he replied. 'Can we?'

'For God's sake!' snapped Becky. 'Can't you be serious for just one minute? There's something up, I just know it. Come on. Let's go in. I'll take the blame if we get caught.' She leaned against the door but it wouldn't seem to move any further. She pushed again, using her foot as leverage and it swung open, creaking on the ancient hinges. 'I bet that's why it didn't shut,' she said. 'Old wood, it's swollen up ...'

'Becky!' Jon tugged on her elbow. 'I think we just got caught.'

A woman from across the courtyard was standing in her doorway, holding a pastel pink watering can, water dribbling out of the spout into a small, potted basil tree. Jon was aware that she was taking more notice of Becky and him than she was of the plant. She began to stride across the courtyard, her brows furrowed.

'Oh, great,' said Becky. 'Fine. Leave this one to me. I hate doing this, but needs must.'

'Excuse me!' the woman said. 'Can I help? I wonder if you're in the right place? I don't think I recognise you.'

Becky smiled. She raised her hand and waved at the woman. *Hello*, she signed. *I'm Becky. We are friends with Cori. Do you sign?*

The woman looked at her blankly. She turned her attention to Jon.

'I wonder ...' she began.

But Jon knew what he had to do. *I'm with her*, he told the woman.

Don't mind us, continued Becky. *It's fine.* She pointed to the house and gave the woman a thumbs-up sign.

The woman looked from one to the other. 'I'll leave you to it,' she said. She backed away and, with one last, confused glance, scurried back into her house and shut the door.

'Thank you and goodbye,' muttered Becky. 'God, I feel bad, but it works every time. Then they wonder how I get some of my stories. Okay, come on.' She hurried into the house and Jon followed, closing the door behind him.

There was a bright, airy hallway with a door leading off to the right; the kitchen, Jon realised. There was also a door to the left leading to a smaller room, with a bunch of flowers abandoned on a bench. Luckily, they were in one of those fabulous water bubble things. Otherwise it would have been one hell of a waste of money. Jon raised his eyebrows and walked into the kitchen.

Becky was already in there, amongst the modern units and the work surfaces cluttered with spice bottles and incompatible crockery. 'I think we need to call Simon and check she's not with him,' she said. 'She's left in too much of a hurry. I'm going upstairs.'

Becky tried to push past him, but Jon blocked her way. 'What makes you say that?' he asked.

'Look! On the bench!' Becky jabbed her forefinger towards one of the alcoves. 'She was halfway through making a cup of tea. Would you leave a coffee half made? I thought you *watched* all these forensic programmes?' She tapped her temples. 'My eyes function perfectly well, you know.'

Jon saw a tea bag floating on the top of a mug and a spoon next to it. The contents of the mug were mahogany, and a bottle of milk was next to the kettle, slowly curdling. He opened his mouth to reply, but Becky shook her head and this time succeeded in pushing past him and racing up the staircase towards what he assumed was the lounge area.

'Call Simon!' she reiterated as she disappeared around a dog-leg in the staircase. 'Ask him if he's seen her.'

Jon ran up the stairs and burst into the room Becky was standing in. It was a pale cream lounge with soft, comfortable, mismatched chairs and a huge coffee table dominating the centre of the floor. There was no sign of anybody.

'Look – more stairs,' said Becky. 'The second floor.' She started up the stairs and Jon looked around the lounge, trying to see if anything else would give him a clue as to Cori's whereabouts. Then there came a shout from somewhere up above him.

'Jon, quick. There's no need to call Simon. He got here before us.'

Jon turned and pounded up the stairs. He came out into a large, untidy room lined with bookshelves and piles of paperwork stacked up any which way they could be.

There was a quietly insistent thumping as a door opened and closed, bouncing back and forth in its frame as the wind outside caught it. And lying on the floor amidst a pile of scattered books and paperwork, with blood trickling out of a cut on his forehead, was Simon.

When he started to come round and the room had stopped spinning so much, Simon found himself on a soft, pale pink rug and felt a wet cloth being pressed against his forehead.

He had the world's worst headache and there was a woman kneeling over him. He squinted and tried to focus on her. She had dark hair. It wasn't Cori. He would know Cori. He tried to sit up and the girl transferred her palm to his shoulder and pushed him gently down again.

'Don't try to sit up,' she said.

'Becky?' he asked. His voice came out as no more than a croak. 'She said you were visiting Lissy.'

'Yes, we are. And Jon's here as well, don't worry,' she said. 'Do we need the police? Did someone break in?'

Simon shook his head. It hurt like hell. 'No police,' he said. 'I need to find Cori.'

'But where is she? Jon!' Becky sat back on her heels and called across the room. 'Jon. Can you come over here please?' Simon felt the floorboards give a little as two feet came and stood by him.

'Has Sleeping Beauty spoken then?' came Jon's voice. 'Okay, mate, what's happened? Tell me all about it.'

Simon closed his eyes and tried to formulate in his head just what had happened. He had come to the house and he'd knocked on the door and ... Jesus! He'd ended up outside on the roof garden, hadn't he? Then he'd come back in and ... what had happened after that?

Cori hadn't answered his calls; any of them. He'd ended up having to go to work at the gallery still wondering what the hell he'd done wrong. And once he was at work, he found that he couldn't concentrate. Then, after a few more calls, he decided enough was enough; he was definitely going to go to her house.

It was just as well Lissy had been at the gallery that morning – she'd covered for him, telling the manager that Simon hadn't felt well and had been suddenly indisposed. After some of Lissy's graphic descriptions, the manager hadn't pried any more and assumed Simon had gone home sick.

Which was probably about the point when he had pulled up in the Mews courtyard.

'Cori!' He had knocked on the door as hard as he could and it wasn't long before she came to the door, dressed in that long, silvery-white maxi-dress he remembered so well.

It wasn't her looking at him, though. Whoever it was had the same outward appearance but there was something in her face that just didn't sit right.

'Cori, can I come in?' he asked. She looked at him as if she was trying to place him somewhere, then she smiled.

She stood back from the door and beckoned him in. 'I was just making a cup of tea,' she said. 'Come on, let's go upstairs and you can have a seat while I make you one too.'

'Cori, what happened?' he asked, hesitating for a moment before following her inside. There was just something about her that didn't add up. She was off, somehow; skewed. In fact, she didn't even *look* like Cori. Not properly. 'You just disappeared,' Simon continued. 'I've been calling you all day. I was worried I'd done something wrong. I woke up and you weren't there and after I thought we were okay last night.'

Cori laughed. 'Oh, no, you've done nothing wrong. Don't worry about that.'

He knew she had followed him upstairs.

Cori looked at him and her greenish-blue eyes suddenly filled with tears. 'But, Simon, everything else has gone wrong,' she whispered, 'and I think I need your help.'

'Anything, Cori. Whatever you need.' He sat down, putting his car keys on the table with a little clatter. This girl, he recognised as Cori; but she was terrified. The fact she'd run out on him filtered out of his mind. All he was concerned about was her; right here and right now.

'You shouldn't have painted that picture, Simon,' she said. 'It brought her into your home.'

'Brought who into my home?' he had asked, confused. 'What picture?'

'Her. Daisy. The other *Ophelia* picture.'

'You weren't meant to see that just yet. I ...' He felt himself blush. 'No. Actually, I have no excuses. I wanted to paint you. I've wanted to do that since the first minute you walked into the Tate. I was going to show it to you last night, but we never got that far.'

'Did you hear me, Simon? I said that it brought her into your home. She's ruined it. It wasn't me. It was her, she ruined it. I'm so sorry. It was a beautiful picture.'

'Ruined it?' asked Simon. 'Nothing's ruined.'

'It's not ruined? But what did she do to it then?'

'Cori, you've been dreaming. The picture is fine. I've

208

done a few too many flowers in the foreground, but I can easily sort that out. I'm just sorry you had to find it like that. I really wanted to be the one to show you. Is that it? Is that why you ran out on me?'

'Dreaming? But it all seemed so real. Hallucinations – that's the next thing, though, isn't it? She's finally got me as mad as she was.' Cori laughed and shook her head. 'She said you shouldn't have painted the portrait. I know they posed at Cheam for it, and—'

'*Cheam*?' Simon was confused. 'Who posed at Cheam?'

'Lizzie and Daisy,' said Cori, 'at John's studio there. They posed there for the *Ophelia* picture.'

'John? You mean Millais? As I understand, the background was painted when he rented that studio at Cheam; but the figure, whoever it was, was painted in Gower Street.'

'It wasn't Cheam?' Cori stared at him. 'But she said it was Cheam. In the diary.'

'Then I think she made a mistake,' said Simon.

'The diary's upstairs,' said Cori. 'Come with me and we'll have a look.'

Simon faltered. 'But …'

'No! Come with me.' She seized him by the hand and tried to pull him off the seat to drag him behind her, up the stairs to the second floor.

Simon stood up and followed her. 'I don't know what we can prove,' he said. 'But, yes, I'll have a look.' He felt slightly confused – Cori's anxiety was manifesting itself in him to a lesser extent, but he had to go with her. Perhaps she would calm down when they had looked in the diary.

'Will you check outside, just in case?' asked Cori. 'I don't think I had it out there, but who knows? I'll look around the room.' She dropped his hand and began pulling things off the shelves, throwing books down and moving papers from one pile to another.

'Okay. I'll go and see if it's out there,' said Simon, even more confused. He turned the key and pushed the door open to the rooftop. He walked out and stood staring at the broken pots and overgrown tubs, trying to think where she might have read it. There wasn't really anywhere comfortable to sit, so unless she stood out here ... He turned three hundred and sixty degrees, very slowly, but he couldn't see where she would have been.

As he came back to face the railings, his back to the door, he saw an old tattered piece of paper lying squarely in the middle of the crazy paving centrepiece. He bent down and picked it up. It looked like a page from the diary. So she *had* been out here.

Then he heard the clash behind him as the door shut. He spun around and saw Cori, way over on the other side of the room. How the hell had she moved so fast?

Then he saw her throw some more papers on the floor, turn and literally run out of the room, heading down the stairs as he battered the door over and over, trying to make her hear, trying to make her come back.

He had shoved the page in his pocket, and tried to open the door; but it wouldn't budge. He leaned down and saw through the gap between the door and the frame the bar of the lock joining the two pieces of wood firmly together; the bloody thing had locked itself.

So he had thrown his weight against the door, again and again. Eventually, and oddly smoothly, considering the lock should have been holding it together, the old door had suddenly given under Simon's constant barrage of battering and shaking.

He had tumbled into the room as the thing flew open; and that was the point where he'd caught his toe on the pink rug, fell over a pile of digital art books and took a nosedive towards the vicious looking corner of Cori's computer desk.

And after that, he didn't remember much at all.

Chapter Thirty-Five

Simon was sitting up now, on the not-so-comfortable computer chair. He was folding and unfolding the bloodstained flannel into a tiny square. Becky was sitting opposite him, cross-legged on the floor and Jon was leaning against a bookcase.

'So, yes, I guess it sounds a bit mad,' Simon said, 'but that's all I remember. I don't know where Cori went afterwards. We spent the night together last night.' He felt his cheeks colour a little. 'Have you tried calling her?' He looked helplessly at Becky, then at Jon. 'Has she answered her phone?'

'I don't think she has,' said Becky, quietly. 'You tried, didn't you?' She twisted around and Jon nodded.

'I've called her numerous times but she isn't answering,' Jon replied. 'I tried twice when you were out, mate.'

'You said you thought she had taken a page out of the diary,' said Becky. 'Have you still got it?'

Simon nodded and winced a little as he felt his forehead throb with the motion. He pulled the paper out of his pocket and handed it to her.

'I don't like it,' Becky said. 'There's some reason for this. Something she was trying to tell us. Otherwise, why take a random page out?'

'I don't know,' replied Simon. 'Perhaps that page meant something. I didn't get too good a look at it after all that. It was messy, I know that much.'

'Oh, yes. I remember this one from when *I* read the diary. I don't know what it said – I kind of flipped past it. It was just a mess and was giving me a headache.' Becky frowned, clearly remembering it from before. 'I thought it was a kind of doodle page.'

Simon also remembered the page had been covered with extremely closely written text that not only filled the pages but went around the sides and into the margins, wrapping around themselves like a snake and falling into all sorts of designs; it had all been intricately patterned, he recalled, and he hadn't had a chance to interpret it.

'Hang on; it's all about Tolworth,' said Becky, suddenly. She was holding the page up and running her eyes across the writing, turning it to different angles and twisting it about. 'Yes – this bit says something about the Hogsmill River. And then she's done a very convoluted squiggle about ... hold on ... the Manor House?' She looked up. 'Isn't this where they think *Ophelia* was painted?'

Simon nodded, then immediately regretted it as the pain shot through his head again.

'Daisy has repeated it over and over on this page, as if she was trying to remember it. It's like she was trying to imprint it visually on her brain. Look.' She thrust the page out to Simon. 'You said Cori was saying something about Millais and a studio at Cheam, weren't you? About where it was all painted; the background and the figures and things?'

'Yes, she was quite insistent about it,' said Simon.

'Then I think we need to go there,' said Becky. She looked straight at Simon. 'I think that's where she is. And I think that Cori might be in grave danger.'

It was supposed to take only thirty-five minutes to drive from Kensington to Tolworth. It felt more like a week.

Simon's car was gone – he hoped that Cori had taken it. Otherwise, it had been stolen from this quiet, upmarket little mews square in Kensington, and that just didn't seem likely.

Jon had told him it hadn't been there when they pulled up, and then let him sit in the front of his car, as if that would make it all better. Becky, relegated to the back, sat forward

212

and clutched the edge of the driver's seat, apparently willing Jon to hurry up.

'It might have been quicker if I'd driven myself!' she eventually exploded after yet another red light.

Jon looked at her through the driver's mirror. 'And how would you driving have affected the red lights?' he asked.

'It's okay, guys,' said Simon. 'Far rather get there safely.' He looked out of the window as the town gave way to the greener views of Richmond and Kingston and, despite his words, he couldn't get there fast enough himself. He had the page of the diary stuffed back in his pocket, almost like a talisman. He wondered briefly whether Cori, in a moment of Cori-sanity, had actually ripped it out and left it for someone to find.

'It's all my fault,' said Becky. 'I should never have given Cori that diary. In fact, I should never have written that damned article! And shut up, Jon. Don't even try to contradict me. I never thought any of this would happen. The problem is, we just don't know what the real Daisy was like. I mean, was she confused? Or jealous? Was she a dreamer? A psychopath?' She shuddered. 'Jeez, she committed suicide and I think I've seen her ghost. It's not a good combination. Can't you go any *faster*, Jon?'

'She did *what*?' burst out Simon. 'And you saw *a ghost*?'

'It might not have been her,' said Becky, defensively, 'but in Whitby I think I saw Daisy. She looked like Cori. Maybe it was just a trick of the light. But Lissy found out that the real Daisy supposedly committed suicide. That's a fact. Nobody knows if it was intentional, but she was found by her art tutor and she'd been dead for a while by then. There were comments about a laudanum addiction as well. And I'm reluctant to say this in the present situation, but I actually feel sort of sorry for her. You can read the inquest and make up your own mind but I don't think she meant to do it.'

Simon opened his mouth to respond, but the words he had planned never came out. 'There's the turn off!' he said instead. He slapped his palm against the window. 'Jon, it's there.'

Jon braked suddenly and swerved into a country lane, Becky began swearing as she was thrust almost out of her seat with the force of it.

But Simon was more interested in what he might find by the river. All that remained now was to see if Cori was actually there. And if she wasn't, God alone knew what they would do.

Part Two

Chapter Thirty-Six

CRANBOURNE ALLEY, LONDON, 1849

It had all started with a bonnet. Daisy had wanted a new one, and demanded that Henry take her into the town to buy it. If she hadn't been in that shop at that particular time, and if she hadn't witnessed history being made, then her story may have had quite a different outcome.

As it was, she was admiring a beautiful, rich green, velvet creation and was turning it around in her hands, insisting on several extra flowers beneath the rim and perhaps the addition of a sweeping veil to hang from the crown; all to be ready for that afternoon.

'I'm sure we can try to achieve that for you, Miss Ashford,' the woman behind the counter told her. 'Let me just check with my assistant. Then we should be able to advise you.'

'Very well,' Daisy said. 'I can't see there being a problem. Can you?' She had fixed greenish-blue eyes on the woman in a silent challenge.

'No, Miss Ashford,' replied the milliner. 'Please excuse me for just one moment.'

Daisy nodded and turned away from the woman. She walked towards a display of cloaks and fabrics, all ready for the new season. She fingered some of the soft, woollen merino and cast her glance over the whole range. She decided to return in a few days and buy a selection of fabric to have made up into some clothing to see her through the winter.

'Where is she then?' A man's voice broke through the silence in the shop. 'You promised me the redhead would be here today.'

Daisy flushed and turned around, ready to berate the man for his rudeness. And how had he known she would be here anyway? It was a last minute decision this very morning.

The young man was standing in front of the counter, leaning in towards the back of the shop. 'Where is she?' he repeated. 'Art won't wait for idle hands.'

'Yet the Devil makes work for them,' said Daisy, loudly.

The man turned around and Daisy saw that he was very young and pale, with neatly brushed dark hair parted on one side and a rather foppish taste in clothing.

He looked at Daisy and seemed to take in her red-gold curls and tall, slim figure approvingly. 'Ah, you, young lady, will do just as well. The name is Walter Deverell. I'm very pleased to meet you. I'm an artist, you see, and I'm missing a model. My friend, Mr Rossetti, is waiting outside. I'm afraid the wonderful owner of this shop dislikes us bothering her staff. But I do declare that we are absolutely fixated on her assistant. She—'

'Mr Deverell!' The milliner marched out of the back room, clutching Daisy's bonnet. Daisy frowned, fearing the velvet would be irrevocably crushed beneath the woman's grasp. 'What have I told you? Miss Siddal is not interested in your so-called art, it is—'

'It is perfectly all right, Mrs Tozer,' said a girl, drifting out of the room behind Mrs Tozer. The girl was holding a piece of flimsy veil material in her hands, and Daisy felt sure it was the piece that had been destined to attach to the very bonnet which Mrs Tozer now wrung fretfully between her hands. 'I shall talk to Mr Deverell; and perhaps to his friend Mr Rossetti as well. I'm sure we can come to some sort of arrangement. Isn't that so, sir?'

There was a hint of flirtatiousness in the girl's voice, but that was not what arrested Daisy's attention. The girl, Miss Siddal, was even taller and slimmer than Daisy and had hair the exact same colour; but whereas Daisy's hair was neatly

217

coiled on the top of her head, with an array of sausage-like curls bouncing stiffly on her shoulders, Miss Siddal's was loose and flowing like an auburn waterfall, right down her back. Daisy felt a little stab of envy. How had *she* been allowed to wear her hair like that? She was surely of a similar age to Daisy herself. And at nineteen, one was expected to look and act as a young lady.

The bell above the shop door went and Daisy noticed another young man hovering in the doorway. She caught her breath – he was beautiful. There was no other word for it. He had longer, darker hair than Mr Deverell, which fell almost to his shoulders in waves, and bright, slightly drooping blue-grey eyes, which were full of mischief and promises. For a moment, he turned those eyes on Daisy. She was half-hidden in the shadows and he perhaps looked at her longer than strictly necessary, a smile hovering on his sensuously full, slightly pouting lips. He took a step forward, then stopped, as if he realised she was not the woman he thought he had spotted.

'Mr Rossetti!' Miss Siddal called his name and the man turned away from Daisy. Miss Siddal bobbed a tiny curtsey and nodded to him. 'I hear you and Mr Deverell are short of a model.'

'We are indeed, Miss Siddal. Or may I call you Lizzie?' He moved forward and took hold of the girl's hand, leaning over and kissing it. The girl giggled. Daisy thought it was more of a simper, if she was brutally honest.

'You should really call me Miss Siddal until we know each other better,' the girl said.

Daisy coughed loudly and they all turned and looked at her in surprise as she stepped out of the shadows. Her gaze rested on the man with long hair – Rossetti. She rolled the name around her head, liking how it sounded. She flicked her eyes over to the girl, Lizzie.

'I'm terribly sorry to interrupt,' Daisy said, stiffly,

'but will my bonnet be ready for this afternoon or not?' Although her voice was measured and calm, deep inside she was furious. How dare that girl interrupt Mr Rossetti when he had clearly been about to approach her? She needed to be reminded of her place immediately.

There was a leaden silence, then the girl choked on a tiny laugh. Daisy felt herself colour in embarrassment and annoyance.

'Oh, I don't know about that, Miss Ashford,' said the girl, still, Daisy noticed, holding Mr Rossetti's hand. The veil was forgotten, abandoned on the counter. 'It depends if Mrs Tozer has time to do it.' Lizzie looked slyly at Mr Rossetti, then at Mrs Tozer. 'Suddenly, I don't feel very well. I think I need to go home.' She coughed, and tapped her chest. 'Dearie me. I'm so sorry, Mrs Tozer. I had better go before I infect the customers.' She had tugged on Mr Rossetti's hand, and cast a glance up at Mr Deverell from beneath her sultry, heavily-hooded eyelids. 'You'd better come as well, Walter,' she said. 'I need two escorts. I'm liable to faint in the road.'

And with that, she laughed and, pulling Rossetti out of the door, ran lightly into the street.

Daisy stared after her. With those two words, *the customers*, that girl had turned the tables on her. She had belittled *her*, Daisy Ashford, in front of those gentlemen. It was unacceptable. And her bonnet would never get done today now. Not since *she* had walked out without finishing it.

'I thought they were going to approach *me*,' said Daisy, looking at Mrs Tozer. 'Not your assistant.' She stopped herself from adding '*a mere shop girl*' at the end of her sentence. She compressed her lips and stared at the door. 'They saw me first, didn't they? I felt sure Mr Rossetti was about to speak to me. How rude. How very rude.'

Mrs Tozer was also staring at the door, shaking her head

and clearly misinterpreting Daisy's annoyance. 'Then you were, as you suggest, very lucky, Miss Ashford,' she said. 'Lizzie has made a huge mistake. No good will come of it. Those young men are untrustworthy and wild; not the sort of young men I would recommend *any* girl to enter a dialogue with. Lizzie will be back with her tail between her legs and I shall have words with her, you see if I don't.'

But Daisy didn't think herself lucky at all. Mrs Tozer had obviously missed the point; Deverell had said *she* could be his model, and Mr Rossetti had been about to speak to *her* when that girl appeared. The young men, the artists, no less, had seen her first and for a moment she had felt flattered and wanted. And if they were ever famous – well. It should have been her who appeared on their canvases. She would never forget that. Lizzie Siddal had stolen her place. And she had stolen Mr Rossetti's attention away from Daisy; and that was simply unforgiveable.

And that was basically how it all started. Or, more precisely it started when Daisy Ashford returned home, went into her bedroom, pulled out her journal and began to write.

Today I met Mr Rossetti in a millinery shop in Cranbourne Alley, London. Mr Deverell, Mr Rossetti's friend and fellow artist, told me that I was to be his next model ...

Daisy lived in one of the most exclusive areas of London. Or, to be more specific, her father owned a property there. The true family home was further south, nearer the coast. Daisy hated the coast. Her father hated London. It worked well for them to be separated. Daisy's father hated almost everything – including Daisy.

So Daisy lived in London surrounded by a small retinue of servants and in the care of nobody. It wasn't the 'done thing'. It just wasn't seemly for a young lady to live alone in such a fashion; but Daisy didn't care and her father didn't care either. She was nineteen; she was, as far as anyone was concerned, of age. Heavens, she could have been married two years ago and nobody would have blinked an eyelid. The only person who might have cared that Daisy was alone, and who had cared for Daisy for longer than he thought he should have done and in ways in which he felt he probably shouldn't care for her, was Henry Dawson, Daisy's art tutor.

Henry was there the day Daisy stormed out of the millinery shop and demanded to know in which direction the artists had gone?

'Where are Mr Rossetti and Mr Deverell? Has that stupid girl gone with them?' Daisy raged. She swept past Henry and headed, resolutely, down the street. It had been raining and she walked straight through the puddles, not seeming to care that it was ruining her white kid boots.

'Miss Ashford!' Henry called, chasing after her as she stalked down the street, craning her neck to see into the distance. 'Wait! Please – wait.'

Daisy's strides were long and purposeful, her hands holding her skirt well up out of the mud.

Daisy did not falter. Her face was set and Henry knew she would not be dissuaded from whatever goal she had set herself; she had always been the same. He had taught her since she was fourteen years old. When she had moved out of the family home two years ago, Mr Ashford had paid Henry a hefty sum as a retainer. Henry had a home in London, and Mr Ashford expected him to be available for Daisy at a moment's notice; for one thing, it saved her father from having to be in contact with her or tidy up any of her messes. For another, it also helped that Henry was often the only person who Daisy listened to or showed any respect for.

Henry had initially wondered why a man who so despised his only child should be so concerned about her, until he had realised it was more the family reputation Mr Ashford was concerned about. But Henry, at twenty-five and just starting to make a proper living wage from his art, had been grateful for the money; and so long as he watched out for Daisy and erased any mistakes, the money kept coming. And, if he was honest, being in such close proximity to Daisy Ashford was no hardship.

But the young lady was dreadfully single-minded. And Henry saw by her face that today was another example of how that single-mindedness affected anything she did. She had obviously latched onto the group of three people Henry had seen laughing and running down the street, and she wasn't going to rest until she found them again.

'Daisy – please. Stop!' shouted Henry. He managed to catch up with her, his height and his stride length more than a match for her, even though she was taller than most females he had encountered. Henry reached out and put a restraining hand on her shoulder.

Daisy stopped and turned around, glaring at him. 'Where did they go, Henry? I need to find them. She was so *rude* to me.'

'Daisy! She's a shop girl. She probably knows no better,' said Henry.

'Shop girl or not, the gentlemen were talking to me before she approached them.' Daisy was positively fuming, her eyes dangerous. 'I need to find them.'

'And what are you going to do when you do find them?' asked Henry.

'Why, I'm not certain at all.' Daisy put her head on one side and opened her eyes wide, looking as if she was really giving the matter some thought. 'I have no idea. Challenge them, maybe?' she said, shrugging her shoulders.

'Challenge them about what?' persisted Henry.

'I don't *know*!' cried Daisy, stamping her foot. 'I need to find them first. Henry, where is our carriage?'

'It's right there, I—'

'Get in it. Now. We'll look for them from the carriage.' She raised her hand and waved at the driver. Obligingly, he urged the horses forward and pulled up alongside Daisy and Henry.

Without waiting to be assisted, Daisy scrambled into the carriage and beckoned Henry inside to join her. 'I would much rather sit outside with the driver,' she said, 'but that seems a terribly common thing to do, and it's the sort of thing that girl would do.'

Henry knew from experience when it was wisest to say nothing, so he simply climbed aboard the carriage. He was barely inside when Daisy gave the signal to move forward and he fell into his seat as the vehicle moved away.

Daisy leaned out of the window shouting directions to the coachman, who wove expertly through the traffic.

'They can't have gone that far,' she said to Henry. 'Not on foot.' She waited a few more moments then shouted excitedly. 'I can see them! I can see that girl's hair! Look – over there! Look, Henry!' Daisy turned her face towards him and he marvelled once again at how beautiful she was. The fresh air had reddened her cheeks, and her eyes sparkled. Her hair had come undone a little and it gave her the look of Botticelli's *Venus*; but no matter. Henry groaned inwardly. Wanting her was like a physical pain that had gnawed at him for years and he felt it would continue to gnaw at him for many more. Well, at least as many years as he knew Daisy Ashford.

'That's it, slow down, driver!' called Daisy. 'Slow down … keep behind them. I want to see where they go. Where are we, Henry? I don't recognise this area.'

'It's Bloomsbury,' said Henry.

'Bloomsbury,' repeated Daisy, nodding. 'Bloomsbury. Excellent.'

The carriage crawled along and they found themselves on a long narrow street, lined with tall, well-to-do houses.

'Gower Street,' said Daisy, looking at a street sign. 'I have to remember that. Oh – look! They've just gone into that house there. The one on the corner. Stop! Stop right there, driver, and wait for me. Henry, you stay here as well.'

Daisy pushed open the carriage door and slipped out. She headed towards the house and Henry creased his brow, wondering what on earth she was going to do. He saw her hurry past the house and up into the alleyway beside it. She hung around the corner for a few moments, and then began pacing the distance across the alleyway, talking to herself. Henry's heart began to beat faster. What the hell was she going to do? She tapped her fingers on her lips thoughtfully, and stopped for a second. Her head snapped up and around as the door opened from the house and two men came out. It was the man with the longer hair and a different man; a man with shorter hair, which stuck up and out in the most eccentric manner.

Daisy ducked further up inside the alleyway and pressed herself close to the wall. At the front of the house, at the top of the small flight of stairs, the men leaned on the door, one of them, the one with long hair, smoking. After a short while, Daisy's body seemed to relax. Then she stood up straight and a smile began to form on her face. She remained pressed against the wall, however, and Henry saw her hand go to her hair. She fluffed some of the strands out and twirled a long tendril around her fingers, still listening to what the men were saying. Henry closed his eyes in despair. He wasn't sure if he wanted to know what had been said there or not – but he was certain Daisy would tell him.

After the two men had returned inside, Daisy took a moment to compose herself, then walked slowly back to the carriage, making sure she walked right past the front of the house. She waved at Henry and he leaned over and opened the door for her. He stepped outside and she offered him her hand, allowing him to help her up the steps.

When she was sitting primly on the velvet-covered seat, she turned to Henry and smiled. She lifted her hands to her head and pulled all the pins out of her hair. The intricate style unravelled and she enjoyed the feeling of it tumbling down her back. She raked her fingers through the stiff little curls and pulled at them to relax them into loose waves instead.

'Miss Ashford ...' began Henry.

'I think it's much more becoming like this,' she said. 'The gentlemen thought that as well, you know.'

'The gentlemen?'

'Yes, Mr Rossetti and his friend, John. Do you know what they said, Henry?'

'No, Miss Ashford.'

Daisy giggled. 'And you never shall know. That's *my* secret.' She laughed again and turned to face the street through the window.

The conversation she had overheard, however, would set in motion the events that would shape her life.

'So you said there were two of them?' John had said.

'Yes. Two redheads,' replied Mr Rossetti. 'I would have taken either one of them. But Lizzie will do for now.'

'For now?' John had cried. 'How *does* your mind work, my friend?'

Mr Rossetti had shrugged his shoulders and leaned back against the door. 'It works on behalf of the Brotherhood.'

'Oh! Well, it's always good to have a bank of these models, I suppose,' said John.

'A bank of them. Absolutely.' Mr Rossetti had laughed and dropped his cigarette on the floor. He ground it into the step with his heel and stared out into the street. 'Her hair is so wonderful. I adore the way she wears it loose. It's far more becoming.'

It was around about that point, where Daisy had definitely known that that Lizzie girl was far less superior to her. It was she, Daisy, they were talking about, of course.

'Dante, I could use her in the painting I am planning,' John had said, thoughtfully. 'I need someone with her attributes to complete my vision of Shakespeare's Ophelia.'

'Most certainly,' replied Dante. 'I cannot think of anyone better for the job.'

'She will be my muse!' John had said expansively.

'No,' replied Dante. 'She will be mine.'

Then the two men had walked back into the house, still talking earnestly, and Daisy had waited until she heard the solid clunk of the door closing behind them before she left the anonymity of the alleyway and walked deliberately past the house. If they saw her, they might come out again and call her. If not; well, she knew where to find them. It would come in very useful when she needed to remind them of her presence.

His muse. She liked that. She liked that very much.

Chapter Thirty-Seven

TWO YEARS LATER
BLOOMSBURY, 1851

To Daisy, her life in London was extraordinary. She had been lucky, she knew, to meet such wonderful people and her time over the last few years had been consumed by frequently locating those wonderful people and contriving to meet them.

As a potential muse, she understood that it was her very duty to be noticed and to inspire them. Who knew what they were painting and creating behind the closed door of the studio? Perhaps it was a portrait of her? Frankly, she would not be surprised.

Henry, though, could get a little angry at times, especially when she decided to divert an outing to try to find Dante or John or Walter.

'Oh, Henry, my dearest Henry. I know them! They don't mind at all,' she would tell him. But Henry would press his lips together in that way he had and, feeling a little guilty, she would then spend some time trying to cheer him up and boost his mood.

And as such, life flew by pleasantly enough

But some days, she had to admit, it was just easier to lose her darling Henry and travel alone. It may have been frowned upon in society – an unchaperoned girl wandering the streets of London – but she didn't much care. Daisy had never much cared what strangers thought of her.

And in fact, Daisy had found a very pleasant walk. It took her all the way up one side of Gower Street, along to Russell Square and back along Gower Street. She walked the route frequently. It took her, surprisingly, past the house on the corner, where sometimes she would rest against the railings and unbutton her boot to rub her ankle, or simply just stop and catch her breath for a moment or two.

It was a very conveniently placed house.

Sometimes, she would see people coming and going at the house. Then she would hurry up a little, depending on which way she was walking along the street, and smile as they passed her. She recognised them, even at a distance; the confident swagger of Dante; the hurried movements of John, as if he were eager to get on with his work; the easy stride of Walter. And there were others too; there was one they called William, who had the most intense gaze she had ever associated with a man, a quiet man called Frederic and more who she never really bothered to get to know. It was Dante and John who interested her most. And then, of course, there was Lizzie – the ever-present Lizzie, who oozed confidence and beauty and something that was just verging on the hint of danger.

Daisy was fascinated by Lizzie – sometimes she would be cheerful, laughing and joking, hanging on Dante's arm or kissing him in the middle of the street. Yet at other times, she was quiet and moody, or had a faraway look in her eye that made Daisy wonder where the girl was. She wasn't within her physical body, that was for sure. Daisy's initial dislike of the model hadn't abated completely, but now she wondered what exactly it was about the girl that captivated everyone she met. Perhaps there were lessons to be learned from her behaviour. So Daisy began to study her and try to learn from her.

It was one such day, when Daisy was walking up Gower Street, that she finally had the opportunity to catch a glimpse of Lizzie's secret world. Daisy lingered around the entrance to the corner house for rather longer than necessary, and had the good fortune to look up and see Dante, John and

Lizzie coming towards her. Lizzie was hanging off Dante's arm as usual, laughing up into his face and Daisy felt a little stab of envy at how easily Dante was charmed by her. Daisy ducked into the alleyway, waiting until they were closer to her, then chose the right moment to step out into the street.

She looked down and adjusted her cuffs and, accidentally, of course, bumped into one of them. It was John. Automatically, he reached out and steadied her, and she blushed and giggled and twirled a strand of her hair around her finger.

'Oh, I'm so sorry,' she said. 'I don't make a habit of bumping into strange men.'

'He's not strange. He's simply an artist. It's part of the job, it's the curse of the creative mind,' said Dante.

Lizzie giggled. 'Artists are *all* strange,' she said, 'and probably cursed. That's why they wander the streets searching out stunners. And you, *you*, my dear, are very nearly a stunner.'

Daisy scowled. 'That's a very unkind thing to say to me,' she began, bitterly.

Lizzie raised her hands and flapped them in front of Daisy, shaking her head. 'Hear me out. I say "nearly" a stunner, because you look like such a *good* girl.' She smiled and leaned closer to Daisy. Daisy smelled a strange, sweet smell on the girl's breath – a little like wine and something headier mixed with it. Cough mixture, maybe. Lizzie looked a little peaky today; she was very white, yet her cheeks were quite flushed. 'You should let me give you some advice on being much *less* of a good girl.' She smiled at Daisy and unexpectedly Daisy found herself smiling back.

Then John cut in. 'Come on, Lizzie,' he said, looking a little uncomfortable. 'Stop tormenting the poor girl. I'm sorry,' he said, turning to Daisy. 'She gets a little odd sometimes.'

'John, don't you think we look alike?' said Lizzie,

suddenly. She stepped over to Daisy and stood by the side of her. She pulled Daisy towards her, wrapped her arms around her and leaned her head against hers.

Daisy was thrilled and shocked in equal measures. She knew their hair would be merging in one glorious fireball, and she knew that Dante had seen that as well. He stood, one arm folded across his body and his other hand placed thoughtfully on his chin. His head was on one side, as if he was assessing them for a painting. Daisy's heart began to beat faster.

She dropped her gaze, then quickly looked back under her eyelashes at him. 'Do you think so, Mr Rossetti? How about you, Mr Millais? Ha!' She laughed, when the men started at their names. 'Yes, I know who you are. I know how talented you both are.'

Dante laughed and clapped John on the back. 'What a girl, eh, John?' he cried. 'She knows us! We are famous at last. Can you see a resemblance, there, John? Any resemblance? At all?'

'Well, yes, there is a likeness,' said John, still looking uncomfortable. Daisy's heart swelled.

'Well, then,' said Lizzie, triumphantly. 'There is another little muse for you.' She released Daisy with a quick hug and stepped back towards Dante. 'And we are right outside your studio, John.' She waved her hand towards the house. 'I'm sure your family won't mind.'

'Lizzie,' said John. 'It's not just a studio, you know. My family have been good enough to let me use our home. I can't let you just invite people in.' He turned to Daisy. 'I'm sorry,' he said, 'I don't know what's the matter with her. Of course, she's jesting. Please excuse her, and once again I apologise.'

'Oh, please, don't apologise to me,' said Daisy, quickly. 'If you wanted me to, I could …'

Then Lizzie burst out laughing. 'Oh, I like you. I like you

a *lot*,' she said. 'Here, have some of this, it'll loosen you up even more. Now *that* would be comical.' She pulled a small bottle out of her pocket and thrust it at Daisy. Lizzie then threw her head back and laughed, before heading up the small set of steps to the front door of the house. 'Come now, gentlemen,' she said, looking over her shoulder at Dante and John. 'To work! And you *know* the studio is on the ground floor, John, so there's no reason *why* she couldn't come in. It's not like she would have been disturbing your family, is it?'

Lizzie blew a kiss at Daisy and waited until John hurried up the steps and opened the door for her. Dante trailed up after them, his hands in his pockets. Daisy watched them, undecided as to whether she was included in the invitation or not. Dante was the last to enter the house.

He turned to Daisy and smiled, fixing her with those haunting eyes; then he pointed his forefinger at her. 'One day,' he said, 'I might paint you.' Then he too stepped into the house and closed the door behind him.

Daisy felt as if she were embedded in the pavement at the bottom of the steps. She watched the door for a moment, then, when she realised nobody was coming back out, she looked at the bottle in her hand. It was more like a phial. She turned it around to read the label. *Tincture of Opium*. How strange. She opened it up and sniffed it, screwing her eyes up as the alcoholic fumes hit her nostrils. That, then, was the peculiar smell on Lizzie's breath. Interesting. She peered closer at the label. One word stood out and her eyes widened: *laudanum*.

'My goodness,' whispered Daisy. She looked around quickly, and tucked the bottle in her purse. She would have to investigate that later, in the privacy of her own home. But the first thing to do was to make her feet move and hurry back to record this momentous occasion in her special journal.

I visited John at his studio today. He has a wonderful studio in his family home in Gower Street. It is on the ground floor, so it means I never have to impose upon the rest of his family when I visit. John has always commented on my likeness to Lizzie; it is a great privilege to be compared to her. She is, after all, the muse to end all muses ...

Chapter Thirty-Eight

'I say,' said Henry, 'the art world is going mad for Millais' latest creation; especially with the idea of Ruskin's patronage behind it. I hear he has already sold the painting – despite it being unfinished – to the art dealer Henry Farrer.'

He was obviously trying to make polite conversation during the art lesson, but Daisy wasn't really listening. She was trying to paint a picture based on an Arthurian legend, a style she very much associated with the Brotherhood. However, her horse didn't look right and her knight's legs were far too short for his body. She laid her brush down in disgust and folded her arms.

'Henry, this is wrong. It's just all wrong. Can you sort it out for me? Please?'

'I don't know why you won't stick to more straightforward things,' said Henry, coming over to the easel. He pondered the canvas for a minute then shook his head. 'No. I can't sort it out for you. Short of making the gentleman stand in a gorse bush, we can't hide his legs.'

'Then a gorse bush it shall be!' she retorted, angrily. She picked up the brush again and rammed it into the black paint. 'And in this horrible, misshapen fantasy world, the gorse bushes are *black*.' She attacked the canvas, jabbing the brush over the picture and smearing paint everywhere. She covered the knight, legs and all, in a thick layer of the stuff and didn't stop until he was indistinguishable from the black horse he was supposed to be standing next to. Then she continued to cover the black horse and was just

233

about to start on the winsome lady, when Henry grabbed her arm.

'Enough!' he said. 'What did all that achieve?'

'It made me feel better!' she shouted. She threw the brush onto the floor, swiftly followed by her apron and stormed out of the French doors into the leafless, unwelcoming garden. 'The Brotherhood *never* have this problem!' she shouted over her shoulder. 'Everything they do is perfect!'

'The Brotherhood have their share of troubles as well!' shouted Henry following her.

'They were *born* talented!' replied Daisy. She sat down on a chair, her back towards the house and Henry, her arms folded again, oblivious to the cold.

'Maybe,' said Henry, 'but they draw and paint from real life, remember. They get their proportions from the models and their inspiration from elsewhere. It's a fine line – if one part breaks down, the other follows.'

'Nothing breaks down for them,' complained Daisy.

'Yes, it does,' said Henry. He sat next to her. 'For instance, I hear that Miss Siddal is unwell. The portrait I have just been talking about has been postponed at an extremely awkward point.'

'What?' Daisy turned to him, suddenly interested. Her attitude changed instantly. She smiled at him and put her hand on his knee. She knew he always liked that, she could tell by his face; and to be honest, she quite liked the power she had within her to do that to him. At twenty-two, she knew she was the most attractive she'd been in many a year. She'd slimmed down over the last two years or so and made sure she'd protected her skin from the sun as much as possible to keep her complexion pale and clear. Sometimes, she would apply just a hint of rouge to her cheeks and lips and liked the contrast between that and her ivory skin. She was also in the habit of applying henna rinses to her hair. She'd often been teased for its natural redness, but now she adored it and loved the fact the henna emphasised the tints in it. She liked to wear her hair loose as well. It was so much better to feel free of the confines of pins and ribbons, she thought.

Daisy imagined Lizzie having the same power over men as she had over Henry, and it made her feel especially allied to the redheaded muse. Daisy moved her hand and squeezed Henry's knee. Talking about the Brotherhood always held her interest and she wanted him to talk some more.

'Dear Henry. I do so enjoy hearing your tales from the art world. I do so love the sound of your voice. Do tell me more about this interesting situation,' she begged, deliberately making her eyes wide and round.

Henry sat back, smiling at her. She could tell he was pleased and would be more than happy to talk a little longer.

'Well,' he began, 'as I say, I hear Miss Siddal is under the weather. She was posing in a bathtub, believe it or not, and they had lit candles beneath it to keep her warm. Millais continued to paint as the candles died down and Lizzie has developed some kind of illness relating to the freezing water. Add to that the death of her brother and she has left Millais in a dreadful pickle. And as you can see, in defence of her apparent near-pneumonia and rumoured weak heart, it is not exactly warm weather, is it? In fact wouldn't you like to go inside and talk about this?' He shivered a little.

Daisy thought for a moment; she thought of Lizzie bravely lying in a tub of freezing water, suffering so John could paint his picture.

She shook her head. 'No. I want to stay out here,' she said. 'Please continue.'

Henry looked at her, surprised. 'Very well,' he said. 'As you wish. So, yes, Miss Siddal is unwell. I hear the portrait is at a desperate place to be left. Millais is beside himself, obviously, but he is well aware that the health of his model is of the utmost importance. There are rumours that her family will insist on him paying her medical bill, poor girl.'

'I say!' said Daisy, opening her eyes even wider. 'That's extremely interesting news. And is John working at his studio?'

'I'm not sure – I believe he had a studio in Cheam while he was working on the painting,' said Henry, 'but I think he may have returned to Gower Street.'

'Cheam?' said Daisy, picking up on the new information. 'In South London?'

'Yes. I believe also he has painted the background extensively using the Hogsmill River in Tolworth.'

'Tolworth?' cried Daisy. 'Oh, I must remember that name. I would like to visit there someday. Will you take me, Henry?'

'I suspect it doesn't really cater for casual tourists,' replied Henry. 'It's simply an interesting area to paint.'

'Still. I would like to visit,' said Daisy. She removed her hand from Henry's knee and looked out over the garden again. 'I hope the background to the portrait is cheerful. What would you paint on it, should you work on a portrait like that?'

'Oh, I really couldn't commit myself,' said Henry. 'As it is depicting Shakespeare's Ophelia, I would want to make it instantly recognisable to the viewer. I'd probably put a variety of flowers in it. '

'Hmmm,' said Daisy. 'Would you put some daisies in it? Because that's my name, you know.' She smiled at him. 'And daisies are supposed to mean innocence and purity.'

'And loyalty and beauty,' said Henry, quietly. 'I would dust the whole foreground with daisies if it were my work.' He smiled slightly. 'Daisies are my favourite flower.'

Daisy sat back in the seat and looked at Henry, fixing her eyes fully on his. '"*There's rosemary, that's for remembrance,*"' she began. '"*Pray you, love, remember.*

And there is pansies, that's for thoughts. There's fennel for you, and columbines.—There's rue for you, and here's some for me. We may call it "herb of grace" o' Sundays.—Oh, you must wear your rue with a difference.—There's a daisy. I would give you some violets, but they withered all when my father died. They say he made a good end." Do you think I make a good Ophelia, Henry?'

'You make a remarkable Ophelia,' said Henry, warmly. 'Bravo. You could easily stand in for Miss Siddal, have no fear about that, Daisy Ashford.'

'You charm me, Mr Dawson,' she said, laughing, 'but I like hearing it. Oh, my.' She raised her hand to her forehead and closed her eyes. 'Henry, dearest, I'm so sorry, but I think I am coming down with an awful headache. Would you mind at all if we continued our lesson tomorrow?'

Henry sat for a moment, then stood up and bowed slightly. 'You and your father employ me.' He sounded crushed. 'It is therefore your prerogative to ask me to leave or command me to stay.' He looked rather disappointed and Daisy actually felt a little sorry for him.

'I would adore you to stay,' said Daisy, 'but I am a little chilly out here after all.' She transferred her hand to her mouth and managed to hack out a cough. 'Please forgive me. Will you come tomorrow morning instead?'

'Certainly,' replied Henry. 'Whatever you wish, Miss Ashford.'

'Oh, don't! Do not call me Miss Ashford!' she said, pulling a face. 'It's so formal. And we are closer than that, are we not?'

'Well, I would like to think so,' murmured Henry. Daisy saw that he blushed a rosy pink colour, right to the roots of his fair hair.

She smiled. 'Of course we are. Dear Henry. I shall see you tomorrow. And, like the Arthurian lady in my terribly ruined painting, I shall allow you, my glorious knight, to kiss my hand.' She held it out and Henry blushed an even darker shade of pink.

'Daisy!' he said.

'Oh, humour me, just this once!' she said. 'I don't ask a lot of you, do I?'

'Well, I beg to differ on that, at times,' he replied, suddenly smiling at her.

Daisy laughed, then she drew back her hand and buried it within her skirts. 'I shan't torture you any more. I think I shall have a little medicine after you leave, and that will cure my headache.'

'I hope it isn't a bad headache,' said Henry, 'but if there's anything you want, you must let me know.'

'I most certainly will,' replied Daisy. She coughed again and closed her eyes briefly. She hoped her cheeks looked fevered, as she imagined Lizzie's would at the minute. Lizzie really was very pale, and a fever might give her a little colour. 'Goodbye, Henry,' she whispered. 'I will see you tomorrow if I am well.' She pressed a hand to her breast and winced as if it pained her deep inside somewhere.

'Indeed, Miss Ashford,' he replied. 'I will see myself out, but first I will escort you to the drawing room and you can sit before the fire to warm yourself.'

She smiled, she hoped bravely, and allowed herself to be escorted by the hand into the drawing room and laid on a chaise longue.

Daisy waited until she heard the door shut and then sat right back up. She locked the door to keep the servants out, then rummaged through a bureau drawer until she found the bottle she was searching for. *Damn!* It was almost empty. Fortunately, she had some more upstairs. She drained the last few drops of liquid and closed her eyes as the blessed calm stole over her and the taste of the alcohol numbed her tongue. One moment more and she was lying down in a deliciously drowsy half-sleep, promising herself she would recover from her illness quickly – she so didn't want to impose on dear Henry. Or was it Dante? No. It was John, wasn't it? It was dear John she needed to help ... oh, she would be such a *good* help. He would be pleased he had approached her. She would be such a *boon* to him ...

In her semi-drugged state, in her own mind, she took the fantasy to its logical conclusion; then she fell asleep for several hours.

And when she woke up, she wrote it all down, because it had all happened, hadn't it? Of course it had. She couldn't possibly have dreamt it – it had all been so real.

I hear Lizzie is indisposed. I offered to help poor John out. He is at a most difficult part of the portrait, in which he represents Ophelia. I can see the background is already perfectly painted and, joy of joys, I see he has added some daisies to the foreground! Oh, how we laughed when I pointed them out to him. He was unaware of the meaning of the daisy. As it is my name, it is something I have considered deeply. It actually means purity, innocence, loyal love, beauty, patience and simplicity.

These are, without exception, qualities I believe I have. I quoted the famous speech from Hamlet *to John, and I ensured I gave the true, wistful voice to those simple words: 'There's a daisy.' Poor Ophelia. I believe, in some ways, a daisy also reflects unhappy love, and this was I feel the crux of the matter between Hamlet and she. John suggested I take the place of Lizzie for the time being, just until she regains her health. Of course, I agreed. I would do anything to help my friends.*

I do so wish I were as talented as Dante and John and the rest of the Brotherhood. Dante was absent for most of the day, I have to say. He was with Lizzie, so I understand. I can confess this to you, Dear Diary, but to nobody else – I do believe Lizzie keeps him on a terribly short leash. Poor Dante, he is trapped by her, yet I am reluctant to raise the matter with him just yet. She is not the most stable of characters and I fear for both their sanity at times. I asked John where he painted the background and he told me it was Tolworth, of all places. I must remember that. If ever I am asked about it at one of our gatherings or at an exhibition, I can say, with great confidence, 'Tolworth! The background was painted in Tolworth! But Lizzie and I were painted in his new studio in Cheam. Now, fancy that!'

Chapter Thirty-Nine

FOUR YEARS LATER
KENSINGTON, APRIL, 1856

Henry knocked at the front door and waited for someone to
let him in. They had no art lesson booked today, but he had
received an urgent message, demanding he come to Daisy's
house immediately.

A maid opened the door and stood back, curtseying at
him as he walked into the house. He was a regular enough
visitor for the household to recognise him, and he did
actually have enough of a social standing, being a tutor and
an unofficial guardian, to warrant a curtsey.

'I'll go and announce you, Mr Dawson,' said the maid.

'Thank you. Miss Ashford is expecting me,' replied
Henry, taking off his hat. The maid bobbed another curtsey
and hurried into the drawing room along the corridor.
Henry stood on the marble inlaid floor of the entrance hall,
enjoying how the sunlight dappled the black and white tiles
with colours from the stained-glass crescent window above
the door. Little things like that, he thought, made him
appreciate his life.

'She'll see you now, Mr Dawson,' said the maid, hurrying
back along the corridor. 'May I take your coat and hat, sir?'

Henry was about to reply when Daisy appeared at
the door of the drawing room. 'Leave him be, Ellen,' she
snapped. 'I need to see him right away.'

'As you wish,' said the maid. She curtseyed again and
hurried away towards the back of the house.

'Henry! Dear Henry!' Daisy's tone of voice changed like
the wind. She held her arms out and Henry took that as an

invitation to walk into the drawing room. It was stuffy and warm in the room, and the sofa cushions showed a definite imprint of a body. She'd obviously been having a little nap while she waited for him. There was an empty glass on a small table next to the sofa and Daisy glanced at it as she waved Henry inside.

'I'll ring for some tea or something,' she said. 'I hadn't realised how thirsty I was. I must have drunk all my water.' She smiled and sat down on the sofa. She patted the cushions next to her and Henry hesitated, hovering near a single chair opposite it. 'Oh, for goodness sake, I think we know each other well enough for you to sit next to me,' she grumbled. 'Nobody is going to criticise your manners in here today. Sit. I need to show you something.' Again she patted the sofa and Henry sat down.

Daisy leaned over him and he caught the unmistakeable scent of her perfume as she took hold of a bell. 'Do you want anything?' she asked.

Henry shook his head. 'No, thank you. I'm only interested in knowing why you felt the need to summon me so urgently.'

Daisy stared at the bell in her hand for a moment, and then put it down without ringing it. 'I don't think I need tea, actually,' she said. 'I'll have some more water later. So, Henry.' She moved a little so she was facing him more fully. 'I want you to see this.' She reached over to the table in front of them and shifted position again. Her hands were trembling ever so slightly as she picked up an envelope and then tried and failed to open it and extract the contents.

'Forgive me, Daisy, but you seem on edge,' said Henry, full of concern for her. She was flushed and there was a slight sheen of perspiration on her face.

'I'm perfectly all right,' she said. She stared at the envelope as if willing it to open itself, then she tried to open it again. 'It's just this letter. Well, it's not really a letter. It's an invitation. My father's birthday is next month and it appears I am invited to a masked ball to celebrate.'

'What? But your father ...' Henry stopped himself before he said too much; before he added *hates you*, to the end of the sentence.

Daisy laughed bitterly. 'Yes. You're correct. He won't usually tolerate me anywhere near his presence. I can only think he has a plan afoot to find me a man and make me respectable.'

Henry's world shifted. This was something he had never considered happening before. Daisy had, in his mind always been his responsibility and always would be. He had refused to contemplate anything else.

'No,' he said, without thinking. 'I can't ...' He stopped again and looked down at his hat. His knuckles were white as he crushed the brim of it, trying to stop himself telling Daisy what he thought, what he felt.

'I know, Henry.' Her voice was soft and she put her hand on his wrist. 'That's why I want you to come with me.'

'What?' He looked up sharply. Her eyes looked huge and quite scared. He felt a rush of love for her and a vital need to protect her at all costs.

'I want you to come. I want you to look after me when I'm there. Goodness only knows what he has planned for me. And I don't think I can cope without ... well. Without certain things.'

Henry didn't dare think that she actually meant him – but he didn't know what she did mean.

'And besides.' And there it was; one of her sudden and inexplicable shifts of emotion. She was smiling now, her voice bright and cheerful. 'I am to be Ophelia. I need you to come with me into town so I can get the costume made up. I want to look *exactly* like her.' Then a flirtatious note crept in. She tilted her head to one side and twisted a curl around her finger. Her hair looked very red today and she suited it loose, thought Henry, momentarily distracted. 'I'll be a beautiful Ophelia, won't I, Henry? You know I'll make the perfect Ophelia. You just have to help me. You will, won't you? You'll help me, Henry, won't you? I need to do a little shopping in town as well, just to get stocked up on essentials for my trip. Are you busy now?'

Henry shook his head, robbed of speech and excuses as he looked at her. She was as excited as a child at Christmas.

'Good. Wait for me one minute. We'll go now.' She leaned into him again and put her hands either side of his face. He couldn't breathe, thinking of the fact her lips were only inches away from his. It would be the work of a moment – all it would take would be ... 'I'll be a beautiful Ophelia. The best Ophelia ever. Just wait and see,' she said, breaking the spell. She dropped her hands from his face and clasped them together instead. Her eyes were sparkling now, the thoughts and fantasies of the dress clearly whirling around her head. 'Let's go right *now*,' she finished and stood up.

She was true to her word. She took barely a minute to call a maid, get her outdoor cloak ready and prepare to leave.

'Come on, Henry!' she called from the front door. 'Let's go and get provisions for this wonderful party!'

Henry had no choice but to follow her.

Chapter Forty

Daisy stood in the corner of the ballroom watching the guests whirl by her in all sorts of ridiculous costumes. Despite the masks, she could tell who almost each and every person was.

Her father lorded it over them all, moving around the floor, enjoying the attention being bestowed upon him. She wrinkled her nose in disgust. He hadn't come near her, of course, but that didn't stop her wondering who he had decided to foist upon her as a potential mate.

A highwayman went past with a giggling milkmaid, followed by Henry VIII and one of his many wives. She didn't know which wife the woman was supposed to be portraying but she still had her head attached to her body, so that was something at least.

Daisy sighed loudly and turned her attention to the drinks tray, which was being proffered by a footman. She took a large glass of wine and pressed herself further into the shadows as she added a few drops of tincture from a bottle she had hidden in her purse. Her hand shook a little as she tipped the bottle up and more liquid than she anticipated went into the glass. She shrugged her shoulders, not really caring, and, turning back to face the ballroom, took a dainty sip.

'Miss Ashford.' She looked up at Mozart or Beethoven or some musician she didn't recognise and blinked.

'Yes?'

'Do you not know me?' asked the musician.

She looked at his ridiculous wig and his pale blue and silver breeches and her eyes settled on the pocket watch at his waistcoat.

Then she looked at his hands. 'Give me your hand, sir,' she said, leaning forwards and holding her own hand out. The man gave her his hand and she took it. She held it in her own for a moment and ran her fingers up and down his long, slim ones. She pressed her thumb into the soft pad at the base of his thumb and turned his hand over so it was palm up. She leaned forward again and, keeping hold of his hand, she led him over to a large candelabra. She examined his hand some more in the pool of flickering light. 'Ha!' She gave a shout of glee and squeezed his hand. 'You, my friend, are an artist. I know this type of hand well. Now, let me see.' She let go of his hand and pressed her fingertip to her chin, tilting her head to one side and looking at him coyly. 'Are you Mr Rossetti?'

The man laughed quietly. 'I wish. No, I am not Mr Rossetti.'

Daisy felt a little prick of disappointment, then she quickly rallied. 'Mr Millais? Really! You've come here to see *me* dress as Ophelia? To echo your wonderful painting?'

'Nor am I Mr Millais,' said the man, laughing again. 'Miss Ashford, you're teasing me. Don't you recognise me?' He made as if to take his mask off and Daisy flapped her hand in front of him.

'No – no, don't remove it yet. Let me have one more guess. Just one more guess.' She held up her forefinger and waggled it. 'One more. Please.'

'Very well. One more guess,' said the man. There was an amused note to his voice. 'Then that is your last chance.'

Daisy pouted. 'Spoilsport,' she said. 'However, I shall guess correctly this time. Hmmm – let me think ...'

'Don't think too long,' said the man.

'Do not hurry me!' said Daisy. 'Ha! I have it. I know

you ... it's Mr Madox Brown. No! Mr Hunt. No! Mr Hughes ... No!' She laughed. 'Oh, very well. Mr Dawson. It's you.'

'The very same,' said Henry. He lifted his hand to take his mask off and this time Daisy did not stop him. She sighed a little, wishing it really had been one of the Brotherhood. How perfect that would have been. Still. She perked up a little. Now Henry was here, he could keep her company; and maybe get her another drink. She realised with an element of surprise that her glass was empty. She looked at it for a second then held it out to Henry.

'Would you?' she asked. 'Please?'

'Oh. Certainly.' Henry frowned as he took the glass. 'I'll have to find a footman. Will you wait here while I go on my quest, fair lady?' He bowed, theatrically.

Daisy laughed. 'Now *you* are the tease. Henry, does my father know you are here? Amongst the guests?'

'I expect so,' replied Henry, sounding a little surprised. 'He knows I came here to look after you. Although I don't think he knows what my costume was going to be. Still,' he said with a sigh, looking at the men waltzing their partners around, 'we are all of an equal rank when we are dressed as we are tonight. I too could be a lord or a sir or someone of importance.' He smiled. 'Never mind, I am perfectly happy just to be here and to chaperone you. Not that I think you need it.'

'That's good. I don't want you to leave my side, Henry, do you understand? I cannot be bothered with all of these people and if you are near me ...' she paced her fingers up his waistcoat and fiddled with the chain of the pocket watch, 'then nobody will approach me. You are the best chaperone I could hope for. But, no, I shan't be waiting here. I shall be outside, I think. I need some air.'

'Yes, your cheeks are a little red,' said Henry, with concern. 'Are you quite well?'

'I'm perfectly well,' said Daisy; although Henry was starting to blur a little around the edges and suddenly the music was coming from very far away. 'I just need a little fresh air. I will see you on the terrace.'

She felt herself stumble and Henry reached out to hold her elbow and steady her. She knew it wasn't just fresh air she needed. Some of her tincture would take those feelings away, just like it always did. It would calm her breathing and settle her nerves. But she didn't have time to wait for another glass of wine; it would have to come from the bottle.

'I'll be outside,' she said, pointing vaguely in the direction of the door. 'On the terrace. Just hurry, will you?'

'I'll be as fast as I can. Are you sure you don't want me to escort you outside first?'

'No!' She realised, as Henry looked shocked and involuntarily stepped away from her, that she had been rather loud. 'No.' She lowered her voice. 'I'm sorry. It's the heat. I will see you outside.' She turned and weaved her way out of the ballroom, banging into several couples and making a few more falter in their steps to avoid her as she headed, single-mindedly to the door.

She didn't care what they thought of her. She never had. But she needed that tincture and she needed it now. Thank God she still had some left in the bottle; and several more bottles secreted away upstairs for the rest of the interminable stay at the ancestral home.

Henry managed to collect two crystal glasses full of wine and followed Daisy outside. He, however, walked carefully around the edge of the dance floor, holding the glasses a sensible distance away from the guests.

He had seen Daisy's less than elegant exit and heard the tuts and comments made as she left the room. Remembering his usual station, he had bitten down his retorts with great difficulty, especially when he heard Mr Ashford – the worst offender – call his daughter 'a disgusting, drunken, trollop'. Daisy might be a lot of things, but as far as Henry was concerned, she had done nothing to warrant any of those titles.

She was anything but drunk. She was tired and hot and probably very stressed. And to be honest, if Mr Ashford was trying to introduce her to a man to make her 'respectable', as Daisy had told him, the last thing Mr Ashford should be doing was to call his daughter those sorts of names in polite society. He was labelling the girl as damaged goods before she'd even had the chance to shine. And she would have shone, Henry knew that. She was what, twenty-six now? A woman in her prime. Henry, on the other side of thirty, found her captivating; even more so here, when she was clearly in need of rescuing from the horrific Mr Ashford and his stuffy, self-obsessed crowd of hangers-on.

Henry felt himself colour; he shouldn't really think such thoughts, he knew that, but what else could he do? If it was up to him, he would sweep Daisy off her feet and take her back to London. They would live out their days happily together and …

Henry stopped suddenly. He was on the terrace now, and, laid out before him in the formal gardens was the grand lake. There was a small jetty and a boathouse at the shore, and the full moon reflected starkly in the black water. Tiny, glittering pinpricks studded the lake surface, identical twins of the stars up above. And on the lakeside, was a ghostly figure, shimmering in the moonlight as it walked amongst the reeds.

'Daisy?' Henry recognised, even from this distance, the flowing hair and the silvery Ophelia dress. Her hands held up the heavy skirts delicately and she was now picking her way out towards the water, pushing her way through the foliage. '*Daisy!*' Henry shouted her name and the girl stopped for a second, looking around her. Then she pressed forwards again.

Henry swore and, slamming the glasses onto the stone balustrade that edged the terrace, he started running towards the apparition. '*Daisy!*' He saw her step into the water and hesitate a moment, before dropping the skirts. They billowed up around her ankles and then her calves, then her thighs – she was going in deeper, walking steadily and determinedly into the centre of the lake. '*Daisy!*'

Now he was on the grassy bank himself – not too far until he reached her, not too far until he managed to grab her and stop her from going out any further. Surely the heat hadn't been that bad? So bad she needed cooling down so completely by wandering into the lake?

The dress was slowing her down, thank God. She had stopped and was looking around her. Henry was in the reeds, feeling the ground give beneath him between tussocks of boggy grass. He called out her name once more, throwing off the wig and the heavy brocade waistcoat – as if that would make it easier to swim.

Then – but for months afterwards, he could never swear that what he had seen actually happened – she turned to her right, threw her arms into the air and seemingly launched herself backwards into the black water.

Daisy fell back into the water, closing her eyes. It was freezing; bitterly cold, and she was soaked through. The weight of the dress was dragging her down and there was a current of sorts. It was pulling her downstream, she was floating away.

She could feel her body shutting down bit by bit. Her toes were frozen, her hands were numb. Her neck felt as if icy fingers were crawling up it, spreading out to the roots of her hair, which was itself being slapped around by the water and floating outwards like a halo. She opened her eyes as the shock permeated her skull and saw the stars and the moon above her, smiling down on her.

She was Ophelia. She was Lizzie. She was invincible.

There's rosemary, that's for remembrance. Pray you, love, remember. And there is pansies, that's for thoughts. There's fennel for you, and columbines ...

'Daisy!'

No. That was wrong. Daisies didn't come into it until much later ...

There's rue for you, and here's some for me.

'I'm coming for you, Daisy. Hold on. I'll save you.'

We may call it 'herb of grace' o' Sundays. — Oh, you must wear your rue with a difference.

'Daisy!'

That's right. Now it's a daisy. There's a daisy. I would give you some violets, but they withered all ...

Strong hands grabbed her under her armpits and she gasped, flailing against the arms and kicking uselessly as the fabric of the dress wrapped around her ankles and tried to drag her down into the water.

'I've got you. I've got you. You're safe. You waded out too far. I've got you.'

Daisy wanted to shout at the top of her lungs: *No! No! I didn't. I'm Ophelia. Look at me!* But her voice just wouldn't work. Suddenly, she became aware of the fact that her teeth were chattering and her nose was running and her eyes were stinging. And she was cold. So cold. So very cold.

She found her voice. 'C-c-c-cold ... so c-c-c-c-cold ...'

'I know, I know. I've got you now. You slipped. You tried to cool down and you slipped. It's all right. You're safe now.'

The voice was Henry's – forever reassuring her, always there to catch her when she fell. Dear Henry. Dear, dear Henry.

'Henry? Help m-m-me. I'm c-c-c-c-old.'

'Come on, now, let's get you to the side.'

She opened her eyes and focussed on him. The silly wig

was gone, and it was truly Henry she saw there; Henry with his fair hair plastered darkly to his head and his white shirt clinging to his body. She gave herself up to him and closed her eyes again. It was Henry who had rescued her, nobody else. She allowed herself to be stood upright and half-guided, half-dragged to the shore, where she collapsed in the reeds, coughing and spluttering and shaking.

'We'll get you into the house. Can you walk? Are you steady, Daisy? Daisy?'

She couldn't answer him, so she didn't. She lay on the ground and let the world dissolve around her again. It was black and calm and peaceful and … a jolt as she was lifted up and hoisted into his arms. She nestled into him and he carried her away from the water and towards the house. She felt the gentle rocking motion as he walked and he murmured nonsense to her, telling her to stay awake and telling her they'd be safe soon.

Her mind slipped away before they reached the house and much after that was a blur. She didn't know how long she'd stayed at the house; she knew they'd taken a carriage home to London even before she could bear her own weight. But the strangest thing was, she had heard a voice, exactly like her father's, saying he would have to add 'insane' to her list of character traits.

She didn't really care. He had said something about 'no longer my daughter' and 'staying away from me' as well. And, actually, that made her very happy.

But she'd heard another voice too; one that whispered to her urgently in her darkest moments and one she couldn't quite place.

I won't leave you, Daisy. I'll never let anything bad happen to you again, I promise. I want to look after you for the rest of your life. And I swear to you, on my life, that I never break my promises.

She wondered if it was Dante.

252

Chapter Forty-One

THREE YEARS LATER
BLACKFRIARS, LONDON, 1859

To Daisy's eternal disgust, she recovered remarkably well from the incident at her father's party. Initially, she languished in her bedroom in her London home, feeling truly like Lizzie.

However, when she ran out of her tincture, she did seem to make a speedy recovery and manage to travel alone, in her carriage, to the pharmacists, to top up her supplies.

There was also initial concern that her heart had been weakened by the exposure, but that was proven to be a false concern. Her lungs in the end were also discovered to be healthy; there was no disease at all. Henry, of course, was a constant visitor throughout those weeks of malady – and beyond. He was relieved his actions had saved her life – even if they had not saved her reputation, her family name and potentially her inheritance.

It was also through Henry that Daisy discovered, quite a long while after that unfortunate lakeside incident, that Lizzie had left the country.

Daisy often wondered, rather obsessively, when Lizzie would be coming back. She had heard that Lizzie and Dante had argued extensively, and that, combined with Lizzie's own ill-health, had necessitated a trip to the continent. Oh, how she identified with the redheaded muse now! Illness would certainly put a strain on one's temperament, as well as one's companion's temperament – although Henry, the closest thing she had to a companion, had been so patient with her and she was awfully grateful. Daisy had also heard that a woman called Fanny Cornforth, a woman of a lower class and even lower morals, had solicited poor Dante on the street and he was finding solace in her. That was simply unacceptable. He was engaged to Lizzie and should act accordingly.

Henry, that wonderful font of information, had also told her that Mr James Leathart had commissioned Dante to finish a painting and that Fanny woman had been depicted in it as a prostitute. Daisy sniffed. She was obviously well matched for that picture, then; but she knew in her heart of hearts that she, Daisy, would be a far better model for him. She really wasn't a prostitute herself, but didn't she have red hair?

That Fanny woman had red hair, but Daisy was far more like Lizzie than she was, especially after her own terrible, wasting illness; she had suffered so badly two, three years ago was it now? She couldn't really remember. But still. If Lizzie was away, then she was obviously the best-placed person to model for Dante. Hadn't she modelled for John? She smiled, remembering it, remembering how cold she had felt that day and how warming the medicine had been afterwards. She had been out for her medicine today, in fact. She had sent the carriage home half an hour ago, telling the driver she would walk a little. She felt a little faint and wished to clear her head.

'Will I call by on Mr Dawson, miss?' the driver had asked, expressionless as always. He was, Daisy knew, used to calling on Mr Dawson for strange, unrelated incidents that she suddenly needed Henry for.

'Not today,' she answered. 'Today I will be quite all right on my own.'

'Very well, Miss Ashford,' replied the driver and headed off. So Daisy had put her head down, felt the comforting solidness of the bottle in her hand, and walked.

Oh, and my goodness me, here she was on Blackfriars

Bridge, just a stone's throw from 14 Chatham Place; Dante's new home and studio. Well, now, if she just sat here for a few minutes, then maybe Dante would come out and find her.

Or maybe she would just have to solicit him herself.

In the end, it was longer than a few minutes. It had been a few hours. But he had come to her eventually.

It was all a bit of a blur, if she was honest. She had her bottle of tincture with her, of course, just to relax her; but she must have taken a little too much. She hadn't eaten either, so the effects were much stronger than usual. But she had no appetite and hadn't been sleeping well, so it was a blessing that she had ended up in such a relaxed, wonderful stupor.

She remembered singing softly to herself and quoting some of her favourite poems to make the time pass more quickly. Then she had sensed someone bending over her and trying to help her to her feet. She had laughed and murmured something about being just like that painting Dante was working on. The person had touched her hair and whispered something to her, then she had felt them scoop her up in their arms. It felt just like when Henry had rescued her from the lake at her father's house. She had closed her eyes and rested her head against their chest, feeling once again the calming rocking motion as they walked. She had come round briefly inside a building, but drifted away again after she felt herself laid on a couch.

And it seemed to be a good while later when she found herself in a carriage, on her way back home. She had practically crawled up the stairs into her bedroom and lain straight down on her bed, where she had drifted off again.

Her dreams had been incredible. She remembered snatches of conversation, laughing and joking. She remembered soft touches and warm kisses, and she remembered the feeling of near completeness as she kissed him and set off on her way home.

When her head cleared and she felt stronger, she pulled out her journal and picked up a pen.

Lizzie has not yet returned from France. None of us have heard from her, yet Dante is convinced she will return. I am not so sure. I have been suffering these last few days, and Dante, being such a good man, has looked after me in his own unique way. Whilst I was staying with him, he painted me; it is not much more than a sketch at the moment but he humoured me. I asked him to make the portrait special, to make it just for me, and he laughed and he did so. I was reluctant to return home, but I could not impose upon him any longer. If only he would write a poem about me as well, I think my life would be quite complete!

Chapter Forty-Two

Lizzie and Dante had been married on the 23rd of May, 1860, in St Clement's Church, Hastings, of all places. Daisy was extremely annoyed that she had missed it.

Apparently, it had been a quiet sort of wedding. They had, so the rumour-mongers said, asked a couple of strangers to be their witnesses. The rumour-mongers also had it that Dante had only married Lizzie as he feared she was close to death. Lizzie had been so frail, poor girl, that she had been carried to the church. Well, she had been convalescing at Hastings, Daisy thought. So clearly she was never going to be strong during that period.

Daisy remembered the stony beaches and the warm seas of the Sussex coast well; that being the area she had spent many, many summers during her girlhood. It was a wonderful place to regain one's health – she was annoyed she hadn't thought of convalescing there herself after her 'Terrible Illness'. Henry could have accompanied her. She and Lizzie could have sat together on the beach, drawing or sewing or simply taking in the air together. They could have kept one another company. But anyway, it was only a hop, skip and a jump from Hastings across the Channel to France, and Dante had taken Lizzie there for a honeymoon. Daisy thought it was wildly romantic. She made a mental note to ask Henry to escort her to Paris at some point as well. He would love to paint the city, she was positive.

She had already made Henry visit Hastings with her earlier that month. It had been a warm beginning to April and Henry had agreed to accompany her, then he had surprised her with a picnic at Fairlight Downs. She smiled at the memory. Then she frowned. He had of course made her paint the place before she was allowed to even open the picnic basket. Sometimes, Henry took his role as art tutor too seriously.

Not that either of their pictures matched the standard of William's, of course. The critics had complained, Henry told her, that William's picture had too much contrast in it. So, as if to prove her allegiance to her friends in the Brotherhood, Daisy ensured the grassland in her painting was much, much darker than the sky, which she then washed with the lightest of blues and refused to add anything else to it.

She had watched in some surprise as the watercolour sky ran messily into the dark grassland beside it and bled into the outlines. It was a dreadful muddle, but she had declared that it was raining that day and her painting, in her opinion, was delightful and revolutionary. Henry had looked at it and agreed. She had wondered if he was teasing her, but his face was terribly innocent and in the end, they'd both ended up laughing.

It had been a lovely trip.

But now, nearly a year after the wedding, Daisy had discovered Lizzie was back in London. So day after day, she sat on the rampart of Blackfriars Bridge, dead opposite Chatham Place, where Dante and Lizzie lived. She sometimes thought about the time she had spent in that house and hugged the secret to herself. Dear Henry. He had been beside himself when she reappeared.

It had been three days, apparently. He was going mad, wondering where she was, and had been walking the streets asking about her. He always showed such concern. She couldn't tell him where she had been, of course. In the first instance, she wasn't quite sure herself what had happened; and in the second – well. It was all rather delicious and private, really.

But today, as with all the other days she'd spent here recently, Daisy had, hidden in her muff, a hip flask full of the tincture. She kept slipping it out and taking a sip, just to calm her nerves while she was waiting for Dante. She cared for Lizzie deeply and this was different to when she had been with him. Good Lord, Lizzie and Dante were married now and marriage vows were sacred. Daisy had to tell him she had heard tales about him and she didn't know if they were true or not. She hoped they weren't true; but she wanted to hear it from him.

The door to their house opened and suddenly Lizzie stepped outside, frail and beautiful as always. Daisy caught her breath. The woman was still elegant, her hair, as always, that silken red waterfall; but her eyes were dead. Her bearing had also changed. She stood awkwardly, Daisy noticed, and looked uncomfortable. One hand brushed against her coat and briefly cradled her stomach. Daisy sat forward and tilted her head to one side. Her own hair, similarly loosened, fell over her shoulders. Surely not? Surely Lizzie wasn't …?

She took another large swig from the flask and, unable to help herself, got to her feet unsteadily. 'Lizzie! Lizzie! Why didn't you tell me?' Daisy shouted. She stumbled across the road. 'Lizzie!'

Lizzie snapped her head around and for a moment her eyes remained unfocussed, before they cleared and fixed on Daisy. 'What in God's name!?' 'What do you want? Why won't you just leave me alone. asked Lizzie.' She began to hurry down the street, away from Daisy. 'Go away!' she cried. Suddenly she stopped and raised her hand to her mouth, painful-sounding coughs wracking her body as she hung onto a railing to steady herself.

'Lizzie – no. Lizzie, I just wanted you to tell me yourself.' Daisy caught up with her easily. 'I've heard the rumours, and—'

'Rumours?' gasped Lizzie, trying to catch her breath. She swung around to face Daisy. 'What *rumours*?' Standing next to her, it was awfully clear Lizzie's chest was troubling her. Her breathing sounded terrible.

'The rumours that your health is suffering and the fact that Dante—'

'You have no right to talk to me about Dante! You have no right at all,' shrieked Lizzie. 'I do not need *you* to tell me about his *lovers*.' She turned abruptly and began to walk back the way she had come, trying in vain, it seemed, to lose Daisy. But Daisy would not be lost.

'Lizzie, I know what will make you feel better,' she said, desperately. 'I know what you need. You're going out to buy some right now, aren't you? It's the tincture, Lizzie. Look! I have some. I have some right here.' She put her hand out and closed it around the top of Lizzie's arm. Her arm beneath the fabric of her coat felt no sturdier than a green stick. Lizzie tried to shake her off, but Daisy clung more tightly. 'Here. Look.' With a flourish she pulled the flask out of her muff, still holding onto Lizzie. 'There's no need for you to go and get any. Just let me come inside with you and we can—'

'No!' Lizzie stopped, but Daisy saw her eyes slide towards the flask. 'No.' Her refusal was less emphatic this time. She gave one last little shake of her arm, but Daisy knew she didn't mean it any more. The strength had all but seeped out of her.

Daisy smiled at Lizzie and snaked her arm around the woman's waist. God, the width of her back was tiny! Daisy made a mental note to reduce her food intake even more. She had to aspire to be like Lizzie at all costs.

'Come on. Take some, it's good for you. And good for the baby as well.' She had no idea whether it was or not, but it made her feel very happy sometimes, so why wouldn't it make Lizzie's baby happy? Oh, how glorious!

Dante and Lizzie were to have a child! Daisy smiled at Lizzie.

'I can't. I shouldn't,' said Lizzie, eyeing the bottle. She reached out a hand, then just as suddenly her eyes briefly flashed back to life and she pulled it away. 'No. Please, go away. I've seen you sitting there day after day on the bridge and I'm *sick* of it.' Lizzie's face was beginning to flush and that horrible angry note that Daisy disliked so much was lending a nasty edge to her voice.

'But Lizzie ...' They had stopped outside the house again, Daisy noticed. She felt tears well up in her eyes. 'I'm trying to help you.'

'You're not! You're not helping at all,' shouted Lizzie. 'Go away!' She began to haul herself up the steps back into the house when the door swung open and there he was: Dante, filling the doorframe and glaring at Daisy with those eyes.

'Dante!' Daisy cried. 'Oh, I'm so pleased to see you. I was just—'

'For God's sake, woman!' shouted the man. He reached out and pulled Lizzie roughly inside. 'Can't you see she's pregnant? And ill?'

'Oh!' Daisy's eyes widened and she stood with her hands on her hips. She felt she was swaying a little, but was too angry to care. 'And that makes it all right for you to have other lovers, does it?' she challenged him. There! That would show him. She knew all about the stunners; all about Fanny Cornforth and ... and ... all the others. 'Dante, even *I* gave you up when I realised what you felt for Lizzie.'

'Look here ...' Dante appeared to be furious. Daisy should have quailed under his glare, but she found herself staring at him, her mouth slightly open, thinking how magnificent he was and it did something funny to her insides. Lizzie's head appeared around the corner, her mouth set in a straight line, her eyes looking longingly at the flask Daisy still clutched.

'Let me pass, Dante,' said Lizzie. She squeezed out of the door and made to head back down towards the street. Daisy knew there was a pharmacist along there who would provide her with the wonderful tincture. But all she could see was Lizzie defying Dante, who had always known what was best for his women.

So Daisy turned her attention to Lizzie again. 'Lizzie, darling, I don't think it's wise, do you?' she said, gently. 'See how upset your poor husband is? I think you should go inside and maybe rest a while.'

'You don't know my husband. You don't know anything about any of us,' said Lizzie. The words were like a knife in Daisy's heart.

'But, Lizzie. I know your husband almost as well as you do. I modelled for him when you were away, and he said—'

'Dante!' Lizzie turned to him. 'Is that right? Is she telling the truth?' She flung out her arm, pointing at Daisy. 'Her?'

'I'm sure I cannot recall …' began Dante.

'You're lying! You're lying!' Lizzie curled her fists into balls and began beating them against his chest. 'Why do you *lie*?' Her body was taken by another wave of lung shattering coughing; instinctively, she stopped pounding Dante's chest and instead gripped onto his shoulders, choking horribly for her next breath.

'Lizzie!' Daisy said. She took a step towards her. 'Please, stop! Can't you see what you are doing to him? To us all?' She shook her head. 'Oh, Lizzie. Here, take this.' She held the flask out and Lizzie managed to let go of Dante. She turned her eyes to Daisy and made a grab for the flask. Dante's hand came out of nowhere; he slapped Lizzie's hand away and knocked the flask out of Daisy's hand. The flask rolled into the gutter and both women made to dive after it. Dante restrained Lizzie who cried out angrily and began coughing again.

262

'In! Now!' the man commanded. This time, he pushed Lizzie into the house and strode in after her, slamming the door shut. Daisy stood up from the gutter, the flask filthy and muddy but safely in her hand.

Her mouth made a small, indignant 'O' shape and she stared at the house a moment longer. 'Well, now. Fancy that,' she said. She looked at the flask and wondered for a moment what she was doing with it. Then she opened it up, took a long draught, and staggered away towards home. She knew exactly what was going in her diary when she got into the privacy of her bedroom.

Dante tells me Lizzie is with child. I am very, very concerned about her. Her recent behaviour towards me has left much to be desired, and I have always, always strived to be friends with her, for Dante's sake. I do feel, Dear Diary, that she is not entirely stable. I have tried to speak to her about it, to tell her how sad it makes Dante, how sad it makes all of us, and she refuses to listen. What am I to do? I have always aspired to be like Lizzie, to be as wonderful and to be as talented and to be as loved as she is. Why can she not see that she is destroying everything I have built for us? She is not the same girl as she was. We have all changed, myself included, and it breaks my heart to see her like this.

Chapter Forty-Three

Henry had been summoned by Daisy that evening. She was sitting in the drawing room, a sketchbook on her knee, filling the page with rows and rows of tiny daisies when he arrived.

Her hair hung in titian waves, brushed until it shone in the candlelight. The crackling fire brought out all the shades of autumn in it and she wore a pale, silvery-white gown, which reflected in her greenish-blue eyes like moonlight. It looked a lot like that Ophelia dress from that awful masked ball, but God, she was beautiful.

'Henry!' she said, looking up as he was shown in. 'How wonderful to see you.' She laid the book down and stood up, coming towards him with her arms outstretched. 'I hope you don't think this is presumptuous, but I wanted to repay you for everything you've done for me. Look.' She indicated the sketchbook. 'See how my art has improved under all those years of your tuition.'

Henry dutifully looked at it. The sketches were not executed very well, but then again she had never been the most talented of pupils. 'Well done, Daisy,' he said. He knew better than to try and correct her artistic endeavours too much. She thrived more on encouragement. 'Perhaps next time we can concentrate on the shading of the petals.'

'The shading. Yes. That would be good. I like daisies. They're my favourite flowers. Are they yours, Henry? Is a daisy your most favourite flower ever?' She tilted her head coquettishly onto one side and smiled at him.

Henry swallowed. 'The daisy is indeed my favourite

flower,' he replied, not quite sure if he was interpreting the context correctly or whether it was simply wishful thinking on his part. 'You know that. I've told you before.'

'Excellent. That's good to hear.' She smiled and indicated the door. 'I've prepared a little feast for us. I hope you don't mind. You've been so good to me, and never mentioned any of my little adventures to Papa. For which I am eternally grateful.' She shook her head, genuinely surprised. 'I'm so sorry I disappeared that time. You must have been very worried. And I'm sorry I almost died at father's birthday party. Thank you for rescuing me.'

'Oh, please. You're safe now and anyway, it isn't my place to say anything uncomplimentary about you to anybody,' said Henry. 'It's the last thing I would want to do. I mean, not that there is ever anything uncomplimentary to say about you.' He cursed himself inwardly. He was doing his usual trick of speaking without thinking; but Daisy simply laughed.

'Dear, sweet, Henry. I know I'm naughty, I know I can be a terrible trial to you but … I can't help it.' She lifted her hand and flicked a swathe of hair over her shoulder. She stood, framed in the doorway, her eyes glittering, looking at him. She plucked a flower out of a display on a small hallway table and held it between her thumb and forefinger, twisting it thoughtfully. 'Rossetti painted a portrait of Lizzie standing like this, you know,' she said. 'He called it *Regina Cordium*. And he did it just after they were married last year. Isn't that beautiful? It means "Queen of Hearts". Only Lizzie is holding a pansy.' She looked down at the flower in her hand and frowned. 'A pansy means "thought", and it means Dante was thinking about Lizzie and she was simply occupying his mind. All the time.'

'I see,' said Henry, not really seeing at all.

'Henry, do you think you could paint a picture of me?'

Henry wanted to tell her that he already had dozens of

small books filled with pictures of her; from her being a petulant adolescent, through to a young lady, right up until the present – when she was a self-assured, sensual woman.

Instead, he pressed the palms of his hands against his thighs and took a moment to collect himself. 'I would very much like to paint a picture of you,' he replied. 'You know you only have to say the word and I would do it.'

'I think I would love being a model again.' A frown flitted across her face, as if she was remembering something painful. 'Only this time it would be different.'

'When have you modelled before?' Henry's voice was sharper than he meant it to be. What was it to him, whether she modelled or not? And why should it matter to him, a person in paid employment to her, whoever the hell she modelled for anyway?

'Oh! Yes. I've done it before. One of my little adventures; the sort that nobody ever gets to hear about.' She laughed ruefully. 'No matter. It was an experience.' She smiled again and tucked the flower behind her ear. She held her hand out. 'Come. See what I have prepared. You've distracted me long enough.'

Henry paused for a moment and took her hand, knowing that on some level this was far too familiar. But what Daisy wanted, Daisy usually got. And she clearly wanted to hold his hand.

Daisy led him into the dining room and stood back to let him see what she had concocted. The table was laid for two people, with a candelabrum in the middle of it; shooting crystal sparks off the wine glasses. The cutlery was silver, polished so it reflected the candlelight a thousand fold and another fire was blazing in the hearth.

'Do you like it?' she asked.

'Daisy! This is ... this is wrong. I'm your tutor. Your father pays me. I teach you to draw.'

'No, Henry, you're more than that,' said Daisy. 'You're

a good friend. You look after me. You do not judge me. Why, I could almost love you.' Again, she tilted her head and smiled. 'Take a seat, Henry.'

Speechless, Henry held out a chair for Daisy, then walked to the other one himself. A maid materialised and ladled some soup into his bowl.

He watched the maid disappear, and eventually he found his voice. 'I don't understand, Daisy,' he said. 'This is —'

'Sssssh. Shush.' Daisy put her fingertip to her lip. 'Don't spoil it. Come now. Eat.'

Henry ate the soup mechanically, but he didn't taste it. He was too busy looking at Daisy through the shadows.

Daisy toyed with a few spoonfuls, but didn't seem to eat any. 'Is it good, Henry?' she asked. 'Here – pour the wine. Soup always tastes better with wine.'

Henry stood up quickly, leaning over the table and pouring her some wine. His own glass was half full, but soon hers was empty. Her eyes were soft in the candlelight, her lips rosy and inviting. Henry's hand shook a little as he filled her glass again and he spilled some on the linen.

Daisy laughed. 'No matter,' she said. She dipped the tip of her finger in the ruby red pool and held it out to him. 'It's a shame to waste it,' she said. 'Take it. No?' She laughed. 'Then I will have it.' She popped her finger in her mouth and sucked the liquid off it, never taking her eyes off him. Henry didn't know where to look, so he looked at her.

It wasn't long before another maid brought the next course. And then the next course came. And then Henry realised that it was time for dessert and all he had done was stare at Daisy and eat very little. Daisy had eaten even less; but there were three empty wine bottles on the table and he really didn't think he had had more than two small glassfuls of the stuff. But he must have done.

Later on as they sat on the sofa with more wine, Henry looked at the woman he – yes – the woman he loved. 'Daisy,

I have to thank you for this,' he said, formally. Too formally. He didn't want the evening to end, but he knew it had to. It was probably a decent time to make his excuses and go. 'I've never been entertained like this before and I appreciate it. Thank you.' He cleared his throat. 'Tomorrow, if I may, I will call on you and instead of us concentrating on your art, I would very much like to do some sketches of you. Some proper sketches.' His face coloured as he thought of all the small books at home, filled with her image. 'And then, once we have agreed on the structure, I would like to paint your portrait.'

Daisy laughed. 'Of course you may do some sketches. It will be my pleasure. But I have to ask you, Henry, why you feel you need permission to call on me?'

Henry stood up. If he sat next to her any longer, he wouldn't be responsible for his actions. Unfortunately, Daisy stood up as well. And damn, she was close to him.

She swayed slightly and giggled. Henry put his hand out to catch her arm and she leaned towards him, pressing her weight against him so his chin was level with the top of her head. Her hair tickled him and she was warm and smelled oh, so sweet and enticing. She reached up and steadied herself by holding onto his shoulder. Then her hand crept around to his back, and she pulled him closer.

'Oh, Henry,' she said, nuzzling into his neck, her hand now tugging gently at his collar. 'Make love to me, Henry.'

'Daisy! I can't – your father employs me.' *Dear Lord!* Her closeness to him, her soft hands playing with his hair, the feeling of her next to his skin …

'My father will never find out,' she whispered. 'This is my house. I can do what I like.'

'No!'

'Yes.' There was a faint hint of alcohol on her breath as she moved closer and pressed her lips onto his. He resisted at first, but she drew him closer and her kisses became more urgent.

Henry was lost; he could do nothing but respond. He pulled her to him and covered her face, her neck, and her shoulders with kisses. So long! For so long, he had been desperate to do this. Instinct took over from reason and he swept her up in his arms.

Daisy giggled, a delicious, musical sound, and latched her arms around his neck. 'Where are you taking me?' she asked.

He didn't need to think twice about the double entendre. 'Wherever I can,' he said, roughly.

'Upstairs. Take me to my room. We won't be disturbed in there.' She laughed. 'But take me there quickly.'

'As fast as I can, my love,' said Henry, his heart thumping in his chest. He shouldered the door and carried her upstairs. She was so light in his arms. Layers and layers of her petticoats crushed against his body and hampered his movements, but he didn't care.

'Here it is. This is my room,' she said as he paused outside a huge white door with a Greek cornice above it.

'I know. God, how well I know that!' he said, and they both laughed.

'Oh, Henry. I'm so naughty,' she said. 'Please forgive me.'

'You can do nothing wrong, my love,' he said. He somehow managed to open the door and stepped inside the room. He kicked his foot back, slamming the door shut and carried her over to the bed. He laid her gently on it like a prize, smoothing her skirts out around her. 'Let me look at you,' he said. 'Just let me look at you.'

She tilted her head back and carefully bent her arms, flinging them out to the sides, her hands curling into loose fists. She closed her eyes and her hair flowed over the white pillowcase like lava.

Henry heard a groan and he realised it was coming from him. 'You are beautiful,' he said.

'Am I a stunner?' she asked, teasingly. 'Am I?'

'You are.'

'Am I as beautiful as Lizzie Siddal?' she asked.

'More so.'

'You're not my first, Henry. I hope you don't mind.'

'I don't care. I don't care tuppence.'

'That's good. Neither do I,' she replied.

Then Daisy opened her eyes and stared right at him. It was like a current vibrated through him. She raised her arms and linked them around his neck. Then, in one sudden movement, she pulled him towards her. He was surprised at her strength, at her urgency.

But he let himself be taken down and then he thanked his lucky stars that fortuitous night that he was Henry Dawson and nobody else.

Chapter Forty-Four

Daisy sat in front of her dressing table mirror, staring at herself, trying to take in the news. A sea of flickering candles reflected in the glass, creating shadows in the room that seemed to mock her. It was all over London already; the fact that Lizzie was dead. The official story was that she had died, early this morning, as a result of an accidental overdose of laudanum. Daisy wasn't so sure; there had also been talk of a suicide note.

Henry had told her the news and she had cried. Then Henry had to leave her to do a silly commission, and he had hated leaving her – he really had. But he told her he would come straight back afterwards. He would be here at three. He had promised her he would back.

The last time Daisy had seen her, Lizzie had been miserable. She had looked dreadful; she was thinner than ever and her whole body seemed wracked with pain. She knew she had lost the baby she was carrying just after they had that awful argument and she kept trying to find ways to help her and support her. Lizzie was so horribly depressed; she could barely leave the house at times. Daisy knew this, because stories spread like wildfire in the wonderful artistic circles she moved in with Henry.

And she herself had waited for Lizzie to come outside and talk to her; she had waited ever so long until one day she eventually spotted Lizzie, trailing along the street looking rather haggard, clutching a paper-wrapped package in her hand. Poor Lizzie! She had taken it out on Daisy when she showed her concern; Lizzie had shrieked at her and accused her of being obsessive. She had called her a monomaniac and told her that she deserved to be in a sanatorium.

Painfully remembering all this, Daisy took a huge, shuddering sob and picked up her pen. Slowly, she began to write, the nib forming the words, but Daisy herself barely aware of what she was even writing.

Lizzie is dead. That is all. I cannot bring myself to comment further. Dante is broken-hearted. I went to him, of course, and tried to offer my condolences, but he was inconsolable. Oh, Lizzie, what have you done? What have you done to both of us? To all of us? There is nothing further I can do and the path I must take is now quite clear. I have always aspired to be like you, Lizzie, you know that. I looked up to you like a sister. We have been through so much together. I have accompanied you on your journey, and now your journey has ended. I hope it was peaceful. I know you left Dante a letter, I know he is still protecting you. He always will. He is a good man. And Lizzie – I pray to God that He shall rest your soul. We will meet again, I am sure, and we will once again be the great friends we were. Goodbye, my love, my sister. Goodbye.

Daisy put down the pen and looked around the room. She had cried until she could cry no more. And Dante – he hadn't wanted her sympathy. He hadn't wanted *her*. She had gone there, gone to Chatham Place after Henry had told her. The others had left. She knew – she had been waiting until they drifted away. And then she had hammered on the door. He hadn't even answered. She had pressed her face against the windowpane, calling his name, trying to find a gap in the curtains; trying to see something. But there was nothing. The curtains were firmly closed, shutting her out. Well. Lizzie had really done it this time. Daisy sat up straighter.

Already more stories were filtering through about the

Rossetti's – the fact they had been out for the evening with the Swinburne's, the fact Lizzie had been drowsy whilst she was there. They'd gone home, he'd gone out, and he returned to find Lizzie beyond help. Despite four physicians being called, Lizzie had died. Daisy rammed her knuckles into her mouth to stop the screams that threatened to erupt. She bit down onto her hand until she broke the skin and tasted blood, but it didn't make her feel any better. And there was due to be an inquest tomorrow. They all had to relive it again.

'Henry,' she whispered, taking her fist away from her mouth. 'Oh, Henry. What would you do, if it were me?' Her eyes filled with tears again. Would he be able to continue? Would he fight to save her life? The thoughts were exquisite, her imaginings beyond romantic.

He would, she was sure, do everything in his power to save her and if he couldn't; oh, he would mourn her. He would mourn her so very much. Yet it was so, *so* frustrating that she hadn't even been able to conceive and *really* experience Lizzie's emotions – and it was not for want of trying. Dear Henry. These past few months had been delightful. She glanced over to the portrait he had finished a little while ago, and, to her mind, she looked an awful lot like Lizzie. As she stared at the painting, a different picture began to form in her own mind.

He will find me here, in my bed. The room is dark and the patterns on the wallpaper do not show in this February dusk. And I am so, so sorry that he has to find me. He shouts and I hear him thundering up the staircase.

He calls for me: 'Daisy! Daisy!' I cannot move. My body is weak and frail beneath the weight of the blankets. My breathing is shallow.

'Please, let me sleep,' I want to tell him. No more pain. Let me sleep, my love, let me sleep... The door into the room slams. I know it is him, but I cannot bear to open my eyes. I am so tired. So very tired. He calls my name again.

Then he screams 'No!' over and over again. Hands seize me; he shakes me, he pulls me out of the bed, hoisting me upwards, calling to me all the time. I flop around like a rag doll, my head lolls to one side. I don't want to open my eyes. I can't open my eyes. He slips away from me and all is silent...

It would be so beautiful.

Daisy stared at her reflection again. Henry would. He would try and save her. He would be here at three. He had promised her. He had never let her down; never.

Carefully, deliberately, she loosened the pins in her hair. She watched it fall down past her shoulders, in rippling waves like Lizzie's had done. Oh, Lizzie. Her eye caught the small phial on the dressing table next to her.

It was almost time. He would be here soon and he would save her.

She would be like Lizzie once again; almost *identically* like Lizzie. Henry would come. He would come and find her and it would be so beautiful.

Does one refer to this as a tisane or a tincture? I do not know. The names and the meanings escape me now. I believe tisanes are made with natural, herbal ingredients, but then so is this. Does it truly matter?

She slowly untied the ribbons of her robe, slipping it off her shoulders and exposing the creamy white of her skin. The shadows were dark in the hollows where her collarbone jutted out and she smiled. Her arms, oh so slender, were just as Lizzie's had been. Her face, she was pleased to notice, had developed that wonderful cheekbone structure Lizzie had. Her nose, however, disappointed her. It was nothing like Lizzie's. Lizzie's was aquiline and elegant. Hers, though, was small and turned up slightly at the end.

She let the robe fall to the floor and reached out for the bottle, pleased to see how her wrists were so defined and that the skin which was pulled tight across her hands was almost translucent. The whiteness of her bones and the blue of her veins showed clearly through the flesh.

Oh, Lizzie.

She took the bottle and uncorked it, putting it to her mouth.

Oh, Henry.

She drank.

Oh, Dante.

Yes. It would be so beautiful ...

Part Three

Chapter Forty-Five

It almost felt as if someone was holding her hand and guiding her down towards the river.

'I'm sorry I had to do it this way. I need you to be here.'

Cori heard the voice but there was nobody with her. She was standing in a field with the riverbank a little way in front of her. She had no recollection of getting here, but she was aware she was holding something in her hand. She looked down and saw a set of car keys, with a Tate Britain key ring attached to them. Her stomach heaved as she realised who they must belong to.

Oh God, I've turned into a car thief now as well!. Her granny would be absolutely mortified, she thought.

'Corisande!' The voice was curt. She recognised it now; it was Daisy. *'What are you waiting for?'* Daisy continued. *'Before anyone else comes, I want to show you where John painted the background. It was all done "en plein air". He told me that he was in danger of being blown by the wind into the water, and becoming intimate with the feelings of Ophelia.'* She laughed again. *'Dear John, he was such a joker, he …'*

Something tugged at the back of Cori's mind. She had heard those words before. Hadn't Simon told her there was a letter? Hadn't Millais written to someone? A lady? A lady who was married to one of his patrons …

Then she remembered. 'Martha. Martha Combe,' said Cori. 'She got that letter.'

'No!' said Daisy. *'I knew all about it before she did. He wrote to me as well. But it was her copy everybody talks about. I don't know what happened to mine. Such a lot of things got lost.'*

'No! No.' Things started shifting in Cori's head. 'No.' She looked at the river before her and the willows that still trailed their fronds in the water. She imagined the portrait back at the Tate and the classic figure of Lizzie Siddal floating down that very same river.

It was okay, she had the car keys. She could go. As soon as she worked out where she'd left the car.

'Corisande? Talk to me. You believe me, don't you?' Daisy's voice sounded small and fretful.

'I want to believe you,' said Cori, turning slowly in a circle, trying to work out where she was. Jeez, she was talking to herself. Truly talking to herself! As well as suffering from phantom laudanum overdoses and hallucinations and … Oh God.

'What happened to you, Daisy?' Cori asked. She'd never found out, had she? Lissy hadn't come back to her yet. 'Where did you go after Lizzie died?'

Trying to quell the idea that was forming in her head, she turned away from the river and looked back across the field to the gate. She would start walking there. It was fine. Daisy had just wanted to show her Tolworth. It was fine …

'I don't want to talk about it,' said the girl suddenly. *'It wasn't like it should have been.'*

The sharpness of the words was like an arrow, stopping Cori in her tracks. She tried to ignore the voice and fought against turning around to look at that river again. She had a bad feeling about that river and she didn't like the images that were flitting into her mind.

The weight of the dress was dragging her down and there was a current of sorts. It was pulling her downstream, she was floating away but the stars and the moon were smiling down on her.

She took a step towards the gate, trying to fight off the nausea and dizziness that was pressing in all around her. One foot in front of the other, that's all it would take to get away.

There's rosemary, that's for remembrance. Pray you,

love, remember. And there is pansies, that's for thoughts.
There's fennel for you, and columbines…

One foot in front of the other, back to the gate. Back to the car.

She was Ophelia. She was Lizzie. She was invincible.

Back to Simon.

'You don't trust me, do you?' said the voice. Cori faltered. It seemed to be coming from right in front of her

'No,' hissed Cori. 'No, I don't.'

'But you're not leaving me. You're coming with me,' said the voice. *'I want to show you how it felt. I promised you I'd do that, didn't I? And I have done. But you need to feel this as well.'*

There was that funny glow again and Cori's heart started beating faster. There was something rectangular on the ground in front of her. It was the diary, lying open with the pages lifting in the breeze. Cori was pretty certain she hadn't brought the thing with her – but then again, she couldn't even recall stealing the car.

The shape of a girl started to form in the light and Cori had to squint against the brightness. It had to be Daisy. She was wearing that silvery-white dress again and it glowed. Her pale, beautiful face was framed by long, fiery hair, tumbling past her waist.

'Corisande, we both know it's all true!' said Daisy. *'You shouldn't distrust me. I modelled for them. And I fell in love. And then it all went wrong.'*

The apparition exploded into a ball of light, then the light got sucked away as if a huge black hole was forming in the field by the river.

The black fog started descending on Cori. She buckled at the knees as the cramps came over her body and the disorientation set in. She could feel herself slipping away and Daisy's mind taking over again.

Of course it was all true. It had happened. It was all real. And this was how it was all going to end.

Chapter Forty-Six

Cori woke up, her head spinning and her body aching all over. She opened her eyes and squinted at her surroundings.

It took a moment for her to realise she was in a darkened room with vague shapes of furniture looking even blacker against the gloom. Somehow, she had been found and they had taken her home. That was good.

She turned her head painfully in the direction of her window, remembering the dress she had hung there on the curtain rail a few nights ago. She really ought to get it put in her wardrobe. There was a scratchy sensation beneath her cheek and she wrinkled her nose as she recognised the pungent scent of rosemary coming from whatever she had lain on.

As her eyes focussed, the dress shape moved and she closed her eyes again, remembering also the draught that had blown through the other night. But it was funny; because she was warm and she could hear a faint crackling, like flames somewhere nearby. Then she realised she could smell woodsmoke too – the unmistakeable smell of an open fire, something she was used to from her granny's big old rambling house up in Northumbria.

Granny would sort her out. She was glad she was back home; she ...

'What the ...?' Cori sat up, her brain suddenly clicking into gear. If she was in her room and the dress was there, what the hell was her granny doing burning logs in her room?

'*It's all right.*' The voice was soft and horribly familiar. Cori's heart leapt and she snapped herself fully awake;

Daisy. Somewhere in the corner of the room, a candle burst into life and the girl was illuminated in the soft light.

And Cori realised she wasn't in the mews house and she wasn't in her granny's house either.

Daisy stood with her arms folded around her middle and a slight smile hovering around her lips. Her face was so pale, the pink blush on her cheek stood out like roses against the snow. Her hair hung in loose, red-gold waves down to her hips, and she was still wearing that silver dress – the fancy one with all the brocade and embroidery on it; the one that looked exactly like Ophelia's dress in the Millais painting.

Cori felt sick. It was as if, she realised, she was staring at herself, only a more beautiful version of herself. Daisy had the same teal-coloured eyes; the same shaped mouth, even. But it all just seemed more perfect on Daisy.

'No. I'm dreaming. I have to be,' said Cori, scrabbling to her feet.

In one swift movement, Daisy was in front of her. *'No you're not. It's all real, I've told you.'* Cori was speechless. She pinched herself hard on the arm and winced as she felt the little nip of localised pain.

'You'll have bruises there tomorrow,' said Daisy. She came closer and Cori backed away, her heel bumping into something on the ground. *'Careful, Corisande,'* said Daisy.

Cori's heart was definitely pounding now. In fact, she was willing to bet it was echoing around this whole … she looked around and swore. It was a bedroom. Definitely a bedroom, but not one she recognised.

Daisy followed her gaze and sighed, the breath coming out of her like a little icy wind that gave Cori goose bumps where it touched her flesh.

'I miss it,' said Daisy, *'very much.'* Her eyes rested on the bed and she sighed again. Then another candle lit up, this time in front of a mirror. Then another one; this time on a bedside table. And another, on the mantelpiece. Soon, the

whole room was bathed in flickering, golden light and Cori found herself hypnotised by it. The candle by the mirror arrested her attention, and she looked in the glass, trying to take in the weird, backwards room that greeted her there.

And then she saw it.

Reflected in the mirror, just behind Cori and situated on the floor, was a heap of what looked like old clothing; that, then, was what she had caught her heel on.

'*It's not clothing,*' whispered Daisy.

'Get out of my head!' hissed Cori. She turned around and looked at the heap. It was crumpled and part of it was smothered in red-gold and ... 'Oh God!' Cori rammed her fist in her mouth and choked back the bile that rose into her throat.

The heap was a woman – a woman lying collapsed and immobile on the floor, her features ghastly white and a terrified expression in her eyes. She lay half on her side, curled up with one arm outstretched as if she was trying to reach the door.

'It's you!' said Cori, looking quickly at the figure and then at Daisy.

Daisy had turned her head away, looking revolted and, if possible, even paler than she had done before. '*I know,*' she said. '*I know.*'

The woman on the floor's eyelids fluttered briefly and closed. Knowing it was fairly useless and probably crazy; Cori rushed over to her and dropped to her knees. She took the cold, outstretched hand, not even thinking about how she was able to touch it. The fingers twitched as Cori grasped it, curling weakly around Cori's. The woman's eyes opened again briefly and met Cori's for a split second. A tiny jolt of life and recognition came into them, before they closed again. Cori didn't know if that made her feel sicker or not.

'Daisy,' she said, trying to rub some life back into the hand, 'Daisy ...' Cori turned her head to the Ghost-Daisy and shouted at her. 'What can I do? What the hell can I *do*?' She felt tears spring to her eyes and the image blurred for a second.

Daisy shook her head, still not looking at them. *'Nothing,'* she said. *'I died alone. And at the very end, I thought Lizzie had come to save me. But it wasn't her, was it? It was you. Henry didn't make it in time, and I thought Lizzie had come back and I would just sleep and when I woke up he would be there. But nobody saved me at all and I died instead.'*

'Daisy …' Cori turned her attention back to the girl on the floor. With a great effort, her eyes opened again and the sweetest smile brushed her lips, before she gave one tiny breath and the life left her body.

Cori felt the hot tears running down her face. She had never seen anything like that before.

She caught sight of a small bottle on the floor, as if it had been dropped and rolled a little away across the rug and the horrible realisation came to her. 'Did – did you do it yourself?' she whispered.

'I did.' Daisy's voice was small and flat. *'And I expected Henry would find me. He was supposed to find me, but he didn't come back in time. I always wanted to be like Lizzie and I couldn't help imagining how it would have felt to be her; how it would have been to be rescued, like Dante tried to rescue her. She was my soul sister. I don't think she knew it, but I did.'*

'Was Henry your lover?' Cori asked, quietly. She smoothed the glorious red hair down, brushed it away from the dead Daisy's ravaged face; because it *was* ravaged. That girl on the floor had a face that was all hollow valleys and jutting cheekbones. There were huge dark circles under her eyes and she was painfully, painfully thin. The Ghost-Daisy was, in contrast, a beauty; a 'stunner', as the PRB used to call them.

There was a little laugh and Daisy was beside Cori in a

swish of brocade. *'A "stunner". You compliment me,'* she said.

Cori opened her mouth to protest at Daisy reading her mind again, but shut it. What was the point? *'And you ask about Henry. If Lizzie was my soul sister, Henry was my soulmate; my one true love. Dante was a passing infatuation. It was beautiful while it lasted, but it should always have been Henry. I just wish I'd realised sooner. And I wish we'd had longer. If I hadn't been so silly ... Look. You'll see him in a minute.'*

Daisy raised a hand and pointed at a clock. The hands spun around and the fire in the grate jumped and settled as if time had, literally, speeded up. Nothing else changed. Cori remained kneeling, but the next time she touched the woman on the floor, she knew the irreversible chill of death had overtaken her and felt unutterably sad.

A knock on the door startled her, and she looked up.

'He's here. Now you'll see him,' murmured Daisy.

There was another knock and a shout; a man's voice calling, as if nothing was untoward and he was just trying to establish where somebody was in the building.

'Daisy! Daisy! My love – are you in there? Daisy?' The man waited a second, then the door burst open. There was a beat – and he stood in the doorway.

To Cori, that was worse even than watching Daisy die; watching the man who loved her rush into the room; watching as he threw himself down on the floor beside her. Listening, as he called her name over and over again.

'Daisy ... Daisy. Wake up. Wake up, my love. Come on ...' He became more and more agitated, taking her by the shoulders and shaking her uselessly. He checked her wrist; leaned over and put his ear to her mouth. Pressed his hand against her heart. *'My love ... No.'* His voice cracked and he leaned forward, his head on her chest now, great sobs wracking his body.

Henry was kneeling right next to Cori. The light from the fire illuminated him as he sat up and raised his face heavenwards, closing his eyes and whispering prayers. In that moment, with his fair hair and his handsome profile, he looked a hell of a lot like Simon.

And all of a sudden, Cori felt as if someone had knifed her in the heart. She stared at the man, a whisper away from him yet invisible to him. She felt his pain and understood, suddenly, what a mess this whole thing was.

Who cared if Daisy had been the model for *Ophelia* or not? Who cared if she had floated around on the edges of the PRB, dropping away into insignificance like the willow fronds Millais had painted? Who cared if her damned diary was real, or a made up part of some delusional life a Victorian woman had created for herself?

All that mattered, really, was that she hadn't meant to kill herself. She hadn't meant to put the man she loved through such anguish. She hadn't meant to commit suicide. It was an accident; a horrible accident and somebody needed to know that. The rest was incidental.

And she should have had help; professional help to deal with her mental health. But what hope did she have? The answers came to Cori with a frightening clarity, as if the images were flowing from Daisy's mind right into her own. Her father had disowned her, she had no friends to speak of, the servants did what they had to do – and her lover could see no wrong in her. Again – what a mess.

This was why she needed Cori. This was why she had found her. From wherever she was, Daisy had seen the connection; she had seen Simon and seen Cori and fixated on them as she had fixated on her connection to Lizzie. And the truth was all that Cori needed to take back with her. *Perhaps it'll be enough for just one person to know the truth. Or maybe two.* Wasn't that what Becky had said once?

Yes, somebody had to know the truth. And Cori did.

'She didn't mean to do it, Henry,' Cori said, quietly, as the man by her side dropped his head and covered his face with his hands. He jerked his head up and stared out into the room, and Cori wondered if, on some level, he had heard her. Then he stood up and with shaking hands took a blanket from the bed. He knelt down again and placed the blanket carefully over the Daisy on the floor, tucking it up around her chin. Then he smoothed her hair back, just as Cori had done.

'I'll get help, Daisy,' he said. *'I'll get a doctor. We'll save you.'* Then he stood up and strode over to the door. He threw the door open and shouted as loudly as he could for help. He kept shouting and shouting, until footsteps hurried along the corridors and people began to crowd into the bedroom.

Cori stood up and turned away, walking into the far corner of the room and being careful not to catch sight of anything in the mirror – she didn't need to see any of that; any of the aftermath.

'They're all shadows,' said Daisy. *'You don't have to look. We can't do anything about any of it. It happened. I hate it. I hate what I did, what I became. What do you call it in your time? A statistic? That's all I was. That's all I was to them. I deserved to die alone.'* Her voice rose hysterically and she began to pace around the floor, the ghostly swish of the dress brushing against cabinets and the bedstead and the fire-set by the now guttering flames. *'I deserved it. My poor Henry … it hurts seeing it all again, but I had to show you. I deserved to die alone, I …'*

'You didn't!' Cori cut in. 'You didn't deserve that. And you didn't die alone. I was there.'

Daisy stopped moving and turned quickly to Cori. *'Say that again?'* she asked. *'Again. Say that again.'*

'I was there,' replied Cori. 'I was with you. Remember? We both saw it again, just now. You saw me when it happened. You weren't alone, Daisy.'

Daisy blinked, wide greenish-blue eyes that, Cori realised

287

again, were the identical colour to her own. It gave her a nasty little chill up her spine.

'*I wasn't? I wasn't alone? Oh, my ... no. I wasn't.*' Then she smiled, the sea change in her mood palpable. If this was what she had been like in life, Cori thought, God bless her. Even Daisy herself mustn't have known how to deal with the see-saw of emotions. But then, it must have just been *normal* to her. Unless that was why she started taking the laudanum in the first place – to calm herself down? She didn't think she'd ever know the reason behind it.

Cori blushed, remembering Daisy's uncanny knack of getting into her head; but fortunately the woman was preoccupied, moving around again, touching everything in the room as if she was rediscovering it all or maybe saying goodbye to it again.

She lingered by a portrait of herself and touched that last. Cori didn't recognise the individual style, but it was similar to a Waterhouse or a Millais, all beautiful detail and rich colours. It must have taken someone a long time and a lot of love and dedication to paint that. Cori thought of the painting Simon had done of her, the one she had discovered in his second bedroom. The other *Ophelia*.

The man who had painted Daisy's portrait had poured as much love and energy into it as Simon had poured into his portrait of Cori. 'I never thought I'd need that sort of studio space again,' he'd told her. 'What I've got here seemed enough. But it's not. Not any more.'

'I need to go back,' Cori said, suddenly, her voice surprisingly strong.

'*Of course you do,*' said Daisy. Her butterfly mind had moved somewhere else and that smile was back again. '*I'll take you, shall I?*'

'Yes. Please,' replied Cori, desperately. 'Daisy?' She took a deep breath. 'What do you want me to do with your diary? When we get back?'

Daisy stared at her, apparently weighing up her options.

Then she spoke in that little lost voice. *'I don't want it forgotten,'* she said. *'Because I think I've been forgotten. And Henry – he kept my picture, but it got destroyed in a fire after he died. So at least he never knew it was gone.'* Her face looked so sad. *'He never married.'* She frowned. *'He should have done, I think. I think I'd like to see him again but he's never been there when I've looked for him. Maybe he thought I meant to do it and can't forgive me properly?'* She was off again, her gaze jumping all over the room in tandem with her thoughts.

Cori tried to coax Daisy's mind back to the present situation. 'And what about your diary?'

'Can you *keep it?'* Daisy asked, fixing her with such a heartfelt look that Cori wasn't surprised to feel the tears building again.

She swallowed them down. 'Of course. Do you … umm … do you want me to try and set the record straight about things?' She didn't know how she could do that, but she would try, if she had to. Could you reopen cases that old?

'Has anyone said, recently, in public, that I killed myself?' asked Daisy. Her voice was harsh but Cori knew it was defensive, more than aggressive.

'No.' Cori thought back to the article. 'There was a story in the newspaper about you, when they found your diary; but all it said was that there was a mystery surrounding the painting of *Ophelia*. It suggested that maybe Lizzie didn't model for the whole thing after all and someone – you – had modelled for part of the painting, when Lizzie was indisposed.' At that Daisy lowered her eyelashes and looked coyly at the floor.

'Then, no.' the response was emphatic and Daisy shook her head. *'No. Because I don't want them delving into my affairs too deeply. I don't want them to start looking at*

my friendship with the Brotherhood. It's too private and too painful – especially after what we went through with Lizzie.'

'Well, fair enough,' said Cori, cautiously.

'I only wanted someone to know the truth about what happened to me – at the end. And you do, don't you? And I don't know – maybe Henry does too. I'd like him to know. You told him though, so that's good. And it's important that you know, because we are the same, you and I. Just wait – you'll see. I need to thank you properly and I know just how I can do that.'

Daisy's attention started to drift off. She was staring at her own body again and Cori knew she was losing her – and perhaps her only chance of getting back to her own life. God, what if she was trapped here; trapped in some other world with only Daisy for company?

'Please. It's over with,' Cori said. 'Daisy. Daisy? Look at me. It's over with.' She wanted to touch the girl to reassure her, but wondered if her hand would fall straight through Daisy's body if she tried to do that – which reminded her that she was in actual fact talking to a ghost in said ghost's ghostly bedroom/death scene.

Cori began to shake. Certifiable. She was *definitely* certifiable.

Daisy turned to face Cori and studied her for a moment. Then she laughed quietly, reaching out one hand to take Cori's.

It was the weirdest sensation, like being held by a snowflake. Then she reached her other hand out and touched Cori's forehead. Cori felt waves of tiredness wash over her, and then she felt herself crumpling up into a heap. The last thing she thought as she drifted into oblivion was that at least there was no pain this time.

Chapter Forty-Seven

'That's my car!' said Simon. He saw it, abandoned on the grass verge a little way along from a gate. He jumped out of Jon's car and ran over to his own, trying the door handles to see if it was locked. It was. He peered into it, trying to see if there was any trace of Cori in there. He saw a purple mobile phone lying on the passenger seat and cursed. 'Her phone's in here, she's definitely around somewhere.'

'You see,' said Becky, 'you could do the CSI thing as well.'

'Yes, but it also means that wherever she is, she can't contact anyone for help,' said Simon. He looked up and across the field. 'Wait! Is that her?' He saw a figure in the long grass, standing quite close to the edge of the river.

He recognised the silvery-white maxi-dress and the long red hair that fell in curls down her back; and he also noticed that she was now picking her way carefully through the grass and walking towards the water.

'Cori!' He shouted her name, but the word was carried across the field and she didn't falter. He swore and climbed over the fence, not bothering with the gate. He started to run across the field, focussed only on getting to the woman before she slipped and ended up in the Hogsmill.

Cori had reached the bank now, and stared down into the fast flowing water. To Simon's eternal horror, she sort of half-slid and half-stumbled down the bank, then actually stepped into the grey, rushing river. The current must have taken her by surprise as he saw her wobble a little, then grab out for a willow branch that hung nearby.

'Cori!' he shouted again, pounding across the grass to her. 'For God's sake, Cori, just stay there.'

He was almost upon her, when she let go of the branch and seemed to steady herself. Then she turned to the right and, throwing her arms outwards, fell backwards into the river.

The water hit her like an icy blast. It was freezing; absolutely freezing.

She knew she went under, as the water covered her face and she started to choke. Her hair wrapped around her face, clinging to her skin and dragging her head backwards until she somehow managed to jackknife her body, and force her head out of the water again. She gulped in air, then tried to flip herself over so she could at least try to swim or put her feet down to save herself.

She flailed around, her dress dragging her back down and gasped, taking in a mouthful of water. She coughed and shook her head to get the hair out of her face, but all she succeeded in doing was getting the red-gold mess wrapped around her even more.

She was going down for the third time, when she heard an almighty splash and almost immediately felt a strong pair of hands grasp her under her armpits and haul her out of the water.

'Oh thank God, thank God!' she cried, hanging onto the strong, firm body that was pulling her upright.

'Cori, what the hell are you doing?'

It was Simon, looking as terrified as she felt. His shirt was clinging to his body and his face was pale. His own hair was plastered to his head and he pulled her close to him. 'Come on. Out of here. Now.' He must have thrown himself in after her, judging by the look of him.

'I don't know. I fell in the river. It was cold.' She was babbling, she knew it.

'Sod this,' said Simon. He gathered her up into his arms and waded back to the shore, Cori clinging to his neck and shivering.

He set her down on the grass, well away from the water and pulled her close. She was shaking and cold, and her teeth were beginning to chatter.

'We have to get you back to the car. There's a blanket in the back,' he said. 'Becky and Jon brought me here, but God knows what would have happened if I hadn't found you. I only knew you were here because of this.' He pulled out a soggy piece of paper from his pocket and Cori recognised the patterns the words made. He crumpled it up and threw it on the ground, then pulled her even closer, as if he was trying to wrap her up and warm her himself.

He stroked her hair back from her face, searching her eyes for answers. 'Why did you do it?'

There was a soft, self-satisfied laugh from behind Simon.

'Why not? You saved her so it proves you love her. That's my gift to you both. So you both know how it feels to be loved like I was loved. Cori – will you tell him now? Tell him I didn't mean it. Tell him. I need him to know.'

Cori could tell by the way the remaining colour drained from Simon's face that he had heard the voice as well.

'Who the hell was that?' asked Simon, looking around for the source of it.

'It's Daisy,' Cori managed to say. 'And she didn't commit suicide. It was an accident. A horrible accident and Henry couldn't save her. That's what she means. I need to tell you she never meant to do it. I think she sees you as Henry and me as herself. She wanted you to save me to make it all right again. Because Henry couldn't save her at the end.'

Cori slid her gaze over to where the diary lay, a couple of metres away from her. The car keys were, somehow, neatly placed next to it. It looked so innocent, yet she knew that it contained the deepest secrets and desires of Daisy

Ashford's existence. She would have to make sure it was safe so nobody would probe too deeply into Daisy's life, ever again.

Cori wasn't one for breaking promises.

'Thank you.'

Daisy's voice was no more than a whisper and Cori instinctively clung tighter to Simon. Then there was a movement on the grass by her feet, and it brought her attention away from the leather bound diary.

The piece of paper Simon had so recently discarded began to roll across the ground, almost as if it was being directed somewhere. There was no wind to speak of and certainly nothing strong enough to lift a piece of wet paper into the air and make it dance across the field towards the river. Then a flash of light caught Cori's peripheral vision and she squinted, turning her head towards it.

She saw that a ray of sunshine had suddenly burst through the branches of the trees, and had thrown a spot underneath the willows into a pool of light. The paper drifted and danced, and ended up tangled in the dropping branches of the willow.

And in the pool of light, was the distinct outline of a woman, holding the skirts of her long dress up and out to the side with one hand, and seemingly balancing herself by gracefully reaching out with her other hand. The sunlight caught off her hair and it shone like fire, rippling down her back to her hips then merging into the silver of her dress. She took a step towards the river, and another step; then paused on the bank.

The woman looked to her left, at the willow nearest to her, and dropped her skirt. She half-turned, facing the tree as a man stepped out from behind it. He bowed low at his waist and then straightened up, holding his hand out to her, the other arm bent behind his back in a very formal attitude. She paused for a second, and then walked towards him. She held out both hands and he straightened up, taking her hands in his.

The two figures took a step towards one another. By some weird law of physics, they apparently merged together in another flash of silver: and in another instant, they were gone.

Cori closed her eyes and hid her face in Simon's chest. She could feel his ribcage moving as he breathed; could feel his arms around her, holding her close.

This was where she wanted to be, she realised. Right here, forever, with the man who had saved her life.

I won't leave you, Daisy. I'll never let anything bad happen to you again, I promise. I want to look after you for the rest of your life. And I swear to you, on my life, that I never break my promises.

'I love you, Simon,' she whispered into the damp cloth of his shirt. 'Don't ever leave me.'

She felt him bury his face in her hair. 'I love you too, Cori,' he said against her damp curls. 'I won't leave you, ever. I promise. And I don't break my promises.'

'I know,' whispered Cori, feeling the tears spring to her eyes, feeling wretched and helpless about Henry and Daisy and for the whole tragic mess they'd ended up in. 'I know you don't.'

Then she pulled away and looked at the river and the willows and the reeds swaying amongst the grass on the bank.

And she hoped Daisy and Henry would find their peace now.

Epilogue

The new Rossetti was, as Lissy had said, the centrepiece of the latest Pre-Raphaelite Exhibition at the Tate. The canvas was smaller even than the *Ophelia* painting, but it was clearly a Rossetti.

'It's crazy to think that something like this could be hidden away in someone's attic for so long and nobody knew anything about it,' said Jon. He and Becky were staying at Lissy's for a few days. Lissy had been determined to get them down to London one more time before the baby arrived and the exhibition had been the perfect excuse.

'You can see *Ophelia* again,' Lissy had said, trying to persuade Becky during one of her visits to Whitby. 'It's a shame if you miss out on the new Rossetti, just because you can't see your toes any more.'

'Are whales generally welcome in the Tate?' Becky had asked, conversationally.

'You're not due until August,' Lissy had argued.

'And the exhibition opens at the end of July,' Becky had countered. 'As I said, are whales welcome at the Tate?'

'You'll be fine,' said Lissy. 'You're just blooming. Do you want me to paint your toenails for you? That always cheers me up.'

Becky had remained unconvinced as to the 'blooming', but had offered her toes to Lissy anyway.

And in the end, of course, they'd gone to London.

'If I have the baby in your perfect house,' Becky had moaned to Lissy as she flopped, ungainly and exhausted, onto Lissy's sofa after the journey down, 'it's your own fault.'

But so far, so good, and they'd all made it to the preview evening. Lissy steered Jon and Becky off towards *Ophelia*, chattering as she went, and Simon and Cori lingered beside the new Rossetti, promising to meet up with the others at the buffet table later.

'You can see why the PRB were deemed revolutionary, can't you?' asked Simon. He pointed out the bold strokes of colour in the portrait.

'See how the light shines on her hair – it's like it's painted out of sunsets.' He looked down at Cori and smiled. 'It's easy talking about Lizzie like that. It's easy talking about my model like that as well.'

'Really?' Cori fingered one of the corkscrew curls that fell down way past her shoulders. 'I always just thought my hair was ginger. I guess I have ladies like Lizzie to thank for the fact people can see past the ginger-ness of it.'

Simon laughed. 'She certainly had a unique sort of beauty. Imagine, though, as Jon says, how this could have been lost for so many years.'

'Mmmm,' agreed Cori. 'Imagine it.'

'And one of the nicest things about it, I think, is that Rossetti's painted the bunch of flowers on the floor so carefully. Look – each petal is individually shaped, and there are tiny, pink stripes through each one. They're beautiful.'

'They're daisies,' said Cori. She looked again at the portrait, a little more closely. 'Daisies. Definitely.' Her heart seemed to stutter for a second and she cast her eye over the model again. It looked like Lizzie. It had Lizzie's hair – but the nose, when you looked a little closer, wasn't quite so aquiline. The girl was half in shadow, the light from the window covering most of her face and the sweep of red-gold hair that fell down past her shoulders doing a good job of covering even more of her features. Cori hardly dared breathe for a second.

'What is it?' Simon asked.

'They're daisies,' she repeated. 'And I don't think her nose is quite Lizzie's nose.'

'But you think it's still Lizzie, yes?' Simon frowned, concerned now.

Cori didn't want to lie to him; but she did. 'I think it's probably Lizzie,' she said, trying and failing to keep her voice measured. 'It's probably not one of his best likenesses. He would want to show the world the real Lizzie. Not this Lizzie. This is probably a practice Lizzie.' Yes, she was babbling again, and she knew it. 'But it's Lizzie.' *The world wants it to be Lizzie. So it is Lizzie.*

'Oh, good. Because for a moment, I thought you might say it was Daisy.' Simon laughed. It was, it had to be said, a rather forced laugh.

'Who knows?' replied Cori. 'Maybe it's even my Aunt Corisande. Who would know the difference nowadays?' Suddenly, she shivered as a thought entered her head: *if it's not Lizzie – or Corisande – and it* is *Daisy, then at least she got her wish. She's been recognised in a Rossetti; as Lizzie.*

'Let's go,' she said, rather too abruptly. 'Let's look at the other pictures again. Then we can head back and you can start moving your canvases and your painting stuff onto my second floor. If you like.'

As Lissy had said, Cori had never been too reticent in the past – but that was before Evan had come into her life and squashed her confidence. Now, however, she had Simon; and she saw no reason to go on as they were going – the odd night at his, the odd night at hers.

'Then, once they're moved in, how about you follow them? Only you're not going to be limited to the second floor, of course. And Bryony has to come as well.' Cori really liked that little tabby, now she was used to her running out of Simon's second bedroom at random moments. And Bryony seemed to like her, which was always a bonus.

Simon stared at her. Then he pulled her towards him and kissed her as if nobody else was in the room.

When he finally drew back, he looked down at her, straight into her eyes. 'I would like that more than anything in the world,' he said, softly.

'Well, we could have moved into your place, but I really think it's time you gave up that lease and stopped wasting money on rent,' replied Cori, ever practical. 'My place is definitely more user-friendly.' She stole her hand into his and was pleased to feel him squeeze it. 'Especially since you fixed the doors.'

Cori looked again at the girl in the portrait and smiled to herself. Then she dragged her eyes away from the painting and looked back up at Simon; her future.

The portrait was in the past. It had lain discarded in her grandmother's attic for over a century and a half, hidden in an old trunk which, according to paperwork also found inside it, belonged to Thomas Hedley-Turner – the original Corisande's husband. Cori had begun tidying the attic in the wake of the Evan break-up, just for something to do to occupy her mind and she had discovered the portrait, stuffed away in a trunk with the locks rusted shut.

When they read the painter's signature, they'd had it valued and then Granny had done a small victory dance around the lounge.

Granny was convinced it was truly the Rossetti portrait of Corisande that family legend had long believed in, but Cori hadn't been too sure. Rossetti had been renowned for seducing a plethora of beautiful redheads. This might simply be one of many. It wasn't exactly an innocent picture; but, as Granny had said, it made a lovely story. Regardless, Granny didn't want the family connection getting out into the public domain or, she said, she'd have no peace at all from Rossetti fans.

Granny had told Cori to do what she liked with the portrait. As far as she was concerned, it was Cori's now, as she'd found it. Call it her inheritance. And what use did her old granny have for that sort of money anyway? The family she had never spoken to for decades would be all over her like a rash if she admitted it.

So, with her grandmother's blessing, Cori sold the picture anonymously and moved to London. Granny's only provisos had been that she buy a house big enough to accommodate her business and to put up her old granny if she ever felt like a trip to the capital.

When she realised how much the Rossetti was worth, Cori had felt horribly guilty, and tried to give her granny the money back. But her grandmother had said no. And she wasn't a woman to be argued with.

Once again, as she left the Tate behind, Cori wondered who the girl in the picture actually was. She still wasn't one hundred per cent sure it was Corisande; and she was fairly certain it wasn't Lizzie Siddal either. But could it actually be Daisy Ashford? Becky's article had been published at a very opportune time and had piqued Cori's interest in the painting even more.

And, thinking about it all now, Cori realised that she felt sorry for Daisy. Daisy had been living in her own little dream world, addled by drugs and obsessed by a woman she could never aspire to be. Rossetti had known her – he must have known her. Maybe he picked her up from the gutter one night when she was having an episode.

Maybe she boldly knocked on his door like she claimed to have done with Millais. Maybe Rossetti had painted her then – and, years later, passed the portrait off to Thomas as a portrait of his wife – having been too busy making love to Corisande to paint her properly. Who knew? Who would ever know the truth of it?

Cori doubted whether Daisy herself had really known much about real life at the end. But one thing was for sure. Daisy had wanted to be noticed – and she had been.

Cori cast one more look over her shoulder as she followed Simon out of the door. It may have been a trick of the light, or it may not have been. But she could have sworn there was a girl standing by the portrait; a tall, slim girl, who wore a long, silvery-white dress and had red-gold hair that shimmered in the light. A man stood next to her, holding her hand. He wore a smart frock coat, a white, starched collar just visible above the lapels. His fair hair was just a little too long to be entirely formal. The girl stood before the portrait, her back to Cori, her head tilted slightly to one side, leaning on the man's shoulder, as if she was studying the picture. Lying on the floor, just in front of the picture was a small bunch of flowers.

Cori couldn't tell at that distance – but she was willing to bet they were daisies.

Thank You

Thank you for reading *The Girl in the Painting*. I hope you enjoyed Cori and Simon's story as much as I enjoyed writing it. The characters from my previous novel, *Some Veil Did Fall* wouldn't let go and I had to write the story to stop them from pestering me. And by doing that, I met the incredible Daisy, who has to be one of my favourite characters yet!

All authors, as well as loving their characters, really value their readers. The road to publication is a magical one and seeing your book out there, being enjoyed by people like yourself, is a fantastic feeling. It's even more special if people like you take the trouble to leave a review. It's lovely to hear what readers think and we all value their feedback.

If you have time therefore, something as simple as a one line review on Amazon, a note on a book review site such as Goodreads or indeed a comment on any online store would be hugely appreciated.

Please do feel free to contact me anytime. You can find my details under my author profile and I very much hope that you'll enjoy my other books as well.

Happy reading, and again, a huge thank you!

Lots of love

Kirsty

xxx

About the Author

Kirsty Ferry is from the North East of England and lives there with her husband and son. She won the English Heritage/Belsay Hall National Creative Writing competition in 2009 and has had articles and short stories published in *The People's Friend*, *The Weekly News*, *It's Fate*, *Vintage Script*, *Ghost Voices* and *First Edition*. Her work also appears in several anthologies, incorporating such diverse themes as vampires, crime, angels and more.

Kirsty loves writing ghostly mysteries and interweaving fact and fiction. The research is almost as much fun as writing the book itself, and if she can add a wonderful setting and a dollop of history, that's even better.

Her day job involves sharing a building with an eclectic collection of ghosts, which can often prove rather interesting.

The Girl in the Painting is Kirsty's
second novel in her series.

Follow Kirsty on:
www.twitter.com/kirsty_ferry
www.facebook.com/pages/Kirsty-Ferry-Author

More Choc Lit

From Kirsty Ferry

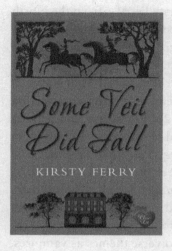

Some Veil Did Fall

Book 1 in the Rossetti Mysteries series

What if you recalled memories from a life that wasn't yours, from a life before …?

When Becky steps into Jonathon Nelson's atmospheric photography studio in Whitby, she is simply a freelance journalist in search of a story. But as soon as she puts on the beautiful Victorian dress and poses for a photograph, she becomes somebody quite different …

From that moment on, Becky is overcome with visions and flashbacks from a life that isn't her own – some disturbing and filled with fear.

As she and Jon begin to unravel the tragic mystery behind her strange experiences, the natural affinity they have for each other continues to grow and leads them to question … have they met somewhere before? Perhaps not in this life but in another?

Available in paperback from all good bookshops and online stores. Visit www.choc-lit.com for details.

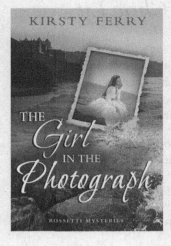

KIRSTY FERRY

The Girl in the Photograph

Book 3 in the Rossetti Mysteries series

What if the past was trying to teach you a lesson?

Staying alone in the shadow of an abandoned manor house in Yorkshire would be madness to some, but art enthusiast Lissy de Luca can't wait. Lissy has her reasons for seeking isolation, and she wants to study the Staithes Group – an artists' commune active at the turn of the twentieth century.

Lissy is fascinated by the imposing Sea Scarr Hall – but the deeper she delves, the stranger things get. A lonely figure patrols the cove at night, whilst a hidden painting leads to a chilling realisation. And then there's the photograph of the girl; so beautiful she could be a mermaid ... and so familiar.

As Lissy further immerses herself, she comes to an eerie conclusion. The occupants of Sea Scarr Hall are long gone, but they have a message for her – and they're going to make sure she gets it.

Read an extract of the Prologue and Chapter One overleaf.

Visit www.choc-lit.com for details.

Introducing Choc Lit

We're an independent publisher creating
a delicious selection of fiction.
Where heroes are like chocolate – irresistible!
Quality stories with a romance at the heart.

See our selection here:
www.choc-lit.com

We'd love to hear how you enjoyed *The Girl in the
Painting*. Please leave a review where you purchased the
novel or visit: **www.choc-lit.com** and give your feedback.

Choc Lit novels are selected by genuine readers like yourself.
We only publish stories our Choc Lit Tasting Panel want to
see in print. Our reviews and awards speak for themselves.

Could you be a Star Selector and join our Tasting Panel?
Would you like to play a role in choosing which novels we
decide to publish? Do you enjoy reading romance novels?
Then you could be perfect for our Choc Lit Tasting Panel.

Visit here for more details…
www.choc-lit.com/join-the-choc-lit-tasting-panel

Keep in touch:
Sign up for our monthly newsletter Choc Lit Spread for
all the latest news and offers: www.spread.choc-lit.com.
Follow us on Twitter: @ChocLituk and Facebook: Choc Lit.

Where heroes are like chocolate – irresistible!

Preview
The Girl in the Photograph

by Kirsty Ferry

PROLOGUE

She dragged the silver-backed brush through her hair, feeling the wild, salty, tangled curls stretch out and pull into the soft waves she was more accustomed to. She longed to be outside, rather than trapped in this gilded cage; she yearned to feel the sea breeze on her face and the sand crushing beneath her bare feet. She didn't belong here, with him, but she knew she had to stay, at least a little while longer …

CHAPTER ONE
Whitby, July, Present Day

'Seriously, it'll be fun!'

'Fun?' Lissy de Luca stared at her half-brother Jon Nelson and pulled a face. 'I suspect it's more fun for the photographer than the model.'

Jon was sitting on the sofa, right next to a picture window which was big enough for the afternoon sun to pour through the glass and make the little lounge in the flat above his Whitby photographic studio glow. 'Look, it's a project I've been thinking of for a while,' he said. 'You know Simon's having an exhibition in Mayfair and he's already said I can have some wall space. I think it'll be great to try and recreate some of the Pre-Raphaelite paintings in photography, and they'll go alongside Simon's work quite nicely. It's just a different form of art, that's all.'

Simon, an artist, and his partner Cori were friends of theirs who lived in London and Jon had just been telling Lissy about their joint plans. He was visibly fizzing with excitement.

'Well, his paintings are marvellous!' Lissy leaned forward and took a biscuit from a plate. 'He's got Cori to model for him and he can recreate all those pictures easily. They'll look so good. I can just see them now, up on that gallery wall. Wonderful.' She nibbled a corner of the biscuit, breaking into the chocolate shell with a view to stripping the chocolate off it in a neat, efficient manner before she hit the actual biscuit inside.

'So, basically, you're implying Simon's paintings are better than my photographs? Well, thanks Sis, I love you too.' Although Jon and Lissy had the same mother, they had grown up together in the household of Lissy's wealthy Italian father; but it had never made any difference to their relationship, which was based on the usual deep love and fiery spats between siblings.

In this instance, Lissy didn't rise to the bait. She licked the last vestiges of chocolate from the biscuit and popped the remaining shortbread circle into her mouth.

She stared at Jon as she chewed. 'I often wish I had a sister instead of a brother. Girls are less touchy.'

'Rubbish! Absolute rubbish. I grew up with *you*, remember, and I now live with two girls and no way are they less touchy!'

'You just proved it; you are far too touchy.' Lissy stood up and stretched. 'Well, as I was hoping to see Becky and Grace and they aren't here, I'm going to go.'

'Oh, sit down. They won't be long. Grace wanted to see the pirate ship so Becky took her out for a wander.' Jon suddenly perked up. 'Maybe she'll bring back some coffee?'

'What? Becky would juggle coffee *and* a three-year old in a coffee shop, just to feed your addiction?'

Jon grinned. 'Hopefully.'

Lissy shuddered. She couldn't even contemplate such a horror. She loved her sister-in-law and her niece dearly, but surely there were limits? The thought of taking Grace into an exclusive café in London, where Lissy lived – well, in fact, an exclusive café anywhere – was inconceivable. There was a hot chocolate place along one of the side streets in Whitby with the blessing of outside tables. Lissy could just about cope with the child there. And that was only because she would usually feed her with a succession of marshmallows and strawberries dipped in chocolate, which did tend to keep her quiet; even if it made her rather sticky and unpleasant afterwards.

There was a jingle from way beneath their feet and it was Jon's turn to stand up. 'Customers. No rest for the wicked.'

He strode out of the lounge and headed towards the rickety old staircase that connected the flat to the shop. The studio dealt mainly with the tourist trade; people would come in to have photographs taken of themselves in period clothing and the twice-yearly Goth weekend celebrations were his busiest times. Luckily the queues of pale people dressed in black and discovering their inner vampire, courtesy of Bram Stoker setting part of his *Dracula* novel in Whitby, didn't bother his small daughter.

Grace often sat on the old wooden counter entranced by the vamps. Sometimes, it had to be said, her piercing, solemn stare would unsettle the customers more than they could unsettle her. It often took a double take for them to realise the thing that was 'off' about her – the fact that, like her father and aunt, she had one blue and one green eye, inherited from her paternal grandmother's line. Her unusual eyes were surrounded by the darkest, longest lashes, and when you matched that with her dark hair and her mother's English Rose complexion, Grace Eleanor Nelson was clearly destined for great, although not conventional, beauty.

'Hey!' Jon's voice, rising an octave and somehow simultaneously softening in tone, floated in from the tiny landing. 'Who is *this* coming up the stairs to my little house?'

'Cap'n Hook,' came another voice – a child's voice. 'But I want a crocodile. Tick tock!' The door to the lounge flew open and a mini-whirlwind came in, sporting a lop-sided eye-patch and brandishing a rubber dagger. 'Bang bang!' The whirlwind came to a sudden halt in front of Lissy and grinned through a mask of something unidentifiably, yes, *sticky*. 'Bang bang!' Cap'n Hook held the dagger aloft and pointed it at Lissy.

'Darling, *guns* go bang bang. That's a dagger,' said Lissy.

'It's a gun today,' replied Hook. 'Hallo.'

'Hello sweetie.' Lissy bent down, intending to kiss each side of her niece's face as she usually did in polite society, but the little girl had other ideas.

Grace threw her arms around Lissy's neck and lifted her feet from the ground. 'Mwaaah.' She smacked a wet kiss somewhere to the side of Lissy's mouth.

Automatically, Lissy put her arms around the child to steady them both and Grace snuggled in to her. 'Come see who Mummy found.' She pointed to the door and bounced in Lissy's arms. 'That way.' Lissy had no choice but to walk towards the staircase, breathing in the faint scent of chocolate and bananas the child was breathing out.

'I don't suppose your Mummy found anyone interesting?' she asked. 'Was it a princess? If it was a princess, maybe it was just a customer.' Grace adored the more elaborate Goths – she loved the long flouncy dresses and the lace gloves, stared covetously at the red lips and had, at times, to be physically restrained from touching the velvet chokers or veils the ladies displayed.

'No princess,' said Grace. She sighed and shook her head. Then she brightened. 'It's a prince!'

Lissy fully expected to see a pallid young man dressed in a top hat and a frock coat as she manoeuvred the unwieldy bundle expertly down the staircase and pushed the door open into the studio.

What she didn't expect to see, was Stefano Ricci.

'Oh, good God!' Lissy's face drained of colour.

Stefano looked at her, his heart thudding – maybe it was panic, maybe it wasn't. But, regardless, he hadn't been sure of what his reception would be. He did notice, however, that Lissy was as immaculate as she had always been. Her dark hair now fell to her shoulders from a severe side parting and a long, dark, choppy fringe hid part of her face. There were streaks of purple and pink in the fringe – on anyone else, Stefano knew, the highlights would be lost in the mass of dark hair. On Lissy, they lay exactly where they should.

He took a deep breath and smiled, bowing elegantly to her. '*Mia cara.*' Then he saw the look of thunder on her elfin face. 'Ah, why would you look so upset, Elisabetta? I have come from so far to see you again. And this – this little girl. She is a doll.' He turned to Grace. 'In my country, which is somewhere called Italy, we would call you *Grazia.*'

'*Grazia*?' The child tried the name out and appeared to like it. Grace was obviously not a shy child. She looked directly at him, a stranger to her, and jiggled, apparently letting her aunt know she wanted to be put back on her own two feet. 'Hallo, again.' She walked over to Stefano when Lissy had done her bidding and stood in front of him, waiting for him to answer.

'Hello,' said Stefano. He held his hand out solemnly.

Grace seized it and pumped it up and down, giggling. 'Mummy,' she said, turning to Jon's pretty chestnut-haired wife, Becky, 'he's nice. I like him.'

'I'm glad,' replied Becky, smiling back. 'He's Daddy's friend Stefano. Can you say that?'

Grace nodded. 'Yes.' She didn't elaborate however, and Stefano smiled.

'Good girl,' he said.

'Yes, I am,' replied Grace confidently. She tugged at the hand she still held and Stefano was curious as she pulled him slightly at an angle and pointed at her mother. 'But you must talk straight to Mummy. Her ears don't work right.'

'Grace!' That was Lissy scolding the child.

'She tries to help,' Stefano defended her. God, the woman looked good. 'How long has it been?' he asked, gently releasing Grace and taking a step towards Lissy with his hands outstretched. His camera was slung around his neck, and he felt the equipment bump against his body. He itched to take a photograph of Elisabetta. Nobody had ever compared to her.

'Not long enough,' said Lissy.

'Yet I think it has been far too long.'

'You *are* joking?' exclaimed Lissy. The child had run back to her now and was patting her legs, trying to get attention and probably hoping for another carry in her arms. She was half bending over to the child, ready to either pick her up or send her off with a flea in her ear, when she looked up at Stefano.

Flash.

'I thank you,' he said. 'You have made my first Pre-Raphaelite imagining come to life. You are the very image of Waterhouse's *Lady of Shalott looking at Lancelot.*'

'I don't believe you,' she hissed. 'You are sneaky and underhanded and ...'

'And you have never forgotten me,' interrupted Stefano, 'and you still feel a passion for me – otherwise, why would you still be so bothered to see me?'

Lissy, apparently, couldn't find an answer.

Coming soon!
Visit www.choc-lit.com for details.